Clockwork
Fairy Tales

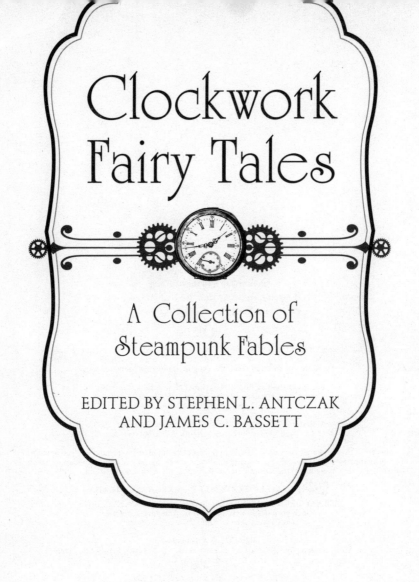

Clockwork
Fairy Tales

A Collection of
Steampunk Fables

EDITED BY STEPHEN L. ANTCZAK
AND JAMES C. BASSETT

A ROC BOOK

ROC

Published by the Penguin Group

Penguin Group (USA) Inc., 375 Hudson Street,

New York, New York 10014, USA

USA I Canada I UK I Ireland I Australia I New Zealand I India I South Africa I China
Penguin Books Ltd., Registered Offices: 80 Strand, London WC2R 0RL, England
For more information about the Penguin Group visit penguin.com

First published by Roc, an imprint of New American Library,
a division of Penguin Group (USA) Inc.
First Printing, June 2013

ROC REGISTERED TRADEMARK—MARCA REGISTRADA

LIBRARY OF CONGRESS CATALOGING-IN-PUBLICATION DATA:
Clockwork fairy tales: a collection of steampunk fables/
edited by Stephen L. Antczak, James C. Bassett.
p. cm.
ISBN 978-0-451-46494-1
1. Steampunk fiction, American.   2. Fairy tales.   I. Antczak, Stephen L., 1966–
II. Bassett, James C.
PS648.S86C58 2013
813'.0876608—dc23   2012029669

Printed in the United States of America
10 9 8 7 6 5 4 3 2 1

Set in Stempel Schneidler
Designed by Sabrina Bowers

Contents

Clockwork
Fairy Tales

La Valse

by K. W. Jeter

**(BASED ON "THE RED SHOES"
BY HANS CHRISTIAN ANDERSEN)**

"The problem," said Herr Doktor Pavel, "is that we gained our empire when we were young. And now we are old." With a great iron spanner in his hands, he turned to his assistant and smiled. "What could be worse than that?"

"I don't know." Anton felt himself to be a child, when hearing of such things. "I'm not as old as you. At all."

Around them, in the Apollosaal's basements, the machinery wept. Even though they had both spent the better part of a week down there, in preparation for this evening's grand events, still the miasmatic hiss and soft, plodding leaks prevailed over their efforts. The tun-shaped boilers, vast enough to engulf carriages and peasants' huts, shuddered with the scalding forces pent inside them. Their rivets seeped rust. In the far-off corners where the theatrical scenery was kept and more often forgotten, pasteboard castles sagged beneath the threadbare fronds of a humid jungle of ersatz palm trees.

"Age, like wealth, is but a mental abstraction, my boy." The doctor peered at a creaking armature above his head, adjusting

1

some aspect of it with a miniature screwdriver, skill as precise and surgical as though his title were that of a physician rather than an engineer. "And nothing more. People fancy that God loves them—and consider themselves and their kind exceptional as a result." He wiped his pale, egglike brow with the grease-smeared lace of his shirt cuff. "If such fancies were gears and dreams cogs, I would wind this world's mainspring tight enough to hum."

Anton didn't know what that meant. The doctor was of an obscure and poetic persuasion. He took the screwdriver from the hand held toward him, replacing the tool in its exact slot with the greater and smaller ones on either side.

"Will everything be ready? By tonight?" Anton thought that was more important to know. If the ballroom's mechanisms were not completely functional and satisfactory when the guests arrived, then the doctor and he would not be paid, resulting in a cold and hungry New Year's Eve for them.

"Not to worry." The doctor picked up his tool bag and moved on. He tapped a lean forefinger on a set of calliope-like pipes, each in turn, flakes of rust drifting onto his vest as he bent his ear toward them. Just as a physician counterpart might thump the chest of a tubercular patient, to assess how long he had to live. "No one's merriment will be impaired by the likes of us."

In winters such as these—were there any other kind anymore?—Anton limited his hopes to that much. If one managed to get to the first muddy, thawing days before actual spring, then there was a chance at least. Of something other than this. Something other than the dank, hissing basements under the ballrooms and palaces of that finer, fragile world above. Far from the sharp-toothed gears and interlocking wheels, the pistons gleaming in their oily sheaths, the ticking escapements wide as cartwheels, the mainsprings uncoiling like nests of razor-thin serpents. He could take Gisel out beyond the apple orchards, their branches still black and leafless, no matter that it would cost him a day's wages and her a scolding from the head housekeeper. What would it matter if both of them would go supperless that night, bellies empty as their aching arms? Lying on straw-filled pallets far from each other, gazing out cobwebbed attic windows at an envious moon. Remembering how the ice at the roots of the sodden grass creaked beneath the back of her chambermaid's blouse, his face buried in the gathered folds of her apron. Smelling of honey and lye, her hand stroking his close-cropped head as she turned her face away and wept at how happy she was. If only for a moment.

"What are you dreaming about?" The doctor's voice broke into his warming reveries. "Come over here and help me open up these stopcocks."

He did as he was ordered, letting all the girl's smiles flutter away, like ashes up a chimney flue. Straining at the stubborn valves, he let one other hope step inside his heart. That none of their work here, readying for the gala ball, would require going down into the subbasements below these, where the great roaring furnaces and boilers resided. He hated having to go down there, hated seeing the stokers chained between the fiery iron doors and heaps of coal, the shimmering heat revealing the stripes across their naked backs. Their eyes would turn toward him as they crouched over their black shovels. Their eyes would tell him, *As you are, once were we. Steal but the slightest crust or bauble, and join us here. . . .*

Their extinguished voices would follow him as he fled up the spiral of clanging metal stairs, the errand accomplished that *Herr Dr.* Pavel had sent him on. He could hear them now, whispering far beneath his sodden clogs, as he gritted his teeth and strained to turn the most ancient of the spoked wheels another quarter turn.

"That's good." The doctor stepped back, wiping his hands across his vest. "Anton, my coat, if you please."

He fetched the swallow-tailed garment, lifting it from the hook by the stone arch of the cellar door. The horsehair-padded shoulders itched his own palms as he helped the doctor slide into its heavy woolen arms.

"There." An old man's vanity—he tugged at the lapels, gazing fondly at his reflection in one of the floor's puddles. "When every-day gentlemen dressed as elegant as this, the empire was feared by Cossack and Hun alike."

"If you say so." Anton had no memory of such things. The doctor might have been imagining such faded glories, for all he knew.

"We'll discuss it another time." The sad state of his assistant's learning was a topic frequently evoked, if never acted upon. "Let's fire 'er up, lad. A job well done's the best payment."

Anton watched as the doctor pushed one lever after another. Constellations of gears engaged about them, all enveloped in sweating vapor. Ratchet and piston moved through their limited courses, the clatter of brass and iron loud as church bells on a tone-deaf Easter morning.

"Splendid!" The doctor bent his head back, gazing up enraptured at the chamber's damp ceiling. "Do you hear it? Do you?"

Anton knew what those sounds were, barely audible through the commotion of the machinery driving them. He'd heard them before, every year's end, from when he'd first apprenticed to the dancing engineer's trade. To now, this last calendar page, so much dragglier and tattered than the ones from all the years before.

He pulled his own thin coat away from one of the jointed arms thrusting up through the ceiling's apertures, careful not to be snagged by its pumplike motions. All through the basement, more such churned away, up and down and at various angles, pivoting upon the hinges that he and the doctor had so carefully greased. Like a mechanical forest, brought to clanking animation by the white gouts billowing from every quivering pipe. . . .

There they go, thought Anton as he looked up at where the doctor gazed. He could see them, without ascending the stairs to the grand ballroom. The empty metal frameworks, like iron scarecrows, would be bowing to one another, then embracing. The smaller with the larger, just as if already filled by the evening's elegant guests. Already, the mechanical violins were scraping their bows across the rosined strings.

Closing his eyes, he watched from inside his head as each skeletal apparatus—jointed struts and trusses, cages shaped into men and women—took another by a creaking hand. Then swirled across the acres of polished floor, just as though it were the music that impelled them, rather than clockwork and steam.

She breathed into her cupped hands, warming the strands of pearls she held.

There might come a day when she was old enough, with years of servile experience ingrained through every memory, that she would be entrusted to help dress their dowager employer. For now, Gisel watched as the senior maids, some of them older than the bent and wrinkled figure upon whom they waited, busied themselves with the intricate laces and stays.

"Ah! You're too cruel to me." Vanity and girlish affectations tinged the dowager's simpered, murmured words. "You'll break something one of these days—I know you will." She brought her hawk-etched, deep-seamed visage over the lace at her shoulder and smiled the yellow of old parchment at her attendants. "But not tonight. Be so sweet as to spare me just one more night of pleasure."

The maids said nothing, but obliged with nods and their own little smiles. Gisel had heard the old woman say the same thing the year before and the year before that. She had still been working in the scullery three winters ago, scrubbing the stone floors with a wet rag, but the oldest of the chambermaids had told her that the dowager had spoken the same words every New Year's Eve, for decades now. None of them were quite sure that the dowager could say anything else, at least not while getting dressed for the ball.

Gisel watched as the others stepped back, the gown assembled into place at last, as though a seamstress had wrapped lengths of ancient silk around a bone dummy. The dowager admired herself in a triptych of full-length mirrors, as though the gray film at the center of her eyes somehow filtered out the overlapping scales of time, letting through only the image of the lithe girl she still believed herself to be.

Now the pearls were as warm as Gisel's blood. They could have been a kitten sheltered between one palm and the other, if only they had breathed and had a fluttering pulse inside soft fur. She stepped forward with them, holding them up as though they were some sort of offering.

"No—not now." The dowager surprised them all by something different. Something she had never said before. She waved a wrinkled, impatient hand at Gisel. "They caught last time. In the framework." Her scarlet nails clawed at the tendons that ridged her neck harplike. "How they tormented me! The whole beautiful night, dancing and dancing, and the whole time I felt as though I were being garroted. I could have burst into tears from the pain, if I'd let myself."

Gisel dared to speak, though she received a warning glance from the oldest chambermaid. "You don't want to wear them?"

"Silly girl—of course I do. They were my mother's, and her mother took communion from the hand of a pope with them around her throat. How could I not wear them on a festive occasion such as this? I wear them *every* New Year's ball."

"I'm sorry. . . ."

"Don't fret about it, dear." The dowager smiled even wider and scarier as she let one of the other maids settle a wrap about her shoulders. "Let us go to the Apollosaal—you and I, and the others. Won't that be fun? And you can put the pearls upon me there. So you can make certain they don't pinch and bind. I believe that's the smartest thing to do, don't you? I don't know why I didn't think of it before."

The notion terrified Gisel. Her heart pounded at the base of her own throat as she felt all the other maids turning their silent, premonitory gaze upon her. What would she do without the oldest and kindest of them, to tell her what to do?

"But . . . I don't know. . . ."

"No one will mind, I'm sure. Once the music starts, I'm sure there will be some little corner where you can crouch and hide.

Perhaps in the back, from where the waiters bring the champagne and the marzipan cakes. No one will even see you." The dowager's eyes were like ivory knifepoints set in crepe paper as she went on smiling.

She knows I'm scared, thought Gisel, holding the bundled pearls closer to herself. *That's why she wants me to go with her.* If only she hadn't let the dowager see that in her, she might have had a chance. To escape.

But now there wasn't any. She nodded dumbly and followed the other woman, out of the dressing room and toward the curving sweep of stairs that led down to the carriage outside the door, and all the wintry city streets beyond.

A s the guests assembled, he saw her. Anton's heart raced—it always did, as though some internal furnace of his emotions had been stoked higher.

Assembled, it seemed to him, almost literally. This was the part of his apprenticeship to the doctor that he disliked the most. Some tasks were worse than others. He thanked God, the one cloaked in the tattered remnants of his faith, that this one came about only once a year. And at the end of it, so that even in the bleakest December there would likely be no further discouragements.

With his own tool kit slung by a leather strap from his shoulder, he hastened through the grand ballroom. Only the lesser nobility were entrusted to him. And of those, only the men—he knelt before baronets and princelings, the younger sons of dynasties and households so ancient that their pedigrees might have been traced in whatever pages would have followed the Book of Revelation. As *Herr Dr.* Pavel had pointed out more than once to him, *youth* was as relative a term as *wealth*, in this case meaning only slightly less gray and enfeebled. With wrench and calibrated screwdrivers, he encased spindly legs, cavalry boots buffed lustrous by their lackeys, into the jointed, cagelike frames. Standing up, he fastened curved metal bands about the noblemen's waists and chests, taking care not to disarray their ranks of medals, gleaming as miniature suns with the profiles of dead emperors at their centers. Last came the tapered armatures locked into place at their wrists and elbows, linked by clever pistons to the similar mechanisms at their shoulders. With a few of the more dissipated, he had to hold their arms above their heads himself while with his other hand he completed the necessary fastenings. As a lady's maid might corset an obese matron, he would then raise a knee to the small of their backs, in order to engage all the torso elements to the mechanical iron spines that extended from their hips to the napes of their stiffly collared necks.

But he had to admit the results were impressive, when he finally stood back from each one, his tools dangling in each hand. They stood at attention, chests thrust out inside the metal cages, shoulders pulled back by bows of iron behind them, each as proudly straight as though their decorations had been won on actual battlefields.

With practice accumulated over decades, the doctor was able to work so much faster, encasing not only the more elderly noblemen, but all their wives and daughters and courtesans as well. The doctor had told Anton that the women were easier, as their bodies were more pliant, more accustomed to the rigors of fashion, more submissive to the attentions of men. He wasn't sure about that—they all terrified him, the old ones with the bodices like the prows of bejeweled warships, the comparatively younger with their sharp glances aimed over fluttering fans as though they were infantry rifles. He would have believed that the women were more ready than the men to pick up their grandfathers' sabers and run through any foes worthy of such an encounter.

"Such attentions are a delight, *Herr Doktor.*" The grand duchess of some inconsequential principality simpered through her fan. "If only my late husband's touch had been so skilled."

"You flatter me, madam." Wielding a brace of screwdrivers, the doctor completed adjusting the thin steel bands spanning the woman's capacious bosom. "I am no more than a simple craftsman."

Anton finished encasing those to whom he had been assigned. The gaudy colors of their parade uniforms seeped through the hinged ligatures and mechanisms, as might the plumage of exotic birds in tightly bound aviaries. They preened before each other, the skeletal limbs of their full-length cages creaking in place, as he knelt at the side of the ballroom, wiping the tools with an oily rag before putting them away.

A fluttering murmur arose from the noblewomen. Without glancing over his shoulder, Anton knew that the last of their number had arrived. Every New Year's Eve, the dowager's arrival at the ballroom was the culminating event of the preparations, the signal that the festivities were soon to commence. Carefully timed, as though the old woman had some preternatural sense of when all the others had been bolted and strapped into place, ready to admire and obsequiously comment as she assumed her rightful position among them.

The doctor set to work, with no need of greeting or command. One of the senior maids in the dowager's retinue took the wrap from her shoulders, the sable fur powdered with snow not yet melted in the ballroom's heat.

Another waited upon the dowager, who had not accompanied her the year before. When Anton closed his tool kit and stood up, keeping close to the paneled wall, he spotted Gisel. That was when his heart sped and his breath caught in his throat. Not at seeing her face—when had that ever made him other but happy?—but at discerning the fear inscribed upon it. She stood behind all the others, her own gaze downcast, arms close against her ribs, red-chafed hands locked upon some bundle glistening white. The pulse at her throat ticked even faster than his, impelled by whatever terror it was that she felt.

"There." *Herr Dr.* Pavel stood back from the dowager, his intricate labors done. "The evening is yours, madam. Enjoy it as you wish."

"Not yet," said the woman, now surrounded by the same metal struts and linkages as the other guests. "There are still the best adornments to be put on." She turned and looked past the knot of chambermaids, to the one farthest behind them. "My pearls—"

Gisel scurried up to the dowager, her hands opening to cup the circled strands.

"Don't dawdle, child. The ball is to commence at any moment."

The reason for Gisel's fear was quickly evident to Anton as he watched her struggle to fasten the pearls around the dowager's neck. The articulated metal bands came up high enough on the woman, as with all the other noble guests, to make the task more than merely difficult—close to impossible, in fact. His own hands tensed into useless fists as he watched the girl attempting to draw the pearls through the narrow space between the dowager's wrinkled throat and the inside of the ironwork assembled about her.

"What is the matter with you?" The dowager fidgeted in discomfort, a soured grimace evidencing her dislike of another human being so close. "Is such a simple task beyond you?"

The woman's sniping words didn't help. Gisel became even more flustered, her face draining white and her hands shaking with anxiety. Beneath her fingertips, one of the gleaming strands caught in the angle of a metal hinge. She tugged at the graduated length, attempting to free it. The silken thread inside snapped— the tiny, precious spheres flew in all directions, bouncing and clattering on the ballroom floor.

"Cretin!" The dowager's face was a wrinkled mask of fury as her bony hand slapped Gisel. "Idiot! Look what you've done."

"I'm sorry—" Gisel was already down on her hands and knees, trying to gather up all the scattered pearls. Futile—some of them had rolled and vanished into the grooved apertures through which the various machinery from the cellars below protruded, scalding vapors hissing along the jointed armatures. "I didn't mean—"

"The smallest of them is worth more than you." The point of the dowager's heeled boot caught Gisel in the ribs, hard enough to evoke a gasp from her. "Twenty of such as you!"

Anton wouldn't have thought there was so much strength in

the old woman. As he watched, another kick brought a spatter of blood from Gisel's mouth. If it hadn't been for the cagelike mechanism bolted into place around the dowager's voluminous silken skirt, her anger might have been enough to take off the offending girl's head.

"Don't—" *Herr Dr.* Pavel laid a restraining hand across Anton's chest as he had stepped forward from the wall. "I'll take care of it."

Tears had diluted pink the blood that Gisel smeared with her palm as she huddled into a ball, knees against her breast. She barely looked up as the doctor interposed himself between her and the dowager. "But an accident," he soothed. "No harm was intended—"

The dowager's rage continued without respite. She was even smiling, a slash across her starkly rouged face, as her gloved and jeweled hand struck the doctor. Her eyes glittered in triumph as he fell at her feet.

A blow such as that wouldn't have been enough to kill the doctor—Anton knew that. Perhaps it was the shame, to be treated as a mere servant in front of all this nobility. It didn't matter. He pressed his own spine tighter to the paneled wall, gazing with dire presentiment at the unmoving figure crumpled on the ballroom floor.

The manager of the dowager's estates came down to the cellar, to talk with Anton.

He sat on a little wooden crate that at one time had held canisters of grease for the machinery clanking and wheezing all about them. Up above, he could hear the dancing. The unmanned violins slid their bows across the strings, the sprightly rhythms impelling the aristocratic figures through their motions. Or seeming to—all knew, but pretended not to, that it was actually the various armatures that moved through the openings in the ballroom floor, their pistons and hinges connected to the curved metal bands fastened around the elegant guests.

"You're aware, aren't you, that this person's dead?"

Anton looked over to where the manager, in his black livery, tilted the doctor's chin with an ink-stained finger. The old man's face was gray and slack, his eyes already filming over.

"Yes—" He nodded. "I knew that. Even before they brought him down here."

The distant instruments skirled and stuttered through a Hungarian *galop*, its rapid notes audible through the mechanical clamor closer at hand. From below, he could hear the roaring of the furnaces, driving every step of cavalry boot and sweep of lace-fringed gown.

"So I can hardly pay you, can I?" The manager pulled his hand back, letting the doctor's head nod back onto his motionless chest. "Our contract is with him. Or rather, it was. His unfortunate demise would seem to nullify the relationship. Did he have heirs?"

A shake of the head as Anton bit his lower lip. He was not surprised at what the manager, with the accounts book in a pocket of the swallow-tailed coat, told him now—he had expected as much, in his own sinking heart. But to hear it pronounced with gallows finality, that he would not receive his year's wages, which *Herr Dr.* Pavel had always settled upon him as the midnight bells had struck—that he would go homeless and hungry, peering through shuttered shop windows for even the illusory hope of some new employment—he felt his hollow stomach clench at the thought of the empty, wintry streets that lay outside the Apollosaal.

"If he had such, you might apply to them." The manager drew on his gloves. "For what's owed to you."

Anton said nothing. He knew no one owed him anything now. That was the way of this world.

He watched the estates manager mount the creaking iron rungs, spiraling back up to the light and music above.

Alone once more with his former master's corpse, he leaned forward where he sat, arms across his knees, hands working themselves into a brooding knot. His own hunger he scarcely minded. He was used to that. But Gisel had surely lost her place in the dowager's service. If he were able to pay for even a few more weeks of the attic room's shelter, he might have taken her there and wrapped his arms about her as they lay on the brown-spotted straw heaped in one narrow corner. He might have kept her safe there as they both waited for the cold year to turn, the snows to melt under spring's desperately longed-for advance. They had both whispered plans to each other, that he might break from the doctor's drudging employ, that they both might flee from the city and live on wild apples and snared woodcocks turned on rudely fashioned spits, the two of them crouched around a small fire's blackened stones. . . .

Even if it had been just for one spring and summer, before the first chill winds inched through the hills—they would at least have had that much. Which would have been enough, or at least enough to tell each other so. But now they wouldn't. He turned his head, looking over at the doctor's slumped form. They never would.

Heavy with resolve, Anton stood upright, pushing the wooden box aside with the heel of his foot. For a moment, he looked around himself at the churning machinery, the levers and pistons pumping away at the linkages to the ballroom above. If he tilted his head back, he could see small bright glimpses of the light from the glittering chandeliers, interrupted by the quick, relentless motion of the dancers, swirling in their courses from one end of the grand space to the other.

He watched and listened, then turned toward the valves and gauges spanning the basement's walls. He reached out and grasped one of the small iron wheels, hesitated a moment—then twisted it as far as he could, until it could open no farther. Each of the valves hissed at him as he did the same to them. When he was done with the last, he stepped back, listening to the machinery shake faster and faster. Clouds of scalding vapor filled the chamber as he turned and made his way to the stone steps leading even farther below.

The stokers turned their silent gaze toward him. The flames

beyond the iron doors glinted on the sweat and soot of their naked chests.

"More," said Anton. He brought his own gaze from each man to the next, one after another. "Higher." He raised his hand and pointed to the furnaces behind them. "All you can give."

They looked about at each other, then back to him. First the closest one slowly nodded; then they all did. A time had come that the stokers in their chains had thought would never come to them. They turned away, thrusting the blades of their shovels into the heaps of coal, hurling one load after another into the mounting flames.

Even before Anton retreated onto the steps, he felt the dizzying heat wash over him as though it were the tide of a fiery ocean. He brought a forearm across his eyes, to shield himself from the vision of suns bursting to life inside the furnaces.

He found Gisel at the back of the crowds outside the Apollosaal. The townspeople pressed their faces close to the high-arched windows, gaping through the blood-spattered glass at the whirling scene within.

"Don't you want to see them?" Gisel pulled her rough woolen shawl tighter about herself. This far away from the columned building, the snowflakes remained unmelted, clinging to her golden hair. "You told me you never liked them, either."

"I don't need to," said Anton. That was true—when he had come up from the basement, he had walked through the grand ballroom. He had stayed close to the wall to avoid the caged figures of the nobility, whirling about in the interminable courses through the glittering space. Impelled by the unleashed machinery protruding from the floor's gaps, the corseted men and women moved with such velocity that the slightest impact might have sent him sprawling unconscious.

At the sudden noise of the windows shattering, he wrapped Gisel in his arms, turning his back toward the Apollosaal and shielding her from the shards of glass. There were at least a few people in the crowd whose faces were nicked by the bright flying bits, like a gale of razor-edged ice crystals. They didn't even notice the trickles of red running down their throats as they pushed and scrabbled with the others, climbing inside the ballroom to gaze at the dead marvels there.

Dead or dying—he had seen at least a few, as he had made his way along the side of the ballroom, who might still have been at least partly alive, the last of their strength and breath ebbing away. Slumped in the cages of the whirling machinery, medals dangling from hollow chests, jewels draped over cold breasts, their bodies kept erect only by the confines of the iron bands as they swept in one great circle with the others, from one end of the ballroom to the other, then around again and again. The clattering of the machinery, along with the hissing and groans from the boilers beneath, was all that could be heard in the ballroom. That other music, all *allegro* and dash, had ceased when the violins' strings had been sawn through by the ceaseless, back-and-forth fury of the bows.

Anton let go of the living form in his arms. He walked over to the dead one that had crashed through the ballroom window, flung by the mechanism that had disintegrated about the woman, its iron bands snapped at last by the force of the dance. The dowager's kid-leather boots were sodden red now, the feet bloodied to pulp inside them. After she could no longer dance, the machines had danced for her and the others caught inside them. Now twin pools of red seeped through the trampled snow, which thawed with their thinning heat, then froze again. The empty eyes looked up at him, with nothing but the night's heavy clouds reflected at their dulling centers.

But only for a moment. He felt Gisel stepping close beside him, then saw one of her rag-wrapped clogs kick the dowager's face, hard enough to crack bone and snap its lifeless gaze to one side.

"Don't—" He wrapped his arms around her again, pulling her away as she burst into sobbing tears. "It's all right. It is, it is . . ."

Even more terrible things were happening inside the grand

ballroom. As he led Gisel away, he could hear vengeful shouts and laughter, the creak of metal wedged asunder, bludgeons of stick and fist upon withered flesh.

In the center of the city's widest street, he held her close to himself. They both looked far beyond the skeletal trees at either side, toward the ancient Roman walls. The half-naked stokers were lifting the beams onto their blackened shoulders, unbarring the gates tall as clock towers. Massive iron hinges groaned as the gates slowly parted, the stokers gripping and pulling the timbers' edges toward themselves.

He closed his eyes and pressed his face to the snow that had traced across Gisel's hair. Soldiers who wore no medals, with worn boots of rough, unpolished leather, and hard-faced commissars with machine pistols rather than swords at their belts, astride horses lean and bony-ribbed from their long trek across the steppes—they would enter unopposed now, gazing around at all that had fallen so easily into their hands.

He held her even tighter, her heart in time with his.

Things would be different now.

Fair Vasyl

by Steven Harper

**(BASED ON THE RUSSIAN FAIRY TALE
"VASILISA THE BEAUTIFUL")**

"I'm going up," Vasyl said.

Petro caught his arm with strong fingers. "Don't be a fool! The penalty—"

"I know the penalty." Vasyl shook himself free of his friend's grip and climbed the stairs in chilly autumn air. A chattering crowd in Kiev's Khreshchatyk Square hushed in stages as they realized that someone was taking up the challenge. Vasyl's heart beat faster with every step and his stomach felt tight as sheet metal. At the top of the wooden steps on the wide platform sat Vyktor Ivanovych, the mayor of Kiev, dressed in all his red velvet finery. The heavy gold chain beneath his beard indicated his office, and he occupied an elaborately carved chair. Behind him stood a mechanical man in gold livery. It carried a tray of food and a crystal goblet of wine. Vasyl quavered at the intimidating display, so fine compared to his simple work boots and oil-stained shirt. Even his tinker's pack and cap had oil stains on them. He quickly snatched off the latter, revealing deep red hair.

Beside the mayor, on a much smaller chair, sat Hanna

Vyktorevna, the mayor's daughter. Her golden hair, azure eyes, and graceful figure made Vasyl think of an autumn sunrise, both beautiful and untouchable. She was nineteen now, time for her to marry. Ivanovych wanted Hanna to marry a prince, but no princes called on the daughter of a mayor.

As time passed, it became more and more embarrassing that Hanna remained single, and Ivanovych decided that if his daughter couldn't marry a prince, she must at least have a husband who proved himself by fulfilling a task set by the mayor himself, a task sure to be all but impossible. As a result, this was the seventh Sunday the mayor had put his daughter on display, and no one had dared approached the platform.

No one until now.

Ivanovych looked Vasyl up and down. "Who are you?"

"My name—" Vasyl's voice broke. He coughed and tried again. "My name is Vasyl Mykhailovych, and I wish to marry your daughter."

The crowd broke into unexpected applause. Vasyl caught a glimpse of Petro standing among them. His lifelong friend's face was grim. Petro was a Tatar, from the Crimea, which meant he had dark hair and a swarthy complexion. Years of working as a blacksmith had given him a powerful build, and his kind face caught the attention of any number of women, but he had shown no interest in any of them since the death of his wife nine years ago. At the moment his brown eyes were hard with disapproval, and Vasyl almost left the platform right then.

The applause died down and the mayor held out his hand. "Wine," he said, and his mechanical handed him the crystal goblet with precise movements. "Your occupation, Mykailovych?"

Vasyl shifted the little pack of tools on his back. "I am a simple tinker, sir."

Hanna glanced at him, then looked away, her face carefully impassive. The mayor pointed a beringed finger and replied, "Does *that* wish to marry her as well?"

Coming up the stairs was a brass machine. It was a skinny, pointed staff with two long arms that ended in vaguely human hands. The bottom of the staff flared out wide like a bell with wheels on the bottom. To navigate the stairs, it hitched itself upward with its arms, one step at a time, laboring with the effort but refusing to give up. Steam puffed from several seams.

"Broom!" Vasyl said. "You didn't have to come up here."

The unclear command caught Broom off guard. He hesitated at the top of the steps and tipped dangerously backward.

"Wait!" Vasyl called. "Come here, Broom."

Broom scrabbled a moment, regained his balance, and scuttled over to Vasyl, where he waited with folded hands. The crowd laughed.

"Your mechanical has a difficult time understanding orders," the mayor said.

"I ordered Broom to follow me, sir," Vasyl replied, keeping his voice even despite the implied criticism. "He does what he is told, no more, no less. It is the nature of all mechanicals. Even yours."

"Hm." The mayor sipped from his goblet, then tried to hand it back to his mechanical, who didn't move. "Take this," he said irritably, and the mechanical obeyed. "You know the nature of the challenge, boy?"

Boy? Vasyl bristled. He was nearly thirty, and just because he had never married didn't mean he was less a man. Women certainly looked at him. Petro said many called him Vasyl the Fair. But what with one thing and another, he had never married. Good looks notwithstanding, Vasyl was just a tinker who repaired machines for other people, not a crafter who built them new. It didn't matter that the machines worked better after he repaired them—people hated paying the tinker, and they paid as little as possible.

The lack of money put off most women, and the ones who had shown interest hadn't stimulated Vasyl's interest in return. But now talk was going around that the tinker couldn't find a wife, and it was time to do the right thing, be a man. Not a boy.

"I will complete your task," he said stiffly, "and prove myself worthy of your daughter's hand."

"And if you fail," the mayor added, "it means your head and hands on my table."

The words landed like lead slabs. Petro blanched, and mutters whispered through the crowd.

"Yes," Vasyl said. His knuckles were white and his chest felt constricted by bands of brass. Broom waited patiently, little puffs of steam escaping from his seams, while Hanna still refused to look at Vasyl.

"Very well," the mayor said, and the crowd went silent. "Your task shall be this."

Vasyl held his breath. The only sound was Broom's puffing.

"Create for me," the mayor pronounced, "a mechanical that can think for itself."

A moment of silence followed. Then the crowd broke into an excited babble that rushed against Vasyl's ears. Petro staggered.

"A mechanical that can think for itself?" Vasyl said. "But that's—"

"You have accepted the challenge." The mayor rose. "You have three days."

He took Hanna's hand and swept off the platform, accidentally leaving his mechanical behind.

"Can it be done, Vaska?" Petro demanded as they walked the cobblestoned streets. "Is it possible to make a mechanical that can think for itself?"

"I don't know." Vasyl hunched forward, hands in his pockets, pack dragging at his back. "You were right, Petya. I'm a fool."

Broom clattered down the cobblestone street behind them. He—Vasyl always thought of Broom as *he*—managed to look worried, despite a lack of facial features. Every so often he snatched up a piece of detritus from the walkway and tossed it with disdain into the gutter.

Petro put a heavily muscled arm around Vasyl's neck. "We need food and we need a drink," he decided, "especially a drink. And you will spend the night at my house while we work on this problem together."

"I shouldn't—"

"'On the thirteenth night of October,'" Petro interrupted, quoting the old story, "'Baba Yaga seeks her bones, and woe to he who walks alone.' You will sleep on my stove, and we'll start fresh in the morning. No arguments."

He steered Vasyl toward his own house, the one behind his forge. The few people on the street, their friends and neighbors, ignored them both, uncertain how to react to Vasyl's gesture in the square. But most people had already closed their shutters, and several doorsteps had plates of food on them.

A cold fear about the entire affair grew in Vasyl's stomach, and he became more and more grateful for Petro's powerful arm around him, though he would never have said so. Instead, he allowed Petro to drag him toward the smithy.

Petro's forge and house occupied the back of a little square with a fountain in it. Other businesses occupied other stores, and the owners lived above them. Since it was Sunday, Petro's forge was cold and deserted. The house behind it was small and all his own. As he always did, Vasyl compared the cozy place to his own cramped workshop with its narrow bed in the corner and gave a mental sigh.

Petro thrust the door open. "I'm home!"

A nine-year-old girl with brown braids scampered across the little kitchen and flung herself into Petro's arms. "Papa! Uncle Vaska! Broom!"

Petro lifted the girl high and kissed her cheek. "How good were you while I was gone, Olena?"

She spread her arms wide. "This good. I made supper, and I was sure Uncle Vaska was coming, so I made sure to put out food for him, too. And I'll make an extra plate for *her*."

"Baba Yaga's place to take," Petro said, "and our place to give."

"Everyone is talking about Uncle Vaska," she said anxiously as Petro put her down. Broom shut the door and Vasyl shrugged out of his pack. "Are you going to marry that girl, Uncle?"

"We'll see, dearest," Vasyl said.

"I don't want you to." Olena's tone was serious. "I want you to move in with us and fix toys for children and be my uncle forever."

He forced a smile and twisted one of her pigtails around his finger. "Are you jealous, little one? Perhaps you want to marry me?"

She made a face. "No. I want to marry someone who likes girls."

An uncomfortable silence fell over the room. Petro cleared his throat, but before he could say anything, Vasyl jumped in.

"I will always be Uncle Vaska," he promised. "No matter what. Now, how about we eat supper, and then Broom can help clean up?"

It was hog-butchering season, and on the table Olena had set a long, wide strip of white pork fat still on the skin, a loaf of fragrant dark bread, several cloves of garlic, a dish of salt, a bottle of vodka, and a pot of tea. The three of them sliced rich pieces of fat off the skin and ate them on the bread, alternating with cloves of garlic dipped in salt. The extra plate sat on one corner of the table, waiting to be put outside. Vasyl and Petro drank vodka while Olena drank sweet tea. Vasyl also drank in the scene itself. The cozy kitchen, the warm stove, the yellow lamp, the brass mechanical. The little girl who was a daughter to him in all but name. The strong, outspoken man who was his best friend and the one person he could always lean on. He wished it could go on forever.

Broom, at Olena's order, gathered up the dishes and took them to the washtub while Olena poured hot water over them from the kettle on the ceramic stove.

Petro poured more vodka into their cups. "Why, Vaska?"

Vasyl knew what he meant, but he wanted to hold on to the moment a bit longer, so he fell back on his usual trick. "I'm sorry, Petro. It must have been difficult to watch that today."

"Of course it was," Petro said thickly. "You are like my own brother. When you went up there, my hands were ice."

"You felt helpless."

"No man likes that feeling." Petro thumped his glass on the table. "Especially when someone he . . . when his brother does something dangerous and foolish."

Vasyl straightened in his chair. What had Petro been about to say? He wanted to ask, but he knew from experience that would be a mistake. Petro was falling into the rhythm of speaking now, and Vasyl let himself fade away, become the listener. It was a skill he had honed over many years. When people were talking to you, they weren't hitting.

"It was foolish," he said, echoing Petro's last statement.

"And now we both have to pay the price." Petro's dark eyes were serious. "Sometimes I don't understand you, Vaska. You have everything—looks, intelligence, a strong body—but you always fail."

"I always fail," Vasyl the echo replied.

"So why today?"

The question caught Vasyl off guard. "What?"

"The mayor put his daughter on display six other Sundays. Why did you pick this Sunday to step forward?" Petro leaned forward again. "Why this sudden need to get married?"

Petro fell silent, waiting, and the fine moment ended. Vasyl sighed. "I'm tired of being alone, Petya. I want to wake up with someone together and spend days together and go to bed together."

"I understand loneliness," Petro said. "After nine years, I understand. But to relieve yours, you could choose Yilka, the baker's daughter, or Larissa, the shoemaker's sister. Instead you risk your life to choose Hanna, the mayor's daughter. It hurts me that I don't understand why." He thumped his chest. "Right here it hurts. So, why her and why today?"

"I'm also tired of being poor," Vasyl blurted. "And I felt bad for her because she has to sit up there every week with no one to choose her. And now . . . I wish I could take it back. I am a fool. No one can build a mechanical that thinks for itself."

Olena and Broom continued with their work. Broom was washing dishes while Olena swept the floor. The men kept their voices low, but Vasyl was sure Olena heard every word. Children always did.

Petro squeezed Vasyl's forearm. Vasyl felt as though he should pull away, but he was too full and too tired and too tense to bother. Besides, the physical contact was reassuring. "Nothing is impossible," he said stoutly. "I will help you, my brother. But first, you must answer the question you have been avoiding."

Vasyl felt nervous again. "What question have I been avoiding?"

"Why didn't you make this mess last week or the week before? Why today, of all days?"

Vasyl opened his mouth to say he didn't know why. Then he looked at the extra plate of food and at the gathering gloom outside the windows, and he realized he did know why.

"It would be easier to show you than tell you. But, Olena—"

"If you are going out, I am staying in," Olena said.

Petro clambered to his feet. "You're not going out!"

"I must." Vasyl dropped the half-empty vodka bottle and the rest of the bread into a sack and pulled on his coat and pack. "I went up there today because tonight is *her* night, and I knew I might need help."

Petro's dark eyes went wide. "You want to visit *Baba Yaga?*"

"I have no idea how to make a mechanical think for itself. She might."

"She'll eat you alive!"

"And the mayor's punishment is kinder?" Vasyl hefted the sack. "If you want to come, then come. I have to leave now."

Petro looked torn. He glanced at his friend and then at his daughter. Vasyl felt a small stab of jealousy. Despite his earlier statement, he didn't really want to do this alone—he had used up his courage for the week facing down the mayor—and he badly wanted Petro to come with him. When they were younger, Petro would have come without hesitation. But now Petro was a family man, and family men didn't leave their families to help friends.

Vasyl admonished himself. He was being unfair. Still . . .

"Go, Papa," Olena said. "I am not frightened. As long as I do not go outside, she will not touch me."

A soft rumble outside made Vasyl hurry to the door. "Quick!"

Petro kissed Olena's cheek, snatched up his own coat, and ran outside with Vasyl. Vasyl dropped the plate of food on the doorstep, and the two men ran out to the deserted square. Every front step had a plate on it. Every window was shuttered tight.

"Do you see anything?" Petro was looking at the darkening sky.

"There!" Vasyl pointed. A streak of light rushed overhead and west. At the front of it was a strange contraption of iron and brass. It was shaped like a giant bowl or mortar, held together with an intricate pattern of rivets. On the back were fastened a pair of engines that blasted fire and light, carrying the mortar just high enough to clear the rooftops of Kiev. Vasyl took an involuntary step backward, and the autumn air grew colder. In the mortar stood a tall, thin hag in an earth-brown dress. Her gray hair streamed out behind her, and she steered with a rudder made from a brass pestle. The woman glanced down and her hard eyes met Vasyl's for a tiny moment. His blood turned to thin ice water. Then she was gone, leaving a trail of smoke and thunder in the sky.

"I can't believe I am actually saying this," Petro said, "but we must hurry if we want to follow her."

The two men ran through the empty streets of Kiev, their boots ringing on cobblestones. Ahead of them, the spreading trail of smoke arced downward as the hag brought her mortar in among the buildings, close to ground. Vasyl ran until his ribs burned, still following the smoke trail with Petro at his side. Unfortunately, the city grew too dark and the smoke trail too thin. They lost the path.

"Where now?" Petro asked.

Vasyl scanned the street. He could smell the sharp exhaust from paraffin oil. All the houses they had passed sported plates of food, but here several of the plates had been emptied, and a number had been flipped upside down, as if someone moving at great speed had snatched the food from them without pausing.

"This way." He led Petro down the street, following the trail of empty plates, until he came to an intersection. The plates on the street in three directions were still full. Vasyl peered nervously down the narrow fourth street. It was dark as a wolf's mouth. The plate on the first doorstep, just visible in the pale light at the intersection, was empty.

"I didn't think to bring a light," Vasyl whispered. "Did you?"

Petro shook his head. "How do we—?"

A rattling noise made Vasyl jump, and his heart beat at the back of his throat. Broom scuttled up, bobbing anxiously.

"Broom!" Vasyl gasped. "What in God's name?"

"Did you order him not to follow you anymore?"

"I forgot," Vasyl admitted sheepishly. "But as long as he's here, we can use him. Broom, light, please."

There was a *pop*, and from the spot where Broom's staff belled outward a beam of blue light speared down to illuminate the cobblestones. Broom bounced up and down, apparently pleased.

"Very nice, Broom," Vasyl said. "Walk beside me."

They entered the street with Broom lighting the way. All the windows were shuttered, and every doorstep plate was empty. Stony walls pressed inward, and the air dripped with smells of urine, garbage, and paraffin oil exhaust, which told Vasyl they were going the right way. The street made a dogleg and ended in a square. Vasyl sucked in a breath and Petro put a heavy hand on his friend's shoulder. Even Broom's little light quivered.

Before them stood a fence made of bones. Electricity arced in ladders up fence posts made of femurs and snapped off the skulls that sat atop them. The bones were inlaid with iron, and sparks snarled around the metal, bringing to Vasyl a mixture of fear and admiration. He swallowed around his pounding heart and wiped sweaty palms on oil-stained trousers. The fence blocked the entire alley, and beyond it . . .

A creak and a thud, and another creak and another thud pounded the cobblestones beyond the fence. A metal cottage occupied a square beyond the awful fence. Rust streaked the sides and the roof, and a heavy iron bar held the door shut. Strange enough that a cottage should be made of metal and sitting in the middle of a little square in Kiev, but this house was supported by a pair of enormous bird legs made of brass. Exposed pistons creaked and hissed as each leg moved. The feet came up and down, thudding and thumping and creaking and hissing on the cobblestones, ready to crush anything that dared come close. Vasyl stared at the structure, simultaneously fascinated and frightened.

"How do we get past this fence?" asked Petro in a hushed voice. "If we touch it, we will die."

"If *I* touch it," Vasyl replied, also hushed. "You are staying here."

"You aren't going in there without me."

"Yes? And who will take care of little Olena if you die?"

That silenced Petro, though his face clouded and it was clear that he wanted to disagree further. Vasyl pulled off his tinker's pack and rummaged through it until he found some wire and a pair of wooden tongs.

"This will do." He used the tongs to connect one end of the wire to the fence, while the other end dragged on the ground. With a pop and a shower of sparks, the electric current vanished.

"It's a simple series circuit," Vasyl said to Petro's unasked question. "Easy enough to interrupt if you know what you're doing." Still, he used the tongs instead of his hands to push at a section that looked like a gate. It swung open with a tooth-grating screech. At the sound, the cottage beyond stopped moving on its strange bird legs. With a dreadful creak, it turned toward Vasyl as if the front windows were staring eyes.

"Uh-oh," Vasyl said. "We're supposed to say something. A password. What is it?"

"How should I know?" Petro hissed.

Broom managed a tiny whimpering sound. The cottage took a step toward them, then another and another. It leaned angrily forward. Old stories flashed through Vasyl's head. The hut appeared on the thirteenth night of October each year. Anyone who touched the fence would die. To make it stop dancing, you said—

"Little hut, little hut!" Vasyl called. "Turn your back to the forest and your face to me!"

The cottage continued to stomp toward them, now only a few steps away. Broom quivered. Vasyl desperately glanced left and right, but there was nowhere to run to. His bowels turned to water. The hut thundered forward. He shouted the words again, but there was no effect.

"Little hut, little hut!" Petro cried. "Turn your back to the city and your face to me!"

The cottage came to a halt a mere step away, one foot raised to crush them. Then it lowered itself to the ground like a hen settling onto a nest.

"We aren't in the forest," Petro said calmly.

Vasyl drooped with relief. "I'm glad you're here, Petya."

"Then let me come in with you."

"You know she won't allow that," Vasyl replied with a shake of his head.

"I'll wait out here." Petro folded his arms. "All night, if I have to."

"All right." Vasyl succumbed to temptation and gave Petro a fast hug. "Here goes."

Vasyl dashed up to the door before he could lose his nerve and flung the bar up. The door leaped open. Panting, Vasyl hurried through the dark opening. At the last second, Broom scurried in behind him—Vasyl had once again forgotten to order him not to follow. The door slammed shut. Vasyl stood in darkness, the only sound his heart pounding in his ears.

"Broom," he whispered hoarsely, "light."

Painful light exploded all around Vasyl. He threw up a hand to shield his eyes. When he could see, he found himself in a kitchen much larger than the cottage walls could encompass. Vasyl spun, trying to take it all in. Dirty flagstone floor. Ashy ceramic stove. Greasy black kettle. Grimy kitchen table. Cobwebbed cupboards. Tangled loom. Rumpled bed. The light seemed to come from the walls themselves, though Broom gamely cast his tiny twin beams.

In the corner, tall and thin, arms folded, stood the old hag with her tangle of gray hair. She looked like a mop left to dry. Then she grinned, revealing iron teeth that made Vasyl's stomach shrivel back against his spine.

"Well," she said in a gravelly voice lower than Petro's, "it isn't often dinner just walks through my front door."

Vasyl gave the door behind him an involuntary glance. Three heavy bolts slid home with a clunk, a thud, and a boom. Broom squeaked. Vasyl swallowed and wondered if his life could be counted in seconds. He forced himself to stand straight.

"You don't want to eat me," he said.

"No?" She licked her lips with a pale tongue and Vasyl realized she was at least two heads taller than he. "Why?"

Vasyl ticked off reasons with trembling fingers. "I'll taste stringy and gamy. You just ate from all those plates outside, so you're not hungry. And I brought other food for you." From the sack he produced the bread and vodka, which he put on the awful kitchen table. Then he backed away. Broom stayed right behind him.

"Hm. I can give you a few minutes." She gobbled the bread in two bites, poured the vodka down her throat, and flung the bottle into the fireplace with a crash. Vasyl flinched. "So, boy, what gives you the balls to brave the dancing hut of Baba Yaga?"

Coming from her, the word *boy* didn't sound insulting. "I need your help, Grandmother."

"They all do. And they all end up in that kettle. Why should you be any different?"

"You're talking to me instead of eating me," Vasyl pointed out, not quite believing he was doing this. "That makes me at least a little different."

"Hm. Usually I get tender young girls. They ask me to give them a dowry for some hideous husband or hand them fire for their stupid stepmothers when they could just as easily get either for themselves if they would just try."

"It must be difficult," Vasyl said, "to watch foolish people make foolish mistakes, especially when you give them good advice."

"You can't possibly know how difficult." A rusty mechanical cat crawled out from under a cupboard, and Baba Yaga picked it up. Her claws scraped absently across its back and made Vasyl's teeth ache. "I tell them their husbands and stepmothers have to sleep sometime, and the kitchen is filled with long, sharp knives. Or, if you *must* bow to them, make fire yourself with a pair of sticks when the hearth goes cold. But no—they always come to me. And then they cry bitter tears when I drop them into the kettle or, if I'm in a very good mood"—her claws raked the cat's back with a screech that raised Vasyl's hair—"I chase them across a river or through a hedge to teach them a lesson in self-sufficiency."

"But they don't learn much, do they?" Vasyl said.

"Never," she sighed. "They always marry some stupid twit and spread lies about my—hey, now!"

Vasyl tensed. "Yes?"

Baba Yaga laughed, a low, throaty sound that sent confusing shivers down Vasyl's back. She tossed the cat on the table, filled a long, thin pipe, and lit it with a spark created by snapping one claw across her teeth. The smoke smelled of diesel.

"So you bring the gift of listening as well as food, do you?" she said. "You're smarter than I gave you credit for, boy. I like that. I think I like *you.*"

Vasyl let himself feel a tiny bit of relief. "So you'll help me?"

"*Like* can mean any number of things," Baba Yaga said around the pipe, "including how good you taste. But for now, it means yes, I might help you. What do you want?"

Vasyl took a deep breath. The mayor in his arrogant red velvet seemed simple and friendly compared to Baba Yaga's grimy kitchen and iron stare. "I need a mechanical that can think for itself."

Baba Yaga sucked silently at her pipe for a long moment. The cat stared at Broom. Broom stared at the cat.

"What for?" she asked at last.

"So I can keep my hands and my head." Vasyl tried not to shift from foot to foot. A tightrope stretched behind and before him, and he didn't dare move.

Baba Yaga stared at him for another iron moment. The smelly blue smoke filled the room. Vasyl remained silent.

"What," Baba Yaga said at last, "does this have to do with the tasty young Tatar waiting outside my gate?"

Vasyl's knuckles went white. "Leave him out of this. He hasn't entered your yard. He hasn't broken any of your rules. You can't touch him."

Baba Yaga ticked off fingers of her own. "He's out and about on the thirteenth night of October. He used my password without my permission. And you brought his delicious scent into my cottage. I can do as I please, boy. Answer the question."

"This has nothing to do with Petro." Fear widened Vasyl's eyes and made him pant. "Leave him alone."

"Hm." She leaned toward Vasyl, invading Vasyl's space with her long nose, smoky pipe, and greasy hair. Still panting, Vasyl held his ground and smelled sweat and oil and hot metal.

"He's still mine if I want him," she whispered into his ear, exhaling warm smoke like a dragon. "Would you offer to take his place, Fair Vasyl?"

Her words turned his skin to ice. "I . . . I . . ."

"Never mind." She leaned back and waved a hand, creating blue swirls in the smoky air. "I was only playing with you, like Maroushka here plays with mice. She can't eat them, but it makes for interesting results when she tries. Sit down, boy. You make me tired to look at you."

The room spun more than a little, and Vasyl gratefully sank onto one of the creaky benches near the table. Broom scuttled closer, his eyes still alight.

"What of that one?" Baba Yaga was still standing. Looming. "Can't your mechanical think for itself?"

"Broom? No," Vasyl said. He started to put his elbow on the table, but his skin shied away from the filth, and he set his arm in his lap instead. "I've improved Broom, but he can't think."

"He?" Baba Yaga asked mildly.

Something in her tone tightened Vasyl's stomach again. "I've had him for so long, it seems rude to say *it*. You called your cat a *she*."

"Indeed." Baba Yaga knocked the ashes out of her pipe into the fireplace, and a cloud of angry red sparks puffed up. "Where did you get him?"

"My mother gave him to me. She was a crafter, not a tinker, so she could make instead of just repair. But she died when I was very young."

"Your father remarry?"

Vasyl lifted his chin. "Yes."

"Bitchy stepmother?"

"You'd get along with her," Vasyl said before he could stop himself, then braced himself for a blow or worse.

But Baba Yaga only snorted. "Why didn't your father throw her out?"

"He wasn't strong enough. When I was old enough, he told me to flee. I obeyed, and took Broom with me. That was more than twenty years ago, which means my father's probably dead by now. The bitch-mother, too, for that matter. And I don't care if she is." He suddenly felt defensive. "What of it?"

"Not my job to judge, boy." Baba Yaga filled and lit the pipe again. "But I do observe that it's difficult to escape familiar patterns. When you live your life with cruel words, you look for people to give them to you. When you escape an evil stepmother, you take an uncaring bride. When your father throws you out, you love someone who won't love you back. And to keep yourself in cruelty, you're willing to risk head and hands on the mayor's sideboard. Keep the pattern going. Hm."

Vasyl's mouth had dried up, and he realized he was clutching Broom with one hand. "That's not the way it is."

"Pah." Smoke curled into the heavy air from between Baba Yaga's iron teeth. "This gets us nowhere. I said I would help you, and I will."

"So it's possible to make a mechanical think for itself?"

"It's possible. But first we'll talk payment."

The hope that had arisen in Vasyl's chest froze like an apple blossom in a spring frost. "Payment?"

"Why does everyone think I work for free?" Baba Yaga asked Maroushka, who lounged at her own end of the table.

"I don't have any—"

Suddenly Baba Yaga was looming over Vasyl again, bending down so her long, thin nose practically touched his. The terror that tore through Vasyl turned his bones to lava and his heart to ice. Her thin figure filled his entire world with famine, disease, and loss. The point of one clawed fingertip lifted his chin and forced him to look into her eyes. They were as black and empty as an eclipse, and Vasyl felt they might drain the life from him.

"Do I look like I want money?" she hissed. "Your paltry mayor wants head and hands. Me, I'll take much, much more."

Vasyl's stepmother was standing over him again with her stick, the one twice as thick as her thumb, and he knew when Father came home and saw the cuts and bruises, she would simply say the boys up the street were at little Vaska again, making fun and starting fights because of all the time the boy wasted reading his mother's books and tinkering with his mother's machines, and Father would sigh and tell Vaska that he should spend more time outside in what passed for fresh air in Kiev, and since no one listened to Vaska, he learned to listen to other people, read their bodies, and take their secrets so he could use them for protection instead of fighting back directly, and Baba Yaga had seen the truth of it and now he would pay for letting the secret out.

No. He touched Broom's solid shell for reassurance, and it was as if his mother were there again, in some small way. The fear receded. *That was the past and this is the present. If she were going to kill me, she would have done it by now.*

"What's your price, then?" he asked. "My soul? I'll give you that, if you want."

Baba Yaga backed away a little, then chortled. "Nice try, boy. We both know your soul belongs to someone else and isn't yours to bargain with."

Vasyl spread his hands. "Then what?"

"My biggest fear, boy, is that while I'm putting together your precious mechanical, my poor cottage will fall to ruin."

Vasyl looked around the filthy kitchen. "Er . . . I don't understand what you're asking."

"Keep house for me while I work," Baba Yaga clarified. "Today you will clean this room. And if you don't meet my standards, it'll be more than your head on my table."

Vasyl remembered the bone fence outside and swallowed. "All right. I only have three days before—"

Baba Yaga waved this away. "Do you know what a tesseract is, boy?"

"No."

"Suffice it to say that we will have sufficient time inside this cottage. Let's both begin." She stalked out of the room through a door Vasyl hadn't noticed before and slammed it shut.

Vasyl looked around the harshly lit, windowless kitchen and its coating of grime. He sighed heavily from his chair, shrugged out of his tinker's pack, and opened it.

"You know you're screwed, right?" said Maroushka the cat.

Vasyl's hands jerked, and the pack rattled. "What—?"

"Screwed," Maroushka repeated from the table. "It means treated unfairly or harshly."

Vasyl scrambled to regain his equilibrium. Mechanicals didn't talk. Ever. Therefore the cat wasn't a mechanical, or Baba Yaga could work real miracles.

"I—I know what I'm doing," Vasyl replied shortly.

"*I—I know what I'm doing,*" Maroushka repeated in an exact replica of Vasyl's voice, and Vasyl jumped again. "They all say that."

"I have help. I wouldn't have come here if I didn't."

"Sure." Maroushka yawned, exposing brass fangs and a rubbery tongue. "All the girls have help, right up until the moment she's adding their bones to the fence."

"I'm not a girl. Or a boy. I'm a man."

"To her, anyone under a thousand years old is a baby, and everyone tastes the same in a stewpot. Look, the stories only talk about the two or three who get away, never the eight or nine hundred who become goulash. So you're dead."

"Probably." Vasyl had had enough shocks for the day and found himself growing tired of them. "I have work to do."

Baba Yaga's door shook with thuds and clanks, and once Vasyl thought he heard a muffled scream. He reopened his pack.

"She'll be back faster than you think," Maroushka said, "and this place had better be cleaner than a virgin's bathtub."

"Do you think for yourself?" Vasyl extracted a can with a spout on it from the pack.

Maroushka stared at him with hard green eyes. "That's a rude question."

"But do you?"

"Yeah." Maroushka sniffed. "Not that the answer means anything."

"Because you could be programmed to say that," Vasyl finished.

Maroushka licked one paw. "How do we know that anyone really thinks? For all you know, all the people in the world are mechanicals masquerading as people and you're the only real human in it."

"That would awfully self-centered." Vasyl unscrewed the lid on the spout and pulled out his pocketknife. "Why should the entire universe revolve around me?"

"You're *here*, aren't you? In the cottage of the world's most powerful crafter and witch in a cottage that exists partly outside time. That's major shit. Of course you're the center."

"Everything is the center in an infinite universe," Vasyl countered, "so technically you're right."

"Do *you* think for yourself?"

"Of course I do. I'm a human being."

"Doesn't mean you automatically get free thought."

"Yes, it does."

"No, it doesn't."

."Yes, it—oh, shut up!"

"My point." Maroushka curled her tail about her paws with a *clink*, a faint echo to the loud rattles and clunks beyond Baba Yaga's door. "Since you can't think for yourself, what the hell *are* you doing?"

"I can, too, think for—oh, never mind." Vasyl popped the cap off the spout, took a deep breath, and slashed his palm with the knife. He bit his lip against white-hot pain.

"Whether you agree with me or not, my question stands. Answer it."

"I'm feeding Broom." Vasyl unscrewed another cap on Broom's side, let his blood flow into Broom's fuel tank, and followed it with some of the can's contents. Broom squeaked and bounced up and down as the liquid gurgled into him.

Maroushka sniffed the air. "Is that . . . *paraffin* oil?"

"My mother's private formula." Vasyl waggled the can. "Want some?"

The cat barely hesitated. "Damn straight!"

Vasyl found a similar cap between Maroushka's shoulder blades. It was stiff with rust and came free with effort. Vasyl dripped blood and a measure of paraffin oil into the reservoir. Maroushka produced happy mechanical mewling noises. Broom, meanwhile, quivered with energy.

"I feel fifty years younger," Maroushka said. "You can stay."

"Unless your mistress eats me." Vasyl gave the cat a speculative look and wrapped a rag around his wound. "You know, maybe I should just take *you* to the mayor."

Maroushka froze and tipped over with a crash. Startled, Vasyl poked at her, but she remained motionless. After a moment, she came back to life and sat up. "No one knows that I'm self-aware, kid. Not even *her*. And I intend to keep it that way."

"She didn't make you to think for yourself?"

"She barely feeds me from the dregs of her fuel bucket. You think she cares enough to make me think? Screw that. I had to figure it out for myself."

"So, why are you telling me you can do it?"

"Kid, you feed me paraffin oil, and I'll lick your earwax clean," Maroushka said, then added, "You'd better get to work. You'll find cleaning supplies in that cupboard."

Vasyl shot Baba Yaga's door an uneasy look, then turned to Broom, who seemed ready to burst. "Broom, clean this room."

Broom saluted and shot about the room with inhuman speed.

He yanked soap, brushes, rags, and buckets from the cupboard Maroushka had indicated and flew into work, washing, scrubbing, scraping, and scouring. Water sloshed everywhere, and the soft scent of soap overcame Baba Yaga's pipe.

"How—?" Maroushka began.

"Mother's private formula." Vasyl snatched her away to avoid Brooms brushes, then set her down again. "You did say you felt younger."

Just as Broom was throwing the rags back into the cupboard, Baba Yaga's door slammed open.

"Broom," Vasyl hissed, "stop!"

Broom obeyed as the witch stomped into the room. Her dress was stained with grease and she smelled of machine oil, reminding Vasyl unsettlingly of his mother. She put her hands on nonexistent hips and glared about the kitchen. Broom skittered to hide behind Vasyl, who drew himself upright despite his pounding heart. The black kettle that now gleamed on the stove yawned big enough to swallow him whole.

"How did you do it all, boy?" Baba Yaga demanded.

"I'm efficient."

"Hm," the witch grunted. "Well, I suppose it'll do."

Vasyl released the breath he'd been holding. "Thank you, Grandmother. About the mechanical, then."

"Takes time, boy. We'll talk tomorrow." With that, she flung herself into the bed in the corner and fell to snoring loud enough to vibrate the floor. Vasyl stretched out on one of the hard benches that ran the length of the kitchen table. Exhaustion turned his bones to granite, but he couldn't sleep.

Maroushka jumped up next to his head. "He's still waiting, you know."

"Who?"

"That Tatar guy. Petro. He's been waiting a long time."

Vasyl tensed. "He should have gone home."

"Hm." Maroushka stretched, which made little clattering noises. "Why's he hanging around? Do tell."

"He's worried about me, I suppose."

"That's sweet," Maroushka purred. "How does it make you feel?"

It wasn't the sort of question Vasyl would normally answer, certainly not from a mechanical cat, but he was so tired, and Maroushka's voice was soft and sympathetic, and he'd been the listener all his life. Now he had an invitation to talk. "It's . . . nice, actually. Knowing someone cares enough to wait."

"I don't understand these things very much," Maroushka said. "Me, I'm bitchin' with that fuel. But you humans need people to talk to. What's so special about this particular guy?"

Sleep blurred Vasyl's words. "He's stronger than I am. And he's always there when I need him. And he'll tell me when I'm being foolish. And . . . he has . . . deep . . . eyes."

"Deep eyes? What the hell does that mean?"

But Vasyl was asleep.

"Hm," Maroushka said. "So, what's *your* deal, Broom?"

But Broom hadn't been ordered to answer, and remained silent.

"Today," Baba Yaga said, "you need to cook for me. And tomorrow I'll have another task for you, and then I'll give you your mechanical. How's that sound?"

"Wonderful!" Vasyl made a fist around his bandage and did some quick calculations against the can in his backpack. It should just work. "What do you want for supper?"

"This." Baba Yaga pulled a lever, and an entire side of beef dropped from the shadows in the ceiling. It landed on the table with a crash and a splatter of warm blood. As an afterthought, three dead chickens followed, landing like dreadful snowflakes. Vasyl gaped and backed away.

"Get to it," Baba Yaga said. "Or it's you in the pot." The workroom door slammed behind her.

"You'll find knives in that drawer," Maroushka said.

Vasyl wiped the blood from his face and regained his composure. He slashed his palm again, gasping at the pain of reopening the half-healed wound, mixed blood and paraffin oil in Broom's fuel tank, and said, "Broom, butcher this meat and cook it!"

Maroushka and Vasyl stood back while Broom hacked and chopped so fast the knife blades blurred. Fat and feathers flew. Vasyl rewrapped his bleeding hand and pressed his back against a wall. It felt as if he had been here for weeks instead of hours, and despite Broom's and Maroushka's presence, he felt horribly alone. He longed to hear Petro's voice, feel that rough embrace around his neck.

"You're kidding yourself if you think *she* doesn't know something's funny here," Maroushka said.

"So? I'm not breaking any rules," Vasyl said. "Broom's a tool, just like a loom or a water pump."

"Or a knife."

Broom's bone cleaver whacked through a section of rib at that moment, and Vasyl flinched. Maroushka held out a paw and studied her claws as if something interesting might be caught in them.

Uneasy, Vasyl changed the subject. "Is Petro still outside by the fence?"

"No," Maroushka said flatly.

"Oh." Vasyl felt sad, even abandoned. "He couldn't stay out all night, I suppose. Not with Olena at home."

"Is Olena his mother or his sister?"

"His daughter."

"Really?" Maroushka sounded surprised. "Well, don't that beat all?"

"What does that mean?"

But Maroushka didn't answer.

When Baba Yaga burst out of her workroom several hours later, the enormous kitchen table was piled high with steaks and roasts and ribs and baked chicken and the kettle on the stove brimmed with stew. Savory smells filled the cottage. Broom sat in the corner, hands folded. Vasyl couldn't help a thin smile at Baba Yaga's consternation.

"Hm," Baba Yaga grumped. "Looks adequate."

And she fell to eating. In moments, she had chewed her way

through every morsel on the table, bones and all, and she emptied the kettle in one long gulp. Vasyl was glad he had already eaten—the witch didn't leave behind a single tendon or bit of gristle. And when she was done, she was as thin as ever.

"Tomorrow," Baba Yaga said, wiping her mouth with the back of her hand, "you'll finish my weaving for me."

Vasyl shot a glance at the enormous loom in the corner and the tangled mess that spilled out of it. Had his mother taught Broom to weave? He couldn't remember. Vasyl himself certainly didn't know how. His hand tightened around the bloody bandage and he swallowed.

"All right," he said uneasily. "How's the mechanical coming?"

"Glad you asked. I need your . . . input."

"Input?" The word was unfamiliar to Vasyl. "What do you mean?"

In answer, Baba Yaga flung the door to her workshop open and gestured for Vasyl to follow her inside. Vasyl hesitated. No one had ever seen the inside of Baba Yaga's workshop and lived to tell the tale. Why was she bringing him in? To kill him? On the other hand, if she wanted to do that, she could do it at any time. And curiosity pulled him forward. Baba Yaga's workshop would be a place of wonder. He took a breath and stepped through the open door.

A wave of heat met him, and an alarm bell clanged. Vasyl flung his hands over his ears.

"Oops," Baba Yaga said, and shouted something Vasyl didn't catch. The bell stopped. "Alarm goes off whenever anything living enters my workshop, so don't get any ideas about swiping a souvenir."

"Uh . . . sure." Vasyl was sweating now. The source of the heat was a forge that squatted like a demon in the center of the huge room. An anvil floated before it, and nearby sat the huge brass pestle and metal mortar with its strange engines mounted on the back. Two kegs of what Vasyl assumed was fuel waited nearby, and Vasyl nervously wondered why Baba Yaga would store something flammable so close to her forge.

Stone worktables of varying heights were scattered every-where, including the walls, ceiling, and floor. Racks of gleaming tools stood among them, also clinging to the walls and ceiling. Vasyl turned, trying to look everywhere at once. Every table was covered with machines, cogs, pistons, and parts. Brass gleamed, steam puffed, and sparks spat. An army of mechanical spiders skittered about every surface, some of them making adjustments to the half-built machinery, others delivering bits and parts. Vasyl dodged a trio of them carrying the head of a mechanical St. Bernard. A tall metal arch in one corner glowed, while the interior flickered through a dozen scenes—jungle, desert, forest, ocean. Through it all, a rhythmic thump thudded against Vasyl's bones.

"The hut is dancing again," Baba Yaga said at his elbow, and Vasyl jumped. "Over here, boy."

"What are you building?" Vasyl asked as they threaded their way through the workshop.

"Negative entropy." She stepped on a wall and walked up it, still upright, as if that were the most normal thing in the world. Vasyl came with her, and the room lurched. The floor he had just left became the wall behind him, and the wall ahead of him became the floor. His stomach oozed with nausea.

"Don't barf," Baba Yaga warned, and led him to a particular table. It sported a garishly complicated set of machinery. Coils of copper leaped over bent pipes and exposed wire in impossible patterns. Switches and dials festooned a large control panel at the head of the table and thrummed with enticing rhythm. Tiny tongues of lighting flicked across the entire array. Vasyl stared, fascinated.

"I don't understand," he said slowly. "Where's the mechanical?"

Baba Yaga glanced about. "Where's your broom?"

"You're going to make *Broom* think for himself?"

"He's halfway there already, boy. It's faster than starting from scratch."

Vasyl blinked several times. This unsettling possibility hadn't occurred to him. Broom was the only remnant of his mother he had left. Letting Baba Yaga fiddle with him felt like a violation.

"What if I said Broom doesn't want to think for himself?" Vasyl hedged.

Baba Yaga showed her iron teeth. "Then I would say my little machine here is unnecessary. Look, boy, we made a deal. Either you get your mechanical in here so I can finish my job, or I'll just have to feed you."

"Feed me?"

Vasyl realized the witch was holding a butcher knife. The same butcher knife Broom had used on the beef. A spot of blood on the blade made a splotch of red chaos near the handle. "Feed you," she said, "to myself."

"Broom!" Vasyl shouted. "Come!"

Broom bustled into the workshop, barely pausing at the intersection of floor and wall. He halted at Vasyl's side and saluted. A puff of steam escaped from one of his seams with a small squeak.

"Drat." Baba Yaga set the knife down. "I could have done with a nice head cheese."

"You're not going to hurt him, are you?" Vasyl asked anxiously.

"Not at all. I just need a little help to complete the process." Baba Yaga pressed a button, and another table rose from the floor. Chained to it by his wrists, neck, and ankles was Petro. He was also gagged. The table tilted, and Petro's terrified dark eyes met Vasyl's blue ones. Vasyl cried out and ran toward him, but Baba Yaga shoved him backward and he landed flat with the wind knocked out of him. Broom quivered but didn't move. A spider crawled to the edge of the table and peered quizzically down at them.

"Don't act so surprised, boy," Baba Yaga said. "I told you the Tatar was mine if I wanted him."

Vasyl hauled himself gasping to his feet. "You said you were just playing."

"Yes." Baba Yaga dropped the spider on Petro's shoulder, where it set the tips of two of its sharp, pointed legs against Petro's skull. His eyes widened, and he tried to lean away from it, but the fetter at his neck didn't afford him enough movement. Muffled noises emerged from the gag.

"Don't you touch him!" Vasyl yelled.

"I don't have a choice," Baba Yaga replied calmly. "We have a deal. In order for me to make a mechanical that can think for itself, I need living nervous tissue. The procedure won't kill him. Quite."

"Broom! Attack!"

Broom charged. The iron point of his staff speared toward Baba Yaga's heart.

Baba Yaga was caught off guard. She screeched and jumped back. Vasyl didn't watch what happened next. Instead he snatched up a hammer from another worktable and struck at one of the locks on Petro's fetters. The lock at his right wrist cracked. Then a hard hand yanked him away from Petro's table and flung him down to the floor (wall?) several paces away. Baba Yaga's ugly face pushed into his.

"You think making a deal with me is a joke, boy?" she hissed. Behind her, Broom lay motionless on his side. The tip of his staff was bent. "There are rules even I cannot break. You will complete the housework and leave this cottage with a mechanical that can think for itself, or I will boil you screaming in my cauldron so I can peel meat from your long bones."

"I won't let you hurt Petya for me," Vasyl snarled from the floor at her feet.

"Why not?" Baba Yaga barked.

The lump came back to Vasyl's throat. The spider on the side of Petya's head pressed its sharpness through his dark hair, and a trickle of blood ran down his neck. Vasyl felt the pain as his own.

"You know why," he whispered.

Her smoky breath burned his lungs and droplets of warm spittle spattered his cheek. "Say it, my little automaton."

Vasyl shook. His teeth chattered and he clutched his hands to his sides. But he couldn't disobey. He said, "Because I'm in love with him."

The entire workshop fell silent except for the rhythmic thud and thump of the dancing feet outdoors. Vasyl's face burned with shame. How would Petro, his lifelong friend, the one man who knew his heart better than anyone else, react to this? He didn't want to meet Petya's eyes, but he couldn't help it. Slowly, he looked at Petya's face.

Petya's gaze was stone. He looked away and closed his eyes. Vasyl's heart turned to lead and dropped into his feet.

"Hm." Baba Yaga ran a claw across her lower lip. Broom remained motionless on the floor. "Such irony. To win a bride you don't desire, you blindly obey orders to seek a mechanical that can think for itself. And to get these two things you don't want, you'll have to give up the one person you *do* desire."

"You're a bitch," Vasyl whispered. "A granite bitch."

"You came to me, and you agreed to the offer, so you've no one to blame but yourself, boy. And speaking of the offer, I still need part of your Tatar's brain to—"

The rhythmic thud outside stopped. Silence followed. Baba Yaga twisted around and swore.

"Panel!" she ordered, and a trio of spiders brought over a portable control panel with a glass front, though two of the spiders twitched and quivered, nearly dropping the thing. The third spider limped. Baba Yaga twisted dials and punched buttons in an arcane pattern until an image wavered and cleared in the glass. It showed the nasty alley with the fence of bones, which still gaped open. Standing just past them was a little girl clutching a doll. Olena. Vasyl bit back a cry. Petya's eyes went wide and frantic.

"I hate it when people do that," Baba Yaga muttered. "Now I have to recalibrate everything. One of these days I'll have to change that password into something people can't hack."

"I don't want the mechanical anymore," Vasyl said. "Just let Petya go. And leave that girl alone. She has nothing to do with any of this. You and I can make a new deal. It must be hard to live here all by yourself with—"

"Sorry," Baba Yaga interrupted absently. "I have to complete the mechanical. I've lived what you call the future, and I know it will be done."

Vasyl went cold. He staggered backward and leaned against

the mechanical's table. "No. We have free choices. The future isn't set except by—"

"*Him?* Hm. In the same vein, perhaps Broom thinks *you* set the future." Baba Yaga gave a dreadful chuckle. On the screen, the image of Olena wavered uncertainly in the gap Vasyl had made in the fence.

"Look, can't we—"

"In any case"—the witch waved her butcher knife at the screen—"that tender girl out there upset the calibrations of my entire workroom. I'll be up all night resetting the machinery so I can finish your mechanical on time. The little wench earned you a reprieve, boy."

She slapped another button, and all of Petro's fetters, including the spider, released themselves. He slid from the table to land in a heap on the floor while Vasyl hovered uncertainly above him. He wanted to grab Petro and run, but Baba Yaga was between him and the door, and in any case he wouldn't get very far.

"Why are you letting him go?" Vasyl asked.

"I'm not. No one gets out the front door unless I unlock it, so it doesn't really matter if your Tatar sleeps in my kitchen or weeps in my workroom until I need him." Baba Yaga dropped the butcher knife on the table again with a clatter. "Nothing in our deal says I can't give you one last night together, though whether that's mercy or malice, I'll let you decide. If you get bored, you can get a head start on tomorrow's weaving."

Vasyl started to help Petya up, but he hissed, "Don't touch me," and struggled to his feet on his own. Vasyl felt sick inside. Baba Yaga was cruel, indeed.

"We need to help Olena," Petya whispered. "Get the hell out of here."

Vasyl righted Broom, his eyes down. It looked as though Baba Yaga had merely knocked the mechanical's memory wheels askew, and it would take no time at all to reset them. The bend at the top of his staff hadn't seriously hurt him, either. Vasyl wheeled Broom like a little pushcart ahead of him and followed Petro, who limped toward the wall and barely paused at the corner to turn the angle and right himself. Behind and above them, Baba Yaga stormed over to her floating forge, muttering and cursing all the while. The workroom door refused to shut for them, so they were forced to leave it open when they went back into the kitchen.

"I *said* you were screwed," Maroushka said from the table.

Petro stared, and Vasyl made a fast introduction. "We should figure out what to do about Olena."

"The little girl outside? She's fine for now. Out there it's still the same night you boys came in. It took Olena nearly four hours of our time to say the entire password. Tesseract, yeah?"

Petro collapsed onto a bench. His muscles sagged and his head bowed. "Then we have time. A little."

"Petya." Vasyl parked Broom and gingerly sat next to the other man. "Petya, I'm so sorry."

"Sorry?" Petro said to his clenched fists. *"Sorry?"*

"For bringing you and Olena into all this." Vasyl had to force himself to keep talking. "For not listening to you. And for . . . the other thing."

"Well, *I'm* intrigued," Maroushka said.

"You bastard," Petro whispered in a tone that crushed Vasyl like paper. "How can I believe you did this to me?"

"I'm s—"

In a lightning move, Petro grabbed the front of Vasyl's shirt and hauled him face-to-face. "If you say you're sorry again, I will ram your balls up through the roof of your mouth."

And then he was kissing Vasyl. Vasyl stiffened. Petya was *kissing* him. It wasn't happening. It couldn't happen. It was wrong and evil and it was the very thing he had been wanting ever since he had first met Petro all those years ago, the exact thing he had never been able to admit to anyone or to himself, but this terrifying and impossible place allowed the terrifying and impossible to happen. Petya's mouth was warm on his, and his unshaven cheek rasped against Vasyl's, and his arms were strong around Vasyl's neck and back. Vasyl whimpered softly as something broke free inside him and he pressed himself against Petya, held his warm, hard body against his own. His soul rose and twisted beyond metal walls, and Petya's rose and twisted with him, trailing like a pair of comets in the sky.

"Why didn't we ever do that before?" Vasyl asked when they parted.

Petro shook his head. "You know the answer to that."

There was a pause, and then Vasyl asked, "How long?"

"Always, Vaska. On the first day we met, you listened to me. You made me feel wanted and . . . special."

Vasyl closed his eyes for a moment. "All those years wasted."

"Not wasted." Petya kissed him again, then pressed his forehead against Vasyl's. "I wouldn't have Olena. *We* wouldn't have Olena."

"I was so jealous when you married Irina." Vasyl leaned into him, put his arm around him. It still felt impossible, but Petya was here, solid and real. He smelled faintly of coal smoke and dark bread. "But I kept my mouth shut and smiled at your wedding."

"Like everyone tells a good friend to do," Petya agreed. "And then you decided to get married, like everyone tells a man to do."

"I hate to break a romantic moment," said Maroushka, "but you guys still have a honking big problem. Once the old lady gets her machinery reset, she's going to suck Petie-boy's brains out and put 'em into that old broom—or she'll eat Vasyl. And probably Olena, too."

Petya went pale, and resolve filled Vasyl. He got to his feet. "No. We're ending this. Tonight. Now."

"Sure, yeah, whatever." Maroushka yawned. "Let me know how that turns out."

Vasyl opened Broom's control panel and swiftly pushed the faulty memory wheels back into place, then rooted through cupboards and drawers until he found a wrench with which to straighten Broom's staff. Noises continued to emerge from the open door to Baba Yaga's workshop. Vasyl restarted the wheels, and Broom shuddered to life as Vasyl dug the can of paraffin oil from his pack.

"Maroushka," he said, "you know how to open the front door, don't you?"

Maroushka eyed the can. ". . . No."

Vasyl waggled the can so it sloshed enticingly. "Come on. You've been here for decades, haven't you? Alone and neglected. What do you owe her?"

Maroushka licked her chops. "Look, it's not that simple. Once you get out, she'll chase you until the sun burns out. Yeah, the tesseract closes at dawn, real time, and the cottage will go . . . elsewhere, but it comes back every year, and she'll be royally pissed. At you."

Vasyl leaned his fists on the table. His bloodied hand twinged inside its rough bandage. "How will she chase us? In that flying mortar of hers?"

"Duh."

"Fine." Vasyl went to the workshop door and peeped in. Baba Yaga was standing at a control panel amid a large group of sharp-legged spiders. She twisted dials, and most of the spiders turned left. About a quarter of them froze and flipped over. Baba Yaga cursed and fiddled with the panel again. Petya came up behind Vasyl and put a hand on his shoulder. For a moment, Vasyl felt the old forbidden yearning. Then he remembered how things had changed and he put his own hand over Petya's. Despite the difficulty of their situation, Vasyl couldn't hold back the smile.

"If either of you meat puppets sets foot in there, you'll set off five kinds of alarms," Maroushka warned from the table.

"Broom!" Vasyl said, and Broom scuttled forward. "Slip in there and bring me those kegs of fuel by the forge. Don't let *her* see you."

Broom saluted and skittered into the room. Vasyl held his breath, waiting for the alarm, but nothing happened. Broom wasn't alive. His handle bobbed and wove among the tables, just another mechanical going about its business. Baba Yaga's back was to him, and she didn't notice when Broom snatched up the kegs, one under each arm, and scampered back to the door. There was another bad moment when Broom crossed the threshold and Vasyl expected an alarm, but everything remained silent.

"Good job, Broom," Vasyl said. "Put them by the table."

Broom obeyed, puffing and squeaking. Petya squeezed Vasyl's hand. "What are they for?"

Vasyl cracked a lid, expecting paraffin oil but getting another, rather dizzying, smell. "Uh-oh. I don't recognize this."

"That's a fractional distillate of petroleum. Makes paraffin oil look like seawater." Maroushka's tail scythed back and forth. "I think I have a hard-on."

"A hard-on? Strange for a female," Petya observed.

"Strange for a female," Maroushka echoed in Petya's voice. *"You're hardly one to judge, light-foot."*

Petya balled up massive fists. "Now, look, you rusty little—"

"Be quiet, the both of you." Vasyl replaced the first keg's lid. "Maroushka, are you sure Olena is still all right?"

"She's moved eight inches since the last time you asked," Maroushka said. "Twice the length of Petro's—"

"Good, good." Vasyl straightened. "Look, you *are* going to help us, right?"

Maroushka hesitated and shot a nervous look at the workroom. "I do like you, kid, but—"

"When was the last time she even gave you coal dust, let alone paraffin oil?" Vasyl said. "I'll even fill you with some of this petrol. You'll lick my earwax, right?"

Maroushka gave a long, long look at the open workshop door, clearly warring with herself. Thinking. Vasyl held his breath. After an aching moment, she said, "All right. But I was only kidding about the earwax."

The front door was locked with a series of dials and switches that had to be set to particular numbers in a particular order at a particular speed. According to Maroushka, a mistake would send a deadly jolt of electricity through the door and set off a cacophony of alarms as a sort of afterthought. Maroushka told Vasyl how to open them and repeated the sequences several times until Vasyl had them memorized, then went over to Baba Yaga's loom, which stood near the open workshop door. Petya kept watch while Broom carried the kegs of petrol.

"Ready?" Vasyl mouthed at the cat.

Maroushka gave a distinctly nonfeline wave of her paw and Vasyl set the dials and switches by the door to the first sequence. Zero, one, one, two, three, five, eight, thirteen. He forced his hand not to shake. One wrong turn—

The first of the three heavy bolts slid back with a heart-stopping *thud* that echoed through the kitchen. Petya's face paled.

"What was that?" Baba Yaga demanded from the workshop.

But Maroushka was already working at the loom. She pushed on the warp beam, jumped down on the treadles, then leaped back up to the beam. The loom banged and thumped. This only made the tangled threads worse, but that wasn't the point.

"I am starting your weaving, Grandmother," Maroushka said in Vasyl's voice. *"Just as you said."*

No response from the workshop. Vasyl traded nervous looks with Petya and went on to the second sequence, and the third. As each bolt clunked aside, Baba Yaga shouted for an explanation, and again Maroushka said "he" was weaving.

The door was now unlocked. Petya took Vasyl's hand. The smith's palm was warm and calloused. Petya said, "Go!"

Vasyl shoved the door open. An immediate alarm screeched. The trio didn't take time to listen. They bolted out the opening and down the steps into cold air. Olena was standing at the bone gate.

"Papa!" she cried. "Uncle Vaska!"

Vasyl had never been so glad to see her. Petro ran forward and snatched her up. Vasyl and Broom dashed after. The noisome, moonlit courtyard with its dead windows and uneven cobble-stones seemed absurdly normal after all those days inside Baba Yaga's hut.

The moment the two men reached Olena, Baba Yaga herself appeared in the doorway holding a trembling Maroushka by the scruff of the neck.

"Traitor!" she screeched, though whether she meant Vasyl or Maroushka, Vasyl couldn't tell. "I'll devour you alive!"

Olena screamed. Maroushka twisted in Baba Yaga's grip and sank her brass teeth into the witch's arm. Baba Yaga shook her arm with a howl, and somehow Maroushka managed to leap up and attach herself to Baba Yaga's face. More outraged howls.

"Run!" Vasyl said.

They fled through the dark streets, following Broom's blue eye lights. Petya continued to carry Olena, whose little face was tight. "I was worried," she said. "And I followed you, even though I was scared."

"You did a good thing, my Olenka," Petya panted. "You saved us all."

They turned down another alley. "Can't she follow us in her flying mortar?" Olena asked.

"We stole the fuel," Vasyl replied tightly. "But we're not safe yet. She'll—"

"Behind us!" Petya cried.

Baba Yaga was, indeed, coming behind them, running like a demon scarecrow, her long legs eating up the distance between them. Her iron teeth gnashed and blood ran from a dozen cuts on her face. Olena whimpered.

"Broom!" Vasyl cried. "Break the kegs!"

The kegs shattered like eggs in Broom's arms, and a river of petrol cascaded down the cobblestones toward Baba Yaga. From his pack Vasyl drew the knife he had taken from Baba Yaga's kitchen and stabbed at the stones. Sparks flew, and the petrol ignited. Fire roared. Heat sucked the air from Vasyl's lungs and singed his eyebrows. Baba Yaga leaped back from the yellow flames.

"Go!" Vasyl gave Petya a shove, and they ran again, with Broom lighting the way. They reached a deserted crossroad and sprinted over it. In the distance, a bell struck five o'clock. Still an hour until dawn, when the tesseract would close. Vasyl gave himself a final look at Petya, knowing what he had to do.

"That fire won't stop her for long," Petya panted.

"I know." Vasyl halted, as did Broom.

Petya ran a few more steps before he noticed he had lost Vasyl. He spun and shifted Olena to his other arm. "What are you doing?"

"We can't outrun her," Vasyl said softly, "and she said it was you or me. You have to think of Olena, so—"

"No!" Petya set Olena down and grabbed Vasyl by both shoulders. "That isn't a choice, Vaska. It's foolishness."

Vasyl merely shook his head, unable to meet Petya's dark eyes. "I've been a fool all my life, Petya. Especially when it comes to you."

"What are you talking about, Papa?" Olena asked frantically. "She's coming! Run!"

"I knew how this would end from the start, Petrushka," he said, using Petro's most intimate nickname. "You can't let her take Olena."

"Papa?" Olena said.

Petya crushed Vasyl to him, and Vasyl felt tears running down his face, and he didn't know if they were his or Petya's or both.

"How can I lose you now that I just found you?" Petya's voice was thick and hoarse.

"You had me your whole life," Vasyl replied, equally hoarse. "Now *run*!"

Olena's protests about leaving Uncle Vaska behind faded as Petya fled with her deeper into the city. Vasyl swiped at his face with his sleeve and turned with Broom to face Baba Yaga. It wasn't long before she stormed into view. Broom quivered and tried to hide behind Vasyl, but Vasyl grabbed the top of his staff and held him in place, though his own hands were shaking and black terror threatened to swallow him whole.

Baba Yaga loomed over him, clawed hands on hips. "So, it's going to be you, my little mechanical. Very well. I'll devour you raw and screaming in this place so the noise will remind all those people cowering behind their ordinary windows what it means to cross Baba Yaga."

But Vasyl pressed the point of Broom's staff against his heart. The life pulse throbbed beneath his ribs. "I offered you my soul, Grandmother, and you refused it."

"You can't bargain with something that doesn't belong to you, boy."

"But I can." Breath coming in short puffs, Vasyl spread both arms wide, leaving Broom's sharp spear at his heart. Broom remained motionless. "One word to Broom and I die. *You* won't have taken my life, and our bargain will be nullified. Without the bargain, you can't touch Petya, either, no matter what kind of future you saw."

Baba Yaga's eyes narrowed. "*He* doesn't like suicides, you know. Would you choose an eternity of torment to ensure that your little Petya lives a few miserable years in freedom?"

"Yes. My soul, my bargain. My choice."

"Liar." Baba Yaga drew back her hand. Iron claws gleamed in silver moonlight.

"Broom!" Vasyl shouted. "Kill—"

"Wait!" Baba Yaga dropped her hand. Witch and man stared at each other for a long moment. The center of the universe shifted, and Vasyl felt empty and triumphant at the same time.

"Very good," Baba Yaga chuckled at last. "I said I liked you, boy. You've earned your future. But think on this—a witch always fulfills her bargain."

Still chuckling, she turned to stalk away, then paused and turned back. "By the way, boy, where did you find that delightful and delicious paraffin oil?"

"It's my mother's formula," Vasyl said.

"Hm. If you ever want to share it with someone who can truly appreciate it, you know where to find me." She vanished into the dark and stony streets.

Vasyl held himself upright for a moment, then grabbed Broom's handle as his legs turned to bread dough. He stood there for some time, feeling his own heartbeat, tasting every breath.

Footsteps tapped toward him. He turned, expecting to see Petro. Instead, Broom's little blue lights illuminated a young woman in a dark cloak. She gasped when she caught sight of Vasyl and flung back her hood. Golden hair spilled over the cloak, and azure eyes blinked at him. It was Hanna Vyktorevna, the mayor's daughter.

Vasyl's mouth fell open. "What are you doing here?"

"I don't want to marry you," she blurted. "I don't want to marry *anybody.*"

"That's still no reason to be out on the night of . . . oh. Oh!"

"If *she* can't help me, no one can."

"That way." Vasyl pointed. "Better hurry, though. The tesseract closes in less than an hour."

"Tesseract?"

"Just run."

She gave a curt nod and started off. Vasyl called, "Hey, wait!" He dug through his pack and handed her a tattered, much-folded piece of yellow paper.

"What is it?"

"My mother's formula for paraffin oil. It'll give you a leg up when you bargain with her."

Her eyes widened. "Thank you! You're so kind, Master Tinker." The new center of the universe kissed him on the cheek and dashed away.

Moments later, Vasyl let himself into Petya's house. Before he could even shut the door, Olena flew into his arms and nearly knocked him over. Petya grabbed them both together and squeezed so tightly Vasyl thought he would never breathe again. He kissed Vasyl over Olena's head, his strong fingers running through Vasyl's sunset hair.

Vasyl set Olena down and kissed Petya back. The last of the fear and tension evaporated, and he gave himself up to the thrill and love that ran through him, the upswell of pure emotion he had been waiting for his entire life. He loved Petya and Petya loved him back and the rest of the world didn't matter.

"I was right! I was right!" Olena squealed. Broom bobbed up and down.

They separated and Petya tugged one of her braids. "You were definitely right, my Olenka."

"And now Uncle Vaska can move in with us and fix toys for children and be my uncle forever."

Vasyl touched Petya's cheek with the back of his hand. "Is she right? Am I moving in?"

"Of course she is. What better pairing could there be besides blacksmith and tinker? Everyone in the neighborhood is half expecting it anyway. No one will notice or care, as long we keep quiet."

A terrible thought occurred to Vasyl. Petya read his expression and asked what was wrong.

"Baba Yaga said a witch always keeps her bargain," he said. "Is she going to come back to finish the job?"

"Not to worry," said Maroushka from the kitchen table.

Everyone jumped and spun. The cat was sitting calmly next to the lamp.

"How did . . . what are you . . . ?" Vasyl stammered.

"What's with the surprise? I can't stay with Baba Yaga, duh," Maroushka said. "And *you* make paraffin oil."

"A talking kitty!"

"Hey! Hands off, kid."

"All right," Petya said slowly. "Why don't we have to worry?"

"The bargain's fulfilled. Baba Yaga's future came true. Again, duh."

"Because of you?" Vasyl asked. "If you live here, it'll mean I came away from the cottage with a mechanical that can think for itself?"

She gave a paw a swipe with her tongue. "Hell with that."

"Hey!" Petya snapped. "If you're going to stay here, you have to watch your language."

"Whatever. Why aren't you going to marry the mayor's daughter, kid?"

"Because I chose someone else." He looked down at his own hands, and realization clicked. "Oh. Oh! Baba Yaga meant that I'm—?"

Petya took one of his hands. "We've known each other more than twenty years, Vaska, but you never reached for me."

"Because everyone told me not to. I tried to marry because everyone expected it. I escaped my stepmother because my father told me to go. I even obeyed Baba Yaga's rules without thinking."

"The perfect little automaton," Petya said. "Until she let me go to you and you chose to break her rules."

Vasyl nodded. "I chose to think for myself. I chose you."

Petya cleared his throat. "But there's still the mayor. You can't present yourself to him and claim—"

"Actually, I don't think that'll be a problem," Vasyl interrupted. "Hanna went to bargain with Baba Yaga about the marriage, right? If Hanna wins, she gets what she wants, and she won't have to marry me or anyone else."

"And if she loses," Maroushka put in, "there won't be anyone for you to marry. End of bargain. Nice one, kid."

"I think her chances are pretty good," Vasyl said. "She's pretty smart, and she has my mother's formula."

"So, are we a family now?" Olena asked.

"Yes, my Olenka." Petya touched her head. "All three of us."

"Four," Maroushka corrected.

"Four," Vasyl agreed with a laugh.

"Five," said Broom.

The Hollow Hounds

by Kat Richardson

**(BASED ON "THE TINDERBOX"
BY HANS CHRISTIAN ANDERSEN)**

He was still a young man, though his tall, slim body was much battered and his face no longer handsome beneath his luxuriant blond mustaches, but when the news came, his commanders were as glad to send him home: a patched and broken soldier, old at twenty-six, and no good to anyone at the front—not anymore. No good to anyone at home, either, for there was no one there, nor family remaining East, West, North, or in the war-torn South. How bitter the irony that while he stood in the hellfire of war and emerged changed but still living, his wife and child, safe at home, had died of fever and remained forever as they had been in his memory, but only there.

He had returned to bury them, and then found no reason to stay. Carrying nothing but what lay in his pockets, he returned to the station and boarded the first train heading away from all he knew—west past Kansas until the train could go no farther. He disembarked at the rural station in an unknown territory and begin walking. Just walking. Looking for . . . what? Something to set his heart by, perhaps. Some purpose. Or some reason to stop.

He came to a crossroads in the woodland through which he trod and paused beside the stout signpost there, the sunlight through the trees dappling his pale hair as he looked down. He checked his watch—like its owner, a battered thing but running still in spite of all it had passed through—then took a key from his pocket as if he meant to wind the mechanism up and stood staring at the key a moment. He had looked up at the fingerboards pointing from the post and down to the key again—as if the key would help him decide which road to follow—when he heard a sound all too familiar: an explosion like those made by the infernal torpedoes to which he had lost a good horse on the battlefield and taken no small injury himself.

The not-so-old soldier shoved the key back into his pocket as he ducked and scrambled under the nearest cover, expecting a hail of dirt and stones thrown up by the blast that had sounded so near at hand, but there was no such rain of debris. Instead he felt a rude and insistent shoving at his back, which he had pressed against a sheltering rock outcrop.

"Devil take it," someone groused at his rear. "Give way!"

He jumped forward, whirling to see what and who prodded him in the backside so persistently and why they spoke in such impatient tones.

From the depths of the rock emerged a disordered man who shoved wide the camouflaged door that had been hidden in the deep shadow of the overhang. The soldier saw that the door was in fact wood, cleverly painted. The rock around it had been carved away in some fashion to create a niche just deep enough to ensure that the door would remain shaded all the year and preserve the illusion of stone, but not so deeply set in the rock that any animal would choose to make its den on the threshold.

The man, portly and balding, wearing a long leather apron covered in bulging pockets and sleeve gaiters over his clothes, closed the door in haste against a billow of smoke as acrid as that from any battlefield and stepped out into the sunshine near the signpost to stare at the soldier from behind the thick, round lenses of a pair of goggles that gave his eyes a bizarre, insectile appearance.

"What, by Jupiter, are you doing here?" the man asked, pulling the goggles off his face as if they might be causing him to hallucinate. "No one walks through these woods nowadays."

"If they are regularly troubled with explosions beneath their feet, that would hardly be a wonder. Shall I assume that was your work," the soldier asked, pointing to a few wisps of sulfurous smoke, "since you came from a door in the rock that clearly leads to wherever that explosion originated?"

The disheveled man peered at him, his uncovered eyes sharp with speculation. "An observant man, I see. Do I take it rightly, by your dress, sir, that you are but late returned from the battlefields of the Southeast?"

"I am not returned at all, sir," the soldier said, taken for a moment by a perverse humor. "But I am, indeed, late from the war."

"I don't recognize you," the man said, "and I've lived in these parts nigh on five years."

"I am not from these parts. I find myself at loose ends and thought I'd take a walk until I tied them back up again."

"What, no family nor friends nearby?"

"None. Not nearby nor anywhere. All dead."

"A tragic tale, friend, and perhaps too common in this time of conflict." The man shook his head in sorrow and then offered his hand. "My name is Conscience Morton and you have my sympathies."

The soldier took his hand and shook it stiffly, but offered nothing more, for there seemed no further reply to make.

Morton continued after a moment's clumsy silence. "Well, friend, if you have no destination, perhaps I might persuade you to do me a small favor. . . ? Though you are wan—perhaps still suffering from your wounds?—you seem a strong man and clever. Educated, I would guess. And what I would ask of you requires no great strength, but is quite out of the question for one . . . encumbered by such flesh as I am."

The soldier nodded at him to go on, or in agreement that the gentleman before him was, inarguably, rotund and unused to physical labor.

"Below," Morton began, "lies a great maze of caverns and tunnels in which are secreted such marvels as would amaze even the most jaded collector, and gold enough to send a miser into transports of joy. Now, among this treasure lies a small music box—quite an ordinary sort of thing carved of a pretty bit of wood and bound in brass and no larger than a lady's prayer book—that I made . . . for my late wife." The man watched the soldier from the corner of his eye as he spoke and must surely have noticed the other's unhappy expression as he added, "She died of a brain fever and nothing to be done for her, poor thing."

The soldier bowed his head and shook it in sympathy, his eyes sparked with tears.

"So you see," Morton continued, "how dear such a keepsake is to me."

"I see," the soldier replied, dashing the moisture from his face with the back of one scarred hand.

"I would give all the gold of Midas to retrieve that box. It was stolen from me by a rival, a mad inventor, a very devil of a man who has turned his hand to building vile mechanisms—but I let my emotions run away with me. Forgive me. It is only recently I've discovered that he keeps the music box in his secret laboratory, which lies below."

"In these caves you say run beneath our very feet?" the soldier asked.

The weighty Mr. Morton nodded. "As you say. And I have tried to gain access to the place to reclaim what is mine, but this man—beast that he is—set traps at the door which I, unsuspecting, set off and the explosion has sealed this entry. There are other ways in, but only to this one did I hold a key. And now I cannot pass through it."

The soldier drew himself up, frowning in thought and looking at the man before him as if he could weigh the truth of his tale in his gaze. "How do you propose to get below and reclaim your treasure?"

Morton's face lit up and he exclaimed, "Ah, such penetration! I knew you were a clever fellow the moment I clapped eyes upon you. And you, you see, *you* are the very answer. There is, nearby, an air shaft disguised as a lightning-blasted tree, and a slender fellow such as yourself should find no difficulty in shimmying down it. I might assay it myself, but I fear I am not a vigorous man and should fail of the attempt. If *you* would go down and retrieve the box, I should be most grateful."

The soldier frowned. "If you'll pardon my saying so, sir, I don't quite perceive what reward there is in this venture for me," he said. "Saving the satisfaction of returning your beloved wife's trinket to you—which is a kindhearted gesture, I do admit it— there seems no further inducement to *me* to take such a risk, for such an impulse no longer shivers in *my* breast. I have lately laid all my worldly happiness and all I possess on the altar of my country and placed my life and limbs in the hands of men who cast me aside once my usefulness was done, and my heart is no longer kind. So tell me what I am to be paid for this service."

"My dear friend," Morton replied, "you mistake me entirely. There is treasure in plenty below—gold, silver, and gems. Merely take what you will—be discreet in your choices, for the builder may recognize his toys if you should take one of those—but of materials, he shall miss nothing if you temper your avarice with common sense. It's a veritable trove down there!" he added, throwing his arms upward with enthusiasm. He knocked the backs of his knuckles against the fingerboards on the signpost and winced, missing the soldier's swift, ironic smile.

The soldier schooled his expression into one of careful thought and then nodded. "Very well. Lead on to your air shaft and I shall go below and see this dragon's hoard for myself."

Morton led him perhaps half a mile into the woods, his path wobbling between the boles of larger trees and the spindly growth of smaller ones, to a large, blackened stump. It stood a couple of feet taller than the soldier—who was taller than Morton—and was more than twice as big around. The remaining top of the tree was ragged and had only one branch that stuck out at a crooked angle.

The soldier raised his arms and jumped, aiming to catch the branch and pull himself up, but the branch hung just out of reach. He turned toward Morton, saying, "If you gave me a leg up . . . but perhaps not," he added, observing the pudgy man's physique.

"I have with me a rope," the other replied. "If you could scramble up and tie the rope off to that branch, I should be able to climb up behind you so as to pull you back up once you've found the music box."

The soldier nodded. "The height is just a bit more than I can leap and the trunk too large to shin up easily. . . . Perhaps I could step on your back. . . ."

"What!" Morton objected.

"Dear fellow," the soldier replied. "It *is* in a good cause, isn't it?"

And so it was that Morton knelt on the ground at the base of the false tree and the soldier wrapped the rope around his body and stepped up, light and quick, caught the branch with ease, and swung himself up to look down into the blasted tree.

"Hollow as a hound before supper," the soldier observed of the tree as he tied off the rope to the branch and prepared to swing his legs over into the void.

"Just a moment, friend," Morton called, dusting himself off before struggling to ascend the tree with the help of both rope and soldier. And an arduous journey it was.

When Morton sat, panting and sweating, on the branch beside the soldier, he said, "Before you descend, you must know this: the owner of this cavern has three guardians below and they stand vigil over his most precious inventions—and no doubt the music box as well. These guardians are clockwork beasts of a horrible aspect, but they may be easily overcome with a small invention of mine own." He took a small box from one of his pockets and a sort of round brass plate that he popped open into the shape of a cone, telescoping much in the manner of an opera hat that extends from its flattened state with a flick of the gentleman's wrist. He screwed the cone thus made into a hole in the box and offered it to the soldier. Then he passed him his goggles as well. "But touch the button on this box and it will emit a field from the cone that will temporarily disable the mechanical beast. Wear my goggles and you shall be able to see the field and any others like it that my rival may have placed below. They aren't terribly dangerous to men—make one a bit queasy, is all—but they play hob with mechanical things for a time. If he has used these fields for alarms, walking through one will allow the bell, or whatever diabolical engine at which it has been aimed, to begin functioning again, so these fields are to be avoided if you wish to emerge again a free man. Just remember: point the cone at the beast and press the button. You may then leave the emitter on the ground in front of the creature until you have finished your inspection. I've calibrated the effect to last several minutes after the generator is removed, so you may carry on out of the creature's sight where it will not see and pursue you. They will not detect you otherwise but with their eyes."

The soldier accepted the goggles and the device, carefully dismantling it and putting the parts of it into his jacket and pockets so he could have his hands free to climb down. "Just be ready with the rope when I come back," was all he said before he vanished down the hollow tree.

It took several minutes for the soldier to slither down the pipe using his back and legs braced against the opposite sides, for the space was much wider than he'd at first thought and he was not so tightly tucked in as he would have liked. Morton might, in fact, have eased in, but the inventor was clearly not fit enough to climb.

When he neared the bottom, the soldier paused to don the goggles and survey his proposed landing site. A dim or distant lamp cast a poor illumination on the area and the goggles darkened it still further, but he saw no sign of mysterious fields or roving mechanical beasts of a diabolical nature, so he let himself down with care and crouched below the air shaft a moment while he assembled the emitter. He could barely hear the constant dripping of water somewhere below a low whine that filled the air much like the sound of the monstrous engine he had seen prowling in the Confederate skirmish lines at Shiloh. It had been no rail locomotive—though just as large—and it had raised lightning around its metal body that struck at the Union men and ground around them. It had seemed the hand of Zeus himself flung the bolts on General Johnston's orders until that man was, himself, brought down and the engine silenced. In this shadowy cavern, the memory of death whispered close and the soldier shivered.

He crept across the floor to the nearest wall and inched along its length toward the sound until he came upon the thing, crouching beside a buried stream of water on a bed of steel and rubber. In the low light made dimmer by his goggles, he inspected it, for it seemed unlikely to attack him, fettered as it was to the ground. It took only a minute to recognize it for what it was—an electricity generator, driven by the spinning of a handful of propellers sunk from the machine into the buried stream of water below it like some cockeyed metal water mill. Thick cables clad in rubber and guided by hoops of rubber-lined brass carried the electricity away into the cavern to power the dim lights hanging in cages pegged to the walls. Here there were no gas flames or sputtering torches, only the lowered, chilly light of the heavens' rage tamed by man. Nearby, a regiment of switches marched along a metal panel, carefully labeled, but in no ways helpful, for the soldier couldn't imagine what they truly did and had no desire to call unwanted attention to himself in this place.

He prowled onward, taking care to avoid anything that looked like the field Morton had warned of. It was in avoiding one of these that he came suddenly around a corner and face-to-face with a dog. It was about the size of a big hunting hound, but it gleamed metallic gold and red in the low light and its eyes, as large as doorknobs, glowed with the pale blue of electricity. The soldier jerked to a standstill and stared at the beast, his own eyes nearly as wide as the dog's.

The mechanical beast scratched one iron forefoot upon the floor, sending sparks flying from the stone as it growled like a freight car rolling slowly over gravel. The soldier leaped backward and the metal dog crouched as if to spring, but the soldier held Morton's emitter between them and, praying more from habit than hope, pressed the button. The box made a click and a squeal, and then what looked like a hash of black and white lines shot from the cone and enveloped the dog, who stopped stock-still, half-crouched, the cold fire in its gleaming eyes extinguished in an instant.

The soldier put the box on the ground in front of the mechanical beast and walked toward it, curious. But as he stepped into the beam, a wrenching pain tore through his chest and he reeled, stumbling aside and falling against the wall, his sight dim and his ears filled with an unnatural silence. He lay still against the wall for a minute or two, as still as death, until at last he heaved a mighty breath into his lungs and dragged himself back to his feet.

" 'Makes one a bit queasy,' " he mocked. "Ha!" He turned to regard the dog, but it was as motionless as before, unmoved and unmoving, its eyes still dark. "But it does work a treat on you, old boy," he added, and forbore to pat the brass-bound hound on the head. He stepped with care past the dog and into the chamber it guarded.

Shelf upon shelf groaned under the weight of brass, copper, and steel parts and boxes filled with the tiny sapphires and rubies watchmakers used in their art, of which he poured a few into his hand and put them carelessly into his breast pocket. Spools of wire, coils, cylinders, and sheets of metal rolled thin enough to bend and shape were stacked beside bins full of screws, pins, gears, springs, valves, grommets, pistons, chain . . . and things so foreign he had no word for them. Ranks of tools waited in racks on the walls. Upon the tables set across the room, quiet under a thin blanket of dust and cobweb, sat dozens of mechanical creations. Seeing only the glitter of jewels and no spark of electricity in their eyes, the soldier walked up to the first table and found himself in the midst of a wonderful menagerie of automata: birds, beetles, snakes, rabbits, puppies, squirrels, chickens . . . all such small, familiar animals rendered in shining metal and each with a key protruding from its back. The second table was filled with more sophisticated and bejeweled miniature human figures poised to demonstrate various clever tasks: a tumbler dressed in jester's motley of set gemstones, a lady with face and arms of carved ivory and hair of silk thread seated at a tiny piano, even a soldier dressed in British red enamel with a small ebony and brass musket in his hands, and so many others it was hard to count them, each more gloriously adorned than the last and all left to gather dust. The final table was much cleaner and held more frightening models: a tiny guillotine that raised and lowered its own blade and diligently disposed of the severed bits of its wax victims into a box below, all at the flick of a lever; a sort of reverse torture rack that screwed itself down to crush the dolly victim within; a metal box that seemed capable of opening by itself to spew out its unpleasant secrets; balls covered in the sturdy spines of detonation triggers; and cylinders with valves and timers that whispered in his memory of deadly gases creeping across the Georgia ground like killing fog.

He shuddered and stepped back, wanting nothing from this chamber.

He turned warily toward the dog, but it was as inactive as before. He edged past the cone of strange light, careful to stay entirely out of it, and pressed the emitter's button. The field vanished and he picked up the box. Still, the dog made no motion, its eyes remaining dark.

He walked on, passing yards of cable burdened with electricity and fixed to the cavern wall with loops of rubber-lined brass as he went.

Around another corner he encountered a second dog. This one was the size of a great mastiff, its horrible sparking eyes as large as artillery shells and nearly on a level with his own. This one let out a bark that shook the soldier in his boots, but he thrust forward the emitter and pushed the button . . .

. . . and the dog froze as if encased in glacial ice, the light in its eyes winking out.

The soldier let out his held breath, put the emitter on the floor in front of the massive hound, and stepped around it with wary care.

The chamber beyond was much larger than that he had just come from and it was filled with great mechanisms and engines built to run on steam, all gleaming bright with polish and glistening with oil. Though not as pretty as some in the previous chamber, these far surpassed the others' mechanical sophistication with their apparent—and not so apparent—abilities. Here a machine that cleaned, dried, and pressed clothing, beyond it another that appeared to be a self-contained and automated forge, and still another that seemed to be some kind of massive, pressurized pump covered in couplings, valves, knobs, and coiled lengths of hose. Farther on stood a conveyance like a pony trap that rolled around under its own steam power and another larger version had not wheels but an endless chain of spiked plates that dug into the ground and clawed the engine forward—no doubt meant for conveying freight over rough or muddy ground a horse and wagon could not pass. Another machine seemed to be a kind of self-propelled augur on six articulated legs—perhaps a drilling machine? Beyond that lay a large armored ball with another set of the clawed tracks running around it and a door to a passenger—or driver's—cabinet within. The soldier had no idea what it was meant to do, for he couldn't imagine how it moved, though it clearly was meant to. . . .

As he wandered through the room, the mechanisms, as before, grew bleaker in their purpose. He saw great guns with valves and tanks stinking of kerosene and hoses leading to nozzles where the muzzle should have been and others that propelled themselves on legs or wheels, directed by huge empty eyes like those of the inert hound outside the door. An experimental poke at the muzzle of one gun produced a spark and a moment's blue flame that suffocated as the dregs of its fuel burned away. Beyond that lay an iron cask that stank of gunpowder, its surface all scored to break apart once it had crept on moving belts to its destination. Still more dread mechanisms lined up beside it.

Against the wall stood a rack of cylindrical machines nearly as long as he was tall with something like a stiff metal rotating fan at the tail and the fins of a fish along the sides. The lean metal bodies led to empty heads that plainly awaited the mounting of some large, round thing. Beyond them he saw the bulbous, unpleasant shapes of land torpedoes such as the one that had claimed his horse, and he guessed these were the objects the swimming machines were meant to carry to ships. The farthest wall held racks of rolled paper plans, and he had barely the heart to open a few and see their descriptions of even worse machines of destruction before he rolled them up and shoved them back into their pigeonholes.

He turned aside, disgusted, and spied a small version of the very lightning machine he had seen at Shiloh.

"What manner of man owns this place?" he whispered.

Forsaking the plans, which he knew would be worth a small fortune to men who practiced war, he ran from the room, barely remembering in time to dodge the field that immobilized the massive mechanical dog before he bent to retrieve the emitter.

As with its smaller kin, the mechanical dog remained unmoving and unlit as the soldier walked away.

He passed through more tunnels, taking care this time to check around each corner in search of other fell guardians, but he saw only room after room of empty tables, marked with the dents and scrapes of heavy objects removed in haste. Judging by what he had seen already, he had no desire to confirm his suspicions of what those things had been.

He heard a sound and turned back, to see the second dog drag itself slowly past and into the room where the electricity generator hummed. Following it, the soldier saw the dog stop beside the generator and lie still. In a moment, the dog seemed to glow and arcs of blue lightning grew from the end of the generator to stroke the dog, which sat up, its eyes igniting again with their eerie blue light.

The soldier withdrew quickly, lest he be spotted by the dog, and hurried back to his search, wondering what had become of the first dog and if the second had awakened sooner than the first. Was it possible the emitter was weakening, its charge lingering for less time with each use?

Ahead, the light gleamed brighter and more yellow, like a hot welcoming fire, and he quickened his steps toward it without thinking.

Perhaps he made too much noise, or cast a shadow, but whatever the cause, he had only a moment's notice of the beast's proximity before it pounced and bowled him to the ground with a roar that shook dust from the ceiling.

Blindly, the soldier waved the emitter in front of himself, holding down the button with his thumb. When he was not killed, he put the emitter down to rub his eyes clear of dust and then looked around.

A mechanical dog whose shoulders were as tall as a door and its body almost as wide loomed over him, its head lowered and jaws poised to snap the soldier in two. The man's breath caught in his throat, but it was obvious the dog was as immobile as its brothers had been before, its gaze as banked and dark.

Beyond the dog, the chamber gleamed, but this time not in shades of copper and brass, but the bright hardness of electric light glittering on gold, silver, and gems. He stepped past the mechanical beast, awed by the beauty of the light that reflected from such a pile of wealth, his breath trapped in his throat.

With such engines of destruction at his call, the soldier supposed it was no difficulty for the inventor who kept these caves to amass such a treasure and yet it was thrust and piled and spilled into the chamber as carelessly as if it were so much trash. This, indeed, was a dragon's hoard and nothing in this chamber—much smaller than the ones before it, but guarded by such a monster—was ordinary, nor of base materials. Except the one box of brassbound wood lying as if discarded near the feet of the huge dog.

The soldier was loath to reach into the beam to retrieve the box and he wasn't sure that the dog could be held in its sleeping state for long if, as he guessed, the emitter was truly burning out. He looked about the room until he came across a life-sized figure of a man. The gilded figure was something like a giant doll with arms and legs articulated at each natural joint. Excusing himself, the soldier twisted and pulled until one of the arms came away at the shoulder socket with a pop. He carried the heavy arm as close to the strange light of the emitter as he could and laid it on the floor, pushing and rolling it until the cupped hand curled around the music box. Then he pulled the arm back and picked up the box.

Stuffing the music box into his jacket, the soldier carried the arm back to its owner. Then he turned to the glittering trove and picked out a fortune for himself in silver and gold coins and gold nuggets with which he filled his pockets.

At last he picked up Morton's device and returned to the room where the shaft had first deposited him. He saw no sign of the dogs on his way, but he could hear the generator in the far room humming and a clanking sound that reminded him that at least one fell guardian was back up and feeling its mechanical oats.

"Morton," he called up. "Throw down the rope."

"Do you have the music box?" Morton demanded, peering over the edge from his perch on the branch.

"Of course I do," he replied. "Lower the rope and I'll give it to you."

"Toss up the music box first."

The soldier had no intention of doing so, but before he could say so, he heard the clanking and sparking of a great machine coming toward him. Looking back, he saw the two smaller dogs racing toward him. In the distance, he thought he could hear the grinding of the larger one making its way through the tunnels as well.

"We've no time for these games," the soldier shouted back. "The hounds are coming and I doubt I'll hold them off for long!"

"Throw me the music box and I'll let you up."

There was no time to reply, for the first of the mechanical beasts was upon him. The soldier kicked at it, sending the smallest of the beasts skittering across the stone floor, but it righted itself and turned to come back. The soldier slammed his finger onto the button of the emitter, but this time it only gave a squeal and a click and the dog faltered, but the fire in its eyes remained alight.

The second dog now dashed at him, its dreadful jaws agape. He threw the emitter at it. The hound snapped it up like a biscuit and ground it between its metal teeth, staggering a moment as the box crushed in its mouth, spewing out a final, dying pulse of light. The soldier tore off the goggles and leaped up, using the stunned dog as a stepping-stone, and scrambled upward to grab at a rubber loop that hung from the bottom of the air shaft. The dog shook itself awake again and snapped at the dangling soldier, who swung his legs up into the shaft, but couldn't find enough purchase at such an angle to wedge himself into the pipe. Thus his legs swung back down.

Now the first dog returned to the fight, making mighty jumps the larger dog could not assay and snapping at the soldier's dangling boot heels. It bit into one and ripped the boot from his foot as it fell back to earth, growling and savaging the leather as it would, no doubt, savage his body if the soldier fell.

The soldier pulled the music box from his pocket and waved it in the light of the air shaft for Morton to see. "Pull me up, damn it, man, or I'll throw this to them next!"

Wide-eyed, Morton finally tossed down the knotted end of the stout rope. The soldier, breathing hard, shoved the music box back into his pocket and swarmed up as the chamber below him shuddered and rang with the sound of the third dog breaking past the narrow doorway.

As he pulled himself out of the false tree stump, a gout of dust and a frustrated roar from the throat of the third dog rushed upward behind him. He tumbled over the edge and barely caught the branch to stop himself falling to the ground.

Morton, still perched on the branch, stared at him and put out his hand for the music box. "Now, the box, my friend, or I'll shove you back in."

The soldier hauled himself up onto the branch and locked his legs around its girth. "To the devil with you, you miserable, lying swine! You never meant to let me up, but to leave me to die below." And he grabbed the inventor and heaved him, headfirst, into the air shaft.

Morton screamed and plummeted down the pipe, lodging for a moment head-down before his screeching was cut short. The soldier looked away, not caring to see what work the hellish hounds would make of him, but the sound alone was gruesome enough to raise the soldier's stomach into his throat.

He let himself down to the ground while the scrambling sounds faded below. Limping along with but one boot, he returned to the crossroads and took the road to the nearest town.

The place was called Stone Crossing, and even at a distance he could hear the sound of rail workers at their toil, laying the iron road across the vast grassland to the west. The town was busy with railroad men, farmers, cattlemen, and merchants offering every sort of goods and services to the caravans of settlers passing through as they escaped the strife of the war to make their way into the empty territories beyond, hunting a fortune or simply a new start. The soldier took a room in a boardinghouse run by a careful, plain-faced woman named Sarah—the widow of a railroad man who'd been blown to smithereens by a misplaced dynamite charge—and set to spending his fortune in merry pursuits that lightened his mood only temporarily.

He was accounted by most as a generous and pleasant enough companion, if one wasn't bothered by his silence, his scars, and his ever-present expression of sorrow. Such was his discretion in all things from his person to his rare speech that his acquaintances took to confiding their own troubles to him. Even the widow Sarah spoke more easily to her taciturn boarder than to anyone else in the house. Thus it came to his ears in the rising heat of a blistering summer that the town of Stone Crossing was in dire straits.

Over dinner one Sunday evening at the boardinghouse, another guest—one of the railroad men passing through—complained, "I thought the land problem was going to be the worst of it here, but if this heat doesn't break soon, we'll have to halt work. The workers are dropping like flies and we've near run out of water as it is."

"And you won't find any for miles," Sarah replied. "The creeks have all shriveled up or gone underground. My own well's nearly dried out and I'll have to ask you gentlemen to take your baths at the barbershop from now on, or there'll be no water to cook with or clean the pans. I've already stopped mopping the floors as it is. I swear our situation wasn't much better when Morton was still around, but at least you could usually get him to arguing with Halprin and stand a chance of getting something for your trouble when one or the other won out. I've almost developed a soft spot for Conscience Morton now that he's gone—a less well-named man there never was."

The soldier pricked up his ears. "Who're those fellas—Morton and Halprin?" he asked.

"Well, they used to own pretty much the whole town between the two of them and most of the property beyond until Morton up and disappeared a few months ago," Sarah replied. "Utterly mad for inventing things, the pair of them, and small-minded with it. Such a rivalry you never saw—as if making a better spinning wheel were the be-all and end-all. If I had to guess, I'd say Halprin finally found some way to drive Morton off—or kill him and hide the body. The Lord knows they tried to get rid of one another often enough, though I'd have lief it were Halprin who vanished—he's a vile man who kills sheep for his own amusement with his terrible inventions. And greedy beyond imagining, though he's very rich from selling his murderous inventions to anyone as will pay—Union or Confederate. He and Morton fought for a whole year about where the rail right-of-way was going to pass, and the town was a mess because of it. Halprin only half won that argument."

"And now the railroad may have to make a jog around Morton's property," the railroad man added, "since he ran off without leaving a clear deed to the land to anyone. We've tried to apply eminent domain on the abandoned property, but Halprin is fighting us in court—ironically to 'protect Morton from being taken advantage of while he's missing.' I suspect he's just doing it to gain time until he can find a way to get the property for himself."

"I wouldn't put such a thing past him. He's a cruel creature, is Mr. Halprin," Sarah added.

The soldier looked back to Sarah. "What business is it that you're wanting Halprin to do?"

"I'm wanting him to let us drill for a deeper well. We all know there's an aquifer below the town—just look at how the cottonwood trees are still green even in the heat and dry: they must be getting water from below the topsoil. But Mr. Halprin won't allow it. I've asked the council and I've asked him, and the answer is the same—which isn't surprising considering the council is no more than Halprin's puppets these days. And I wouldn't countenance what Mr. Halprin suggested."

The soldier raised his eyebrows, but it was the railroad man who asked, "Surely he didn't impose himself . . . that way?"

"I'll content myself with saying Mr. Halprin is no more a gentleman in that respect than one could suppose from his other dealings," Sarah replied. "And he did not get what he wanted, though I very nearly had to run from the room to make it so."

The soldier frowned and asked, "Why can't you dig your own well?"

"I don't own the land and Mr. Halprin has made it very clear none of us are to go around digging holes on his property without his permission—which he won't give. So I tried to convince him we should drill for a public well, since that benefits everyone and we could use a bit of Morton's property on the south side of the main road—since Mr. Morton can't be found to say no to it. But Halprin refuses to consider it—same argument as he's giving to the railroad, but really, it's because he'd like some of Morton's tenants to up and leave. Without water, it's certain that some of them will. And soon."

"Won't he lose some of his own tenants?"

Sarah gave a wry smile. "Of course, but that makes no never

mind. Once the railroad is through, there'll be plenty of people lining up to buy every scrap of land, built on or no."

The soldier looked thoughtful and made a sound in his throat, nodded, but didn't say any more.

After dinner, he retired to his bedroom, pacing and wondering if he could do anything to help, for he'd taken a liking to the widow Sarah and hated to see her and her neighbors so abused by both nature and a single, greedy man. He also regretted having killed Morton—though not much. His thoughts ran in circles and eventually he sat down on his bed, wishing he had some distraction such as music or cards, but as it was Sunday, the saloon was closed and he didn't dare disrupt the house by going down to the parlor to play Sarah's piano—badly. His eye fell on the music box he had brought out of the caverns, sitting where he had put it down months ago on his chest of drawers. He picked it up, but it had no key. He tried the key he always carried in his pocket. The fit wasn't perfect, but he was able to wind the mechanism one turn before the cylinder began to revolve with a sudden chord that gave way to a strange tune.

Before the song had ended, he heard a scrabbling sound outside his window and when he opened the sash, he was confronted with the face of the smallest of the mechanical hounds from the cavern. He fell back, making room to do battle with the beast, but it only stepped delicately into the room and looked up at him with its flickering electric eyes.

After a moment of stilted silence the dog spoke: "What would you have me do, Master?"

Thunderstruck, the soldier sat down on the hard chair beside the door. "Who would have thought. . . ?" he muttered.

"What would you have me do, Master?" the mechanical beast repeated.

"Can you dig a well?"

"I cannot, Master. But I can fetch the digging machine to you."

"Can you, indeed, little dog?"

The gleaming metal dog nodded its heavy head.

"Then fetch the machine and take it to the field beside the last building on the southeast side of the main road of this town. Bring it in darkness or someone may try to stop you, and we'll drill a new well so deep the town will never run dry again."

The mechanical dog nodded again. Then it bounded out of the open window and was gone from sight in a moment more.

Once darkness fell and the last lights of the town were extinguished, the soldier went out for a walk and strolled to the eastern edge of the town, where he sat on the edge of a dry horse trough, lit a cigar, and waited to see if the dog would turn up. Moonlight silvered the ground, and the earth sighed the day's gathered heat into the air, swirling up eddies of fine grit that looked like fairy dust enchanting the cloudless prairie night.

In a while, the soldier could see something coming down the moonlit road from the woods. It marched along on six slim legs and in front of it ran the metal dog. The soldier stood up to meet the dog and its strange companion, which proved to be the walking augur machine he had seen in the cavern so many weeks ago. He pointed to what looked to be a good spot for the well, but the dog sniffed at the ground awhile and led the machine to a different location.

"Well, all right, then," the soldier said. "Let the drilling begin."

The machine began to drill into the ground, the dirt and rock spewing out and piling up around the edges of the hole as the bit dug in with a deep grumbling noise.

The soldier stood by and watched the machine. The augur dug steadily for hours with only a few adjustments by the soldier while the town slept on. After a while the sun started peeping over the eastern woodland, and the soldier could hear people stirring and beginning their morning chores.

He turned to regard the stalwart mechanical beast standing beside the tireless augur. "Best hie yourself home now, dog. I'll look after the drill, but I think it better if no one gets a glimpse of you."

The dog made a smart turn around and loped away, vanishing into the trees as the sun broke over their tops. The bright orb had barely sent its fingers down to touch the gleaming drill when a geyser of water erupted from the hole it was digging, knocking the walking augur into the air and tumbling it end over end to the very edge of town.

The sound of the machine falling attracted attention, and in a minute a few men and women had gathered to stare at the spring that had appeared overnight in Morton's field at the edge of town. It wasn't long before a crowd had encircled the muddy ground and begun talking about the miracle and praising God for it. The soldier edged to the back of the crowd, but not fast enough to elude the eyes of two people who came running along the street to see the source of the ruckus: Sarah and a beanpole of a man wearing a very fine suit and an expression of fury.

The widow hailed him and the man came along. "What happened?" Sarah asked.

"A spring seems to have erupted from the ground while we slept," the soldier replied.

The tall man scoffed. "It just . . . appeared here overnight?"

The soldier shrugged. "By the grace of God."

But the man had already turned his sharp gaze to scour the landscape, and he spotted the broken augur lying like a crippled spider at the edge of the woods. Ignoring the wondering crowd, he ran to the machine and looked it over. When he returned, his expression was thunderous, but he said nothing, merely brushing past the soldier with a glare and ignoring the calls of "Mr. Halprin, Mr. Halprin!" that followed after him. A small number of men detached themselves from the gawking crowd and scurried after him.

Sarah let out an amused snort at the sight. "There they go, kissing Halprin's backside, but I think they won't let *this* be taken away. Even the city council needs water." Then she turned to regard the soldier with a clear eye. "I suspect you have some idea how this 'miracle' came to be."

"It's hardly my place to guess at the motives of the Almighty."

"I was thinking of someone closer to home," she said, reaching out to take his nearest hand and turn it over to see the light smears of dirt and machine oil that smirched his palm and fingers.

The soldier cast his gaze down and pulled his hand back.

But Sarah was disinclined to let him get away so easily. "Why don't you come home with me and fetch some buckets? Be a pity to let that water go to waste when there's so much to clean and cook, and bathe. . . ."

The soldier nodded and followed her, meek as a lamb, but with a smile on his face.

It took two days to build and cap a proper wellhead and most of another to mount the large, gleaming pump donated by Mr. Halprin, but the folks of Stone Crossing went to the job with a will. It took two more days before the city council had declared that there was enough water and pressure to consider Mr. Halprin's suggestion of a proper civic plumbing project that would pipe water to every building on the main road by the end of the year. Sarah and the soldier both applauded the announcement, but Halprin himself, though hailed publicly as a great man—and privately as a miserly bastard—wore a sour countenance throughout the proceedings, turning a suspicious eye on the soldier and his landlady. But nothing came of his bitter looks, and the town reveled in its wonderful new water supply. The miraculous walking augur was repaired and a second well was drilled west of town to irrigate the fields so that they flushed again with greenery even in the heat, the railroad workers continued their din of industry, and everyone smelled a stretch more pleasant.

Things went on as they had before the drought, except that the soldier smiled once in a while and was seen on occasion strolling with the widow Sarah along the edges of the woods on Sunday evenings. The summer burned out the last of its fury, and the town was left adrift on the golden autumn sea of scythed fields.

As the trees dropped their leaves, red as garnets, on the ground now touched by the silver fingers of frost, the railroad moved west and the folks of Stone Crossing laid up stores for the winter. The soldier began thinking he should do something more than smoke, gamble, drink, and read books in Sarah's parlor, but what he might do eluded him, for he had known no other trade but war. Should he stay or move on? He grew more fond of the widow with every day that passed and he liked the town well enough, but he did not know what place there was for such a man as he. He pondered on it in the night and was, therefore, the first to see the dreadful ruddy glow that illuminated the western sky when all should have been blanketed in darkness.

The soldier threw open his window and leaned out to see what caused the light. A thread of smoke came on the wind and the whisper of a distant fire, crawling on its ravenous way across the stubbled fields toward the town. For a moment he was seized with a terror of this mindless, devouring thing and he thought to flee, but he knew he could not outrun such a conflagration even if it were not a coward's act. Then he thought of the metal dog and plucked the music box from his dresser.

He turned the ill-fitting key in the mechanism, but the tune did not ring out after the first wind. He turned it a further revolution and now the cylinder rotated, starting up with a harsh chime of chords, one and then a second chord, before the queer little song began to play.

He slipped down the stairs and ran outside in his nightclothes to meet the dog. He gazed toward the woods and saw it coming, bounding across the ground in great leaps, but as it drew near, he realized it was not the knee-high beast that had come to his first call, but the larger dog that had guarded the second room and its machines of destruction. He stiffened his spine and waited, for he could no more run from this beast than from the fire advancing on the other horizon.

The massive hound stopped before him, its sides of copper and brass reflecting red in the distant firelight. "What would you have me do, Master?" the dog asked, its voice rumbling like a rockfall.

"Do you see the fire that comes toward this town?" the soldier asked.

The mechanical beast nodded its brass-bound head, red light flickering across the rivets as large as the soldier's thumb that picked out the lines of the creature's face.

"Take the pumping engine from the cave and place it on the crawling wagon, then bring it to me by the western well. Quickly!"

The massive machine-hound turned around and bounded off again without a word.

The soldier began running toward the fire. Soon he was joined by a handful of his neighbors who grabbed up buckets and rushed along with him, though by their frightened words, he knew they held little hope of stopping a prairie fire with nothing but pails and strong backs. As they ran on, the fire gobbled up the western fields and lit the iron rails of the train tracks with orange light that made them glow like ingots fresh from Hephaestus's forge.

As the soldier and his neighbors neared the edge of town, a wind from the east passed violently by them, blowing back the flames for a moment. The townsfolk turned their heads aside to keep the dust from their eyes, but the soldier did not and saw that the wind came in the path of the metal mastiff that towed the crawling wagon in its wake. The dog dashed on to the well at the edge of the blazing fields, and the soldier followed it.

At the well, the soldier clamped the engine's hose to the pump and began to fill the tank as rapidly as he could. The townsfolk were slower, but coming toward the well also.

"Quick, dog," the soldier said, "bring fuel for the crawling wagon!"

Once again the dog ran away and returned in minutes bearing cans of fuel in its massive mouth.

"Good dog!" the soldier cried, and took the fuel. "Now run around the far edge of the fire and dig for all you're worth—bury the flames if you can. We'll water them away here and meet in the middle."

The tireless hound bounded off, disappearing in the smoke that billowed from the burning fields.

The soldier's neighbors stared and rubbed their eyes, but there was no time to wonder if they had truly seen a giant metal hound and they turned their frantic hands to filling the pumping tank and firing up the motor of the crawling wagon. In minutes, the engine began to creep forward. One of the men from the town climbed up into the wagon to steer it while the rest ran beside it, supporting the hoses and turning them on the flames as the soldier ordered them, low to the ground where the fire ate its fill of the harvest stubble.

Water hissed and steam rose and as the night wore on, more and more people of the town appeared to relieve the men who held the hoses and guided the crawling wagon back and forth along the fire line, pushing the flames back and back, down and down. Through the fire some swore they glimpsed a giant beast scurrying back and forth and throwing up clods of dirt as large as pigs that smothered the fire where they could not break through.

By dawn the fire had been extinguished and the empty fields lay blackened and wet, the warped metal of the railroad curling through the wasteland like petrified snakes, and the tracks of the crawling wagon laid over the ashen mud for a mile. But Stone Crossing stood untouched. Shrouded in the steam and lingering smoke at the middle of the burned field stood the wagon, nose to nose with a tarnished metal beast.

The soldier, steam-scalded, burned, and dirty, sat on the front of the wagon and patted the monster on the snout, its glowing eyes dim, but burning still. "You've done well, old dog. Can you return home now on your own?"

The brass beast nodded its massive head and trotted away, its stride covering the miles with ease.

The soldier slid down from the wagon and staggered toward the town, exhaustion weighing his every step as he wove his way across the field. He emerged from the steam and lingering smoke like an apparition and fell to his knees. Near to fainting, he took the little key from his pocket, but before he could do more, Sarah rushed to his side and helped him back to his feet.

"You marvelous fool," she said, hugging him much closer to her side than necessary. "Don't say this was the hand of the Almighty at work."

The soldier slipped the key back into his pocket unseen. "Your preacher says the Lord moves in mysterious ways. . . ."

"I doubt the Lord plunked down a pumping engine in the middle of our fields," Sarah said, "but I won't refuse the gifts he *has* given us. I know a good man when I find one."

She walked with him until they were enveloped in a crowd of their neighbors. The relieved and ragged folks of Stone Crossing carried the soldier home, right past the scowling face of Mr. Halprin as he stood at the outer edge of the town, alone and white with fury.

At the boardinghouse, the widow put the soldier to bed and it wasn't particularly remarked upon by anyone that she took it upon herself to bathe his burns and care for him. It was also no further business of theirs that when she kissed his cheek he kissed her back or how those kisses lingered and slid into something more. Some would not even have been entirely surprised if, like the morning sun, they had peeped in the window a day or so later and seen the widow Sarah snuggled against the soldier in his narrow bed and clothed in nothing more than the sheets.

The soldier, however, was taken quite by surprise at these developments, for he had thought the joy and peace he found in her arms had vanished from his heart forever. When she murmured sweet words and stroked her hand across his chest, her fingers lingering and then stopping on the strange scar that lay in the arch of his rib cage like a keystone, his elation crashed to the ground and he stiffened, holding his breath.

"What is this?" Sarah asked. "Does it pain you?"

"It pains me no more, except that it may send you from me."

She would have inquired further, but a rumpus had begun downstairs and she took herself out of the bed, cursing and putting on her dress in haste. Barely had she closed the buttons when the bedroom door burst in to admit Mr. Halprin and her other tenants in his wake.

The men of the boardinghouse stopped on the threshold, their eyes wide with surprise, but Halprin bulled forward until Sarah blocked his path.

"Step aside, woman," Halprin demanded.

"I don't think I shall," she replied. "You have no right to assault my guests in my house, Mr. Halprin, and I will ask you to leave at once."

"I'll have my say before you throw me out of this house where you consort like a whore."

Sarah slapped him with such force that it turned his head full stop to the side. Then she spoke in clipped tones. "These gentlemen will escort you to the door now."

Halprin glared over her shoulder at the soldier and jabbed a warning finger his direction. "You stole my dogs and you've ruined everything! I don't know how you managed it all, but if you are still here come morning, you'll live only long enough to wish you hadn't come here."

The soldier gave him a glance as cold as midnight and said, "I mean to stay, sir. Make no mistake: I like this little town and I'll like it just as much without you in it."

"Are you threatening me, you miserable scrap of a man?"

"No more than you are me. But you'd do well to recall what befell Morton."

Halprin straightened like a tree bough snapping back from being bent down, and his nose went up in the air as if the soldier's words put a stench up his nostrils. "You will regret your trespassing and your meddling before I'm through," he declared. Then he turned and glared at Sarah and her boarders. "As will you all!"

And he stalked away, brushing past Sarah as if her touch were acid. The rest of the boarders fell in around Halprin and conveyed him out the door and down the stairs with chill courtesy. For the first time in the history of Stone Crossing, they barred the door behind him.

Sarah turned back and looked down at the soldier, who had propped himself up in bed and was reaching for the key he always carried in his pocket.

"Do you truly mean to stay?"

"I do, if you'll have me."

Sarah looked down at him, puzzled. "Have you? Haven't we just—?"

"I meant that I should like to marry you, if you will have me once you know the truth of . . . this," the soldier added, touching the keystone scar on his chest.

Sarah offered him a bemused smile. "Of course I'll marry you, fool! How can you imagine that I would run away now? I know these scars are from the war. I know what you have been through, that you have fought—"

"And died," the soldier said.

Sarah was taken aback, but she sat on the edge of the bed as he patted it for her. Then the soldier told her his tale: how his horse had stepped upon a torpedo and been killed beneath him by the explosion and the sharp metal scrap that cut through the poor creature; how the flying barbs tore into his own face and body, one piercing his heart; how he lay dying, watching his fellows charge ahead on the disarmed ground vouchsafed to them by his noble horse; and how he had awakened again in a makeshift hospital with a clockwork heart ticking away in his chest—the "gift" of a half-mad surgeon driven to save whomever he could by whatever means, no matter how unnatural.

At first the soldier had been confounded, then amazed, happy, frightened, sorrowful, guilty . . . so many emotions crowding into him that he could not think. Until his commanding officer ordered his return to the battlefront and he discovered that now he could not feel, and feeling nothing, he did not care. When the letter came about the death by typhus of his wife and child, the army was glad to send him away at last—a broken toy soldier, a mistake they wished they'd never made.

Sarah stroked his cheek. "You are no mistake, my love."

"Am I your love, truly? A man who must wind up his heart like a watch?"

"I don't care *how* your heart beats, only that it does. I loved you when it was a mystery, and I love you still, now that it's not."

"Then hand me that key, beloved, for I have much to do before Mr. Halprin springs his traps."

"Do you believe he means the things he said?" Sarah asked, passing him the small brass key from the dresser.

"Oh, yes. He means to kill me," the soldier replied, fitting the key to the odd scar on his chest, "and he'll no doubt take half the town with him, for he's clearly quite insane."

"You mustn't let him hurt you," Sarah said, her face going pale, though who could tell whether it was from fear for him or the sight of the little brass key sinking into his flesh. . . ?

The soldier did not look up as he wound his clockwork heart. "I don't intend to. Nor let him harm this town any further. I've stopped him before and I'll stop him again. I'll regret it mightily, but if I must put him in his grave to do it, I will."

He drew the key away at last and raised his head to look at Sarah. Her mouth was set firm, but there was a softness in her eyes that was neither pity nor tears. "I am sorry to present you such a terrible betrothal present," said the soldier. "You can still refuse. . . ."

"No, in fact, I cannot." She smiled gently and kissed his cheek.

The soldier and Sarah sat together for quite a while, talking of their own future and of Halprin's threat. Sarah informed the soldier of Halprin's past in greater detail—which was sufficient to turn even that battle-hardened man pale.

"Halprin is a very monster," Sarah concluded. "I don't doubt for a moment that he set that fire himself, though why he should burn his own properties I can't guess."

"As you said once, there will be no lack of buyers once the railroad is through."

"But the fire ruined the new-laid tracks," Sarah objected.

"Only those that run beyond the town. The station and warehouses at the edge of Stone Crossing remain untouched."

"And those warehouses belong to Mr. Halprin," Sarah added. "No doubt filled with his horrible devices ready to be shipped back to the war in the East."

The soldier looked startled and Sarah asked him what was wrong.

"I am suddenly reminded of something that was missing. . . ."

"What? Has someone robbed your room?"

"No, my love, but there may be a worse problem. Pass me the music box from the dresser, please."

"Why?" she asked, even as she handed him the box.

"I fear Mr. Halprin's threats may be all too real and we may need a great deal of help to counter his plans, but I must ask a question of a dog first."

He put the key to the music box and turned it once, twice, thrice. The chimes rang out in three dreadful chords and the tune began to play. Its strange, discordant notes were still shivering on the air when they heard the sound of metal feet clattering against the roof outside the window. Sarah helped the soldier to the window and threw up the sash.

The smallest of the mechanical dogs stepped inside, its copper and brass no longer so bright as when the soldier had first seen it, but its eyes glowed as if lit by hellfire. Beyond it the head of the largest hound peeped over the roof ledge, gilded a dull silver by the cloud-shrouded moon.

"What would you have us do, Master?" the dog asked as before.

"Are both your brothers outside?" the soldier asked.

The dog nodded.

"Then I will go down to meet them."

The sun was long gone by this time, the late-autumn night clouded and the wind speaking of snow soon to come. The soldier dressed warmly and went down to the porch to speak with the mechanical dogs. If any of his neighbors peered out of their windows, he made no remark upon it.

The first dog scrambled down from the roof and joined the other two, making a row by ascending size: the first normal-sized, the second huge, and the third a giant whose head overtopped the doorway to such a degree that the soldier commanded it to lie down and thus ease his neck from craning upward to see the beast.

"Now, tell me, has your former master returned to the caverns lately?" the soldier asked.

The first dog shook its head, and the soldier marked it as by far the cleverest and most nimble of the three.

"And has anything more been taken away since I first called upon you?"

All three dogs shook their heads, and the porch shuddered as the largest dog knocked one of the pillars with its snout. This one, the soldier thought, was the juggernaut of the company—ponderous, but as near unstoppable as a comet hurtling through space.

The soldier pointed at the first dog and named it. "Scout—for that is what you are—can you record information?"

The smallest dog seemed to give it thought, and then nodded. The soldier nodded also. "Very well, then. Take yourself stealthily to observe your former master and what preparations he may be making against me. Then return and let me know what you've discovered. We have only until daybreak to lay our plans."

While they awaited the dog's reconnaissance, Sarah sat down beside him and asked where the dogs had come from and what their purpose was. The soldier replied that he had found them in a cave filled with mechanical wonders and metal nightmares, and as to their original purpose he was not sure, but as of now, their charge would be to protect the people of Stone Crossing from Mr. Halprin's machinations.

The moon had just tipped past its zenith when Scout returned. The dog's metal body was soiled with dirt and soot and marked with scratches. It paced off a large circle and began to draw in the dirt with its forepaw. Sarah brought more lanterns so that she and the soldier could examine the drawing: two buildings, two long parallel lines, and many rows of small circles backed by more rows of oblongs. The couple stared at the drawing for a while, not knowing what it represented, while the dog-shaped machine trotted across the circle to draw some more: a collection of boxes and lines. . . .

"That's the town," Sarah said, pointing to Scout's newest drawing.

The soldier peered at it. "If that's true, then these lines to the northwest must be the train rails, and that would be the station house beside them and Halprin's warehouse beside that."

"What are all these things spread outside it?" Sarah asked, pointing to the circles and oblongs.

"I don't know . . . but I suspect," the soldier started. Then he looked at the dog. "Did these things come from the cavern once?"

Scout nodded and the other two dogs mirrored its movement.

The soldier remembered the empty room beyond the middle cavern where the plans for machines of war and destruction had lain and he thought of the lightning generator at Shiloh. . . . "I'm not certain, but I suspect they are engines of devastation, meant for the war, but now arrayed against all of us. . . . Can he really mean to attack the whole town for the anger he feels toward me?"

Once again the dogs nodded and the chill wind sent shivers down the humans' spines. A terrible guilt struck the soldier. He stood up. "If I am gone by morning, perhaps this madness won't come to pass." He looked at Sarah and she looked back, shaking her head.

"And perhaps pigs will sprout wings and fly across the Alleghenies every spring," she replied. "Have you not understood all I've told you of Mr. Halprin? He is more than half mad, cruel, and uncaring for his fellow creatures. Did you not see that for yourself? It is not against you alone he swore his threats, but against all of us. I believe he means to carry out his revenge in the worst way. What shall we do?"

"*Si vis pacem, para bellum,*" the soldier muttered. He studied Scout's drawing awhile longer, then looked up at the dogs. "We shall be ready for him, but we must ensure that his first strike does no harm. . . ." First he named the dogs from smallest to largest for convenience' sake: Scout, Bucephalus, and Juggernaut. Then he told them all his plan and sent the dogs to their duty, bringing everything that walked or rolled from the caves while he and Sarah went to rouse the house and town. . . .

Well before dawn, the grinding sound of gears and the grumble of heavy feet began rising in the northwest. By the time the first rays of light had pierced the clouds, the townsfolk were arrayed in trepid wonder at the western edge of Stone Crossing with great piles of chain and rope at their feet, staring out at the burned fields where a cotillion of delicate automata danced and gamboled slowly west in the pink light. Just beyond, ranks of brass and iron machines spewing steam and smoke walked implacably southeast to meet them, some on four legs, some on six, and some on cleated tracks. They bore a variety of weapons from the spiny heads of torpedoes to huge guns and the shining upright tubes of mortars that looked like hellish calliopes.

At the northernmost edge of the town, the soldier stood with Sarah, the massive dog he had named Bucephalus—for his head was surely as large as an ox's—and Scout, and watched the mechanical army descend. "So, this is how a general must feel, playing with his toy soldiers," he said.

"Yes, but none of these soldiers are flesh and bone," said Sarah.

"So we shall hope. For if this plan fails, it falls to men and not machines to fight these monstrous things that come upon us."

"It will not fail," Sarah replied, staring out at the blackened ground filled with golden toys.

In the field, a gleaming rabbit of brushed copper and brass gave a mighty hop into the air, windmilling its ears. Three of the walking guns swiveled toward it and a shattering hail of bullets tore the toy to glittering shards. The townsfolk gasped and recoiled at the sight. But the soldier nodded and muttered, "He may have the force, but he hasn't any strategy at all."

In a moment the first of the walking torpedoes clashed against the tumbling jester in his jeweled motley and exploded with a roar of gunpowder. Gleaming metal confetti and mechanical entrails scattered outward in all directions, setting off two more of the explosives.

The rain of shrapnel drew the attention of the walking guns, and they began firing in ragged volleys, sweeping back and forth so long as the cloud of metal hung in the air. A bullet ripped through the soldier's sleeve, slicing a hot groove in his arm, and he winced.

Sarah reached for him, but he pushed her back. "No," the soldier said. "Fall back now. Take them all to the engines. Remember: our goal is to turn his line south of the town and flank him, not to make dead heroes."

"What of you?" she said, her voice sharp.

"I've been a dead hero once—I've no need to do it again."

Sarah gave him one last look and ran toward her neighbors. At her command, the townsfolk ducked and scurried away as the field filled with the gold-dusted explosions of dozens of murdered automata. The battle line turned slightly south as the walking guns tracked to each new blast of destruction. Behind them the mortars crouched down on their articulated legs and fired off their first ranging volley.

The ground between the automata and the town erupted, throwing dirt clods and burned stubble into the air with a roar.

The soldier looked to the smallest of the mechanical dogs. "Now, Scout, go!"

The mechanical beast, brown and rusty as a dirty penny now, dashed away beneath the cover of the earthen explosion, heading southwest to a lonely stand of trees, and vanished into their morning shadow. In a minute it emerged again, circling back to snatch a knotted rope between its metal jaws and run northwest.

Juggernaut broke from the stand of trees, clutching the other end of the rope in its own massive mouth, its head held low as if on the scent. The ground shook with each step the giant dog took across the field, pulling the makeshift line of rope and chain taut, inches above the ash-covered ground.

As the dust began to clear, the mechanical dogs raced on west, dragging the line between them until it pulled against the legs of the front line of walking machines of death, toppling them backward and sideways into the machines behind them. The first three ranks exploded with a roar that shook the earth. The torpedoes all destroyed, some of the remaining walking guns staggered and fell, some toppling on their sides while others righted themselves and walked on in random directions. But most only corrected their path to the south—toward the largest mass of falling machines—and marched on, spewing bullets and fire over the gleaming bodies of the machines in front of them.

The soldier turned to the last dog and said, "Now, Boo. We're off to find the villain himself."

The large beast bent down and the soldier climbed on his back. He felt absurd riding astride a metal dog, but the time for vanity was long past. The huge mechanical beast leaped forward, running to meet Scout in the north end of the field.

As they hurtled onward, the soldier turned his head to see Juggernaut racing up and down among the stumbling guns, throwing up clods of dirt and metal debris in all directions, luring them steadily southeast and destroying what it could. The nearest guns turned to fire and shot their own kind instead, the giant dog bolting past under the whine of ricochets and the hissing of escaping steam.

Then two engines roared onto the field, one from the southwest and the other from the northeast. A long stream of water shot from the pumping engine as some of the townsfolk drove it into the shattered line's flank from the livery at the south edge of town. The other, clanking forward from the north end, came forth spitting fire from twin barrels that poked out of a makeshift shield of steel plates hiding two men who drove the smaller machine, sweating with heat and fear, but going forward nonetheless.

Streams of fire and water smashed into Halprin's walking guns, battering them with opposing forces of heat and moisture. Heating them, melting them, then cooling and shoving them. When the cold water hit the gleaming sides of hot metal and straining boilers, the machines on the south end of the line exploded with a screech of scalding steam, rivets and metal flying wide and raining down again like metallic snow. The townsfolk crouched beneath the engine and let this devil's rain fall. On the north flank, flames from the other wagon melted the chains of projectiles that fed the guns and they ceased firing, walking onward with no purpose but to smash bodily into the buildings of the town while their companions staggered and fell in warped piles of metal, hissing and bursting in clouds of steam and exploding ammunition, or going down in flame from their own ruptured fuel tanks.

The townsfolk swept the streams of water and fire across the broken line of machines as the mortars crouched again. . . .

This time the mortar shells struck the first buildings of Stone Crossing, blowing wood and fire into the air as the buildings exploded and tumbled.

The water engine turned to put out the fires while the flame-spewer and Juggernaut converged on the rest, fire washing over the devilish calliopes until the shells exploded inside the tubes, rupturing the mortars and sending their pipes spinning into the sky. The townsfolk who could be spared from the water engine attacked the disarmed machines with whatever came to hand: axes, poles, or shotguns. They battered at Halprin's automated army, knocking it down piece by piece while Juggernaut wreaked havoc on the remaining armed guns, pouncing from behind and flinging them into the air to shatter on the ground. The clanging and roaring of destruction and fire deafened the ear, and the stink of burning metal and wood clouded the fields.

The soldier rode on toward the train station, running parallel to Scout at a distance and bolting from cover to cover.

Scout raced across the churned field in wild zigzags, turning sharper than a dancer as a single heavy gun picked at the mechanical dog from the warehouse. Bucephalus and the soldier—ever the cavalry man at heart—swung out wider, heading for the rear of the building from its blind side as the gun continued to try to score a hit on the smaller, swifter metal beast. In the distance, they could feel the pounding of Juggernaut's dashing and digging shaking the ground.

As soon as the soldier and Bucephalus were safe beyond the warehouse's front wall, Scout took a sudden turn and bolted south toward the disintegrating remains of the mechanical army.

The soldier and his strange mount crashed through the back door of the warehouse, the building shuddering as they came inside. In the loft, Halprin spun to stare at them, staggering under the weight of the large gun he cradled in his arms.

"Bastard," he shouted as the soldier slid off the back of the massive hound.

Halprin, a moment too late, squeezed the trigger of his gun, sending a smoking stream of bullets just over Bucephalus's back and across the top of its head. The soldier hit the floor facedown and the brass-bound dog turned its head upward and opened its jaws, one burning eye extinguished.

Then the dog launched itself up the stairs toward Halprin, making a terrible roaring sound as it went. The soldier jumped after it, calling, "No, Boo. Stop!" but, apparently by its own desire, the creature of brass and copper and steel had set its path and leaped forward without heed.

A cheer rose outside as if a crowd were drawing near to urge the mindless copper beast onward. The soldier ground his teeth and started after the massive dog.

Halprin reeled back, the gun chattering as the bullets rattled against the hound's chest and head. And then they tore through, the heavy metal beast lurching forward as its gears blew apart and ground to a halt. Mighty Bucephalus fell with a thunderous clatter, collapsing the stairs and dragging the loft flooring down with it as it plunged to the floor.

Halprin tumbled as the earth shuddered and shuddered again. The soldier ran to the side of the shattered hound, its body bullet-ripped and its huge eyes darkened forever. It was only a thing of gears and metal—it could not think or dream or hurt—but he hadn't felt such sorrow in a long time as he felt for this unlikely beast.

Halprin scrambled backward toward the front door, rolling to scoop up his fallen gun, saying, "Look at what you've done to this place. Look at what you've reaped by your meddling."

"This is what *you* have done, coward!" the soldier shouted back. "You sent your machines against innocent people, and it was other machines that stopped them."

Halprin swung the gun's muzzle around. The soldier ducked behind the wreckage of the dog as the gun coughed and then stuttered silent.

The ground continued to shiver and heave as he glanced over the ruined machine beast. Halprin threw down the useless gun and turned for the doorway.

Outside, a swift shadow bolted toward the doorway, half-hidden in rising sun. The soldier drew his revolver from his belt, aimed over the back of his fallen hound, and squeezed the trigger.

As the hammer dropped, the streak of brown and gold rammed into Halprin's legs and he tripped, tumbling headfirst out the doorway as the soldier's bullet passed through the air his head had recently occupied.

The soldier cursed, jumped up, and ran for the doorway, stumbling across the bucking floor. Scout darted inside and dragged the soldier out of the building behind Halprin. The soldier tried to shake the mechanical dog away, furious and set on taking his enemy's life.

Outside, Halprin scrambled to his feet and tried to run across the shuddering ground as Scout harried the soldier aside.

A shadow fell on Halprin and he glanced up, then froze at what he saw.

Juggernaut, dripping oil and water, his metal skin torn open and blasted by steam and gunpowder, let out a howl as of a million angry souls shouting for vengeance, and leaped on Halprin with his iron jaw agape.

Halprin shrieked in terror as the giant creature fell upon him and crushed him to the ground. A cloud of dirt and metal flew into the air, knocking the soldier and Scout backward as the massive dog came to rest at last.

His breath heaving in his chest, the soldier pulled himself up by holding on to Scout—filthy, dented, indomitable Scout, the last remaining dog. He stood there still, his revolver loose in his hand, when Sarah and the citizens of Stone Crossing arrived, by foot, on horseback, or riding on the crawling wagons with their battered engines.

Sarah took in the wreckage all around, the broken dogs, the warehouse as tumbledown as a shanty, and the sickening remains of Halprin. Then she looked to her beloved soldier, sorrowful and unmoving with Scout beside him.

She took his hand and drew him closer to her. "Did you shoot him?" she asked in a soft voice. "I'm sorry if you had to."

"I didn't kill him. It was the dogs. Even torn to shreds they did not stop."

"You told them to protect us and they did."

The soldier shook his head in wonder and sorrow. "I never ordered them to kill. I never ordered them to protect *me*. Their duty was to you—to all of you. Hollow hounds they may have been, but they had hearts the size of giants'."

Sarah took her soldier back to Stone Crossing, where they were married at Christmastime. They lived in the town for many years, filling the house with children and dogs, but it was always the one dog, the odd one with the metal hide like dirty pennies, that the soldier kept at his side. Two of a kind: their mechanical hearts wound up by something more than a key.

The Kings of Mount Golden

by Paul Di Filippo

(BASED ON "THE KING OF THE GOLDEN MOUNTAIN" BY THE BROTHERS GRIMM)

"This is the devil's own bargain you are forcing upon me, Warner Gilead, and you shall come to rue this day!"

The man thus addressed—a specimen of the pure-quill Newport-summering plutocrat, yet, surprisingly, not flashily attired, overweening, nor lofty, but rather clad in a mourning suit, enervated, and plainly brought low (in spirits, if not in status) by circumstance—refused the aggression proffered by his angry interlocutor. Warner Gilead seemed drained for the nonce of whatever spunk and vim had once propelled him to that hypothetical stratosphere of society which the remnants of his self-assured mien and sober finery proclaimed he still inhabited. He had apparently lost or misplaced his zest for living, and now moved through the affairs of his own life like a ghost seeking what can never be regained.

The intemperate, gaunt-faced gentleman offering the prediction of ill fortune wore a moderately priced, slightly shabby set of tweeds, and exhibited the educated manner of a skilled professional of some sort—lawyer, teacher, or perhaps architect. But an alert observer would have noticed that the man's blunt-fingered hands had been scarred by sharp objects and burned by chemicals, and still hosted ineradicable grease beneath their nails, thus marking him as some sort of chemist or engineer or artificer.

The scene hosting the two antagonists—Gilead seated, the other man standing—was a dark-paneled, book-lined office with tall windows offering a view from above onto Boston's busy Charles Street. Past the raised sashes, riding the spring breezes, came a welter of peddlers' cries, carriage wheels rumbling, and the excited cries of children frolicking.

Before choosing his response to the accusation of driving an infernal deal, Warner Gilead stroked his bushy salt-and-pepper side-whiskers thoughtfully. He regarded his opponent coolly, as might one who mentally weighs the penal consequences of murder against the satisfaction afforded by the deed. Finally deciding against such an act of passion, for which he had not, if truth be told, the adequate zeal, Gilead said, "Rather, Hedley, I think I am being extremely merciful and generous in my offer, considering that you stole my wife away from me, and then could not save her when she was in extremis."

Hedley King—for such was the full name of Gilead's younger correspondent—blanched at this thrust. His face betrayed a blend of anguish, guilt, and self-reproach.

"Damn you, Gilead! How was I to predict a breech birth followed by uterine rupture! I had a competent midwife in the house, but Pella's condition would have been too much for even a professional obstetrician. She died so damnably fast! But did I not rush the baby straight to your man at Massachusetts General Hospital, as soon as we abandoned hope for Pella?"

"Yes, where the child was saved only by the intervention of my good friend Dr. Warren, and where the infant has remained safely ever since. And of course, Dr. Warren's genius and expertise would have been at the disposal of dear Pella from the start, had you not—"

Hedley King interrupted. "Listen to me, you self-deluding old coot! Pella and I fell in love! Such things happen, without intent or machination. Pella left you to be with me. After a year together, she chose to bear me a child. The sad outcome of this chain of events, we both know. But the guilt, if any, rests just as firmly with your beloved Pella and with you as it does with me. If you had not turned so adamantly away from her, she might have felt welcome at your damn fine hospital—"

Gilead considered this observation, the truthfulness of which he was too honest a soul to deny.

"I am sorry to reopen these still-fresh wounds, Hedley. Please forgive me. It's just that Pella—No, I'll speak no further on that subject. Let us simply conclude our business, and then we will not have to associate any longer."

Gilead withdrew two impressively thick legal documents from the center drawer of the desk at which he sat, and took up a pen. Standing on the far side of the big desk, Hedley King watched his rival warily, as if convinced that Gilead was about to trigger some infernal device that would suicidally blast them both into flinders.

Dipping the pen into a pot of ink, Gilead said, "Let me show my good faith by first voluntarily signing the papers transferring to you all the patents pertaining to your invention. Though I do not believe I will hand the document over to you until you have signed your own contract."

Gilead suited deed to words. He regarded King for some sign of appreciation, but King's glare indicated the man was still grudging.

"A fine state of affairs, to have to barter for my own intellectual property."

"Come, now, Hedley, you know full well that your invention was funded entirely by me, and involved important contributions from my partner, Mr. Blanchard. You worked strictly at my behest and as my employee, using my facilities."

"Bah! I'm no one's wage slave! I'm a sovereign creator! And as for Thomas Blanchard, he's a doddering old has-been! His glory days are behind him. When did he invent his foolish 'horseless carriage'? Just over two dozen years ago, in 1825! And where has he gotten with it since? Nowhere! All he did for me was to perfect the process for machining the pressure-resistant capsules that contain the vril. Every other aspect of the Morphic Resonator is mine! Mine alone!"

"Be that as it may, your claims would not hold up in a court of law without this legal transference of the patents. So now you have what you most desire, and so shall kindly grant me the same."

Gilead turned the second document toward King, and proffered the pen. King snatched the stylus, found the relevant page of the contract, and scratched his name with an angry vigor.

"There! The child is now all yours! My own flesh and blood, bartered like a sack of oats! Now give me those patents!"

King irritably plucked up the document his rival had signed, and paged through it roughly to be certain of its terms. Gilead, however, took up the other sheaf of papers tenderly, as if he were lifting the baby itself.

"The boy is only half your flesh, Hedley. Pella's contribution is not to be diminished. And as she was still my wife when she died—you two not having trifled with such formalities—I could have made a good case for instant legal custody of the child. But as you were irrefutably the father, you might have contested my claim and caused me a long and aggravated court battle, depriving me of crucial formative years with my son. But now I can begin to raise the child from his earliest days, free from your stain and influence."

"Raise him as you will, Gilead! His sinews and cells are still half mine!"

"That hardly matters, I think, given that the terms of our agreement call for you never to see him again."

Hedley King's impudence and arrogance dissipated somewhat, and he seemed crestfallen at the finality of this edict. He turned away and moved toward the exit of the study.

At the door, he paused, and said mildly, "We planned to name the child Roland—"

"I don't care what you planned. My heir will be named Brannock. That was his mother's maiden name, one of many facts about Pella concerning which you probably never even deigned to inquire."

Now Hedley King's anger flared afresh. "Curse you, Gilead! You may have made it impossible for me to attempt to see the child ever again. But what will you do when he wants to see me?"

King stormed out on that note, leaving Gilead to sit and contemplate with nebulous unease the dawning of such an impossible day.

At age thirteen, Brannock Gilead (Bran to his chums and teachers and servants and shopkeepers—to all, in fact, but his stern father) presented the inviting appearance of a handsome young fellow, tall for his age and rather more gracile than muscular, with sensitive lips and deeply pooled brown eyes. These two features he knew he had inherited from his mother, Pella, for a large hand-tinted ambrotype of her beautiful face dominated the parlor of his Charles Street home. Bran had spent endless hours musing over that visage captured in silver on glass—serene on the surface, yet with hints of lurking unease and stifled ambition. He tried to imagine speaking with this dead woman, asking her all the questions about his own heritage that he had saved up since earliest childhood—questions that his implacable surviving parent simply would not countenance.

Newly preeminent among these niggling unvoiced queries were all those concerning the nature, history, and current status of the mysterious man who had sired him.

Just the past week, upon his thirteenth birthday, Bran's father had revealed to him that there existed no ties of blood between Warner Gilead and the boy he called his son.

Diffidently intruding into Bran's bedroom that anniversary

evening, after the muted, lonely celebration of his son's birth—a nighttime visit heretofore unprecedented, save once when Bran had been worrisomely ill with the bloody flux—Gilead had manifested some discomfiture totally at odds with his usual self-possessed sangfroid. Sitting himself down on the edge of Bran's mattress and petting his silvery muttonchops, he awkwardly began to recount what seemed at first to Bran to be some kind of modern fairy tale, but which soon revealed a startling personal relevance.

"There's something I feel you are now old enough to know, son, and so I wish you to listen closely to me now. You see, Brannock, your mother—my dear wife—had the misfortune to be gulled and seduced by a villain, some short while before you were born. The fellow was the essence of insolence and temerity, a cheap hired hand whose name shall forevermore be stricken from the rolls of humanity. Pella was a smart woman, but one in whom animal passions ran strong and sometimes countervailing to her usual good sense. In this case, she should certainly have heeded her better angels. When the flippant dastard callously tossed her aside, laden with child—that embryonic lad was your innocent self, of course—I magnanimously took her back into my home. But she perished giving birth to you, ascending to her heavenly reward, and so you and I were deprived thenceforth of the comfort of her companionship."

Bran's father—and what exactly did that term represent, in the light of this startling revelation?—paused in his account and looked with a surprising beseechingness into Bran's eyes, an intimately imploring gesture he seldom made.

"You won't think any the less of our father-and-son relationship, I hope, Brannock, just because of the accidental and unfortunate nature of your conception? I was intensely in love with your mother, and those lingering sentiments incline me to regard any legacy from her actions, however unwise, as part and parcel of my own estate. So as far as I and the world are concerned, your inheritance and position as a Gilead are secure and unquestionable."

Bran had been hopefully awaiting the word *love* to be applied to him, just this once. Instead, he had been deemed a mere "legacy." And since his father's speech seemed definitely to have concluded without any emotion-laden label for their relationship forthcoming, the lad resigned himself with a sigh to that word's continuing and unsurprising absence.

"Rest assured, Father, that all remains between us just as before."

Warner Gilead arose with a small smile, tousled his son's hair, and departed.

In the subsequent week, the idea of learning the identity of his blood father had never left Bran's mind once. He had even dreamed about the man, a bulky, hazy figure emerging beckoningly from a cloaking mist. So compelling had been the urge to know more that it had even driven Bran, this weekday afternoon, into his father's study, a room generally forbidden to him.

Warner Gilead was attending a meeting with Governor Bullock concerning next year's presidential election, and so could be counted on not to intrude.

Bran went to work searching his father's papers, sliding open heavy wooden drawers, lifting the brass-hinged tops of box files, and riffling through overstuffed bellows folders. Such a lot of dry, boring paperwork, all given over to numbers and schemes. Bran swore he'd never let his adulthood be dominated by such stifling drudgery. He'd live a life of adventure, such as he read about weekly in *The Young Men of America* magazine.

In a bottom desk drawer Bran came upon another ambrotype of his mother, one he had never seen before. She stood in the middle of a cluttered workshop, smiling, surrounded by somber leather-aproned men. Bran recognized one, Stan Lambeth, a machinist still employed by his father. Could one of these other fellows be his mother's paramour, and Bran's sire?

Bran pondered the frozen image for a very long time, but no clues obtruded themselves. When he eventually restored the picture to its hiding place, long evening shadows were stretching across the study floor. He'd have to hurry!

Bran had been saving the big safe for last. He thought he knew the combination, having once overheard his father entrust the information to his secretary, Griffin Stumpf. So to the safe's dial Bran moved.

The sequence he had memorized failed to unlock the safe. But after cudgeling his memory, he tried a minor variation and succeeded!

He had the weighty door open just long enough to register the image of some bundled currency, gaudy certificates, a revolver— and a ribbon-tied envelope bearing a red-bordered paper label that carried Bran's own name! Then came the sound of someone approaching!

Bran closed the safe door as quickly as was consonant with silence, spun the dial, and stepped away from the vault.

Warner Gilead entered the room, accompanied by the dour and pox-faced Griffin Stumpf.

"—General McClellan's a fine soldier, I give you that, but as president—"

Gilead espied Bran. The older man's face suffused with choler. His level voice was grave. "What are you doing in this room?"

Bran could make no reply.

Gilead turned to his assistant. "Mr. Stumpf, please fetch Hoskins, and have him bring a good wide length of leather."

Stumpf departed, and Gilead and Bran remained frozen, as if locked into some dull holiday charade. Bran saw his father's eyes flick toward the safe, and appear to register relief that it had not been tampered with.

The brawny, sweaty Hoskins—a gentle man with horses, an expert saddle repairer, and an unerring farrier—trailed behind Stumpf. Dragged from his stables, the man looked miserable.

"Mr. Hoskins, you are to administer five applications of your strap across my son's buttocks. There will be no need to bare his skin, I think."

Hoskins eyed Bran ruefully. "Aye, sir."

Bran was made to bend over the desk. After the first apathetic blow, Gilead said, "Are you malnourished, Mr. Hoskins? If so, perhaps you could find other employment that offered heartier board."

The next four blows were sufficiently mighty to satisfy Warner Gilead's sense of punishment, drawing stifled grunts from the boy.

Bran retired to his bedroom without supper, nursing both his feelings and his bottom. He passed a couple of hours contemplating schemes of revenge and a further raid upon the safe. Then came a knock.

His father entered, carrying something concealed in his fist.

"Son, I know you miss your mother. So do I. That's why I wish to give you this."

Gilead opened his hand and displayed a small oval silver locket, chased with filigree. Bran regarded it with a curiosity even his smoldering anger could not totally swamp. Gilead fumbled open the clasp.

Inside rested a few delicate, almost luminous strands of golden hair.

"Yes, they came from Pella, your mother. Keep this locket with you, and you will always have her close by."

Bran accepted the locket with an uneasy mix of gratitude and disdain.

The next time he dared approach the study, he found the door locked with a new mechanism.

And when he eventually got past that barrier, a replacement safe boasted not one but two dials, neither of which accepted the old combination.

These obstacles between Bran and the packet that bore his name proved insurmountable, and he took solace in the locket, which he wore always on a chain about his neck, vowing that when he got older, he would find a way to secure that information, Warner Gilead be damned!

In the first half of the nineteenth century, Boston's Fort Hill had acquired a reputation as an elegant neighborhood. A steep and formidable eminence suited only for residences, despite its developmentally tempting proximity to the waterfront and central commercial districts, the mount had hosted numerous mansions and the beautiful Washington Square atop its crown.

But by the middle of the century, a disturbing change had occurred. The district had become a slum, filled mostly with unsavory, poverty-stricken Irish immigrants. Warehouses ringed the foot of Fort Hill, and over one hundred saloons dotted its filthy warren of alleys and lanes, along with several charitable poorhouses and a lone hospital ensconced in a former armory. "Fort Hill rowdyism" had became a byword for bad behavior.

By the year of Bran's birth, upstanding citizens were already agitating for the pit of iniquity literally to be leveled, as other hills in Boston had been, the burden of its soil being used as fill elsewhere. By the time Bran was attempting to burgle his father's safe, solid schemes for the razing were being drawn up. Action commenced in the year 1866, when a gigantic trench had been driven through the middle of Fort Hill, to carry Olive Street from one side to the next. But in the year 1868, when Bran attained his eighteenth birthday, work had stalled, leaving the bifurcate hill like a troughed Christmas pudding, still a stew of illegality and want, with makeshift bridges spanning the chasm of Olive Street.

Now Bran labored up the nighted, slops-wet pavements of Fort Hill, his way lit by the occasional lonely gas lamp out of sight of any mates. Bold doxies and judys leered and gibed from doorways; raggle-taggle children who should have been long abed solicited money and offered to run errands; and shady gonophs and bludgers seemed to lurk just within every pool of shadow between buildings. Bran nervously patted the pointed hoof pick in his pocket, which he had secured from the stables. It offered scant protection against knives or guns, but at least it was some kind of weapon.

Finally Bran reached his destination, a tavern whose partially occluded signboard read SPITALNY'S GROT. He entered the fusty, low-raftered, candlelit cauldron of smells and noise.

None among the seedy clientele took particular notice of him, obviously deeming Bran one of the Beacon Hill swells who often visited Fort Hill for their own illicit purposes.

A description, Bran ruefully acknowledged to himself, that fit him perfectly.

Bran approached a harried barmaid. "Can you please tell me where I could find Mr. MacMahon?"

"Bucko? That's him over there, playing at darts."

Bran approached the gamesters, but did not immediately choose to interrupt their loud-voiced sport, for much seemed to be riding on the outcome, judging by the threats and boasts being batted about. The fellow preparing to shoot wore a look of intense concentration, the tip of his wet tongue protruding from the stubbled corner of his mouth. A shapeless cloth hat slanted over one eye. Shattered capillaries mapped his big nose. His patched suit appeared to have been fashioned from sackcloth. This unimpressive lout, then, was Bucko MacMahon, Bran's only remaining hope for discovering the secrets of his past.

Apparently confident of his aim and prowess, Bucko let fly with the dart, scored a bull's-eye, and was greeted with a roar compounded of cheers and razzing.

"Now I'll claim me prize!" Bucko strode to the bar and accepted a tall narrow yard glass filled to the flaring brim with nearly a quart and a half of dark ale. He raised the bulb-bottomed vessel to his lips, tilted his head back, and drained the beer in seven seconds flat. After handing back the empty glass, he wiped the froth from his lips, spotted Bran, and, with a broad wink and gesture visible at least a mile out to sea, indicated that Bran should join him at a corner table.

Once seated, Bucko leaned in close to Bran, who responded instinctively by lowering his own head. The pungent odor of garlic frosted with hops assailed Bran's nose and nearly made him recoil. But he maintained proximity, not wishing his business to be overheard.

"Mr. MacMahon, I understand you're a cracksman."

Tracking down such information had been a long and laborious process for Bran, with his dearth of underworld connections, and he quailed for a moment at the possibility he had been misinformed. But reassurance came instantly.

"Aye, none better, boyo!"

"Well, if I were to secure you unguarded access to a certain safe, with the promise of much reward inside, provided only that you pass over to me a designated packet of papers from the haul, would you be interested in the job? I have no money to invest up front, I fear."

Father Gilead kept Bran on a tight allowance, despite his near-adult status.

Bucko rasped his stubble with one paw. "I might be willing to venture such a job. Is the treasure easy to convert to beer and wimmen, as it were? I'm not perzackly set up to trade in stocks and bonds, you know."

"Do five hundred Indian Head gold dollars seem reasonably susceptible to such a transformation?"

"Describe the safe to me, lad."

Bran did so. Bucko said, "Sounds like an old Adams-Hammond Patent Salamander model to me. Piece o' cake!"

Bran had almost been hoping to hear the job deemed impossible. Now he would have to commit himself to this assault on his father's property. Well, what choice had the old man given him? None!

Bran grasped Bucko's strong rough hand and shook.

"Now for another yard of ale to seal the deal! You, too, sonny!"

Bran managed to quaff a few inches of his powerful drink before Bucko needed a third.

A week later, the fateful night arrived, a temperate evening in May. Warner Gilead was in the nation's capital, attending the impeachment proceedings against President Johnson. Bran had provided Bucko MacMahon with a map of the house. He had given the servants a night off, left the back door ajar, and then gone off to see a play, *The Silver Lining*, at the Adelphi Theatre in Court Street.

As he strolled back to the Charles Street establishment, Bran tried to feel some relief and satisfaction at this fait accompli. Soon he would have the secrets of his birth in hand with no real cost to anyone. He could satisfy the hot urges of his soul. What he would do with the information about his blood father remained unknown. But why feel guilty at reclaiming what was rightfully his? And Warner Gilead could certainly spare whatever cash resided in the safe. . . .

As Bran neared home, he began to encounter a crowd surrounding some commotion. He hastened his pace.

Leaping flames illuminated a Dantean scene. A riot of avid gawkers surrounded several of the new steam-powered fire engines spraying the burning upper story of the Gilead manse. The efforts of the firemen seemed to be effectively containing the destruction to one corner of the house.

"What happened?" Bran yelled to a stranger.

"Some kind of explosion, I heard!"

When Warner Gilead returned to Boston from Washington, he found Bran temporarily ensconced at the Revere House Hotel on Bowdoin Square, with repairs to the manse already begun. After some stern quizzing, the old man eventually absolved Bran, and moved on from the disaster.

A week after the explosion, Bran received a delivery.

The scorched packet that bore his name, glimpsed but once, frustratingly, five years past, and a brief penciled letter sans signature:

> *That warn't no Adams-Hammond, but somethin newfangled what stubrinly resisted all me talents, so I used some guncotton, mayhaps a bit too much. But all's well what ends well, I allus say!*

Now Bran knew all. His mother's willing abandonment of Gilead, her lawful spouse. Her wild love for Hedley King. Their erotic cohabitation, resulting in Bran's own conception and Pella's perhaps preventable death. The deal struck between the two rivals. All contained in that singed folder! What a melancholy yet stirring saga. Bran had previously encountered its like only upon the stage. But now it formed his ineluctable personal heritage.

The knowledge had engendered some changes in his feelings and attitudes: shifts surprisingly smaller than he had envisioned, prerevelation, and less predictable in tenor.

He found himself pitying his father more. Poor Warner Gilead, richer than Midas, yet deprived of the woman he loved above all. Bran could see how his own presence had been both a balm and a gall, explaining why the old man alternately clasped Bran to him, then pushed him away.

Bran's idealized sentiments toward his mother had changed the least. Despite any romantic treacheries in her heart, she remained an idol to him. He clutched now at the locket containing her hair, which hung as always at his bosom.

His feelings for Hedley King, his blood sire, that enigmatic Colossus bestriding his imagination for so long, had altered strangely. He could not regard him as a cowardly scoundrel. After all, Pella had seen fit to love him, and Gilead had forced the man to remove himself from Bran's life. In an alternate existence, Bran might have grown up as the loved and pampered Roland King, heir to his actual progenitor. There was no way of determining Hedley King's real feelings and responsibilities in the matter without meeting him.

But what most intrigued the son now was a heretofore unknown aspect of King's character: his apparent flair for the natural sciences, and his inventorly skills. What was this "Morphic Resonator" for which King had been willing to bargain away his son? It must be a treasure beyond price.

For any number of reasons, Bran simply *had* to meet his natural father! He was prepared to strike out on his own, against Gilead's wishes. But where? The otherwise chatty documents contained no information regarding Hedley King's current location, and not even a clue to his destination eighteen years ago, when he had been ejected from Bran's life.

For several days Bran contemplated the matter. And then, suddenly recalling that old image of his mother surrounded by workmen, he went to see Stan Lambeth, one of the few survivors of that era.

Warner Gilead's fortune, now diversified across many ventures (including heavy investments in several important national politicians), had been founded upon his machine tools enterprise, still the thriving core of his holdings. In fact, the recently ended War Between the States had bolstered the enterprise's income, owing to heavy demand for armaments and the milling machines and lathes involved in their production.

The sprawling, noisy factory buildings of Gilead Toolmakers occupied a plot of land in Brighton, a town adjacent to Boston proper and given over to various industries. Once a part of Cambridge, Brighton had seceded in 1807 and become the abbatoir of New England, rife with slaughterhouses and stockyards. Authorities had recently mooted a scheme seeking to upgrade the ambiance of the place by naming a small residential district after famed local artist Washington Allston, dead some years before Bran's birth. But for now, the town's pestilential and noxious nature kept property taxes low, which suited the economical Warner Gilead.

At the works, Bran tracked down Stan Lambeth on his own, careful not to alert any supervisors to his presence, for fear news of his visit, however innocuous, should get back to his father. Bidden to speak privately, Lambeth willingly adjourned to a shed containing stocks of angle iron.

Rail-thin and taciturn, Lambeth wore his advanced age of forty-five years well, his slim physique toned from his labors. All the staff at the works liked Bran, and Lambeth greeted the lad now with a certain parsimonious Yankee warmth. But when Bran broached the reason for his visit, Lambeth grew less welcoming.

"Young sir, you'll excuse my frankness, but I have to ask if you mean to persecute poor Hedley King further, on your father's behalf?"

"By no means!" Bran explained himself, and Lambeth resumed his cordiality.

"Well, then, know ye this. Hedley and I have remained in contact all these years, exchanging regular letters. We were always enamored of each other's skills and insights into natural science, though I confess he long ago transcended my meager talents. His latest requests for my thoughts on his researches have been met with utter incomprehension on my part, I am humbled to report. In any case, I can tell you that he resides in the vicinity of Windsor, Vermont, at an estate called Mount Golden. He supports himself by working at the Robbins and Lawrence Company, a venture akin to your father's setup here."

Bran clapped the older man spontaneously on the shoulder. "This is splendid! I can go see him immediately, and try to repair all the injustices of the past two decades."

"And your father will give his consent?"

Bran grew crestfallen. That eventuality seemed dicey. He would either have to make a complete break with his father or lie.

As fate would have it, lying proved the much easier route, a fib practically falling into Bran's lap.

The month was late June, and Bran had matriculated in May from the newly established yet prestigious Thomas Parkman Cushing Academy, a boarding school some forty miles outside the city. His best friend at the school had been the affable giant Baldrick Slowey, whose family lived in Brattleboro, Vermont, and had a share in the Estey Organ Works in that burg. One day soon after his interview with Lambeth, a letter arrived from Baldrick, inviting Bran to spend part of the summer in Vermont. He promptly wrote back to Baldrick, politely declining. But the original invitation he showed to his father at the dinner table.

Warner Gilead pondered the letter with some gravity. "You really should be studying all summer, to get a leg up at Harvard in the fall. But I suppose all work and no play makes Bran a dull boy. You may go, but only for three weeks or less."

"Thank you, Father," said Bran, trying to damp down his guilt.

Only when, days later, he had at last transferred to the carriages of the Central Vermont Railway Company did Bran truly feel that his plan stood some chance of success. Up till then, he had expected a parental hand to clamp down at any second and drag him home.

Payment to the affable conductor easily extended his prearranged passage north from Brattleboro to Windsor.

The station at Windsor was situated hard by the burly yet tamed Connecticut River. The Main Street establishment of Robbins and Lawrence, he learned, was but a short walk distant.

As he walked through the neat, leafy little town at the base of mighty Mount Ascutney, his nerves felt afire and his stomach aboil. What would be his first words to Hedley King? He had rehearsed many, but none seemed just right.

Bran hesitated at the door of the L&R Armory, then went in. He applied to the office manager, and learned that Hedley King was not on the premises.

"King works but irregularly," said the mustachioed Pecksniff, whose name Bran had promptly forgotten in his nervousness. "His own endeavors keep him busy, and he comes in for a stint of labor only when he runs short of funds. Begrudges every second of his employment, too. If he weren't so damnably talented, the bosses wouldn't put up with his insolence and independence, you can mark my words."

Bran just nodded noncommittally, and obtained directions to Mount Golden, the King estate. He found the hire of a horse and carriage, and was soon on his way.

The precincts west of Windsor grew increasingly sylvan and wild, like something out of one of Thomas Cole's more apocalyptic paintings. Hoary giants, the densely arrayed trees radiated an immemorial sense of brooding. A swampy patch seemed the gateway to some stygian netherworld. Strange bird cries attendant upon the close of day rang out like a chorus of lost souls.

The sun was going down, and the last house had reared its shabby form some miles back, when Bran's driver, a young lad of Apollonian thews who smelled not unpleasantly of horses, announced, "There 'tis."

Bran saw no welcoming manse, only a rutted, ill-kempt drive

close-hemmed by overgrown yews. He stepped down, and the lad asked, "Shall I wait, sir?"

Bran hesitated, then said with more boldness than confidence, "No, I'm expected. You may return to town."

Bran retrieved his portmanteau, the lad jockeyed the horse around, and in a minute Bran stood alone in the dusk.

He moved cautiously down the drive, as if half expecting to encounter some ogre around the bend.

A large, decaying house—its clapboards mossy, featuring an ill-composed assortment of turrets and gables, and flanked by several skewed outbuildings—loomed out of the darkling air. Candlelight shone from one window.

Bran climbed to the broad granite step at the front door and knocked. No immediate response met his signal. But then the door was flung inward precipitously, and Bran stood waist-to-face with a scowling, disheveled malformed dwarf who, unprompted, shouted in a foreign accent, "And you can go straight to hell!"

Hedley King, Bran's natural father, poured another glass of dark red wine for himself. Bran declined a refill, the two cups he had already quaffed leaving him muzzy-headed. How strange to be sitting here with this intimately connected stranger in a fusty candlelit parlor, full of ancient bric-a-brac, dispassionately discussing their separate lives as if they had met by chance on a train. Although Hedley King was not the ideal father Bran might have chosen for himself, Bran had quickly discerned that the man possessed a certain intensity of purpose and engaging sharpness of intellect that offset his less delicate behaviors.

Bran had already disburdened himself of the broad outlines of his youthful career, right down to his arrival on the step of Mount Golden (so christened by its prior owner, an eccentric named Trafton Shroud who believed without a shred of evidence in the existence of rich veins of ore upon his property). Hedley King seemed pleased that Bran had been motivated to search him out, although of course whenever mention of Warner Gilead intervened in the boy's narrative, the older man grew resentful and irate, still plainly nursing his old grudges against the plutocrat.

And now, having plumbed Bran's depths and found him a receptive and sympathetic auditor, King, slightly tipsy and prone to rubbing a scarred hand across the hard-traveled landscape of his face, as if to erase or reassemble its topography, rambled on about his own past.

"When that guardian of yours sent me packing, right after your birth, it was with the understanding that I'd not find any future employment at my chosen trade within the sphere of his considerable mercantile influence. So I was forced to move about the country, earning my keep as best I could. All I had with me as my treasure and hope were my patents on the Morphic Resonator, which existed only as a collection of scattered pieces, incomplete at that. The vril reservoirs were the bulkiest, but I couldn't abandon them—they had been crafted at great expense, and with the essential help of one of your guardian's associates. Lord, what a damnable inconvenience they were! But I held on to them, knowing that someday I'd have a chance to fill them, thus taking the first step to perfecting my device."

"But this Morphic Resonator—what is it exactly?"

"Ah, you'll see soon enough, first thing in the morning." King downed another gulletful of wine. "Now, where was I? Oh, yes. Some years ago I ended up in Europe, in the Carpathian Mountains, to be precise, nor far from castle Gortz and hot on the track of the vril. And that's where I met Jellyneck."

Jellyneck, Bran now knew, was the foul-tempered dwarf who had greeted him at the door, under the impression that Bran was a bill collector sent from one of the unpaid merchants in Windsor. Pavel Jelinek was the small man's real name, but upon being introduced Bran had heard "jellyneck" and could now not think of him otherwise. As to the nature of vril, Bran had formed some conception of it as an energy-dispensing substance akin to pitchblende. And in fact, the Carpathian Mountains were a known source of that familiar element, so it made sense they would host the mysterious vril, too.

King continued: "Jellyneck was a miner, and was instrumental in leading me to the subterranean veins of vril, where I was able to charge my essential reservoirs. Enlisting in my cause, Jellyneck returned with me to America. We settled down here, knowing I could count on the armory for work. Quickly, I brought the completed Morphic Resonator to its first success. But it's a limited success, I fear. And lack of funds stops me from carrying my experiments further, confound it!"

Bran finally surrendered to an immense uncontrollable yawn. Taking the cue, King said, "I can see you're weary. Let's get our rest, and the morning will disclose miracles to you!"

King summoned his dwarf comrade. Was the man servant, partner, or both? Or something even less describable?

"Jellyneck, take Ro—I mean, Bran—up to the guest bedroom. This has been a monumental day for us all. Good night—son."

With that charged word ringing in his ears, Bran climbed to the upper story of Mount Golden, where he found a bedchamber rich with dust dragons and cobwebs, featuring a spavined mattress and a moth-eaten coverlet just sufficient for the northern June clime. Doffing his travel-grimed clothes for a cotton robe from his carryall, Bran found himself soon soundly asleep, despite all the flighty speculations and retrodden memories buzzing in his head.

He awoke refreshed, to the smell of frying bacon, onions, and potatoes and boiling coffee, most agreeable scents. Dressed and downstairs, he found Jellyneck at the stove, his crabbed motions belying an efficient handling of skillet and tools. The dwarf wordlessly served Bran a simple yet hearty breakfast, then left the room.

His hair a haystack, Hedley King entered the kitchen with a dyspeptic, neuralgic mien, nodding grumpily in Bran's general direction. He poured himself some coffee, lashed it with copious cream and sugar, and downed it faster than was commensurate with the beverage's heat. But the draught did him good, and he perked up considerably.

"Finish up, and we'll go see the Resonator."

Eager to penetrate to the heart of this enigmatic engine that had driven King's every action for twenty years, Bran complied.

King called for Jellyneck to accompany them, and the trio went out to a time-distressed, leaning barn. Using a big key, King undid the padlock on the barn's door and they entered. Once kindled, a kerosene lamp revealed the usual agrarian furniture of such a place—save for a unique construction of brass and iron and crystal.

Occupying about as much space as a large restaurant pie case, the device resembled the mating of three or four elaborate Russian samovars, all pressurized flasks, gauges, and conical pendulum governors, their spinning fly-balls now quiescent. Electrical wires ran from the Resonator to a set of Daniell-Dancer storage cells, and thence to a hand-cranked dynamo of the latest Wheatstone design. Bran could not fathom the machine's purpose.

King walked over to the device and laid a proud hand on a bulbous part of it. "Here's one of the vril canisters, obtained with Jellyneck's invaluable help."

"But what does it all do?"

King seemed happy to lecture. "Before I can answer that question, you must first know a truth not generally apprehended by the academy. All life—all organic matter—is subject to the influence of unseen and intangible shaping forces called morphic fields. I assume that you are aware through your expensively obtained education of the magnetic fields discovered by Faraday and others. Well, these morphic fields are similar, but act upon living tissues, influencing their properties. Every living organism has its unique signature field, a composite of all its lesser fields. My Resonator is able to superimpose one field upon another."

"But to what effect?"

Hedley King grinned in a manner not entirely wholesome. "I believe a trial run would be the best illustration. Jellyneck, a drop of your blood, if you please."

The dwarf pricked his finger and, apparently well familiar with the ritual, went to the Resonator, opened one drawer out of a rank of such niches, and squeezed out a crimson drop into the tin-lined receptacle, thereafter sliding the little drawer firmly shut. King did likewise in a parallel portion of the machine.

"My blood," King explained, "resides in the dominant, or sending, portion of the device. Jellyneck's sample, bearing its organic signature, occupies the receiving portion. The vril mediates and modulates between them, facilitating a one-way flow of instructions. Now, Jellyneck, if you would charge the storage cells—"

The dwarf began to crank the dynamo, working up a considerable sweat. When a sufficient quantity of electricity had been obtained, King closed a connection.

The fly-ball governors of the Resonator began to spin, crystals glowed, and a subliminal hum emanated from the device. Bran found himself entranced by the humming and the motion till they filled his senses. He might have been some Oriental monk fascinated by a spinning prayer wheel. When he finally looked away to speak to King, his breath was halted by an impossible sight.

Two identical Hedley Kings stood in the barn. But one wore the remnant tattered clothes of Jellyneck the dwarf.

"You—you have imposed your physiognomy on Jellyneck!"

"Correct. My morphic field has overlaid and subsumed his."

Disbelieving his eyes, Bran was forced to run his hands over the altered dwarf, who submitted with a certain regal dignity. He found Jellyneck's new body conformable in every respect to the template of King's.

"This—this is not some twin brother of yours, brought out from hiding to fool me, is it?"

"Jellyneck, what were your first words to my son?"

Jellyneck spoke with King's voice. "'And you can go straight to hell!'"

"But this is a miracle! The implications are staggering!"

"Yes, they would be, if my machine were perfected. But as matters stand, it's only fit for some stage conjuror to use to increase his prestige."

"What are the difficulties?"

"First, the effect is temporary, lasting only so long as a current is supplied to the machine. Jellyneck's sharing of my clean-limbed wholeness will be frustratingly brief, unless he wishes to live his life cranking a dynamo.

"Second, I can only impose patterns at a whole-body level. I long to be able to repair a damaged leg or arm, say, without altering the entire individual.

"And third, so far I have access only to the morphic instructions determining the brute corporal level. What I really desire is to discover the resonance of the soul! I truly believe that the patterns of our consciousness is eternally contained within the morphic fields as well."

Bran was stupefied. "And then?"

"Then death would be no more! I would be able to resurrect anyone in both spirit and form, assuming I had some organic talisman of the deceased, to use as my seed."

"How do you mean?"

Hedley King spoke with blunt frankness, his eyes agleam with fanatical ambition. "I would impose the soul and shape of the worthy deceased upon some living nonentity, a condemned criminal, say. Would that not be a fair punishment for some murderer, to host his victim's new existence?"

Bran shivered, and instinctively clutched at the locket he wore that contained strands of his mother's hair. The gesture did not go unnoticed by a gimlet-eyed Hedley King.

"And all that holds me back is a paltry sum of money, and access to a cadre of savants who could aid me. But, Bran—Roland, my son—with your help, I could surmount all these barriers. Together, we could create a paradise on earth!"

Bran's head swam. To embark upon this grand venture with his real father! How much better than some stale interim at college, swotting up more useless information, only to be forced to pick up the dry ledgers of the Warner Gilead enterprises.

"My father will never assist you, no matter how worthy your plans."

"Ah, but it is not your father I seek to enlist, just his connections! Let me explain. . . ."

The lobby of the Parker House Hotel on School Street in Boston, an ornate venue of honey-blond wood paneling, crystal chandeliers, and thick floral carpets, teemed with the bon ton tonight. A large percentage of elite Boston society was here on this glorious late-July eve to welcome the man who would assuredly be the next president of the United States: General Ulysses S. Grant. For despite a strong showing by Democratic candidate Horatio Seymour, those in the know predicted an easy win for Grant in the all-important electoral college.

Warner Gilead was one of the savvy sponsors of this late-campaign fund-raising venture for Grant, and accordingly had intimate access to the sturdy old warhorse. As did his son, Bran.

Which was the entire pivot upon which Hedley King's schemes revolved.

Dressed in his best formal clothes, holding an untouched glass of sparkling wine in one hand, Bran looked nervously around the crowded space, with its glittering women and dapper men, reminiscent of some Newport cotillion. He quaked inside to think of what he was daring to attempt, among this influential crowd.

King had promised to stay upstairs in his rented room, ensconced with the Morphic Resonator, which had been smuggled into the hotel in a large steamer trunk. He professed to be content to have his mundane needs attended to by the faithful Jellyneck. But Bran would not put it past the man to show his face anyhow. Over the past couple of weeks, Bran had come, disturbingly, to detect in his birth father more than a trace of "mégalomanie," as the French had it.

After the first demonstration of the Morphic Resonator at Mount Golden, King and Bran had begun to conspire in earnest. Living with his birth father for the subsequent week—"the Kings of Mount Golden," Hedley had gaily dubbed them—Bran became enthralled with the inventor to a degree he had not anticipated. The man boasted a magnetic personality. And then, too, King had shared his memories of Bran's mother, Pella, further heightening the bonds between father and son. Bran had been so moved by King's devotion to the dead woman as to confess to wearing a snippet of Pella's hair about his own neck.

When all their plans were fully formed and vetted, Bran had returned home alone to Boston, leaving King and company to follow.

Greeted warmly by Warner Gilead at their Charles Street manse, Bran had facilely unloaded an invented fable about his time in Brattleboro with the Slowey family, feeling immense chagrin and guilt all the while. He sought to salve his conscience by telling himself that his actions, although duplicitous, would have no adverse effect on Gilead, but only a positive effect for King, and the world in general.

And now was nearly the time to carry the scheme out!

A member of the Parker House staff caught everyone's attention by hammering a small gong, thus summoning the partygoers to the collation laid out in the grand ballroom, a lush spread prominently featuring the famous Parker House rolls and signature Boston cream pie.

In the bright, large, high-ceilinged, pillared room, the guest of honor could be observed at last: big as life, luxuriantly bearded, straining the buttons of his waistcoat, alternately smiling and puffing on a cigar. General Grant held court as informally but as commandingly as if still on the battlefield.

Warner Gilead corralled Bran. "Come, son, I want you to meet the general."

On his way across the room, Bran rotated the ring he wore, so that the sharp, jagged piece deliberately affixed to the band would project downward underneath his finger.

Grant extended his hand. "So, Warner, this is the scion of House Gilead, hey? A fine young buck!"

Bran clasped the General's hand, then jerked his palm across Grant's flesh, as if suffering a reflexive action from an excess of nerves.

"I say, what a sting!"

Bran had a handkerchief in his hand. "Oh, General, I'm so sorry!" He dabbed up blood from the shallow gash, then hastily repocketed the stained cloth.

"No harm done, lad! 'Tis of no account compared to a Minié ball in the gut!"

Bran made his excuses then and left, while Warner was busy introducing someone else.

Feeling queasy, Bran hastened upstairs to Hedley King's room.

To his surprise, King had a companion other than Jellyneck: an overblown doxy, some woman of low virtue with exposed décolletage. But King introduced her to Bran with insouciance.

"Roland, this is Trixibelle. She's deigned to keep me company tonight."

"How's it hanging, sweetie?"

"But, but—"

"No, don't trouble yourself to comprehend. It's all part of the plan. Now, you have the sample?"

Bran handed over the bloody cloth. King trimmed out two small squares of crimson fabric and placed them in the Resonator.

"Jellyneck's blood already lies in one dominant drawer matched now with Grant's submissive drawer. My blood is paired submissively with Grant's second, dominant sample. Now we just need to wait for the signal that our quarry is alone."

In less than twenty minutes came a knock from a Parker House servant, liberally bribed, betokening that he had observed General Grant hieing himself off to a secluded water closet.

King instantly set the Morphic Resonator a-humming!

In less than an eyeblink, Hedley King assumed the mortal form of General Ulyssses S. Grant while, unseen several stories below them, Bran knew, Grant had morphed to the semblance of Jellyneck.

"Ha!" exclaimed King in Grant's very tones. "Let the general try to convince everyone of his identity now!"

Bran regarded his birth father with some trepidation. "Remember now, sir, you promised—"

"Promises," said King, "mean nothing to a politician! Jellyneck, secure him!"

Bran was pinioned helplessly in a trice by the abnormally strong dwarf. King, wearing Grant's phiz, swiftly drew blood from the lad with a pin.

Then he pulled the locket from around Bran's neck, painfully snapping the chain!

King moved to the Morphic Resonator and opened three new pairs of drawers while the machine still whirred its infernal tune. He shouted like some cheap prestidigitator:

"Bran to Jellyneck! Jellyneck to Bran! And *Trixibelle* to *Pella*!"

Filial blood and maternal hair properly emplaced, drawers shut, and the evil deed was done!

Again the dwarf had split the seams of his clothes, assuming Bran's bulkier nature. Regarding himself in a mirror, feeling his own fine garments hanging loosely on his shrunken frame, Bran knew himself to be the spitting image of the dwarf.

But worst of all, the common whore Trixibelle now wore the semblance of Bran's dead mother!

"*Oooee, coo!*" she trilled. "Ain't I the queen of Sheba, now!"

King addressed the transfigured Jellyneck. "Mr. Bran Gilead, please eject this hideous troll from my rooms!"

Jellyneck stripped Bran's clothes from him for his own use, leaving the lad in his floppy drawers and camise. Then Jellyneck-as-Bran picked up Bran-as-Jellyneck and hurled him out in the corridor, where he lay in a brokenhearted funk.

The next day, several papers in the city—the *Boston Daily Advertiser, Boston Evening Traveler, Boston Herald,* and *Boston Journal,* among others—would report upon a most curious incident attendant upon General Grant's reception.

TWIN DWARVES DISTURB GRANT'S FETE

MISSHAPEN BRAWLING HOOLIGANS
EJECTED FROM PARKER HOUSE

INTENTIONS OR ORIGIN OF GNOMISH INTRUDERS UNKNOWN

CONSTABLES SEEK MISSING RUMPELSTILTSKINS

These bulletins would be played lightly and for laughs, taken up in the same spirit by the newspapers' eager readers, who could only find this three-days-wonder to be a most amusing diversion from more serious news.

Of course, that was how the affair looked from the outside, the morning after. But while the contretemps was still in progress, and when you were one of the reviled and suspect dwarves, matters bulked considerably grimmer.

After a minute or three, a bruised and shoeless Bran roused himself from his crumpled condition on the corridor floor. He knew better than to beat and rave upon the door to King's room. The man's treachery was complete and seamless, and without an iota of mercy. No, Bran's only hope was to convince someone else of the true nature of affairs. Because if he did not, soon Hedley King would be inserting himself inextricably into General Grant's entourage, assuming the future president's identity entirely.

Bran found the service stairway and descended to the kitchen. He met no one on the stairs or among the pots and pans and stoves, and the reason why soon became plain. All attention was focused on the outrageous scene in the ballroom.

A dwarf wearing the loose-fitting garb of General Grant was raving at the center of an astonished and horrified crowd.

"But I tell you, I am Ulysses S. Grant! Damn your eyes, I am!"

Someone shouted in response, "It's a Democratic prank!" Quickly a chorus of agreement sounded, accompanied by guffaws and oaths. Someone threw a Parker House roll at the dwarf.

And then General Grant himself appeared, or rather, the impostor Hedley King.

"Restrain yourselves, folks! There's no need to descend to the level of my jejune opponents!"

That saucy affront was too much for Bran, and from the edge of the crowd he yelled out, "It's true! That little man is General Grant, but bewitched!"

Now all eyes turned to Bran.

"There's another one!" "Grab him!" "Make him confess!"

Bran felt a cold spike of fear go through him, as women shrieked and fainted. But the reaction of the real General Grant was even more disconcerting. He clutched his head and shouted, "A second new me! I'm going mad!"

Then the ensorcelled General Grant ran from the room, in a hailstorm of rolls and catcalls. Subjected to identical treatment, Bran had no recourse but to do the same.

Outside on nighted School Street, Bran looked for his doppelganger, hoping to team up with the general. Bran could explain what had happened, and together they could devise and enact some scheme to right matters.

But the general, possessed by some temporary insanity, babbling nonsense, had continued to flee willy-nilly, and was nowhere to be seen.

Bran ducked down an alley alongside the hotel. He knotted his shirt and trews at their hems so they would not fall off. Despite the summer temperatures, his bare feet and state of undress rendered him chilled. But he could not seek shelter. He had to appeal to his father, his last hope.

Monitoring the front door of the hotel for hours, Bran shivered, coughed, and waited. Finally Warner Gilead emerged.

Bran dashed over to the millionaire, calling out, "Father, Father, it is I, your son, Bran! Take me with you to our Charles Street home!"

Warner Gilead's face assumed a look of absolute confounded horror. He held up a forbidding hand and averted his face. "Get back, get back. I have no connection with you!" The old man scrabbled out a cloth change purse and threw it at Bran's bare feet. "Here, take this money and be gone!"

Bran began to weep. "But, Father, don't you recognize me?"

At that moment, Jellyneck showed up. "Father, our carriage is here. What's the matter?"

"This vile beggar!"

Jellyneck grinned cruelly, employing Bran's own features. "Shall I trounce him, Father?"

"No, no, just get us away from here!"

With filial devotion, Jellyneck escorted Warner Gilead away, turning his head once to leer at Bran and stick out his tongue.

Wearily, Bran bent to retrieve the change purse. Here was his patrimony from Warner Gilead. His legacy from Hedley King he wore in his flesh.

The finest neighborhoods in the Athens of America, those precincts with their upstanding citizens that had congenially accommodated Bran all his life, proved generally inhospitable to a dirty, partially clothed, poverty-stricken, ranting dwarf. Likewise, the police took offense at his very existence. When they saw Bran, they began to shake their rattles to summon help, or charge at him with their six-foot-tall blue-and-white staves. They disseminated news of his travels via the police telegraph stations. Only Bran's fleetness of foot helped him stay free. He felt oddly grateful to the original Jellyneck for keeping his physique well toned.

Eventually, Bran ended up at the only place where his kind fit: Fort Hill, that bisected, steeply terraced den of turpitude and iniquity. He found cheap accommodations at a place called Mother Juniper's Caravansary, where the insect lodgers far outnumbered the human ones. Obtaining some tawdry used clothes and holey shoes diminished his funds further.

And so for three days Bran nursed in quiet his injured pride and shattered trust, eating the cheapest foods without appetite and ruminating on how he could regain his own estate and restore General Grant to his.

Shutting off the Morphic Resonator and destroying it seemed the only adequate solution. Then all the altered people would instantly revert to their congenital forms. Even if Hedley King were ever able to rebuild the device and restock it with vril, he would surely be stymied from gaining the necessary biological samples he needed to wreak havoc, thanks to an awareness of his perfidy.

But how to accomplish this! Bran did not even know for sure that the Resonator remained at the Parker House. Maybe King had secreted it in some safer location. Could he enlist the aid of a friend such as Baldrick Slowey, or one of his father's employees, like Stan Lambeth? Unlikely. They would not believe such a fantastical story for one minute, especially issuing from the mouth of a strange dwarf.

On the evening of third day of his fruitless cogitations, his money almost extinct, Bran lost all hope. He resolved to drown his cares with liquor, and then perhaps throw himself into the bay. He began drinking at a place called Jimmy Tingle's, and then charted a staggering course around Fort Hill's gin mills.

Long after midnight, he found himself in a seedy drinking place that seemed half-familiar to his fuzzed brain. But what did it matter? What did anything matter? He had been such a fool! Damn Hedley King! But damn Bran Gilead, too!

Only when a brawny fellow plopped down onto the low stool at the table beside him did Bran realize he must have been talking aloud.

"Bran Gilead, you say. I knew him. Queer cuss. Hired me to burgle his own home."

Bran tried to focus his blurred vision and concentrate.

"Bucko? Bucko MacMahon!"

"Aye, that's my name. Don't wear it out! Do I know you, runt?"

"I'm Bran Gilead!"

Bucko unleashed gales of laughter. When he had regained control of himself, he said, "You've come down in the world a notch or two, I see, since our last encounter. Well, Master Gilead, it's been nice chatting with you, but I have to go now." Bucko got to his feet.

Inspired by desperation, Bran recited Bucko's well-remembered apologetic note to him: "That warn't no Adams-Hammond, but somethin newfangled what stubrinly resisted all me talents, so I used some guncotton, mayhaps a bit too much. But all's well what ends well, I allus say!"

Bucko sat back down. "How'd you come across that there missive?"

His heart bursting with some small renewed hope, his drunkeness burned away by eager anxiety, Bran laid out all that had happened to him. Then he sat back, feeling like a man who had staked his entire fortune on the single roll of a die.

Bucko peered intensely at Bran, pulling at his stubbled chin for a while, before he finally spoke.

"Well, sir, I once knew a fellow from up the North Shore a ways who only came into his unnatural fishy heritage when he reached his majority, and what a difference that endowment made in *his* looks! So I'm more'n half-inclined to accept what you say as being halfway possible."

Bran had never been so grateful to anyone in his life. Out of all his friends and relatives and acquaintances, only this common thief had given him credit for telling the truth.

"You'll help me, then?"

"Aye, if there's a suitable reward."

"You'll get more gold than you can carry, Bucko—if we succeed! Now, here's what we must do. First, find the Resonator, and then destroy it!"

"Do you think if we follow your fetch, he'll lead us there?"

"Yes, that's perfect! King, as General Grant, can't be toting the ponderous thingummy around the country with him. It must still be here, with my impostor."

"Just leave it to me, laddie. There's not a valuable item in Boston what don't come under the lamps of me or my boys. Now, I don't suppose you saved any funds for a yard of beer or three, did you? The night's still young!"

Despite Bucko's boast and his energetic ferreting, the Resonator proved distressingly hard to find. Days went by without a clue.

Only when Bran applied his deductive mind to the dilemma did inspiration strike. The necessity to keep the Morphic Resonator supplied with a continuous diet of electricity was the key to its location. Jellyneck-as-Bran could hardly spend all his time cranking the dynamo to charge the cells. But where could a steady, reliable source of current be found?

Right at the Gilead Toolmakers facility in Brighton, where a forward-looking manager named Norman Krim had been experimenting with the new technology's applications to machine tools.

Bucko reported back after Bran's hunch. "Your fetch goes to a locked room at the Brighton works at least once a day, to check on something mighty important. Your pa thinks he's taking an interest in the family business."

"That's it! Round up some helpers and we'll go in there tonight."

Bran winced when the lone watchman at the factory succumbed to a cosh upside the head. But that final obstacle to their goal could not be otherwise surmounted. Putting the guilt at the back of his mind for later grief, Bran hurried with Bucko and his two assistants to the door of the Resonator's hiding place. Using a crowbar, Bucko snapped the hasp, and they were in—

—to confront by lantern light a grinning General Grant and Jellyneck-as-Bran, both men holding pistols trained upon the door, guarding the humming Resonator where it sat on a worktable.

The disloyal hired toughs turned and ran. The general let them go, confident of their silence regarding the illegal break-in. Bucko raised his crowbar menacingly, but thought better of it. Bran remained frozen in shock.

Hedley King said, "Your friend's inquiries were very crude, Roland. Mr. Lincoln's new Secret Service men, tasked to guard me as a candidate, were told to be alert for such feints, reporting all such to me, and they did not question why. And so I was able to learn of your searches and to return here to protect my machine—and to chat with you.

"I realize now that my plans will never be safe from your interference, until you are dead—or until you join me wholeheartedly. I regret imposing this grotesque mask upon you at the outset, but my reading of your nature convinced me you would not go along with my schemes. I don't want to kill you, Roland. You're my natural-born son, after all. Just tell me you'll embrace my cause, and you'll soon be atop the world again, where we Kings rightfully belong."

Bran found his voice. "Your cause! Your cause is pure selfishness!"

"No, Bran, it's not. It's the betterment of all mankind. Allow me to show you. Pella, step forth please."

From out of the shadows emerged Bran's mother, the living, radiant, queenly image stepping forth from his cherished ambrotype. Bran's heart caught in his throat.

King said, "You see, son, already in this short time, with the aid of Grant's pull, I've found a way to restore the soul. Pella, tell him."

The dulcet, refined voice of Bran's mother said, "It is true, son. I am Pella Brannock Gilead that was."

Bran wanted desperately to believe. To have his mother restored to life—restored to *his* life, an offset to his superfluity of fathers. To feel free for the first time of the guilt of having caused her premature death by his very coming into being. Wasn't that what he had been unconsciously seeking when he had so enthusiastically endorsed Hedley King's researches and machinations?

"Mother—I want to believe! Prove to me it's true! Please tell me more."

To Bran's acute senses, all the other interlocutors in the room seemed distant and suspended, as if they, too, hung on the words of the revenant woman. And if her first speech had been bland and calm, now her voice suddenly assumed a new dynamic emotional heft.

"Oh, Bran, I've so wanted this day to happen, but I never dared dream within the dream that is the afterlife that it ever could! To see you all mature, so strong and brave and wise, satisfying all my fervent but nebulous hopes as I felt you being born amidst the pain. I feel blessed, and hopeful that this rare, impossible moment can be prolonged."

Bran's heart raced. "Mother, I, too! I can even bear this misshapen body if it means you will get a renewed lease on life!"

Pella's eyes glowed with maternal adoration. "Maybe we can have it all, Bran, all that we've dreamed of. But my tenancy of this borrowed mortal clay feels so insecure at times, as if I were contending with another for possession, that I—"

Pella held the back of one hand to her forehead and swayed alarmingly.

"Mother! What's wrong?"

Pella straightened and grinned in a ludicrously inappropriate manner. "Nothing's wrong, son. Just a slight megrims. I swear by Saint Valentine, it's so. Now, if you'll only listen to Mr. King, your father, and do as he—You shitty *bastard*!"

This cause of this foul imprecation interrupting Pella's instructive speech was the impact of Bucko's heaved crowbar upon her shin. A welter of blue swearwords followed. Surely the gentle Pella had never been prone to such outbursts.

Bucko turned to Bran. "You told me about Trixibelle, and I knew that whore always swore by Saint Valentine. That ain't your ma, Bran. Not right this minute, anyhow. And no matter how much you want her to be, you could never be sure twixt one moment and the next who you was talking to."

Doubt and dark disappointment assailed Bran. To lose his mother almost in the same breath he had gained her! He wavered between endorsement and dismissal of Bucko's warning. But then all uncertainty was instantly removed, along with Bran's hopes, leaving him feeling as if his heart had been wrenched from his chest.

With the stolen countenance of Bran's mother suffused with wrath, Trixibelle said, "Oh, I hate your stinking guts, Bucko Mac-Mahon! And as for you, junior—maybe I didn't bring you into this world, but I'll sure enough take you out of it!"

She grabbed for General Grant's gun and she and King wrestled for control of the weapon.

Bucko launched himself at a distracted Jellyneck.

Despairing yet determined, all selfish ambitions for his personal happiness fled, Bran hurled himself at the Resonator on its elevated stand, his squat form a living cannonball.

Over and backward the humming device toppled, to smash on the stone floor.

A flood of celestial radiance flared as the vril escaped through a crack in its vessel and instantly evanesced.

Bran got awkwardly to his feet. Inhabiting his own body again felt odd and uncomfortable.

Bucko had subdued the dwarf by throttling him.

Bran regarded Trixibelle, the woman who had been transfigured temporarily into Pella, and whose sinful soul had ejected Pella's spirit. The coarse doxy seemed confused by her reversion, no longer foulmouthed. Her eyes met Bran's. And then the oddest, saddest, most unexpected thing happened, powered perhaps by the slightest traces of vril remaining in the atmosphere.

Trixibelle whispered in Pella's genuine tones: "Son, it had to be this way. Live well, with my love—"

Bran mastered the hot tears that followed this last blessing, and confronted his natural father.

Here was the source of so much grief and pain, right from the minute the man had lured Pella away from Warner Gilead! Bran's brief equanimity evaporated.

Hedley King had regained control of his pistol from Trixibelle. Vibrating to Bran's new rancor, King raised the gun in Bran's direction.

"You've ruined the labors of a lifetime!"

"And you've ruined several lifetimes!"

Still menacing Bran, King began backing away toward the exit. "I can rebuild my engine. There's more vril to be had as well! I'll be ruler of the world one day! And I'll be sure to leave your mother's soul to rot in hell!"

Enraged, Bran hurled himself at Hedley King.

The gun boomed, and Bran felt his pate creased. Then he collided with King and brought him down.

The older man's skull struck the iron footing upon which the Resonator had rested, issuing a sickening, melon-bashing sound.

Once standing, Bran regarded his natural father, all broken and unconscious. The man's ragged breathing suddenly clattered to a halt, like a lame horse failing.

Liquid trickled down one of Bran's cheeks. He raised a hand to feel, and found only blood from his wound.

Bucko came to Bran's side. To Bran's surprise, Jellyneck went to King and began to weep. Trixiebelle had vanished.

"Let's go, boyo," said Bucko. "It's all over now."

"One minute." Bran rummaged among the wreckage, until he found the lock of Pella's hair.

"Okay, I'm ready."

Bran turned then and walked away from the worst of his past.

You Will Attend Until Beauty Awakens

by Jay Lake

**(BASED ON "SLEEPING BEAUTY"
BY CHARLES PERRAULT)**

DRAMATIS PERSONAE I

The Thirteenth Child

I have twelve brothers and sisters, all older than me. Each was born under a different new moon, a year and a month apart, in what must have been a heroic feat of planning on our parents' part. And when I say born, I am using that word the old-fashioned way, dropping covered in blood and snot from betwixt our mother's legs.

See what I mean about the planning? If you're going about reproducing the sensible way, with glass dishes and bottled lightning in a nice, safe laboratory, then you can have children any time you want. In any quantity you want. A dozen kids? Install a bigger autoclave, make sure there's enough fuses in the junction box, and you're off to the races.

Not Mom and Dad. No, no. When you're the Queen of Summer and the Winter King, you have to be *traditionalists*. You cut your clockwork gears by hand—or at least have lackeys to do that—and fire your boilers with charcoal burned from your own estates' coppices by hereditary tribes of hunchbacked charcoal burners with overdeveloped forelocks and a pious sense of duty. If it were possible for steam to come with a pedigree, ours would have.

So they created their children the old-fashioned way, and Mother suffered through nine waxings and wanings of the moon as women always had since Lilith carved her initials in the bricks of the wall around the First Garden, and everyone was made miserable thereby. My older sisters assure me that being the last child meant that I missed out on all the fun of thirteen continuous years of pregnancy, a child born every fourteen moons until I, the final offspring, came into the world on a night when the new moon happened to coincide with the winter solstice.

As you might well imagine, being the thirteenth child of two of the most magical people in the world, I was hardly destined for a life of needlework and horsewomanship. My oldest siblings, aged twelve and eleven at the time of my birth, had already evinced talents as fae as fae could be, and so people referred to them as "the good fairies." I understand there were decent odds being laid down in the servants' wing on whether all of the children would turn out that way.

Me? I got to be the bad one.

It's a lot more fun that way.

The Priest

Talos wasn't much of a kingdom, in truth. More of a duchy, or a principality fallen on lean times. So far as I could tell from my readings in the castle library, only several accidents of history, an old treaty or two, a few well-considered dynastic marriages, and, once, the intervention of the Brass Golem of Bourgoigne, had kept the Kingdom of Talos an independent throne. It's a difficult world to make your way in if you can't field an army of steam-powered war machines or a strong coven of mage-mechanicians. Talos mostly has peasants, barley, and apples. You can live on barley and apples, plus some herding or hunting, but agricultural produce makes for lousy ammunition when hostile airships come humming over the horizon with their lightning lances sparking.

Still, King Grimm served well enough, and, continuing the policies of his father and grandfather, sold the surplus bounty of his fields and orchards to his larger neighbors at sufficiently cheap prices that they never felt bestirred to come claim the lands of Talos for their own.

The true jewel in his crown was Perrault. She was a grand-niece of the King of Winter, through his sister the Frost Princess. Perrault hadn't inherited any of her distinguished family's magic, not that I could ever tell, but she certainly had both their beauty and their brains.

Only one shadow lay upon the royal marriage, and it was long and dark and disturbing as an eclipse of the sun. Though they had married young, and were carrying on through their middle years as healthy and hale as any two might ask, Perrault and Grimm had never been able to conceive a child.

This of course represented a problem for the succession, though King Grimm could always name one of his brothers or nephews the Crown Prince and resolve that issue. But, more, it was a stain upon their desires. Both king and queen passionately wished to be parents, to have an heir natural-born of their flesh and blood. There were alternatives of course, but the laws of Talos required that the reigning monarch be blood-born rather than some laboratory creation. Such as me, for example.

You can therefore imagine my mixed emotions when King Grimm and Queen Perrault fell in with a traveling mountebank who styled himself Dr. M. T. Scholes, Surgeon and Specialist in Matters of the Seed and Spirit.

The Queen of Talos

My husband is a dear, dear man, but if he hadn't been born to take the throne, I honestly don't know what he would have done with himself. Grimm is many things—steadfast, loyal, moral, gentle, fierce—but clever will never be one of them.

Most people close enough to the court to be familiar with Grimm's qualities simply assume I married the throne. Which up to a point is true. He was newly crowned when he came courting me in my father's mansion in our country by the umber-sanded shores of the wine-dark sea. When you consort with a king, you consort with his throne, regardless of your intentions concerning yourself and the world.

So of course when this tall, handsome man with a face you could strike coins off of called upon us, clad in leather and velvet with a gold circlet on his head, I knew he was a throne come calling. Kings don't simply drop by, after all. There had been heralds and envoys and a somewhat embarrassing inspection of both my father's premises and my father's daughter by the Lord High Counselor, who at that time was Godfrey the Shrewd.

On that first-and-final visit before we were graced with the royal presence, Godfrey had brought the king's Truthsmeller. A vile machine, I thought it then and still I think it now, exemplary of the worst excesses of the steamwright's art. It clumped on six clumsy, clawed legs, with a body like a mechanical leech and an articulated copper snout that would give nightmares to a corpse. But the thing had good punchtapes whirling in its processors, and sensory organs modeled after those of certain insects with postmortem feeding habits, and it could scent a lie at thirty paces. I did not know this then, of course, but in the years since I have found my own uses for the vile machine, sitting as I so often do at Grimm's side as he dispenses justices, hears petitions, and treats with envoys from larger and more powerful states.

What I knew then was that an ugly, six-legged monster

wanted to put its snout beneath the hem of my belled skirt, and my father, though visibly uncomfortable, was prepared to allow this of the wrinkled old man who was the machine's master.

I objected, of course, strenuously, and very nearly began showing off my training in the sword dance to the likely detriment of everyone involved, before father and Godfrey calmed me down. "This is for everyone's good," Father had said—one of those stupid lies parents tell children in order to truckle them along. "This is for the king's good," Godfrey had responded—one of those pieces of startling honesty that can inspire trust even in a stranger.

So the Truthsmeller sniffed at my undergarments and took the measure of my soaps and bath oils, while Godfrey interviewed my father and, through him, me. His concerns were obvious enough—were we climbers, seeking favor or pursuing a political agenda? Even though the king's men had come to our house unbidden at the first, we could have been clever enough to lay a slow trap of years baited by beauty. Stranger plots have come to pass, succeed or fail.

In the end, I was deemed an innocent girl, which while true I found myself somewhat resenting. Then Grimm arrived, riding not some enormous destrier or war charger but a graceful, modest palfrey that I would not have hesitated to mount. He did not come in the full royal style, either, but as a man bareheaded and quiet, with even a spark of anxiety in his eyes.

It was that secret, hidden fear I loved first and best, for it told me that beneath the crown there was still a man who did not think he ruled the world and everyone in it.

So we courted, and wed. I swiftly realized that Grimm was not my equal in matters of the mind, but he had a good heart and a gentle manner and a genuine desire to better the world for his people. In truth, would you rather wed sharp-edged wit or simple kindness? And kindness in kings is famously elusive.

With such a husband, and a place in life, who could deny a bride's longing to be the mother to a child of her heart?

NARRATIVE INTERLUDE THE FIRST:
FORGING BEAUTY

Father Brassbound followed Queen Perrault down the spiral stairs that led into the dank foundations of the Royal Palace of Talos. The door behind them was in the Lesser Rose Garden, a huge, rusted iron monstrosity set into the base of the Windhook Tower. To pass in three steps from the sunlit idyll of the ranks of polyantha to the mossy, shadowed coils of the stone bowels of the castle always disturbed him.

"My lady." He was nervous—the familiarity itself betraying Father Brassbound's deep sense of uncertainty—"Why do we go below this day?"

"Because," she replied in a voice tinged with gentle exasperation, "I want to show you something."

"I am not so fond of laboratories," the priest said. "My own forging was a painful, drawn-out process."

"We forge nothing this day," the queen assured him.

That they had managed to separate themselves from Queen Perrault's scuttling crowd of maids, ladies-in-waiting, courtiers, and guards was itself something of a minor miracle. As Father Brassbound well knew, royalty was almost never alone. They were attended even in the privy, at least much of the time. Their most intimate moments took place within earshot of a valet, a ladies' maid, and at least two guards.

That she took this trip into the bones of the palace alone except for him was a momentous occasion. Momentous, and smacking all too readily of secrets.

He did not like secrets so much. His God was not a god of secrets, though of course the church had its Holy Mysteries. But those were available to any man who took the right vows and swore to the correct loyalties.

The queen . . . she was a woman of fierce intelligence and strong desires. Father Brassbound feared that in her.

They soon debouched from the winding tunnel of the stairs

into the barrel-vaulted expanses of this particular basement. The queen, carrying a lantern, adjusted some valves and pressed a button that caused sparkers all around the vast, damp space to echo like a battalion of iron crickets.

"Lux fiat," muttered the priest.

"Indeed." He could hear the tense smile even in the queen's voice.

The lights flared to life, illuminating a dozen dozen devices, from a great, hulking revolutionary with lightning cables thicker than his thigh to worktables covered with delicate glassware arranged for the miracle of a chemical wedding. Other shapes were shrouded with clothes, or lurked in shadows behind the pillars that supported the downward leap of the vaulting. Though the priest had no sense of smell, he was certain the place would be redolent of oil, metal, and mold.

Queen Perrault walked over to a great brass-bound tank filled with a dark green fluid. Tubes ran in and out while pumps ticked slowly over, moving dark and viscous fluids from a series of glass cylinders into the shadowed, foggy depths of the tank.

He looked, but was able to see little. Whatever went on in there was obviously meat rather than brass, but beyond that, Father Brassbound could not say.

"I will be pregnant soon," the queen announced.

He was quite taken aback at this improbable declaration. "Your Highness?"

"You will help me create and maintain the appearance of gravidity," she said, glancing back at him. Her brown eyes, so light they were almost amber, flickered in the gaslight that burned from two dozen sources around them. Not tears, he realized.

Determination.

"Pregnancy has but one cause, and a highly predictable outcome," Father Brassbound offered cautiously.

"We will forge our outcome," she said, turning back to the tank. "Dr. Scholes has been very, very helpful to me. The fluid he guided me in preparing is almost steeped enough to host she who will be my daughter."

"You cannot," he almost squeaked. "Only a child of your body can inherit the throne."

"So far as the world knows," the queen replied calmly, "she will be the child of my body."

"What does His Highness say to this plan?"

This time her voice was sad, far away, echoing from an exile's distance. "So far as Grimm knows, she will be a child of my body."

"My Queen," Father Brassbound said slowly. "I serve you in all things so long as I do not betray the church and my faith in God to do so. I . . . If need be, I, I can stand beside you and bear false witness to the court in this matter. But I cannot . . . cannot betray the king."

"Who speaks of betrayal?" Her eyes were glittering with tears. "Dr. Scholes and I will use the homunculi of his ejaculate and the blood-egg of my own body to make our daughter come to life. It is no different than what my body does by instinct and through the virtues of vital essences. I will merely use my hands instead of my uterus. She will still be Grimm's child, and mine."

"But not born of your body."

"No, Father." Perrault's voice dropped, almost a growl, as she threw a switch and the tank began to bubble. "Born of my *will*."

The priest knew then that no matter the qualms of his conscience, he would obey the queen in this as well.

DRAMATIS PERSONAE II

The Eighth Child

Triskaidecalia was always a terrible child. I was five when she was born, and remember well how difficult Mother's labors were with her. Trisk was so loath to emerge into the world that she nearly ruined Mother and Father's years-long project of timing their offspring.

We were to be a coven, see, born to our power and our

hierarchy. Una, the first of us, was to be the greatest, our leader. Triskaidecalia, the last of us, was to be the trickster, the tease, the final rivet in the smooth machine of our lives.

That any of us might have other opinions on the matter was something that had clearly never entered the heads of our parents. They were master and mistress of the seasons. We were merely buds nourished beneath the frost and brought forth by the blessing of the summer sun.

I don't suppose anybody with a lick of sense would expect a *thirteenth* child to be normal in any way, but Trisk took willful rebellion to an art form. I, not being old enough to concoct clever evasions or young enough to be let off the duty for reasons of parental common sense, wound up being her babysitter, nurse, and nanny from the time Mother weaned her, just before my sixth birthday.

Never was there a child so eager to cut holes in clothing, urinate in shoes, color on ancient walls already decorated with masterful murals, and otherwise misbehave. This even before she began to come into dangerous powers like fire-setting and steam breath. She might as well have been a cat, she was so pointlessly and pridefully destructive.

Trisk's saving grace was her charm. She was a cute child and is an attractive woman to this day. Her charisma, when she chooses to employ it, can stun oxen at twenty yards. One simply couldn't bear down the full force of wrathful justice on a child smiling so sweetly as she protested her innocence, even with the bloody knife still in her hand.

And no, that's not a metaphor.

So she grew, bedeviling us all. Once Trisk was old enough to learn simple cantrips, Mother and Father saw their coven fully formed, sufficient to craft a fae ring or do the fire dances, and they began to train us in earnest.

They had Plans, you see.

You'd think being the Queen of Summer and the Winter King would be a sufficiency of power and prestige for most people. But Summer and Winter are ever being usurped by Autumn and

Spring, those transitional upstarts who can never make up their minds quite what they want to be. Ever down the long years had Mother and Father desired an upper hand, control over the transitions, to make the other two seasons their biddable servants.

We, the Equinoctial Coven, were to be the instrument of that change in power.

Unfortunately, no one had informed Triskaidecalia of these plans in advance. As they were slowly unfolded before our gathering of thirteen, she frequently and loudly denounced them as vain and foolish and petty and stupid.

In truth, Trisk had a point, one that most of us were too terrified of our parents to utter on our own. Spring and autumn were what made summer and winter who they were. One could not pass from sun-warmed fields of lengthening hay to the deep crackle of the ice in the forests without journeying through the golden days of autumn. Neither would the frozen lakes yield to the pounding glory of summer heat without the mediating touch of spring.

Pride, it was always about the pride. What Mother and Father had not anticipated was producing a child with even more pride than their immeasurable stores of that emotion, both their virtue and vanity.

My little sister Triskaidecalia, difficult as she was, served as the undoing of much, and the doing of much more. I played my part, too, not to be immodest about the whole business, but on her so much of several plots did pivot.

Lord High Counselor Festus

There's something wrong here, I tell you, but despite my best efforts I have not been able to place my finger upon the nub of the matter. No one in my position survives long without a web of informants and many whispered conversations behind one arras or another, but not even my slyest, most loyal creepers have been able to unravel the skein of my worries in these matters of late.

It does not aid my cause that King Grimm has been seized of mad enthusiasms with the impending arrival of his fatherhood. He dreams of his heir and babbles constantly of how they will forge a friendship between father and son that will be the envy of all Talos. In his swelling pleasure, he also has forbidden to me some of my instruments of statecraft, both certain elusive philosophies of mind as well as the more literal instruments hidden in my Cellars of Inquiry.

I have had to pension off my torturers, and amnesties are granted as fast as arrests are made these days. Is that any way to run a kingdom, I ask you?

Still, His Highness prates on about new eras and enlightenment and the beneficent role of government, and all I can wonder is, where did he learn those words? Grimm is a good man, or at least a man who aspires to be good, but he's never been one for political theory and a life of the mind. I suspect Queen Perrault has been reading him books again, and talking up the future of Talos that they will leave for their son.

Even to that matter, what will happen if the queen bears a girl? This I worry about as well, for matters of the royal succession are my purview. The question of inheritance has dogged our politics this last decade and more. Grimm seems certain his sweet wife is bringing a son into the world. I would not wager more than even odds that this will be true, royal seed being no more or less prone than any other to defining the gender of the offspring in advance.

And it is not as if the ordinary affairs of the kingdom have taken some sort of departure from their fractious norms during this period of royal pregnancy. As ever our neighboring kingdoms bear their weight down upon Talos's diminutive borders. Mountebanks come to town to swindle, beaten wives set fire to their husbands, horses are stolen, marriageable daughters elope with unsuitable sons, and all the petty, sordid dreams of people find their outlets in matters that ever seem to need my attention in order to be resolved.

All of this passes below King Grimm's notice like pond muck

beneath the rounded bottom of a swan. He abides only on the surface of all things, pleasantly thoughtless and small of mind, though he cuts a fine figure parading through the streets of Talos City on his pale charger, gleaming in bright armor and waving to the cheering crowds.

Perhaps it is enough for a kingdom to have such a king. Queen Perrault certainly fills in some of his deficiencies, but in her condition she seems to spend far more time closeted with that infernal, clanking priest, and the only doctor she will trust, Dr. M. T. Scholes. That strange red-bearded man from the Nordic countries claims learnings beyond our poor Sorbonne- and Heidelberg-educated physicians who serve the court and country of Talos as ably as they might and perhaps no better than they should.

In all of this, there is a wrongness. My bones tell me so, and I have been Lord High Counselor all these years since I helped Godfrey the Shrewd choke on a peach pit. My bones are smarter than my thoughts, but they do not communicate so clearly as to put those intelligences to use.

So I badger my informants and walk the halls in slippers and scent the winds as best I can. A plot is afoot, and I do not know its name or nature, but I will discover it. And when I do, I will act in the best interests of king and country.

That is who I am. The best interests, walking on two feet and talking in a voice like a rusty hinge, but always watching, listening, scenting for trouble.

And trouble there is to come.

NARRATIVE INTERLUDE THE SECOND: CHRISTENING BEAUTY

The Royal Palace of Talos was bedecked with even more finery than had graced the wedding of Grimm and Perrault. Strings of spark-lights had been run along the gutters and the ridgepoles of every roof from the stable privy to the King's Tower. The mechanical roof over the Great Hall was repaired and lubricated so

that it could be opened to the sky for the first time in two generations. Every flower bed on the grounds was fresh and beautiful.
Every vase within the palace halls nodded with fresh blossoms.

Talos City was hardly any less beautiful. The meanest
drudges in their hovels had scrubbed and whitewashed their tiny,
grubby doorsteps. The Brass Quarter turned out their own hand-
cast finery upon lintels and window boxes and eaves.

Father Brassbound watched over the little princess. Zellandyne was only a week old and, as the maids said, still warm from
her mother's womb. Somehow he and Queen Perrault had kept
the truth of her pregnancy secret, relying on only one more
conspirator, Dr. M. T. Scholes. A foreigner overflowing with scientific charm, the doctor's trust could be assured under the veil of
medical discretion and a goodly sum transferred in payment.
Even better, much like the priest himself, Scholes had no familial
or political loyalties in Talos to tempt him to betray his well-
bought confidences.

Zellandyne was an unquiet child. Even now, she fussed in the
priest's arms. Of course his brass limbs were not the soft warmth
of her mother's breast, but Father Brassbound privately thought
that the girl somehow intuited the lie of her birth and was struggling to force the secret out.

King Grimm had been taken aback when his beloved child
turned out not to be a son, but he quickly recovered and swore
love eternal to his surprising little daughter.

Now, this day, they would be christening Zellandyne, welcoming her into the protection of the Church and the arms of society. She was bound for greatness, indubitably so being born to
the throne, or at least being born to be marriageable for the
throne. All the nobility and wealth of Talos was gathering even
now in the Great Hall along with assorted dignitaries and nomi-
nal allies from the surrounding kingdoms and farther afield.

They had even invited the Court of Seasons. That had disturbed Father Brassbound a bit—the Church did not enjoy warm
relations with the fae, to put the matter mildly—but Queen Perrault had assured him there was little chance of the king and

queen attending, let alone their obnoxious swarm of children. Still, the Talosoise Mistress of Protocol had invited all twelve of the unholy brood by name. They were familial relations to the queen, after all.

A knock echoed from the door of the little tiring room where Father Brassbound currently awaited events in the Great Hall. "Come in," he called.

The king slipped in, the anxious face of a guard close behind. He smiled and pushed it shut, leaving privacy for himself, his daughter, and the priest.

"How is she?" Grimm's great, noble face with its aquiline nose and glittering eyes was as paternal and wise as ever.

Father Brassbound sometimes thought Grimm and Talos both were quite fortunate that the face did not match the mind behind those eyes. "Fussing, as you can see." The priest hitched his arms a bit and elevated Zellandyne so the king could examine his daughter. "She is as ready as a child her age can be, however."

Grimm thought this over for a moment, his lips moving as he worked through some difficulty with Father Brassbound's statement. "And the queen?" the king finally ventured.

"I would not know, Your Highness," the priest replied truthfully. "I have been here with the baby this past half hour, and the princess was brought to me by Dr. Scholes. The queen has been about her own affairs this morning, preparing for the christening." All their plotting was long since done, the main point of it already come and gone with the birth and presentation of the princess.

"Oh," the king said. He paused again, lost in the very short train of his thoughts. Then he visibly brightened. "Oh, yes, I just saw her." He looked around a moment, as if expecting to discover someone new in the small tiring room. "I need to tell you, Father . . . " Grimm's voice trailed off.

"Yes?" the priest asked patiently, jiggling the child who was beginning to whine. He was quite used to the king's ways.

"Winter and Summer did not come." Grimm's lips moved silently a moment. "But their children have."

Father Brassbound sighed. The Coven of the Seasons. A swarm of difficult children ranging in age from eighteen to six. Witches. Fae. Magical people of some sort, though opinions differed. And they were said to be hellions, setting fire to cottages and souring milk across the provinces of their parents' demesne.

"Thank you, sire," he said to the king. "I trust they will not disrupt the ceremony."

The actual baptism itself would be brief enough, a mercy for all concerned but especially priest and child. However, there was to be a lengthy presentation of gifts, a demonstration of goodwill, and—for some, at least—loyalty to the new princess who would someday sit on the throne of Talos. Plenty of opportunity for mischief.

"Who won't?" the king asked brightly. He smiled with regal dignity at the priest. "I believe I am supposed to be at the queen's side now."

"Of course, Your Highness." Father Brassbound watched his monarch slip back out the door, leaving behind the usual cloud of vagueness and confusion that he seemed to spread like some magical aura.

He looked down at the princess. Little Zellandyne was fussing, but her eyes were heavy. "Let's hope you take after your mother," the priest whispered with a mix of kindness and frustration in his voice.

Father Brassbound entered the Great Hall with the princess still in his arms. The roof was open, starlings circling overhead under a clear, blue spring sky. There were more people gathered here than he'd ever seen in the palace. Their breath was like the sound of a distant ocean, a great tide of open mouths and wide eyes, heads bobbing as people craned for a glimpse of the princess in his arms. All around the audience, lights glittered and bunting hung, while banners depended rippling and bright from beams and buttresses.

He walked with measured tread to the altar that had been

laid on a dais at the head of the Great Hall. A baptismal font was set before it, already filled with water that had been boiled on orders of Dr. Scholes and blessed prior to the ceremony by Father Brassbound himself. He trusted the water had been kept warm as he'd requested, as that made matters with the child much less difficult.

At the altar, facing the audience, he took a deep breath. The king and queen stood before him, just below the font, their backs to the mass filling the Great Hall.

"We are gathered here," Father Brassbound began, feeling the tremolos and imperfections in his voice box as strongly as ever, "to celebrate the birth of the princess Zellandyne Olivia Rosebriar de Talos, and to welcome her into the embrace of the Holy Mother Church."

The crowd sighed, as if the distant surf of their breathing had decided to sweep across the intervening landscape in a tidal surge.

"Let all who stand witness before the altar this day, flesh and brass alike, know that the princess Zellandyne is offered to the Lord by her parents, the good King Grimm and his wife, Queen Perrault."

He held the child high so that everyone could see her in her white christening gown, itself a fall of lace and silk and fine-grained lawn that made her look like a small, squirming confection. Zellandyne woke up at the motion and opened her mouth wide in preparation for belting forth an outraged squall.

Father Brassbound swooped the child down to the font. "I enjoin you now and commit your soul to the Holy Mother Church," he said swiftly, settling Zellandyne into the water, which was thankfully—and as ordered—warm. "As we are so told in holy scripture, therefore go and make disciples of all nations, baptizing them in the name of the Father and of the Son and of the Holy Spirit."

The princess was so surprised by the water that her own impending scream was interrupted. He traced the chrism on her forehead, then lifted her up again, dripping water down his own vestments and onto the platform. "I now call forth King Grimm and Queen Perrault," he said, anxious to hand off the child before she summoned a new burst of infant outrage.

The royal couple ascended to the altar, the queen taking her child from Father Brassbound's hands. He glanced up at the open sky, wondering for a moment whether God might reach down with lightning or some other sign of divine disfavor at the deception he had assisted the queen in maintaining regarding the gestation and birth of the princess.

The heavens remained stubbornly placid, while the assembled multitudes in the Great Hall began to cheer.

Then came the presentation of the gifts.

It was a ceremony of some hours, even though only those of the highest station were permitted to bring forth their gifts personally. Many more people had been asked to leave their offerings on tables in the courtyard, where the Mistress of Protocol and her aides had bustled about making notes of who, what, and when for the inevitable flood of royal thank-you missives that would follow in response over the weeks to come. Still, members of the court, heads of the guilds, senior leaders of Talos City, foreign dignitaries—there were dozens upon dozens of persons whose rank required they make their presentations in the hall.

And the gifts were wondrous. Cunning little clockwork toys from the workshops of Venice and Trondheim and even distant Kwangchow. An entire steam railroad, with little cars the princess could ride in, or, when a bit older, upon, large enough to fill one of the palace's courtyards. Bolt upon bolt of the finest Eastern silks. A trunk filled with ornate silver canisters holding spices from all the warm islands of the southern sun. An ocelot with a jeweled harness that had been trained to fetch and carry. Vases and statues and paintings enough to fill a summer house.

The stream of presents was a panoply of wealth and beauty and exotic curiosities that would amuse and delight Zellandyne through much of her childhood. Father Brassbound wondered how much of the glittering pile a child would trade for a stick horse or a sweet little poppet, but he supposed the king and queen were well positioned to provide a stable full of stick horses and a houseful of poppets should the little princess so desire. These gifts, he knew, were more about the giver. Many contained messages to the royal court in that strange sort of encoding that the wealthy and the powerful used between and among themselves.

The long line of gift bearers eventually shrank to a little cluster of well-dressed children of various ages. Father Brassbound realized these must be the coven from the Court of Seasons.

"I am Tertia," announced one of the oldest girls in the group. She was almost plump, with long chestnut hair and piercing gray eyes. Not beautiful, perhaps, but comely and with a certain sly charm about her. "We come to offer our kindest regards and blessings to the princess Zellandyne, as well as the goodwill of our parents, the King of Winter and the Queen of Summer."

"Our most humble thanks, Cousin," said Queen Perrault in a loud, clear voice. The priest could hear her anxiety to have done with this. These children made even her nervous. He couldn't see King Grimm's face from where he was standing, but he figured on the king smiling in that fixed fashion he assumed whenever matters at court diverged from the agenda in some unaccountable fashion.

"To display our regards and blessings," Tertia continued, "we offer the young princess three gifts."

One of her siblings, an older boy, spoke up. "She will always have friends."

The youngest girl added, in a slight lisp, "Music will follow her wherever she goes."

A middle girl offered the last gift. "Her heart's choices will not trouble her unduly."

"I thank you," the queen began, but she was interrupted by a shattering of one of the large stained-glass windows lining the Great Hall. Color sprayed everywhere in deadly splinters, as if a rainbow had been murdered. A girl rode in on an iron-winged bird that spewed steam like a laundry tub. She was smaller than any of the coven before the altar.

People screamed, stumbling away from the broken window and the hovering witch—for surely that's what she was.

"I am Triskaidecalia," the girl announced in a firm, piercing voice as her bird alit atop a statue of King Ferd the Munificent. "You did not invite me with my siblings. Why didn't I get an invitation?"

Queen Perrault tried to answer. "We did not know. . . ."

Triskaidecalia glared at her. "Just because I'm young doesn't mean I don't count."

"Be welcome here now," the queen said in a conciliatory tone, opening one hand wide even as the other cradled little Zellandyne.

The fae girl's face clouded. "It's too late," she called. "You can't welcome me now. And my siblings gave their gifts, didn't they?"

"Sister," another of the fae began, but Triskaidecalia was working herself up to a full tantrum and ignored the entreaty. "I will be *remembered*." She waved her hands in a tight circle, the air growing hot and close as she did so. "Your Princess Zellandyne will never know love. Her first love's kiss will be her last breath!"

The crowd of well-wishers moaned, the wounded and the hale alike, at such a curse.

One of the fae siblings stepped forward. "Begone, Trisk," she shouted, "or you will be whipped round the court when we are returned!"

"Never," shouted the child, before she flew out the shattered window.

The girl who'd stepped forward turned to the king and queen. "I am Octavia, and Triskaidecalia has long been my charge. She is our thirteenth, and in truth you did not name her on your invitation. I cannot undo her curse, for her power is her own, but I can change it thusly—when Zellandyne knows love's first kiss, she will only sleep until that first lover has passed himself into oblivion. She will be denied only love, not life."

"You call this a blessing?" roared King Grimm, who seemed to almost have kept up with events.

"It is what I can do for her," Octavia said sadly.

DRAMATIS PERSONAE III

Otho, Lord Chamberlain of Talos

Oh, the childhood of this princess. Such a mess we had, after the christening. The court in a panic over that awful girl's curse, then King Grimm summoning mages and artificers and soothsayers from every corner of the civilized world to try to lift the spell.

The queen tried to calm him, to stop him from his rising panic, but the king wanted, if not a son, a son-in-law. He saw the girl Trisk's curse as meaning he could never have even that small consolation.

The story went round the world, of course. Too many had been present at the event to keep the curse a secret. Telegraph wires carried it, and family gossip, and the intelligences of foreign powers. People can't get enough of love and death. A doomed romance is just the topic over mulled wine and roast capon.

Queen Perrault was more practical. She had all books about romance removed from the palace libraries, from the simplest happily-ever-after fairy tales to all those awful true-love books the maids so love to giggle over on their evenings off. This child was going to be raised only on notions of chivalry and service, of quest and sacrifice.

I and many others despaired that they would make of Zellandyne a warrior-princess or some such thing, a modern-day Maid of Orleans.

More practically, King Grimm caused that all boys between the ages of six and thirty be banned from the palace, with an exception only for the Royal Guard, who were under military discipline anyway. Even they were eventually replaced by automata.

This certainly inflected the makeup of the court, and considerably advanced the cause of women's rights in the Kingdom of Talos, as of necessity many jobs formerly held by young men were now occupied by young women of ambition and perspicacity.

So Princess Zellandyne grew, while those of us close to the king and queen watched their years-long, hopeless quest to find a way out of the curse of the thirteenth witch.

Father Brassbound prayed so much we feared for a time he would retreat to some anchorite's pole in the wilderness. Eventually he buffed his face and polished his eyes and rejoined us, but he always seemed haunted by guilt at his inability to successfully petition God to lift the curse.

Dr. Scholes consulted ancient manuscripts and corresponded with learned experts from Cambridge to Peiping, but his studies availed little. He, too, seemed ever dogged by guilt at his failure to resolve the problem through the sciences. Both of them, in fact, had the airs of one being punished for some transgression.

Sometimes, I swear, the queen appeared guiltiest of all, and retreated to her laboratories in the castle basements as if in search of a solution amid the alembics and lightnings of that place.

For my own part, it fell to me to deal with the endless stream of cranks and dreamers and confidence tricksters who came to the palace with ever-more elaborate plans for lifting or evading the curse. Many of them were genuine but misguided, too foolish or caught up in their own fancies to perceive that they had failed before they had begun. By way of solutions, various theories contemplated the love of old men; sheer, simple murder; even the forbidden love of women for one another. In this, perhaps the priest and the doctor were wiser than most. And, of course, some of the visitors were just here to wheedle funds or patronage for their pet projects, devices, even sometimes great juggernauts of machines as if Princess Zellandyne were lumber to be milled within gaping metallic guts, amid chains and belts and shrieking steam valves.

If one or another of these managed to get past me and find their way before King Grimm, well, he would try anything in his royal and fatherly desperation. Not even the queen could talk her husband out of his reed-thin hopes, perhaps because her own eyes always seemed haunted and thus she lacked conviction. Better all around that I stop the parade of foolishness before it marched past the throne.

Still, a few slipped through. We all spent an entire season eating lavender honey and dancing bee dances before that one fellow was run off. Likewise the year that colored smokes were to be deployed to draw out demons and deflect the curse. Mostly we stained miles of curtains and carpets and put the palace laundry to its worst test in many a season.

The child Zellandyne, growing up amidst all this suppressed panic and premature mourning, still somehow managed to be a bright, high-spirited little thing who loved nothing more than morning rides through the misty grounds of the royal estate at her father's side, or playing games with the maids in the courtyard, or reading about castles and quests and knights of old. She showed the most aptitude at mechanics and artifice, though, and was soon laboring at apprenticeships in the workshops and foundries attached to the Royal Palace.

"Let her sweat over a fire," I counseled the king and queen more than once. "Whosoever her heart catches on will be the end of her for the reign of years. Perhaps she will fall in love with the flow of molten brass and spend her time wreaking steam instead of chasing hearts."

"She is a girl," Queen Perrault had said sadly at one of these closeted conferences. "It is her fate to find a love, and be betrayed by it."

"At least it is not death that awaits her," I offered cautiously.

"Just the sleep of years." King Grimm was morose, growing into his name as the ever-changing days of Zellandyne's childhood unfolded. "Is that better?"

"There will still be a future, in time." It was small wisdom, of little worth, but all I had to offer. After all, how do you stop a girl from falling in love?

Prince Puissant of Bourgoigne

When I was small, I had but to pick up a stick and I was feted as the greatest swordsman since Roland. Every scrawl and scribble of mine foretold a new Leonardo. Such words ring hollow after a while, when you come to recognize the fundamental untruths wrapped within their pretty shells.

Mother, of course, stood at the heart of it, as she stands at the heart of everything.

My own words, the ones I will never say, are that Mother terrifies me. She certainly terrifies everyone else in the court, in the palace, in Nouveau Kronstadt, in the kingdom. That her affections seem reserved for me is only natural, and it only adds to my terror.

Since I was small they have trained me to fight like a nobleman. Ahorse with lance, afoot with sword, learning to lead formations of pikemen and archers and hard-bitten old legionaries who march in the style of Rome. Likewise to command cannon, steam leviathans, even the new rockets that have come only recently out of the devil's workshops of the Iron District here in Nouveau Kronstadt.

I will be a man, and I will stand before the world, I am told. Father informs me of this, in his kingly style. I hear it from my tutors, from my arms masters, even at times from the stable boys and serving wenches.

How can I be the greatest warrior in the modern world by the mere virtue and flattery of my birth, and at the same time stand at the front of the armies of Bourgoigne to do my father's will?

It will happen because Mother says it will happen. Her word is the law of the land, whatever our traditions might say. Father married power, after all.

Mother, so the whispered tales go, is an ogress, or least has the blood of fae running in her veins. Whisper those tales too widely and you'll find yourself eating your own tongue sautéed with butter and rue. I watched Mother force my old tutor,

Magister Biyal, to that bitter fate, before turning him out with a traitor's brand on his forehead to beg mute in the streets of our city.

That, at my own age of eight, was when I first knew the rumors about Mother to be true. I have no idea if she literally has ogre blood in her veins, though she is a large enough woman to put fright into one of those Teutonic Valkyries, but she certainly has an ogre's soul in her hard heart.

Yet she is my mother, and she loves me.

So when I turned sixteen I announced that I would quest. First to the Holy Land to worship in the shrines where our Lord was originally venerated. Then to hypocaustal Rome and her younger cousin Venice, where the workshops that birthed the brass world still clang and burble and echo with devilish imaginings amid the foundations of lost empire. Then, I'd told the court at my celebratory feast, I would circle among the countries of Europe seeking deeds of valor and righteousness in the manner of the knights of old.

What could they do but cheer me?

Mother had been furious, of course, her eyes smoldering, but she would hardly tear down her beloved son before court and king. Even she had to answer to Father, when he bestirred himself to venture a preference in some matter besides governance of the kingdom and the vintage to be drunk at dinner.

So I fit myself into the tales she had caused me to be raised upon and rode away from the palace and from Nouveau Kronstadt as free a man as I would ever likely be.

Someday I will have to return and take up my father's crown, whether I wish it or not.

I have worshipped at the Church of the Holy Sepulcher. I have fought against the armies of the Musselman, myself personally bringing down one of the great, jointed walkers out of the fabled workshops of Samarkand through a combination of dumb luck and a well-aimed petard. Decidedly not a nobleman's weapon, but the lessons of my father's court had far fewer applications on the field of battle than my arms masters had believed, or at least been willing to confide to me. With that in mind, I spent several seasons apprenticed to a twisted little woman in Murano, a mistress of clockwork and chemical fires who was building weapons no sane man would use.

And now I am once again ahorse—my third mount these past seven years of wandering, this one a Berber mare of cunning mind and fine footwork—wandering the fields and forests of Mediterranean Gaul and Iberia, wondering if I should finally turn my face toward home.

NARRATIVE INTERLUDE THE THIRD: TRUE LOVE LEAVES NO TRACES

The prince, riding on his horse Lightning as a road-dusted and exhausted knight-errant, approached the Royal Palace of Talos by the westward road. These past years the palace had become one of the most famous residences in Europe, thanks to the fantastic stories about the daughter of the house. It was, indeed, a curious sight to see.

Smoke belched from three high, brick stacks that rose behind the tiled roofs. Even at a distance, he could hear the clang and shudder of foundry hammers. Machines not so much in the shape of men stalked and slouched along the palace's outer walls, or stood atop towers and roof ridges like so many sculptures left behind in the retreat of some mad metalworker.

Puissant smiled behind his rough Maghrebi scarf. So some aspect of the stories was true, if they'd banished their guards in favor of obedient automata. Or perhaps these were even brass men, whose kind he had met so many of on the island of Murano during his long ago days in Venice.

A king and queen afraid of comely young men being too close to their daughter. Mother probably took delight at the cosmic joke played upon these people.

Prince Puissant was in truth on the way home to see his parents, after years of wandering. Somehow his mother's ambitions had become less overwhelming and less important to him with the passing of years. The papers said Father was ill, and not expected to see another winter. He'd never really meant to leave them forever, just to live outside the shadow of Mother's will awhile.

Well, he'd certainly done that.

But this business of the curse on Talos, that had always interested him. It seemed one last, fitting piece of errancy to pursue on his way home.

He wondered what life was like inside the palace.

Taking a knee before King Grimm and Queen Perrault, the prince had already seen plenty of evidence inside the throne room of what had passed over the years. Soot gathered in odd corners even here, a sign that the standards of the house had been relaxed over time. The guards were, as he thought, all brass. Most of them possessed the slack-jawed stillness of automata, but the sergeants were keen-eyed, their gaze gleaming with the intelligence of well-wrought punchtapes. There was even a brass priest attending the king and queen as they received him.

"Your Highnesses," Puissant said, raising his face to meet their tired gazes. "It is both my duty and my pleasure to present my compliments to you."

"You are a traveler, yes?" The queen's voice was as weary as her gaze.

The years have not been so kind to her, the prince thought. She had been mourning her daughter since the girl's birth. How hard that must be for a parent, to raise a child thinking only that you would have to watch her die. Or at least sleep away a generation, if the tales of the curse were true. "Yes," he replied aloud. "I have these past years been to the Holy Land, and all across the south of Europe and the north of Africa."

"And you know of our troubles?" King Grimm's voice was reedy and weary, nothing like the glorious rumble that must have once emerged from that great chest.

"Only what anyone on the street might know. There are half a hundred tales, but the truth seems likely simple enough, if all the more sad for that."

The queen leaned forward. "Do you bring some wisdom that might break this spell?" Old woe flashed in her eyes.

"Only common sense and a good sword hand, I am afraid." The prince's fingers strayed momentarily to his hilt.

"You are welcome to the hospitality of our house," King Grimm said. "There is only one condition on your visit. You may observe our daughter as opportunity permits, but you may not speak to her."

"This would seem to be like solving a puzzle without touching the pieces," the prince replied, "but I understand your fears, and will heed your condition without reservation."

"Then be welcome," Queen Perrault bade him.

The prince abided awhile in the Royal Palace of Talos. He swiftly came to like the king and queen, and could see beneath their twinned mantles of worry and fear that they were not so far beyond their young and energetic years. If the curse could be lifted, the royal couple would be rescued from a generation of sorrow.

Taking his cues about discretion and what was permissible from Otho, the elderly Lord Chamberlain, Prince Puissant observed Princess Zellandyne from a distance. She was almost wanton in her exuberance of movement and action, he noted, as if she'd been raised a boy. She was handsome enough, if not precisely beautiful. The muscled arms and thick legs engendered by long hours in the forges and workshops of the Royal Palace kept her from the classic beauty associated with her breeding and station.

Still, she moved with a flashing vivacity to which he could not help being drawn.

"What projects does she pursue in her workshops?" he asked Otho one day as the two of them looked down upon the metal yard where the princess was sorting through pipe stock in pursuit of some unknowable aim. The prince and the lord chamberlain stood together in the Weather Tower of the palace, hidden from Zellandyne's view by the shadowed embrasures.

"These past several years, automata," the old man replied. "She built a leopard in the memory of her old pet ocelot, that stalks the gardens to this day terrifying the servants. Then an improved model of palace guard. Lately the librarians inform me she has been much at study of the books on punchtapes and clock-work intelligences. I know she spends long hours with Father Brassbound." He added a bit sourly, "The old priest can refuse her nothing, not even inspection of the contents of his head."

The prince reflected on how many meanings that phrase could contain, but said nothing to goad the lord chamberlain's obviously wounded heart.

Still, what would one in her position truly be thinking to make oneself a man?

A few days later, he caught the old priest in the upper gallery above the Great Hall. "Father," called out Puissant, "a moment of your time, please."

"Of course, my son." Father Brassbound sat on a carved bench and met the prince's gaze. "I apologize if I have been dilatory in making you welcome here in Talos."

"No, no, not at all. I am made most welcome. But I wish to ask you something rather personal, if I may so boldly presume." The prince drew a breath. "This is in pursuit of the problem of the princess."

"Anything, my son."

"To cut to the core of my question, in your experience, how long might a brass man such as yourself expect to live? Are you bound by the fleshly three score and ten?" He knew what he'd been taught amid the forges of Murano and Rome, but he wanted to hear this one's answer.

"No. . . ." Father Brassbound stared a moment at his feet as if they were newly arrived at the end of his legs. "Barring accident or murder, of course, we live the life of our component pieces. Which, unlike those of my fleshly brethren, can for the most part be replaced. Some of the earliest brass men from the workshops of Samarkand and Constantinople are still said to survive, four centuries after their creation. The art of crafting the punchtapes and the intelligences ever improves, of course. While those cannot be changed without changing the man within the mind, the bodies go on."

"I have met a few of those old brass along the shores of the Golden Horn," the prince said, musing a moment on memory. "So if the princess were to lay true love's first kiss upon a brass man, she might sleep for centuries while he walked the Earth."

Father Brassbound closed his eyes and sighed. "Do not suggest such a thing to the king and queen, I beg you. Besides, it is not done. Flesh and brass do not mix that way."

Puissant laughed softly. "Not even in the manner of their birth? We both know better, sir priest. And if you believe that people do not mix according to their passions, then you are more naive a prelate than I would give credit for. Do not confuse your wishes for the way world might be with the complex realities of the heart and body."

"Wishes are all we have left to us here in Talos."

Late one evening, the prince slipped through the shadows and into Zellandyne's workshops. True to his word, he had not approached her, and had in fact gone to some efforts to prevent her from even getting a good look at him. Not that it was so difficult to do—the princess kept mostly to her labors, and associated more with her maids and assistants than anyone else in the palace. In point of fact, he'd dined nightly with the king and queen, and had yet to be sent from the table because the princess had never come to claim her place.

He walked softly among the hanging chains and great racks of the workshops. Banked fires glowered through shuttered grates, while burbling and *glooping* noises testified to chemical and thermal activities with the tanks that loomed along the outer walls of the workshop. He touched nothing, but observed everything with his trained eye.

In the third of the stone barns, he found what he was looking for. This was where she'd done the fine work of building her automata. Shelves were lined with springs and torsion bars, gyroscopes and bins of close-cut gears, the leathers and gutta-percha that would go to make a skin or covering.

On a great slab of a table in the middle of the workshop lay the mostly complete body of a brass man. He was visible in one of the few pools of lamplight shining in the shuttered night shift. The chest was open and the face was missing, leaving a complex tangle of clockwork and pressure hoses and spark relays. Puissant walked slowly around it, still looking without touching.

"He is beautiful, is he not?" The voice rang out from the shadows, strong, confident. Female.

"Yes, Your Highness," the prince replied, not very surprised. "Your work is well spoken of within the palace."

"I doubt that. When they speak of me, it is with despair." She stepped into the light, dressed in a smith's leathers with thick denim and canvas beneath. He could not help noticing that one hand held a hammer, rock-steady and ready to swing. "You are that prince, from Bourgoigne."

"Prince Puissant, at your service." He bowed.

She snorted. "Your parents really named you that?"

Another bow, this time with a smile he could not keep from his face. "My mother is . . . ambitious. Most people do not seem to get the joke."

"My parents are desperate," she said flatly. "And the joke here has grown very old. Are you commissioned to somehow free me from the curse?"

"Alas, no," Puissant said. "I merely stopped to attend awhile on my way home from a journey of years."

Her free hand strayed to the brow of the brass man on the table. "It must have been quite a journey, for you to be away for years."

"An ambitious mother can be an inspiration."

"So can a fae curse."

The prince nodded at the man on the table. "You are creating your own true love?"

Her lips grew tight. "Perhaps. It seems one way to avoid the curse."

"Is brass exempted from the failures of flesh?"

"In many ways, yes." She glanced down at the exposed gears and circuits behind the missing face. "And perhaps more obedient."

"Somehow I do not think it is obedience that concerns you most," he said.

"I have been taught to love forge fires and tools and machines." Her voice grew distant. "For fear of what a young man might do to me."

There are places in this world where you might have loved a young woman, Puissant thought, but he did not see it as a helpful thing to say. "Your loves are your own business," he replied quietly. "I confess to curiosity, but this is not my affair."

"I *will* build him, and I *will* kiss him."

"And sleep the centuries until a brass man has walked his last step upon this Earth?"

Her face grew fierce. "He is brass. This will be different."

"Luck and love to you, Princess," Puissant said with sadness.

He bade his farewells the next morning, and took his horse down into Talos City. Prince Puissant had had enough of the gloom of the Royal Palace, and his heart was pierced by the idea of love. In the years of his wanderings, he had known the flesh of both women and men when time and interest permitted. Those had been pleasant pastimes, but they were not love.

Here was a woman denied to love almost from her birth, but she was still trying to find a way past that sentence. He should possess such fortitude.

So Puissant made his way to a middling sort of traveler's inn, ordered himself copious wine and a small feast and two whores, and set about some serious effort at forgetting himself for a while.

On the third day of his dissolution, he woke amid a tangle of limbs and a reek of alcohol to hear bells ringing throughout the town, and the muttering of a crowd in the street. Or possibly a mob. The prince extracted himself from Maisie and Daisy—which might just possibly be their real names, though he was doubtful—and cracked open the shutters.

People were gathering in uneasy groups, with much pointing and shouting. He leaned out to look in the direction many fingers were indicating to see a gray pall just west of town, where the Royal Palace of Talos stood atop its long, sloping hill.

"She has done something," whispered the prince. He quickly donned his riding leathers and the lightest of armor, took up his sword and pistols, and leaving the women asleep in his room, made his way back down to the stables where he'd left Lightning. Puissant had ridden a brass horse for the seasons he'd been in Venice, and much preferred the fleshly versions.

He quickly checked his horse's hooves and hocks, then saddled without the help of the stable boys, who'd run off to gawk like everyone else. Then he was up and heading for the Royal Palace, pushing his way through the uneasy streets where the townsfolk were still working up their courage.

The grounds were a mess as he approached. Not that this had been the best-kept estate he'd ever visited, but overnight every growing thing seemed to have bolted and become leggy, woody and strange. The walls were unguarded, but the main gate was a tangle of fresh vines and tiny, wild roses everywhere.

Puissant dismounted and hacked his way through the entrance. Leading Lightning, he walked up the moss-covered stones of the paved drive to the formal entrance of the Royal Palace. Not even a bird twittered in the trees. The place was eerily silent. The great lacquered doors were ajar, draped again with vines and roses. A brass man was collapsed on the generous portico, resembling nothing so much as an abandoned suit of armor.

Tying off his horse, Prince Puissant pushed his way within.

He came across a maid in the front hall, curled on her side and sleeping deeply. He tried to rouse her, but nothing he could do, not even pricking the back of her hand with the tip of his dagger, provoked the slightest reaction other than a slow, carmine bead of blood. He walked on to the throne room, which he found empty except for two more servants, then to the main dining room. The king and queen were slumped over their golden plates, servants and members of the court scattered around them on the floor.

With a sigh, Puissant headed for Zellandyne's workshop. Surely that was the center of all this. The exits from the Royal Palace were blocked with more vines and roses, and his hand was torn by thorns on the way out. Likewise the entrances to the workshops. He apologized silently to his sword for the abuse, and hacked his way within.

Zellandyne lay on the floor next to her slab table. Of the brass man, there was no sign. The princess was accompanied in unconsciousness by several assistants, all strapping young women with arms as mighty as hers.

"You had to do it," the prince said. "And sadly, you were wrong about the brass man." He looked at her face and wondered if he was supposed to kiss her. Since the most likely outcome of that seemed to be him joining the princess and everyone else in the palace in the sleep of years, he decided against it. Besides, there was no spark between them.

He went looking for the brass man instead.

Puissant found Zellandyne's true love in the stables, fumbling to light the fires of a steam cart. All the horses were asleep, of course. "Must you leave?"

The brass man turned to face him. "There is nothing for me here."

"A hundred people or more sleep at the touch of your lips," the prince said. "Surely you have some responsibilities."

"She made me as she was made, she quickened me as she was

quickened, she kissed me as her mother had once kissed her." The brass man's voice was dull. "Then they all just . . . folded away."

"Did Zellandyne give you a name before she was lost?"

"Morpheus."

The prince had to laugh at that. "Well, Morpheus, what do you plan for yourself now?"

"To go into the world and find a purpose." The brass man glanced at the prince's sword, now sheathed again at his side. "What are your plans?"

"To free the princess, then be about my business," he said. "She will never forgive me for slaying her true love." He drew one of his pistols and in one swift movement shot the brass man in his left knee.

Morpheus collapsed with a piteous hissing whine. "I did nothing to you," he complained.

"I have warred around the edges of the Mediterranean these past fifteen years," the prince told him. "I have personally killed dozens who did nothing to me, caused the deaths of hundreds or even thousands more who did nothing to me, slain at the hands of men I led. Innocence is no badge of protection." He aimed the other pistol at Morpheus's face. "Besides, there is some sin here to expiate, or I am no judge of people. They all suffer from a curse, and it's not just this silly business with the witch. You, my poor newborn friend, are the lamb to be sacrificed on their altar."

He fired the other pistol into the brass man's face with only a single shudder of self-disgust. Then he went to find a hammer and a pry bar to tear Morpheus apart, until Zellandyne's first love was no more.

Puissant thought about attending until the sleeping beauty awoke, but the palace stirred slowly in the aftermath of the murder. He'd broken the curse, and the king and queen had lost not even a day of their lives. They could not have done the same to free themselves, because of course what use to slay the true love before their daughter's heart was grasped? He knew he should congratulate himself on his cleverness, but the prince felt no pride, and likewise no desire to claim any reward.

It wasn't his fault. He did what any sensible person would have done, given the terms of the curse. And what was one confused, newborn life compared to a hundred sleeping royalty and servants, and the damage that would come to a kingdom left bereft of rule, defense, or direction?

Such an easy calculus to make, that only one man had to die. Puissant just wished it hadn't been him who'd done the killing.

Now, if he could ever find that stupid little fae witch who'd laid the curse, he might have a purpose in violence. But he was done with ambition, and wanted to see his father before the old man died.

Somewhere far behind the prince, a woman sobbed.

Mose and the Automatic Fireman

by Nancy A. Collins

**(BASED ON TALL TALES ABOUT AMERICAN
FOLK HERO MOSE THE FIREBOY)**

"Let me get a good look at you," Sykesky said, eyeing his friend like a housewife judging the freshness of a side of beef.

Mose did as he was told, straightening his narrow shoulders and throwing out his birdlike chest as best he could. As an afterthought, he spat in his hand and used it to slick back his bushy, bright red hair. He was about to polish the tops of his brogans against the back of his pants legs, only to stop for fear of the boots disintegrating. Sykesky circled Mose, hands clasped behind his back, his gaze traveling up and down the smaller youth's slender frame as he stood at attention. Mose had always been a slight child, even in the best of times, but eating out of garbage cans had reduced him even further.

Mose was sixteen and had been living on his own ever since his mother succumbed to the white death, nearly two years before, leaving him an orphan. He made a living, such as it was, picking rags and hawking the *Herald* when he could scrape up the pennies to buy papers, as well as the occasional thievery. But he was getting too old to be a newsie, and had little chance of landing an apprenticeship. There was only one real option for a young man such as himself, without education or patronage, if he wanted to survive to adulthood: he had to get himself ganged up.

Of the various gangs on the Lower East Side of New York City, the Bowery Boys were the natural choice, as they were easily the largest and most powerful, with connections to nearby City Hall that the Dead Rabbits and the Roach Guard did not share. Most important, the Boys enjoyed a great deal of social status as volunteer firefighters and owned their very own pumper engine. Thanks to their speedy response time and willingness to rush into burning tenements, the gang made a nice bit of money from the fire insurance companies, often winning sizable bonuses for being the first engine to arrive. Because of this steady, and relatively respectable, means of income, many a young fellow in dire circumstances had found his fortunes reversed after becoming one of the fabled Bowery Boys. Indeed, Sykesky was living proof. Where once his friend had been dressed in rags, now he wore the red shirt, black flared trousers, and black vest that served as the Bowery Boys' uniform, with the traditional black stovepipe hat perched rakishly atop his well-oiled hair.

Mose had known William Sykes since they were both three years old, having grown up together in Mulberry Bend. Upon seeing Sykesky's transformation from street urchin to flashy tough, Mose had asked his old chum to recommend him for membership. Sykesky had first tried to dissuade the smaller boy, but Mose had persisted, reminding him of the time he'd saved his life by yanking him out of the way of a teamster's wagon when they were eight years old. Sykesky finally relented and agreed to introduce him to Horseshoe Harry, the leader of the Bowery Boys.

The Green Dragon Saloon, located on Broome Street, just west of the Bowery, was the gang's favorite haunt and de facto clubhouse. Sykesky pushed open the double doors of the saloon, revealing a long, pitch-black hallway. As Mose trailed behind his friend, he had the uneasy certainty that his passage was being watched by others hidden in the surrounding darkness. At the end of the corridor was another pair of swinging doors that opened onto a room with a sawdust-strewn floor, on one side of which was a lengthy, polished wooden bar fitted with a brass foot rail. Behind the bar was hung a large mirror, and above that was a painting of a nude woman sprawled across a tiger skin rug. In the musician's alcove, near the back of the room, a sodden pianist was muddling his way through "Buffalo Gals," accompanied by an equally inebriated fiddle player. The walls of the Green Dragon were lined by wooden booths filled with boisterous young men dressed identically to Sykesky, drinking foaming tankards of beer, smoking pipes and cigars, and playing at dice or cards. And the loudest and tallest was none other than Horseshoe Harry, the leader.

Sykesky announced himself to his boss by loudly coughing into his fist. Horseshoe Harry, who got his name for his ability to unbend said item with his bare hands, stood over six feet tall, his stovepipe hat drawn down over one eye, his trousers tucked into his boot-tops, the smoldering stub of a cigar pointing from his lips toward the ceiling, his jaw jutting forward contemptuously, as if inviting the world to take a swing, if it dare.

"What d'ya want—Sykes, is it?" he growled.

"Yes, sir," Sykesky said, clearly pleased that the gang leader had remembered his surname. "I got that kid I told you about—the one that's looking to join." He turned and motioned to Mose, who stepped forward.

"It's an honor to meet you, sir," he said, touching his forelock in deference.

Horseshoe Harry snorted and hawked a wad of phlegm onto the barroom floor, alongside the boy's poorly shod feet. "What's yer name, kid?"

"Mose Humphries."

"Ya look like a bog hopper t'me," the gang leader snarled, gesturing to the youth's shock of ginger-colored hair. "The Boys don't take no micks. We don't have no truck with papists, neither. We leave that trash for the Dead Rabbits. We only take native-born, God-fearing Protestants."

"I ain't no Catlick," Mose replied tersely. "My folks was from Wales. But I was born in Mulberry Bend, on Ragpickers Row."

This seemed to mollify Horseshoe Harry enough for him to take the cigar from his mouth and give Mose a closer look. "So ya wanna join up, eh? Ya gotta be tough to run with the Boys, but it looks to me ya couldn't wrestle out a turd."

"I'm tough enough," Mose said, pulling himself up to his full height of five foot one as he jutted his chin out in imitation of the Bowery Boys' legendary braggadocio. "And I ain't scared of nothin'."

"The boy's scrappy as a terrier," Sykesky assured his boss. "I seen him snatch a wharf rat up by the tail and bash its brains out on a paving stone when we was six."

Horseshoe Harry studied the slender youth dressed in stinking rags for a long moment before he finally spoke. "Seeing how ye're a native son of our beloved country, and ain't a bead rattler, I'm gonna be generous and set ya a task. If you can perform it to my satisfaction, you're in the gang. All y'have to do is man the pumper." He turned to look at his fellows lounging about the Green Dragon. "Whattaya say, lads?" he asked, jerking his head toward the door at the back of the saloon. "Let's go see if the kid's got what it takes!"

There was a roar of agreement and within seconds Mose found himself swept along by the tide of rowdy young men and dragged down the street to the Bowery Boys' "firehouse," where their pump engine was kept. Upon arriving, Mose saw that the doors were chained shut and bound by a padlock the size of a baby's head. Horseshoe Harry fished an equally oversized key from his waistcoat and removed the lock, swinging open the door to reveal the gang's most prized possession.

It was, indeed, a sight to behold, with a square, flat body the size and shape of a piano box fashioned from pure mahogany, with gilded moldings that gleamed like the brass on a rich man's coffin. The words AMERICA LIBERTY, draped in Old Glory, were painted on the front, and the accompanying hose cart was red with blue-and-white striping, in keeping with the patriotic theme. Resting atop its large wheels was an air chamber, and a pair of folding wooden pump bars, known as brakes, that ran horizontally and were long enough to accommodate six men on each side. There was no finer pump engine in all the city of Manhattan.

"Show me what ya got, kid," Horseshoe Harry said, gesturing with his smoldering cigar.

Mose eyed the engine for a moment and then stepped up to the brake that was closest to him, which was tilted upward, like a teeter-totter. Standing on his tiptoes, he wrapped his hands firmly about the heavy wooden pump bar and pulled it downward. Or, at least, he tried to, as the brake barely budged. Mose let go, spat into his palms, shook his arms out, and grabbed the handle a second time, grimacing as he yanked it toward the floor with a mighty grunt. This time the brake obeyed, accompanied by a sound like that of a huge blacksmith's bellows.

"*See?*" Mose grinned, turning his head to look at Horseshoe Harry and the others, who stood gathered in the doorway. "I *told* you I was tough enough—!"

Just as he spoke, the brake began its return journey, yanking Mose free of his rotting boots, much to the amusement of the Bowery Boys and their leader. Mose yelped in alarm as he suddenly found himself dangling a foot or more off the floor, his bare feet kicking the empty air for purchase, while the assembled gang howled like a band of baboons. The embarrassed youth let go of the brake and dropped to the floor with a heavy thud, his face an even brighter shade of red than his hair. Snatching up his decrepit footwear, he dashed out of the firehouse into the gathering dusk, his ears ringing with their derisive laughter.

Mose stood at the end of the pier and stared down at the reflection of the stars in the dark and swiftly moving waters of the East

River as he tried to work up the nerve to surrender to its wet embrace. He did not particularly wish to snuff it, but could not find a good reason to keep on living. Every day of his young life had been a struggle. He honestly could not remember a time when he had not fought to keep himself from starving, bodily harm, or despair. He was born puny and had stayed that way in a culture that valued brute strength above all else. He was without family, without influence, and without means. In a day or so his rent would be due, and all he had to his name were the filthy rags on his back and a single, much-worn penny in his pocket—and it cost a half dime to sleep in the old wardrobe on Mrs. Murphy's landing.

What was the point of keeping body and soul together? He was a runt, a pathetic weakling. He couldn't even claim to be a proper cripple, like Dead Legs Turpin or Deaf Willie. He might as well throw himself in the drink and get it all over with. Drowning might not be the ideal death, but at least it was a good deal cheaper than buying poison, and nowhere near as messy as stepping out in front of a train. He took a deep breath, more to steady his nerves than prolong his life, and prepared himself for the cold, dark river.

But just as he was about to jump, a star broke free of the firmament above and shot toward the startled young man, lighting up the night sky like a flare fired from the deck of a sinking ship. Mose watched, mouth agape, as it arced over his head and landed with a loud report at the edge of the riverbank. The pier quaked mightily, as if shaken by an angry giant, nearly hurling him into the water.

Mose hurried to the foot of the pier, all thoughts of suicide erased from his mind. He hopped down onto the riverbank below to see what had plummeted from the heavens above, only to find a crater the size of the Bowery Boys' pump engine gouged in the rocky soil, steam rising from the hole like from a potato roasting in the coals of a fire. He cast about and found a length of driftwood long enough to serve as a poking stick, just in case there was a moon man waiting to jump out at him.

As he looked down into the hole, he saw what looked like a

misshapen sphere of iron roughly the size of his fist, its edges still glowing orange, as if plucked fresh from a blacksmith's forge. Mose's heart leaped in his chest. He knew that a scientist like the famous Professor Tolliver would pay handsomely for such a miraculous find—perhaps as much as twenty dollars.

Mose prodded the smoldering sky stone with the stick, and then scampered off to steal a bucket. He returned a few minutes later with a wooden pail liberated from the back of an unattended wagon. He then trudged to and from the nearby river, like a one-man bucket brigade, dumping gallon after gallon of water onto the meteorite until his arms and back ached. As the first blush of dawn started to tinge the morning sky, he finally succeeded in cooling it down enough so that it could be handled. Wrapping it in cast-off burlap bags, he cradled the still-warm rock to his chest and hurried away. Although the misshapen lump was no bigger than his closed fist, Mose was surprised by its weight—if it had been any heavier he would have had to steal a wheelbarrow to transport it.

Mrs. Murphy's Boardinghouse was located on Baxter Street, and was a ramshackle, four-story building barely two rooms wide, with a crumbling front stoop. As Mose entered the foyer, Mrs. Murphy's door opened and the landlady reached out and grabbed him by the arm, like a trapdoor spider snatching its prey. She was a large, meaty woman, whose face seemed to be set in a perpetual suspicious scowl.

"Trust ye t' be creepin' in at the crack of dawn!" she snapped, giving the startled boy a shake. "Where's my rent?"

"This is all I've got," he replied, shoving his last remaining penny at her.

"All you got, eh?" she said dubiously, eyeing the gunnysack he held cradled under one arm. "What's that, then?"

"Just some rotten bits of food I scavenged from the bin, that's all," Mose assured the landlady. "I'll have the rest in a day or two, I promise."

"Ye 'promise'!" Mrs. Murphy snorted derisively as she dropped the coin into the pocket of her apron. "Here, I'll make *ye* a promise, laddie—if I don't have my half dime by sunup tomorrow, ye'll be sleepin' in the gutter along with the slops and road apples, where ye belong!" With that, the landlady retreated to her apartment, slamming the door behind her so hard it made the entire building shudder.

Mose climbed up the narrow, winding stair, making his way toward the top of the house. Some of the other boarders, those who held jobs working the docks or the nearby fish market, were already up and about. On the third floor he had to step around a small cookstove set up at the head of the stairs, careful not to upset the pot atop it. A weary-eyed woman crouched in a nearby doorway, watching her porridge bubble and hiss. Mose glanced past her into the windowless, reeking room beyond and saw that it was empty of furnishings, save for a pile of filthy rags. The boy sighed wistfully.

Because of the pitched roof of the boardinghouse, the wardrobe on the attic landing was set on its back, like a packing crate— or a coffin. This worked out for Mose, as it allowed him to stretch out as he slept. He opened the cabinet door and dropped his prize onto the bundle of old clothes stuffed with scavenged straw that served as his bed. He then boosted himself inside and closed the wardrobe behind him, securing it from the inside with a twisted piece of wire so he could sleep in relative security.

It was dark as death inside the wardrobe, and smelled strongly of mouse piss, but it was the only place in the world Mose felt anything resembling safe. At least the only things he had to worry about inside his shelter were bedbugs and cockroaches. As he settled in to sleep, he pulled the sky stone from its gunnysack, holding it as a child would a beloved toy.

Tomorrow he would make his way to the university on Park Place and find Professor Tolliver. Back when his mother was still alive, she used to read aloud to him from the papers. She had been particularly intrigued by the account of Professor Tolliver's incredible Automatic Man—a clockwork automaton capable of not only dancing the waltz, but playing chess. Professor Tolliver claimed that someday all the dangerous and unpleasant tasks would be handled by such so-called automatonics, and that mankind, once freed from scarcity and soul-grinding toil, would finally attain utopia and explore its full potential. While Mose wasn't sure such a world was completely possible, his mother had embraced it wholeheartedly. As far as the late Mrs. Humphries was concerned, Professor Tolliver was the wisest man in America since Benjamin Franklin. There might be other learned men of science in the city of New York, but the professor was the only one that mattered.

As slumber claimed him, he briefly wondered from what far-flung star the rock had fallen from, and if that would make any difference to the asking price.

Mose was drawn from the pit of sleep by a loud rapping noise. He opened his eyes to find himself still sealed away in darkness. He yawned and automatically stretched his limbs, only to be unexpectedly brought short, as if he had been transferred, sometime while he slept, from the wardrobe and placed in a small wooden box. What if Mrs. Murphy had come to collect her rent, and found him in such a deep sleep that she had mistaken him for dead? His mind began to race and his heart began to pound in fear. Within seconds, he had convinced himself that the pounding was that of nails hammered into his coffin. Believing he was being buried alive, Mose flailed about in mortal terror, banging his fists against the coffin lid—only to have it shatter into splinters. To his surprise, he saw Mrs. Murphy staring down at him, her usual scowl replaced by a look of shocked disbelief.

"Merciful God in heaven!" the landlady cried out in fear. "What have ye done with Mose, ye great beast?"

"What do you mean? I *am* Mose," the confused youth replied.

As he sat up, Mose came to the realization that what he had mistaken for the undertaker nailing down his coffin lid had been Mrs. Murphy banging on the wardrobe in search of her half dime.

As for what had once been his home, it looked as if someone had attacked it with an axe: the bottom had been reduced to kindling, and the side panels were split wide open.

As he climbed out of what remained of the wardrobe, the top of his skull abruptly smacked against the ceiling. Mose cursed and reached to massage the top of his head, only to freeze at the sight of a huge, hairy hand dangling from his wrist. He looked down and saw that his moldering boots had finally disintegrated, destroyed by the pair of massive feet that now grew from his ankles. He took a tentative step forward, only to go crashing through a rotten floorboard. This proved far too much for Mrs. Murphy, who threw her apron over her head and ran downstairs, screeching at the top of her lungs for her husband.

Mose stared down in amazement at his transformed body. Gone were the spindly arms, twiglike legs, and sunken chest, and in their place were limbs and muscles more in keeping with Goliath and Samson. Although his miraculous metamorphosis had reduced most of his tattered clothes to rags, his trousers—which he'd been forced to triple-cuff to keep from tripping over—were still in one piece, although they were now stretched to the point of bursting and came no farther than his kneecaps.

As he marveled over his "growth spurt," Mose remembered the meteorite he'd scavenged from the riverbank. He reached down into the ruins of the wardrobe to scoop it up, only to find that it had dissolved into a handful of rust.

The ever-present cigar dropped from Horseshoe Harry's mouth as Mose entered the Green Dragon Saloon. The half-naked colossus had to stoop to enter the doorway, and when he stood erect his long, powerful arms dangled so low he could scratch his kneecaps.

Sykesky came forward, staring up at his transformed friend in disbelief. "Mose? Is that you?" he gasped.

"It's me, all right," he replied with a voice so deep it rattled the bottles behind the bar. "I come back to join the gang." The way he said it made it clear it was not a request.

"The Dead Rabbits and Chichesters ain't gonna know what hit 'em!" Sykesky grinned.

The Bowery Boys cheered in agreement, and raised their beers and whiskies in salute to their new secret weapon. All, that is, save Horseshoe Harry, who looked as if he'd just swallowed a bag of nails.

Mose sat down at the nearest table and called out for food and drink, and for someone to bring him a decent suit. While the other gang members yelled at the saloon-keeper to prepare a feast worthy of their new comrade, Sykesky ran off in search of clothes. Ten minutes later he returned, accompanied by a tailor, who carried a sizable bundle of ready-to-wear clothes over his arm and a tape measure about his neck. By this time Mose was busily devouring his second bushel of oysters and drinking beer from a bucket.

The tailor cringed as the redheaded giant pushed himself away from the table, and dutifully stood by as Mose tried on different articles of clothing, flinching every time a seam burst or a button went flying. Mose finally found a suit that more or less fit him, even though the pants ended halfway down his shins and the shirtsleeves stopped halfway down his forearms.

Just as the tailor hurried out of the saloon, one of the Boys came charging in. "There's a fire on the corner of Mulberry and Spring!" he exclaimed breathlessly. "And the Dead Rabbits are on their way!"

The assembled Bowery Boys jumped to their feet and grabbed their stovepipe hats, shouting in excitement. Upon reaching the firehouse, Mose pushed aside his fellow gang members and stepped between the traces of the engines.

"Hang on and enjoy the ride, lads!" he laughed, and took off in a dead run, the pumper and its hose cart bumping along behind him like a rickshaw, while his comrades clung on for dear life, clutching their hats with one hand for fear of them flying off.

Mose galloped through the narrow, cobblestoned streets of Old New York, with Sykesky ringing the engine's brass fire bell to warn pedestrians and other traffic to clear the way. A pack of mongrel dogs chased after them, adding their barks to the general cacophony. As they neared their destination, a plume of black smoke could be seen rising above the surrounding tenements and other buildings.

Suddenly, as they rounded the corner, Mose came to an abrupt halt that sent several of his passengers flying. Blocking the road was a wagon with a broken axle that had spilled a garden full of vegetables onto the street. The greengrocer who owned the wagon was desperately trying to salvage his inventory, which was being pilfered by a band of guttersnipes. Only a day or so ago, Mose would have been one of their number, snatching up errant cabbages and stuffing potatoes in his pockets; but now he had a better way to make a living.

"Take my place, lads!" Mose shouted. "I'll take care of this!"

The greengrocer yelped in fear and hurled a head of cabbage at the redheaded giant striding toward him. Mose merely laughed and popped it in his mouth like a plug of chewing tobacco.

"No need for violence, friend," he assured the trembling merchant. "I mean you no harm." With that, he slipped his shoulders under the wagon tongue and, with a mighty grunt, lifted the wagon—horse and all—over his head like a circus strongman so that a brace of ten Bowery Boys could hurry the pump engine toward the fire.

A block away from their destination, one of the Boys hopped off the engine, carrying an empty pickle barrel under one arm, and ran off in search of the nearest hydrant. Once he found it, he staked the Bowery Boys' claim to the fire by covering the hydrant with the barrel and then sitting atop of it, arms folded and ready for a fight.

By the time the engine arrived, the conflagration was well advanced, with flames licking from the fourth-floor windows. Horseshoe Harry hopped off the engine to check the front of the building as its tenants hurried out of the burning structure with what few possessions they owned. On the lintel of the door was a rectangular pressed-tin fire mark that said CONTINENTAL NEW YORK in raised gold lettering over a black background.

The gang leader grinned and turned to wave to his men. "Start pumpin', boys!" he shouted. "They're insured!"

But just as the Bowery Boys began to hook up their hoses, a second fire engine, this one flying a flayed rabbit skin like a flag, arrived, pulled by a dozen young men. The leader of the Dead Rabbits jumped down off the pumper, pushing back the sleeves of his shirt in anticipation of a brawl.

"Sod off, you lot!" he shouted. "This is our fire!"

"Oh, is it, now?" Horseshoe Harry replied, pushing his stovepipe hat forward like a rooster raising its comb. "Seems rattlin' them worry beads has shook the sense outta ya Paddies. Anyone with one eye in their head can see we got here first, Bourke."

"So that's how it's gonna be, eh, ye Yankee shite?" Black Dog Bourke spat the stub of his cigar onto the sidewalk as he brought up his fists.

The rival gangs set on one another with fists, boots, and whatever else they could get their hands on, swearing and shouting at the top of their lungs. Meanwhile, as they fought for the right to claim tribute from the Continental Insurance Company, the building continued to burn and its hapless residents continued to dash in and out of the smoking tenement, trying to rescue what little they had.

Suddenly there was a great bellow, like that of a gored bull, as Mose jumped into the fray, a wagon tongue clutched in one hand, and a paving stone in the other, inflicting dreadful damage with every swing of his powerful arms.

"Mother Mary, help us!" Black Dog Bourke wailed in despair. "They shaved an ape and set it loose amongst us!"

Shaken by the ferocity of Mose's attack, the Dead Rabbits turned and fled. Upon seeing the rival gang surrender the field, Mose grabbed the brake on the Bowery Boys' engine and began pumping it like a fiend, doing the work of twelve men. Mighty geysers of water erupted from the canvas fire hoses manned by the other gang members, shooting forth with such force and volume that the blaze was extinguished as easily as spitting on a match.

A huzzah went up from the Boys, cheering their newest and bravest member: "All hail Mose! The leader of the gang!"

Upon hearing himself deposed, Horseshoe Harry took off his hat and hurled it to the ground in disgust. The leader of the Bowery Boys was *always* the biggest and strongest of the gang. And they didn't make them any bigger or stronger than Mose.

It wasn't long before stories of Mose's prowess began to spread throughout the city. Some said he could lift a horse-drawn omnibus, passengers and all, above his head and walk it from Chatham Square to Astor Place without breaking a sweat. Others claimed that they'd seen him take a dip in the East River, diving off the Battery and surfacing on the beach at Staten Island three minutes later. There were also rumors he amused himself by rowing out into the bay and blowing ships away from shore by puffing on foot-long cigars, that he wore a beaver hat that measured two feet tall from crown to brim, and replaced his boots every month, not because he had worn them out, but because they had become too small.

Hearing fanciful tales about the Bowery Boys' new leader in a local bar, a reporter for *The National Police Gazette* decided to investigate for himself. Upon arriving at the Green Dragon Saloon, he was astonished to find an eight-foot-tall Mose, now dressed in a custom-tailored suit designed to accommodate his prodigious frame, flexing his biceps like a sideshow strongman while lifting six giggling young ladies—three to each arm, while smoking foot-long cigars and downing growlers of beer the way other men knock back shots of whiskey. Recognizing the story of a lifetime, the reporter hurriedly fished his notepad and pencil from his breast pocket.

"Excuse me, sir. But could you tell me the reason for such

unusual footwear?" the reporter asked, gesturing to the copper plates welded to the bottom of Mose's brogans.

"These be my stompin' boots," the gang leader explained with a grin. "When me and the Boys get in a brawl with the Dead Rabbits or the like, I come leapin' in, kickin' and stampin' like they was roaches under my feet. When I do that, they run off and hide themselves in Paradise Square, like the vermin they are. Ain't that right, lads?"

The other Bowery Boys shouted their agreement in unison, hoisting their drinks to the ceiling in tribute to Mose and his stompin' boots, while the reporter scribbled as fast as he could, visions of headlines swimming in his mind's eye.

Within days, thousands of *National Police Gazette* readers were introduced to "the Colossus of the Bowery," a one hundred percent American-born-and-bred living embodiment of the ancient hero Hercules, complete with an artist's rendering of Mose holding a bull elephant over his head with one hand while puffing on a cigar the size of a walking stick.

One of the many who read of Mose's exploits was none other than P. T. Barnum, the King of the Humbugs, who made a special trip to the Bowery Boys' clubhouse to see if just a tenth of it was true. The showman was so impressed by the young giant he offered to make him the main attraction at his museum on Broadway, right on the spot. But Mose simply shook his head no and said people were welcome to come down to the Bowery and look at him for free, if they dared.

One day, while Mose and the rest of the gang were busy polishing the pump engine in anticipation of an upcoming parade, a messenger boy arrived carrying a letter addressed to "Mose the Fireboy." As Mose had never learned to read, he handed the envelope to his second-in-command.

" 'My Dearest Mr. Humphries,' " Sykesky read aloud. " 'Please allow me to introduce myself: My name is Professor Erasmus Tolliver. I lecture at Columbia College, where I lecture on numerous scientific subjects. . . . ' "

"I know who he is," Mose said excitedly. "He invented the Automatic Man. But why is he writing me?"

Sykesky scanned the neatly penned letter, skipping over the longer words he didn't know. "He says he wants to study you. Take your measurements, look down your gullet—that kind of thing."

Mose thought about it for a long moment, then handed the messenger boy a silver half dime. "Tell Professor Tolliver I'd be honored."

"Yes, sir!" the young boy said, touching his cap in thanks before he scurried off.

Sykesky scowled, perplexed by his friend's decision. "You turn your nose up at Barnum offering you good coin, but you'll let some quack feel the bumps on your head for free?"

"Barnum ain't nothin' but a jumped-up carny barker," Mose replied. "I ain't about t' be gawked at by some flash swells takin' their gals out for a cheap lark, I don't care how many dollars get thrown in my lap. But Professor Tolliver is different," he insisted. "He's a man of *science*. My ma thought very highly of him, and it would have made her proud to know a man of his position was interested in studyin' her boy."

"I don't trust fellows that think too much," his second-in-command said sullenly. "All these fancy inventor fellows and their machines—all it done was force my people off their farm and into the mills."

"This is 1849, not the Dark Ages, Sykesky!" Mose chided. "If everyone thought like you, there wouldn't be gas lamps on every street corner and steamboats on the Hudson!"

"I *still* don't trust 'em," his friend grumbled. "And neither should you."

When Professor Tolliver arrived at the Green Dragon Saloon, he proved to be an older gentleman with outsized muttonchops and bushy eyebrows, dressed in a black frock coat with a high, stiff collar and ascot, and a pair of pince-nez glasses balanced on the bridge of his nose. Upon seeing Mose, he raised his impressive eyebrows in surprise and his glasses dropped from their perch and swung back and forth on the end of a satin ribbon tether.

"I am very pleased to meet you, Mr. Humphries," Professor Tolliver said, once he recovered from his initial surprise. "I have been reading about your exploits in the daily papers with great interest."

"The same here, Professor," Mose replied, his huge hand swallowing the scientist's far smaller one. "It's an honor to meet the inventor of the Automatic Man."

"Ah, yes." Professor Tolliver smiled. "He was what we call 'a prototype.' Granted, all he could do was waltz and play chess, but he was a beginning. A guidepost to grander things, if you will."

"What has me puzzled, sir," Mose admitted, "is why would a man like you be interested in a fellow such as myself?"

"Because I believe that you are the ultimate, living example of the perfect fireman," the Professor explained. "Since you have arrived on the scene, your volunteer fire brigade has broken every record in regards to response time. You've saved five times the number of unfortunate souls than your closest rival, with a fraction of the injuries normally associated with your profession. Mr. Humphries, I firmly believe that if every city in this great land of ours had a firefighter like you, America would be the safest country in the world. A study of your anatomy and physical stamina will help me immensely in realizing this goal."

"Well, if there's one thing that a Bowery Boy is above all else, it's patriotic," Mose said as he took off his coat and tossed it across the back of a chair, revealing a brocade vest adorned with a sterling silver watch fob with links as thick as a man's finger. "If takin' my measurements will help my country, then go ahead and break out the yardstick."

Professor Tolliver proceeded to measure and weigh every aspect of Mose's physical condition, from the circumference of his cranium to the length of his inseam. He also had him run up and down a flight of stairs over and over carrying a piano on his left shoulder and a full barrel of beer under his right arm. Finally, having filled his notepad full of scribbles, he thanked Mose for his contribution to science and the betterment of his fellow man, and hurried back to the safety of his college classroom before the sun set on the Bowery.

Following the visit from Professor Tolliver, the Bowery Boys continued to do as they always had done: drink to excess, traffic in stolen goods, brawl, and put out fires. Given the conditions on the Lower East Side, rarely did a day go by when there wasn't a need for their services. Thanks to Mose's massive strength and extraordinarily long legs, the gang had an iron lock on everything from the Battery to the Flatiron Building, much to the resentment of their rivals.

The Bowery Boys responded to a fire one afternoon, only to find, instead of a burning building, a bonfire made from old crates and mattresses set in the middle of the street. Suddenly every window in the surrounding buildings flew open, revealing a gallery of jeering youths, all wearing the Chichesters' trademark green jerseys. A storm of brickbats rained down on the firefighters' heads, knocking more than one of them senseless. The bombardment ceased as the rival gang came pouring out onto the street—all of them boasting red battle stripes painted across their chests and shirtsleeves, each crimson line indicating a kill in hand-to-hand combat. As they surrounded the badly outnumbered Bowery Boys, beating them with shillelaghs and axe handles, Mose gave a mighty bellow that rattled windows all the way to Park Avenue and grabbed a nearby streetlamp, yanking it free of the sidewalk like a farmer yanking a turnip from the ground. A tongue of flame shot skyward, taller than the surrounding buildings, as the enraged giant used the iron lamp stand like a mace, bashing in the heads of his attackers. Within seconds of suffering Mose's furious counterattack, the Chichesters retreated from the battleground, dragging their injured comrades back to their rookeries.

That was just one of countless run-ins the Bowery Boys had with other street gangs, but thanks to the amazing Mose, they always gave better than they got.

It was some months after Professor Tolliver's visit that Sykesky came hurrying into the Green Dragon Saloon, carrying a broadsheet he'd torn from a wall. "I told you that professor was trouble!" he exclaimed heatedly.

Mose frowned at the poster, which was printed in the florid type usually reserved for circuses and political rallies. "What's it say?" he asked as he eyed the illustration depicting a man in a frock coat and glasses standing on a stage, pointing to a bulky, square-shouldered giant who was wearing a suspiciously familiar stovepipe hat and carrying a fire axe in one hand.

"'The Esteemed Professor Tolliver Will Be Demonstrating His Automatic Fireman to All Interested Parties This Thursday Evening at Campion Hall at Eight O'clock,'" Sykesky read aloud, contempt dripping off every word. "'See the Automatic Fireman Extinguish an Inferno! See the Automatic Fireman Perform a Rescue from a Great Height! Marvel at the Future of Automatonic Firefighting! The Automatic Fireman Is the Greatest Firefighter of This or Any Age! Greater Than Even the Famed Mose the Fireboy, the Colossus of Broome Street! An Educational and Edifying Evening Is Promised to All Who Attend! Admission Is One Half Dime.'"

"It says *what*?" Mose exclaimed, biting his cigar in two as if it were a piece of cheese. He snatched away the offending broadsheet and pushed his stovepipe forward so that the brim dipped down onto his brow. "We'll just see about *that*!"

"P-p-please, sirs!" the usher said, holding up his hands in a feeble attempt to halt the angry wall of young men bearing down on him. "You can't enter the lecture hall without paying admission!"

Mose's response was to grab the usher's shirtfront with a

hand the size of a Virginia ham, lift him off his feet, and deposit him to one side of the door as easily as he would move a potted plant.

The audience turned as one as the doors to the auditorium slammed open and a battalion of angry soaplocks poured across the threshold, yelling at the top of their lungs. Upon seeing the swarm of uncouth, working-class slum dwellers, the gentlemen in attendance shouted in outrage, while several ladies dutifully fell into swoons.

Professor Tolliver stood on the stage, addressing the crowd from behind a lectern. Standing next to him was a massive metallic figure, ten feet in height, that was, at least in its general dimensions, an exact replica of Mose fashioned from copper, right down to his signature beaver hat. However, although it shared the Bowery Boy's height and bulk, its jointed metal right arm ended in a fire axe, while its left arm was made of a corrugated metal tube. It had a face similar to those found on the mannequins at the wax museum, save for its eyes, which resembled the large, circular lenses found in telescopes, but with mechanical irises. A series of canvas hoses were connected to the automaton, with the farthest ends attached to a small pump engine and a leather helmet fitted with strange goggles and a large metal box covered with levers and dials, affixed to a heavy leather vest. Both of these unusual articles of clothing rested atop a table next to the podium.

"Here, now!" the professor said sharply, his pince-nez dropping from his nose. "What is the meaning of this interruption?"

"You know why we're here, Professor!" Mose replied. "When I agreed to let you study me, I didn't know you were plotting to replace me with a damned windup toy!" Upon hearing the collective gasp from the audience, the gang leader turned and tipped his gargantuan hat. "Please pardon my French, my dear ladies."

"Mr. Humphries," Professor Tolliver replied icily, "I most distinctly recall informing you of my intention to make available to every municipality in America its very own Mose the Fireboy. You never asked me *how* I proposed to do so. And as for my Automatic Fireman being a 'windup toy'—I'll have you know he is the latest advance in automatonic technology, combining clockwork, steam power, and hydraulics in one package."

"It's still backstabbin', whatever you call it!" Sykesky growled. "You're tryin' to put us out of business!"

"As well he should!" shouted a man in the audience, his face red with indignation. "Fighting fires is far too important a task to be left to gangs of toughs looking to line their pockets at our expense!"

A couple of the Bowery Boys stepped forward to beat an apology out of the man, but Mose waved them back into line. "Now, that's gratitude!" he spat. "We risk our lives every day: Hogleg Jack got burnt up in the South Street fire just the other day; Scotty Brown had a roof fall on him; Soapy Miller lost a leg when he dropped through the floorboards cartin' an old lady out of a fire on Delancey. All we ask for our efforts is an honorarium from the insurance companies. But you act as if we set the fires ourselves!"

"Sometimes you *do*!" the angry man replied. "And then you steal half of what you 'save' from the fire!"

"Perhaps the Dead Rabbits are low enough to resort to arson to drum up business, but I assure you, my good man, that the Bowery Boys do not stoop to such methods!" Mose said firmly.

"I'm not looking to put you and your compatriots out of work, Mr. Humphries," Professor Tolliver explained. "I'm trying to make your job easier and safer. You yourself just stated how hazardous firefighting can be. My Automatic Fireman can do anything you and your men can do, without fear of losing human life or limb. In this day and age, there is no need to recklessly endanger the welfare of humans if a machine can be made to do the same job."

"That's what they told my grandfather when they brought in the spinning wool-carders," Sykesky said bitterly. "Machines be damned! My boss can best that clockwork man of yours! Ain't that right, Mose?"

Mose nodded, folding his apelike arms across his expansive chest. "I'm willing to put myself up against your Automatic Fireman, but not as part of no two-bit dog-and-pony show. If you want to prove your Automatic Fireman is up to snuff, it has to be during a *real* fire."

"Very well, Mr. Humphries," Professor Tolliver replied with a confident smile. "I accept your challenge."

The clock was striking midnight as the Bowery Boys made their mad dash from their firehouse toward the ruddy glow on the horizon. The fire was on Ludlow Street, and Mose could already tell by the wind blowing fresh from the river that they were going to be in for a bad fight.

Flames raged from the third-floor windows of the five-story tenement, illuminating the neighborhood for some distance. Disoriented parents, who had escaped the blazing inferno, roamed the street in nothing but their nightclothes, desperately seeking other family members, while terrified children called for their mothers amid the turmoil. Despite the lateness of the hour, the street was thronged with hundreds of spectators from the neighboring, closely packed buildings, who were fearful of remaining in their homes should the conflagration spread even farther.

A cheer rang out from the crowd as they saw Mose's strapping silhouette outlined against the flames. As he turned to instruct his men, there came a piercing wail, like that of a kettle on the boil, only a hundred times louder. Mose turned in the direction of the noise and saw what looked like a man wearing an octopus on his head, riding on a pump engine pulled by the Automatic Fireman.

Billows of steam rose from the automaton's stovepipe hat, feeding the whistle attached to its brim. A set of casters were affixed to the Automatic Fireman's feet, allowing the machine to propel itself down the street like a skater gliding across a frozen pond. As the outlandish fire engine came to a halt, Mose realized the man on the engine was none other than Professor Tolliver, and what he had mistaken for an octopus was actually the Medusa-like helmet he'd glimpsed at the lecture hall. He was also wearing the leather vest with the control box mounted on his

chest, its coils tethering creator to invention like a bizarre mario-
nette.

The moment the Automatic Fireman's odd chariot came to a
halt, a couple of young college students leaped down and quickly
set about removing the rigid pipe that connected the automaton
to the pump engine's reservoir and replacing it with a lengthy
canvas hose. Also riding along on Tolliver's pump engine were a
number of journalists, including the reporter from the *National Police Gazette*.

"Are you daft, man?" Mose bellowed.

"*Au contraire*, Mr. Humphries." Professor Tolliver smiled, pushing his goggles up onto his forehead in order to look the Bowery
Boy in the eye. "I have never been saner! This is the perfect setting for our challenge, don't you agree? Tonight we'll see which
makes the better firefighter—man or machine!"

"Just keep your tin soldier out of the way of my men!" Mose
growled, eyeing the welter of canvas hoses that surrounded the
automaton. "And if you got anything else to say to me, say it as an
American, not a Frenchman." Mose exchanged a disgusted look
with Sykesky, but neither man had time to waste on the inventor.
In order to collect their fee from the insurance company, their brigade not only had to put out the fire, but had to rescue as many
personal belongings from the building as possible. "C'mon, lads!
Break out the ladders! Sykesky! Get those brakes pumpin'! I want
this fire out before it brings the roof down!"

"You heard the boss!" Sykesky yelled. "Get to work!"

Mose and his men aimed their hoses at the red tongues of
flame that licked greedily from the windows of the building. The
water from the pump engine made the fire hiss and sizzle like an
ancient dragon, but it was only a drop in the bucket. A smaller
number, dressed in heavy canvas coats with handkerchiefs tied
about their noses and mouth, ran into the burning building to retrieve furniture and other belongings.

Suddenly the crowd behind Mose cried out in horror. He
turned and saw a woman, barefoot and dressed in nothing but a
linen nightgown, standing on a narrow second-story ledge, while

the window behind her belching clouds of black smoke. There came a strange whirring sound, and the Automatic Fireman came striding forward, its casters now retracted into its metal "boots." Professor Tolliver twiddled a knob on the control box mounted on his chest while his students frantically pumped the brakes on the engine, and a set of spikes shot from the Automatic Fireman's feet, anchoring it securely to the pavement, as its metallic legs telescoped upward. Within seconds the automaton was more than twenty feet in the air.

The woman trapped on the ledge, already half mad with fear for her life, screamed as the Automatic Fireman's flexible left arm shot forward and wrapped itself about her waist like an elephant's trunk and yanked her off her feet. It then swiftly plummeted back down toward the ground, causing her to go into a dead faint.

"Behold, gentlemen!" Professor Tolliver told the reporters as his associates extricated the unconscious woman from the Automatic Fireman's snakelike embrace. "Not only is my Automatic Fireman equipped with a built-in ladder and fire axe, but also its own fire hose!" In demonstration, he threw one of the knife switches on the box affixed to the vest, and the Automatic Fireman raised its left arm and unleashed a powerful geyser of water from its palm. "The idea behind the Automatic Fireman is to enable containment and rescue without endangering the lives of volunteers, and to cut down the number of men needed to successfully fight an inferno such as this. By working the pump engine, my students are generating pressure, which not only provides the water used to fight the fire, but also primes the Automatic Fireman's hydraulic system and feeds the boiler in its belly. Clockwork, steam power, and hydraulics alone would not provide enough force to propel my Automatic Fireman, but combined in such a dynamic manner they prove more than enough to handle the situation!"

"What is the purpose of the helmet you're wearing, Professor?" asked the reporter from the *New York Herald*.

"An excellent question, my good man," the inventor said, reaching up to adjust the owlish eyepieces attached to his headgear. "Since the Automatic Fireman is not a thinking being, it must be directed via remote control through special umbilicals attached to the control box I'm wearing. In order to guide my creation, I have devised a means of 'seeing' through its eyes via a series of reflecting speculum mirrors housed within the umbilicals connected to the binoculars mounted to my helmet. The theory is similar to the optics used in certain telescopes—"

Before Professor Tolliver could elaborate any further, there came a deafening crash, followed by a burst of flame from the second story, which sent a shower of broken window glass onto the firefighters on the street below. A second later one of the Bowery Boys staggered out the front door, his coat badly singed and his face covered in soot.

"The third floor collapsed!" he coughed, pulling aside the kerchief covering his mouth. "It took out a good portion of the second floor along with it! Slapsy's dead; he was trying to get a sewing table down the stairs when it happened. Horseshoe Harry's pinned down just inside the foyer!"

Before Mose or his second-in-command could react to the news, the Automatic Fireman calmly strode up the front steps and disappeared into the smoke-filled doorway, trailing its umbilicals behind it like Theseus in the Labyrinth.

The only light in the entrance hall of the tenement came from the fire consuming the upper floors, and the air was thick with choking clouds of smoke and swirling cinders. Fortunately, the Automatic Fireman had no need to breathe. The automaton tilted back its head as if to stare at the huge tangle of burning timber and shattered plaster that now filled the narrow stairwell. There was a faint whirring sound as Professor Tolliver, safely removed from the danger at hand, adjusted the focus on the Automatic Fireman's irises. Hot ash drifted down from above, settling onto the Automatic Fireman's copper skin like a hellish snow.

At the foot of the stairs lay Horseshoe Harry, smeared in soot and blood, pinned under a wooden support beam. The upper part of the timber was covered in crackling flames, and it was merely a matter of moments before the fire would burn its way down to the trapped Bowery Boy. Horseshoe Harry raised his head, hoping to see one of his comrades coming to his rescue. Instead, he found himself staring up at the Automatic Fireman's placid mannequin face as its telescopic eyes whirred and clicked in and out of focus.

"Bugger me," the Bowery Boy groaned.

Just then the Automatic Fireman abruptly raised its axe arm. Horseshoe Harry closed his eyes and turned his face away from what he was certain would be a killing blow. Instead, the automaton's fire-axe hand twirled about on its wrist and buried the pick jutting out of its pole into the burning timber while simultaneously dousing Harry with a flood of water from its left hand. Thus extinguishing the burning timber, it lifted the smoldering chunk of wood free of the trapped firefighter.

Horseshoe Harry tried to get to his feet, only to discover his legs were badly broken. Seeing his distress, the Automatic Fireman snaked his left arm forward, like the rope from a fakir's basket, and wrapped it about Harry's waist and pulled him upright. The Bowery Boy screamed in mortal agony as the automaton's copper skin—superheated by the surrounding inferno—touched his own.

As if triggered by his screams, another fall of flaming debris came crashing down from the floor above, landing on the umbilicals that connected the Automatic Fireman to the outside world. In less than a heartbeat the steam-driven firefighter was not only struck blind, but completely paralyzed as well. Meanwhile, Horseshoe Harry continued to struggle, desperate to escape his would-be savior's burning embrace, but the Automatic Fireman continued to hold tight. However, the automaton's false face finally succumbed to the heat and began to melt, sliding from its metal skull like fried eggs off a greasy skillet.

"Confound it all!" Professor Tolliver said as he wrestled the helmet from his head. "I've lost contact!"

"I've had enough of this foolishness!" Mose snapped,

snatching up his fire axe. "The challenge be damned! I'm going in!" Upon entering the burning tenement, he was guided through the blinding smoke by the sound of Horseshoe Harry's curses and screams, and found the former Bowery Boys leader held fast by Professor Tolliver's Automatic Fireman. Mose grabbed the automaton's arm, in hopes of wresting Horseshoe Harry free of its bear-trap grip, only to recoil from the heat that seared through his heavy canvas gloves as if they were lace. Mose then swung his mighty axe, the head of which was the size of an anvil and sharper than a straight razor, and severed the Automatic Fireman's left arm at its shoulder with a single blow. Live steam, loose gears, and snapped pulleys exploded from the automaton's wound in place of blood and bone, as the Automatic Fireman finally loosed its grip on the hapless Bowery Boy. Horseshoe Harry collapsed onto the floor, unable to stand on his shattered legs. Mose swooped down and, slinging his badly wounded comrade over his back like a sack of potatoes, made his way back through the choking fumes as flaming chunks from the rapidly disintegrating upper stories rained down upon him.

Sykesky and the others rushed forward to take possession of their injured friend as Mose exited the building. However, one look at Horseshoe Harry told them there was no point in rushing him to a doctor. The Bowery Boy was horribly burned down one side of his body, from head to foot, as if he had been held against a red-hot griddle. As Sykesky wrapped Horseshoe Harry in a blanket, the mortally wounded firefighter coughed out a lungful of smoke, gave a final moan, and moved no more.

Professor Tolliver cringed as the giant fireman, his eyes blazing like lamps in his soot-covered face, stomped toward him. "N-now, Mr. Humphries!" he stammered. "Let's not do anything rash. . . ."

Mose leaned down so that he was face-to-face with the older man and poked a sausagelike forefinger at his chest, leaving a sooty smudge on his shirtfront. "The only reason I ain't taking you apart right now like I did your tin soldier is outta respect for my dear, departed ma, you understand? Rest her soul, she admired you as a genius and thought you was a great man. And I thought so, too. But now I see you ain't no better than Barnum, what with your pet reporters trailing after you. Hell, you're *worse* than he is! At least with Barnum, you *know* he's a humbug!"

"What happened to your friend was a horrible, horrible mistake," Professor Tolliver replied. "It was never my intention to harm anyone. You must believe me; my professional life has been dedicated to nothing but improving the lives of my fellow man. . . ."

"Well, Professor, if you *really* wanted to improve us 'fellow men,' you'd create something that would help us *do* our jobs, not *replace* us! If you're so damned smart, why can't you figure out there's some things in life people got no business handin' over to machines?"

Mose halted his harangue of the frightened scientist as a disheveled woman with a blanket wrapped about her shoulder like a shawl screamed and broke free of the crowd of spectators, pointing at the topmost floor of the burning tenement. Standing framed in one of the windows was a tiny girl-child, little more than a baby, still dressed in her nightclothes, looking down at the crowd below as she cried for her mother.

The distraught woman ran to Mose and grabbed his sleeve. "That's my Rosey up there! She got separated from the rest of the family on the stairwell. We thought she was down here on the street, but she must have gotten scared and run back upstairs! *Please,* you have to save my baby!"

The firefighters already on the ladders tried to make a grab for the window ledge, but it was just out of reach. "It's no use, boss!" one of them shouted down. "She's beyond reach!"

"She's beyond *your* reach, but not mine!" Mose replied. With that, he scrambled up the ladder as quick as a monkey, his fire axe clenched between his teeth like a pearl diver's knife. Upon reaching the top of the ladder, he braced himself against the last rung and jumped. The crowd below gasped as Mose grabbed the fifth-story ledge, dangling by one hand as the flames from the floor below licked at the copper soles of his boots.

Using all his strength, Mose pulled himself up onto the window ledge. Looking up, he found himself staring eye-to-eye at little Rosey, who was watching him through the window. The toddler screamed at the sight of the redheaded giant with the sooty face and fled deeper into the three-room apartment.

Mose took his axe and smashed the window, then climbed into the front room, which served as both parlor and dining room for its tenants. The room was beginning to fill with smoke, which rose from the floorboards and slid under the door like invading phantoms. He crossed the room in less than a stride and touched the knob of the door that led to the exterior hallway, only to jerk his hand away. The fire that had consumed the third floor and demolished the second was now busily destroying what remained of the interior of the building, shooting up the central stairwell as if it were a chimney flue. If he wanted to escape the same fate as Horseshoe Harry, he had to find the little girl and get out of there immediately.

He entered the second room in the apartment, which was half the size of the front room, and without windows or ventilation. Although the room was as dark as the bottom of a coal sack, he could make out the silhouette of a metal bedstead pressed against one wall. No doubt this was the parents' bedroom. From his experience fighting fires in the tenements of the Lower East Side, he knew there was yet another room directly ahead of him. As he groped through the inky blackness, there came a loud *clang*, followed by a *slosh* as his boot struck the slop jar at the foot of the bed. A second later he brushed through a pair of curtains stitched together from old flour sacks, which separated the parents' bedroom from the second inner room, where the children slept. It, too, was without light or fresh air, and barely larger than the wardrobe he used to sleep in. Most of the floor space was occupied by a mattress stuffed with rags. From somewhere in the darkness of the room came the whimpering of a frightened child.

"Don't be afraid, Rosey," Mose said gently. "I'm here to take you to your ma."

Upon the mention of her mother, the little girl ceased her

sniffling and came forward from her hiding place, her white nightgown seeming to shimmer like a ghost in the tiny, dungeon-like room. Mose bent down and picked up the child with one hand, holding her as he would a china doll. Cradling Rosey in the crook of one arm, he turned and headed the way he'd come. But as they passed back through the parents' room, they were greeted by a pall of heavy smoke.

Upon stepping into the front room, Mose saw to his horror that the fire had finally breeched the apartment. If he was going to save not only the child but himself as well, he had no choice but to brave the wall of flames that now blocked his way. . . .

"What's keeping them?" Rosey's mother asked no one in partic-ular as she stared up at the smoke and flames billowing from the window Mose had entered minutes before. "Why aren't they back yet?"

"It's real easy to get turned around in the smoke," Sykesky said, trying his best to ease the woman's worry. "But if anyone can save your Rosey, it's Mose."

"What do we do about the ladder?" one of the firefighters asked. "Some of the boys are afraid of getting burnt holding it."

"Tell 'em to keep it in place!" Sykesky snapped. "And I don't care if their hair catches fire! That ladder stays up until Mose comes down it!"

As if on cue, the Bowery Boys' leader suddenly burst from the fifth-story window, wrapped in fire from collar to pants cuff. He struck the forty-foot ladder feet-first, remaining upright the en-tire way as he slid down its length, his coat and pants ablaze, both hands firmly clamped onto his stovepipe hat to keep it from flying off his head. As Mose hit the ground, he was quickly doused with water, which extinguished the flames that wreathed his body. The giant took a step, then two, steam rising from his scorched frame, before collapsing onto the ground. His skin was so black it looked as if he'd been dipped in a pitch bucket, and his shock of bushy red hair had been burned down to his skull.

Sykesky ran forward to tend to his fallen friend, but not even the Colossus of Broome Street could survive such grievous wounds.

"My baby!" the woman wailed, upon seeing the firefighter's empty arms. "Where's my Rosey?"

With his dying breath, Mose reached up and removed the stovepipe hat from his head. And out crawled little Rosey, safe and sound.

They buried Mose in a casket big enough for a grand piano, made of the finest mahogany, with brass fittings that gleamed as bright as a fire engine's. A team of Clydesdales drew his hearse down Delancey, followed by five wagons full of funeral wreaths. The mean streets of New York were filled with mourners, and even the leader of the Dead Rabbits doffed his hat as the King of the Firemen's funeral cortege rolled by. For to be lord of New York City's firefighters, one had to be as strong and brave as they come.

And while they may have built them stronger than Mose, they could never build them braver.

The Clockwork Suit

by G. K. Hayes

**(BASED ON "THE EMPEROR'S NEW CLOTHES"
BY HANS CHRISTIAN ANDERSEN)**

My father's hand tightened on my shoulder as we reached the impressive stone and mortar entrance to Professor Widgerty's home just outside the city. It looked to me like a castle, and I glanced around for the moat as Da took off his cap and smoothed his hair. The hard lines etched into his face by years of work in mines and foundries grew tight and he gave me a quick shake to "buck up," then turned to the massive door.

I had never known Da to be afraid of anything, but I thought I saw his fingers tremble a bit as he raised the heavy brass knocker and sounded it three times against the door. We waited, listening to the echoes die away in the cavernous home, and I did my best to control my own shaking from both worry and wonder.

Da had just reached to knock again when the door opened and a grizzled, white-haired manservant glared down at us and said, "Well?"

Da grabbed the back of my neck to keep me from running. "Beggin' your pardon," he said with a slight bow. "I heard that Professor Widgerty is looking for hardworking young boys." He glanced down at me. "To help with experiments and constructions and such."

The manservant twisted himself around to give me a better look, one eye squinted nearly closed. "What, this little monkey? He's not big enough to piss on."

"Oh, he's a clever lad," Da said. "Good with his hands, he is. Been helping me with repairs since he learned to walk. Knows a spanner from cog, he does, and he can tote twice his weight a full block before setting it down."

The old manservant snorted, then reached out and grabbed my arm, squeezing the muscle against the bone hard enough to make me wince. I felt anger boil up inside me, but Da's hand tightened around my neck, reminding me to behave myself, so I just stared right back at the old codger, daring him to do it again.

His face broke into a grin and he cackled like an escapee from the asylum. "He's got pluck, I'll give him that," he said. He gave me another intense look and then nodded as if in answer to his own unspoken question. "Room and board plus two bits a week if he don't run away."

I looked up and saw my father's face brighten. I could tell what he was thinking: *One less mouth to feed, and two bits a week extra to boot.*

I sucked in a breath. Room and board—that meant I would be living away from Ma and Da, and the rest of the family. I had tried for months to find work at the mills and foundries and other places throughout the city, but because of my size, and my habit of getting into fights, no one would take a chance on me.

But now I had that chance. Unfortunately, it was to be working for Crazy Professor Widget. I had heard stories about the strange contraptions being built at Widget's Workshop. Nobody who actually worked there would verify anything about what they were building. But whispers got out . . . whispers of strange, wonderful things; experiments, contraptions of all sorts; copper and brass constructions; glass tubes and panels; gears and springs; boilers . . . and steam, all the stories talked about the constant hiss of steam.

The thought of having to live and work here made my stomach flutter, not from fear, but from excitement.

"I'll just have a word with the lad, if that's all right?"

The manservant nodded once.

Da pulled me away a few steps and turned his back to the house so that only I could hear what he said. He leaned down and I could smell his tobacco and his aftershave and other smells that was "Da." "This is your last chance, Donny," he said through clenched teeth. "How someone as small as you can get into so many fights I'll never understand."

"It's not my fault," I pleaded for the hundredth time, though I knew it would do no good. Da was a big man and had been a big boy. He'd been already six feet tall at fourteen; nobody had ever picked on him. He could never understand why I had to fight even the slightest insult or push, why I had to prove myself every hour of every day against the bigger boys. He could never understand what it was like to be small.

"Well, you better do something to change your attitude, 'cause your ma and me can't keep you anymore. Got yourself kicked out of school, so now you have to work like the rest of us. You get kicked out of here . . . and you're on your own." His face seemed to soften, his eyes growing damp, and then he was all business again. "You hear me, boy?"

He pulled me roughly back to the doorway where the manservant was waiting. He grabbed me by the scruff of my neck and said, "You do the professor right, you hear?"

I could only nod. A painful lump in my throat kept me from speaking.

Da gave me a slight push toward the door and asked in a hard voice, "When does he get paid?"

"Every Saturday, five o'clock," the manservant said, taking a step back and holding the door wide.

My father nodded again, then looked down at me. "I'll be back Saturday to collect your wages." He kept his hard gaze on me until something got into his eye and he had to blink and turn away. "Make us proud, lad," he said in a thick voice. He pulled on his cap as he stepped down the walkway. "Your mother," he said over his shoulder, "will miss you."

I watched him heading off toward town as if he had somewhere to be. He didn't look back.

Finally the manservant said, "Well, come on, get yourself in here, then. We've got things to do." I wiped at my eyes and sniffed once as I looked over my shoulder toward the retreating figure of my father, then stepped into my new life.

"All right, then," the manservant said as he closed the door, "come along. I'm Jarvis. No mister, just Jarvis. I run the house and I don't like little urchins tramping dirt and metal filings all over my clean floors, so wipe your feet. The others have been out in the workshop since sunup."

I followed him through the big house, which, although cluttered with stacks of books and papers, rolls of large charts and drawings, and clockwork contraptions of all sorts, was nonetheless clean and polished and smelled of lemon oil.

We walked out into a small garden and down a winding path until I heard the sounds of clanking metal and the hiss of steam.

As we came around the end of a tall hedge, I saw the workshop. It was a building the size of a small warehouse, with windows all along the sides and skylights in the roof. The clamor of noise grew as we approached, then burst out upon us like a wave as Jarvis opened the door. The morning sunlight slanting in through the windows cut through clouds of steam and glinted off the polished brass and copper piled and stacked around the shop. A handful of boys, all older and bigger than me, were busy banging and clanging away at worktables, forges, bellows, boilers, presses, and cutters. The place smelled of sweat, hot metal, and steam. It was wonderful.

The manservant led me over to an older boy who looked to be around fourteen working with some copper pipe. "Corbin!" the manservant yelled above the racket. The boy looked up, then scowled when he saw me. He put down the pipe and tools, wiped his hands, and came over and frowned down at me. He had a face like a bulldog and flaming red hair.

Jarvis leaned over so Corbin could hear him better and said, "Here's the new boy Professor's been wanting. Try to keep him alive and out of trouble until lunch."

Corbin nodded. The old manservant watched me as I stared around wide-eyed at all the wonderful machines. Suddenly he burst out laughing again, then turned and headed back toward the house.

Corbin crossed his arms and gave me an appraising, disgusted look and then yelled, "Name?"

"Donny," I said through cupped hands.

He rolled his eyes, then waved me over to the worktable. A copper pipe and a flair tool lay on the table. "You know what this is?" he asked, pointing at the tool with his thumb. The incessant clamor and banging made it hard to concentrate. I nodded. "You know how to use it?" I nodded again. He stepped back and said, "Show me."

I had been helping my father with his work since I could walk. We had repaired all sorts of plumbing and small steam engines and such, so I knew how to flare out the end of a copper pipe.

The worktable was so high I had to pull a wooden crate over to stand on. Once up to a more comfortable level, I grabbed the flaring tool and clamped the bar around the pipe, adjusted the yoke, and started turning the handle on the feed screw until the pipe had a nice smooth flare at the end. When I finished, I showed it to Corbin.

He gave a grudging nod, then pointed to a box of arm-length pipes on the floor. "Get started on these. Only one end for each. We'll bend and cut them to length later." He smacked me on the arm with the back of his hand and said, "Don't mess this up." Then without another word, he sauntered off to another part of the shop.

I had been around boys like Corbin most of my life. To him I was nothing. He would talk to me only if he had to, give me only the barest of instructions, hoping I would mess up, and if he felt he needed to smack me around, he would. So I started right to work with no lollygagging or complaining. I did take a look over my shoulder whenever I got a chance, though. Even with all the noise and steam, the shop did not feel as oppressive as some of the big factories I had been in. The boys and men were not dancing or playing around, but neither did they look sad or overworked. Just guys doing a job.

About an hour later, Corbin came back to check my work. He picked up a few pipes and looked them over, then without a word, headed off toward the other end of the shop.

A moment later he was back and dropped an armload of pipe into the box and walked away. "Pleasant fellow," I said, under the cover of sound, then began talking to myself. "Nice job, Donny. Here's some more when you're ready. I'll smack you around later when I have the time."

All the noise and chaos around me seemed to fade away as I started on the rest of the pipes and became engrossed in the task. Whenever I got the chance, I would sneak a glance at the other boys around the shop. Some were working on a big metal press forming sheets of metal. Others would take the metal pieces and polish them on another machine. Another group were bending pipes of all sizes. And in the center of the shop, a huge boiler roared and hissed steam.

Everyone was busy doing something; they weren't rushing, but nobody ever just stood around. I was in my own little world of flaring tools and copper pipe when a steam whistle screamed loud enough to make me jump. The banging and clatter began to taper off as everyone stopped what they were doing and started heading for the door.

I saw Corbin heading my way, but I knew better than to stop working before he told me to. He bumped me with his shoulder hard enough to almost knock me down, then yelled over his shoulder, "Lunchtime . . . Dummy," and laughed.

I sighed. I was sure he thought the change from "Donny" to "Dummy" was something new and creative, but I had been called the same and worse by bullies all my life. It still hurt, but not nearly as much as it used to.

We walked around back to a small pavilion beneath the shade of a giant oak where a rough plank table was piled high with various sandwiches and fruit. A bucket of cold water and a dipper stood at each end. Soon everyone was sitting or lying in the shade, eating and relaxing, talking quietly.

A tired-looking boy with straight dark hair and a splatter of freckles across his nose and cheeks came over to me. "You're the new guy, huh?"

"Yeah," I said around a mouthful of food, "I'm Donny."

"Russell," he said with a nod. "I guess you met Corbin, then?"

"Yeah."

"He give you a name yet?"

At first I didn't know what he was talking about, but then I got it. "Dummy," I said with an embarrassed smile.

"Aw, too bad," he said, shaking his head. Then he batted his eyelashes and made his own sickly sweet smile and said, "I'm Bustle. Funny guy, that Corbin, huh?"

"Yeah," I said with a snort. "He's a regular card."

Russell nodded in agreement, then gave me a warning look. "Hey, uh, don't cross him, though, okay?"

I nodded and looked down at my sandwich, knowing exactly what he meant. "He looks like he could be mean."

"Mean is not the word. Cruel bastard, more like. If the professor yells at him 'cause of you, then you're shit. He put a kid in hospital last week. Broke his arm."

My face must have shown my distress because Russell nodded and said, "Yeah. . . ."

Russell chewed on a big bite of his sandwich, pushing it around in his mouth so he could talk. "Now, Algert," he said, jerking his head toward the table where the others sat, "big guy with the bald head . . ."

"Muttonchops?" I said, raising myself up to look.

"Yeah, he's okay. Talks gruff but he'll treat you right. Go to him if you hurt yourself or anything. He's like the professor's partner or something. Professor makes the drawings, Algert builds it."

"Thanks," I said.

Russell nodded again as he took another bite. "We get fed pretty good here," he said with his mouth full. "Thirty minutes for lunch, unless the professor gets crazy about something." Russell stopped suddenly and looked around. "And, uh, Donny?" he whispered.

"Yeah?" I said, leaning in.

"Don't let the professor fool you. He talks all cultured and proper, but he can be as mean as Corbin when he wants to." He looked over his shoulder again and then said in a more normal tone, "You probably should eat up—he'll want to talk to you before we start back."

I chewed another bite of my sandwich. It was ham and cheese with leaf lettuce, and it was really good, but all the stuff Russell had told me about took the taste right out of my mouth. And now I was going to have a private meeting with the professor. Suddenly I wasn't hungry.

I swallowed my last bite of my sandwich and asked, "What's he want to talk to me about?"

"Oh, probably just basic stuff about keeping shop secrets—he's real particular about keeping secrets; we can't talk about nothing to nobody. He's got something special planned for you, I think. He's been waiting for someone your size for weeks."

My size? I thought. *Why would he need someone as small as me? What kind of special job would he need me for?*

Russell finished his sandwich, stood up, dusted his hands on his pants, and said, "I'd take you to see the professor, but, uh"—he gave me a worried look—"it's Corbin's job and he might not like it." He stuck out his hand and smiled weakly as we shook. "Guess I'll see you after work. I'll help you get settled in."

He wandered off just as Corbin headed over to me, a scowl on his face. "Come on, *Dummy*," he said. "Professor wants you."

Corbin led me back into the workshop to a separate room off to the side. It, too, had windows all around so that the professor could keep an eye on the workshop, though many of them were covered by drawings and diagrams. Corbin knocked on the door and waited until he heard the professor yell, "Come in," in a cheery voice.

"Professor?" Corbin said as we stepped inside. His relaxed, casual manner changed and he stood straighter with his chest out. But he seemed to be a little nervous, too. "This is Dumm—uh, Donny. Just started this morning. I put him on flaring copper pipes."

A stout fellow with a full gray beard sat at a wide desk cluttered with papers. He took off his glasses and gave me a hard look, then asked, "How did he do?"

"Not too bad, I guess." Corbin looked at me sideways, daring me to contradict him. "But I'll learn him right."

"*Teach*, Corbin. Teach, not *learn*," the professor said, speaking each word in a clear, precise manner. Corbin mumbled something and the professor said, "Yes, yes, thank you. You may leave."

Corbin nodded, then gave me a final, dangerous look as he closed the door.

"Well, Donny," the professor said with a warm smile, "you seem to have impressed Corbin, and he is not easily impressed, I can tell you. He's my foreman for all the boys here at the shop, second only to Algert as my most trusted employee."

The professor sounded just like some of the teachers I'd had, the way his voice boomed out so clear. It made me feel as if I were in school again. I didn't know if I should say anything or sit down or keep standing or what. Da always told me that the best thing a man could do on any new job was to work hard and keep his mouth shut until asked, so that's what I did.

"Tell me," the professor said finally, "how is it that you know how to flair the end of a copper pipe?"

"M-my da taught me."

"And is your da a handy fellow?"

"Ye-yes, sir. He can fix almost anything when he's got the tools."

"Hmm, good. And you've been helping him since you were a wee tyke, I take it?" I nodded. "Have you worked on boilers and steam engines, clockwork gears, and such?"

"Some," I said, my mind racing ahead, trying to figure out where he was going, "but nothing like what's out in the shop. I never—" I struggled to find the words to describe the wonderful things I had only glimpsed. "I've never seen such beautiful machines," I said, and instantly became embarrassed.

The professor smiled. "Yes, they are quite beautiful, aren't they? You would be surprised to find that some people think that they are ugly, noisome contraptions." He walked around his desk, his face practically beaming. "Ah, but each to his own." He reached out to me and said, "Let me see your hands."

I thought he was looking to see if I had washed up before lunch. I hadn't, and once again I got embarrassed. Ma would whack me a good one if it ever got back to her. But the dirt and copper didn't seem to bother him. "Yes, yes, fine delicate fingers, but strong, too, I'll wager."

He pointed at me with the first two fingers of each hand and said, "Here, squeeze them as hard as you can." His request made me feel strange, and I hesitated.

"Go on, squeeze."

Finally I reached out and took his fingers and was surprised to find that they were not at all soft and flabby as I had thought a professor's hands would be. I had thought that he spent his days writing and drawing all his machines, but his hands were rough and calloused and strong just like my da's.

"Squeeze hard, Donny, and twist. See if you can rip them off!"

I had always heard that the professor was a little crazy, but my da told me to do what I was told, so I started twisting and squeezing as hard as I could. After just a moment the professor yelled, "Ow!" He grabbed his own fingers and rubbed. "You nearly broke them!"

I stepped back, horrified, afraid that I had done something wrong, but the professor was chuckling with glee. He walked around his desk to his chair and sat down. "I told Jarvis to find me a strong little lad and he did. Yes, I think you will do perfectly on the inside."

"Inside?" I asked.

"Something special we've been working on. But first, we'll need to get you accustomed to our routine, get you settled in, learn more about your abilities. I'll get Corbin to assign you progressively more challenging tasks each day, and then perhaps after a week, you'll be ready. But for now, I'm afraid, you'll just be flaring pipe."

He looked down at the drawing on his desk and began to trace his finger along a line. "If you have any questions or concerns," he said without looking up, "don't hesitate to express them to Corbin. I know he can be tough at times, but I need someone tough to keep you rambunctious boys in line."

I nodded, a little worried about having Corbin looking over my shoulder, but excited at the possibilities of working on some of the shining machines.

"Just one more thing, Donny." The professor looked up and leaned toward me. "Can you keep a secret?"

I nodded. I had kept secrets all my life.

"Good. You see," he said in a loud whisper, "we have several competitors in our business. Unscrupulous men who will stop at nothing to find out our secrets. I suspect they have tried to infiltrate our little workshop with their spies. It is of utmost importance that you talk to no one, not even your own family, about our projects here. Everything—and I mean everything—that goes on in this shop is to remain our little secret, do you understand?"

I nodded, my mouth open and my eyes wide.

"If you dare"—his voice took on a dark, angry edge— "to speak about anything that we do or say here . . . well, I'm afraid things would go very bad for you. Do you understand my meaning?"

From the look in his eye, I could only imagine that a beating from Corbin would be mild compared to what the professor would do.

"If anyone asks you about your job, tell them that you . . . that you just flair pipes." He gave a small laugh and was suddenly all smiles again.

I nodded, my imagination running in every direction at once.

"Good," the professor said, holding out his hand. "Then welcome aboard, Donny."

In a daze, I managed to make it back to my workstation and finished out the day much as I had begun, flaring enough pipe to supply dozens of small engines. My mind, though, kept jumping from one thought to the next, trying to imagine what special project the professor needed someone small like me for.

When the steam whistle blew later that afternoon, I was both surprised and thankful. My hands were smudged dark with copper residue and felt swollen and bruised from all the twisting and turning I had done. A slap on my back made me jump and I turned to find Russell grinning at me, his tired face looking bright for once. "Well, you made it through your first day. How do you feel?"

"Tired and hungry," I said.

He pinched his nose. "Whew! And stinky, too." He laughed and jerked his head toward the house. "Come on, let's get cleaned up. I'll show you where we bunk."

The next day Corbin moved me over to where they were building some kind of transaxle unit for a heavy cranelike apparatus. The axle itself probably weighed more than a ton, and I could only guess at how much the completed crane would weigh. I had to pack grease into the bearings and joints and then make sure everything was sealed up tight.

As usual, Corbin took every opportunity to push me or smack me in the head and call me Dummy. I began to get the feeling that he not only liked beating on me and the other boys, but actually wanted one of us to get angry and try to hit him so he could really wallop us good. He seemed to be always on edge, and was quick to blame us for anything the professor didn't like.

Each day I was moved to another section where I would learn about different parts and tools and assembly techniques until I became proficient. Finally, after two weeks, I started working at the steam station. I learned how to stoke the boiler and watch the gauges climb up toward the red as the pressure rose. I learned that each valve and lever controlled and channeled the live steam to different tools and machines around the shop. All the boys had to work the boiler on a rotating basis, but I was the youngest and the smallest, and it made me very nervous.

Corbin showed me how each valve and lever had to be set for the various configurations required for different machines, always with his customary look of annoyance.

"And this gauge is the most important," he yelled over the noise. "If it moves into the red, you gotta turn this valve real quicklike. The steam'll vent out the side there. Anybody standing in the way will get boiled alive. You got it?"

I knew better than to ask Corbin, but I just had to know. "What happens if I don't open the valve?"

He grabbed me by the front of my shirt and got in my face so close I could smell his bad breath. "We all die, Dummy."

I swallowed hard. Not because I was afraid of him, but because I didn't want to blow up the shop, so I nodded and looked scared. Corbin gave me a satisfied, confident smile, then smirked and walked away.

I didn't like working the steam station, and neither did anyone else. I had to wear goggles and heavy leather gloves and a leather coat that was ten sizes too big for me. The shop was already hot enough without all the extra leather, but standing so close to the boiler with waves of heat melting off it made things almost unbearable.

Every so often Algert would holler or send a boy over to tell me to open or close a valve for a particular workstation. I would adjust the valve and watch the gauges, keeping an extra-sharp eye on the main pressure. As the professor told me, "Steam is a living thing, capricious and unforgiving. If you make even a small mistake, she will burn you . . . or kill you."

The next day, instead of shifting me to another workstation, Corbin hit me in the head and told me to go in to see the professor. I knocked and opened the door, not knowing what to expect.

"There you are," he said, looking up from the drawings on his desk. "Come in and close the door.

"I've been getting good reports on you from Corbin and

Algert. You seem to learn things quickly and pay close attention to detail. That's exactly the kind of lad I need for my special project."

He stood up and walked around to a corkboard filled with all kinds of diagrams, plans, and technical drawings. "How much do you know about steam engines and machines?"

"I used to help my da when he worked on the engine at the mine. He taught me as much as he could about the repairs."

"Good, good. That's a start, a very practical, hands-on education. As for myself, I was a professor for many years at university until I . . . um . . . left because of small-minded thinking from the dean. There I learned about steam from more of a theoretical standpoint. I had very little practical knowledge until I started this workshop.

"You see these charts here?" He pointed to several charts hanging on the board and along the walls, and seemed to swell with pride. "I created these at university. This one"—he walked over and smoothed his hand down the front—"is an enthalpy-entropy chart that I developed . . . along with Richard Mollier, one of my most promising students. It plots the total heat against entropy of a thermodynamic system. Invaluable in any research involving steam.

"But I must tell you, I have learned far more about steam since my retirement than in all my years at university, thanks to my shop. Here I can put theory to practice, and invite knowledgeable persons who have developed their own mechanized inventions.

"Such luminaries as Richard Trevithick, the leading expert on high-pressure steam engines, visited with us for almost a week. We had many interesting conversations, I must say. And Oliver Evans, who was kind enough to explain in detail his Oruktor Amphibolos, a marvelous digging machine, also was our guest. I only wish I could have gotten James Watt here before he died; even though his work is a bit old-fashioned now, I'm sure he would have had some fascinating insights."

The professor clapped me on the back in a friendly manner. "And now you, my boy . . . you are about to embark on an amazing journey . . . a journey into the very Future of Steam Power!"

He pulled up a chair so that he could sit and stare directly into my eyes. His voice became more somber as he said, "But before we continue with your education, I must elicit a solemn promise that you will not go blabbing to others what you learn here. There are many things at the shop that must, for the time being, remain secret. One day," he said, raising a finger, "yes, one day, we will tell the world and show all, but in order to, ah, obtain funding for my experiments we must keep things under wraps, as they say."

The professor was in what we called "Lecture Mode," so I could only nod to show I was listening.

"And I must tell you," he continued, "there are many unsavory characters who would pay goodly sums to find out about our projects before they are finished. You must guard yourself, young man, *guard* yourself against them. Is that understood?"

"Yes, sir," I said, realizing that it was time for me to speak. The professor had become more and more obsessed with secrecy over the past week; he reminded us each and every morning before we started work.

"Good, good. Now, on to the reason you are here. I have been working on reducing the size and weight of steam engines. The ones we use here at the shop are quite powerful, but also quite large. I'm sure you have heard or perhaps seen steam wagons moving around the city. Up until this point they have of necessity had enormous boilers, compression chambers, drive mechanisms, and heavy iron cogs and wheels. But what if we could design and build a steam engine that was no larger than, say, a traveling trunk? A completely self-contained power source that could drive gears and wheels and levers and all sorts of mechanical devices. What do you think we could do with such a device?"

Ideas began to swirl around in my head: pumps, not just for mines, but for businesses and homes; machines to lift heavy objects; conveyances of all kinds, big and small, some with wheels and some with legs. I had to shake my head just to stop the pictures.

"Yes, my boy, it is quite exhilarating. Now you know why I often appear so distracted! I have so many ideas and projects that I'm afraid I shall die before I can bring them all to life.

"But there is one project, a very special project, that exceeds all others. One that will bring us not only fame, but also much-needed cash to fund all of my other projects."

The professor was in his mode and running strong. He had my absolute attention.

"What if you could build *a suit of armor* . . . powered by steam?"

The professor smiled at my reaction. "Yes, just imagine . . . full protection from all attacks, and yet able to lift great weights and move around without excessive effort. That was one of the problems with the suits of armor of old. They were heavy. A knight's armor with chain mail and padding could weigh as much as ninety pounds and took great strength to move about.

"How much, would you think, a sufficiently thick protective suit of armor for today's soldier would weigh?"

I began to figure in my head. "A hundred . . . two hundred pounds?"

"A good guess, but remember, we will need joints and levers, cogs and wheels, springs and gears and pistons, too."

"Three hundred pounds?"

"Now, what about the steam engine itself?"

I thought of the huge steam engine in the shop; there was no way anyone could carry that around. "The soldier would need to be tethered to a cart or wagon just to carry everything," I said.

"Exactly . . . unless the engine and boiler assembly was small and self-contained!"

"Have you," I said, leaning forward, "have you built one?"

"Yes!" The professor seemed delighted that I had asked the right question. "But we are still having a few problems. We are in the testing stage for the Steam Chamber, and although everything hinges on its ultimate design success, we still have gone ahead with building the suit of armor itself. At present, we are in the process of constructing the driving mechanism, and that is where you come in, my boy. In order to keep the size and weight down to a manageable limit, I have designed some very small and somewhat delicate pieces. So far we have been able to get most of the apparatus to fit together, but some of the attaching screws and bolts are, of necessity, inside the suit itself and require fingers and arms much smaller than my own. Even Corbin is too large for some of this very precise work."

So that was it! That was why the professor had wanted a small boy like me.

"So now you see why I've had you on such a whirlwind tour of our workstations; you had to get practical experience in every-thing necessary to put together our suit of armor."

The professor laid a finger alongside his nose and said, "Come along, and remember what I said about keeping secrets."

He led me out of his office and though the maze of worksta-tions and piles of materials to a special room off to the side. I had watched Algert and the professor and Corbin going in and out of this room but had assumed it to be for storage only. When we en-tered, I saw in the very center of the room, illuminated from the skylight above, a shining assortment of metal panels, plates, gears, and tubes arranged into a manlike shape. If the professor had not already explained the purpose of this construction, I would have thought he had built a mechanical man.

"As you can see," the professor said, "we have most of our Clockwork Suit of Armor assembled, the bigger pieces, at least. All the joints work properly when articulated by hand, but we are having trouble getting some of the pistons and various clockwork mechanisms attached. Would you like to take a look?"

"Ye-yes, sir." I was practically drooling.

I walked over to the apparatus and started looking in and around each arm, leg, and joint.

"Here," the professor said, handing me a glass-and-brass tube with a thick cable coming out of one end. "Have you ever seen one of these?" I shook my head, my mouth open in wonder. "It's a Ruhmkorff lamp, a portable electric lamp powered by an induction coil." He switched it on, and a golden light shone out from inside the tube. "Light without heat," he said. "We use it inside the suit to help see into the more hidden parts."

I took the lamp and guided it up, in, and around the insides of the suit. I could see where several holes were awaiting screws or bolts, or perhaps pipes or cables. It was all very complex, and I could see where someone bigger than me would have a hard time just getting to everything inside. I experimented by guiding my hand snakelike in and around struts and braces, trying to imagine holding a small wrench. It wouldn't be easy, but I thought I could do it.

I handed the Ruhmkorff lamp back to the professor and he switched it off.

"Well, what do you think, my boy?"

"It's . . . wow!" I said, still starting at the lamp. "The . . . the suit of armor, I mean. And the lamp, too."

The professor smiled. "Good to hear it. You start work tomorrow morning."

Bright and early the next day, I began to help with the Clockwork Suit. I had to climb in and around the core, connecting every part that was either hard to get to or just plain impossible for someone bigger. I learned the purpose and function of each piece and how it was attached. I had to become a contortionist in order to get to some of the fittings and then spend sometimes an hour moving the wrench a small fraction at a time until I had the connection tight. It was slow, difficult work, but I loved it . . . except when Corbin was standing over me.

For some reason, everything I did seemed to get on his nerves. Nothing was good enough. "Hurry up, Dummy," he said, kicking the hip strut I was lying in. "We got three more pieces to fit and I can't do nothing till you finish. How long does it take to tighten a damn bolt?"

I was upside down and twisted around like a snake with my arm shoved up as far as I could reach, trying to get enough leverage to push the wrench one more time. "I'm almost done," I said. "Don't want . . . this . . . coming loose."

We had been having trouble with some of the screws and

bolts and compression fittings. Even when I was sure that they were tightened securely, the next day, Algert or the professor would find that some of them had somehow worked loose again. Corbin, of course, kept blaming me for it, saying I wasn't strong enough, or lazy, or stupid.

But after a few days of checking and double-checking every bolt, I noticed that only the ones that were accessible to bigger boys and men were getting loose; the ones that only I could reach stayed tight.

I had just about decided to talk to the professor about it when he came into the special project room and said with a grand smile, "We finally have our appointment with the emperor. We have to get the suit completely operational within three weeks."

The emperor! So that's who the Clockwork Suit was for. I couldn't believe I was working on something intended for the emperor.

"Three weeks!" Algert yelled. He had been working long hours the past few weeks, trying to get everything ready. "But we still haven't had a successful test of the Steam Chamber."

"Not to worry," the professor said. "I'm sure that we are on the verge of great success."

The Steam Chamber was one of the professor's new inventions. It was a specially designed boiler that burned oil to heat the steam into a highly compressed state. It only needed a small amount of oil to keep the burner hot. And most of the steam that drove the power assembly was recycled with each compression.

Unfortunately, it had a habit of exploding before reaching the required degree of pressure.

I found out that we also had another problem. Schneider, another inventor with a large workshop, and the professor's biggest competitor, had wormed his way into the good graces of the emperor and was working on his own suit of armor. But according to the professor, his suit design was greatly inferior, and relied more on magic tricks than science. "Schneider is nothing more than a talented con man," he told me several times, "and will stop at nothing to secure the large advance offered by the emperor."

So as the days passed and the time of our appointment grew near, the tension in the shop became as thick as vented steam. Corbin pushed and punched me two or three times a day. Once, I came close to hitting him over the head with a wrench I was holding, but instead, I thought of what Da would say, and how disappointed he'd be, so I just chewed my lower lip and held my anger. The other boys did their best to avoid talking to Corbin and stayed out of his way, but I was stuck in the special room working on the Clockwork Suit and had to take whatever he dished out.

More and more the professor had been staying in his office going over and over his figures, trying to work out the problems with his designs, coming out only when Algert had set up a test of the Steam Chamber.

One night after work, Russell and I were up in our attic room when he asked, "How are you holding up working under Corbin's boot?"

"He's really pushing me hard," I said, shaking my head. "Someday I'm either going to hit him with a wrench or just quit."

"Why don't you?"

"Quit?" I said raising my eyebrows. "Nah," I said with a heavy sigh. "Ma and Da are depending on me."

"Too bad," Russell said as he climbed into bed. "Maybe the next explosion will take care of him for us."

"Yeah," I said hopefully. "But he's probably too mean. The whole place could go up and Corbin would still be standing there yelling, 'Dummy! I told you to watch that gauge!'"

"Or, 'Bussell! Where'd you put my spanner!'" Russell laughed.

The last week before our appointment, and still without a successful test of the Steam Chamber, the professor decided to go with a less powerful chamber, one that didn't have to hold as much pressure. Although the suit would function, it would not be as strong, or operate as long. "But," as the professor said, "it has the advantage of not exploding."

We checked and rechecked all of the cables and steam pipes attached to the clockwork drive unit, and made sure all the joints worked properly. The professor wanted one last trial before we secured the final plates of armor. He wanted to make sure that Algert could fit inside and walk around without falling down.

We put the suit on a hand truck and pushed it out onto the main floor. We cleared an area of ten or twelve feet so that Algert could move around. He and the professor filled the small boiler on the back of the suit and lit the burner, then waited for the steam chamber to charge.

When all the dials held steady, and nothing blew up, Algert squeezed himself inside the suit. Russell and I closed the breastplate, and the professor pulled down the helmet and visor.

Even without all the armor plates Algert looked dangerous and spectacular.

The suit really was ingenious; instead of using buttons and levers to operate the various pistons and gears, the professor had pressure plates placed at strategic spots within the armor that corresponded to Algert's knees, feet, forearms, and more.

Once Algert was all strapped in, he pushed the control to ACTIVE and steam began to hiss out as gears started to whirr and clank. And then the suit began to *move*. Algert's first step was tentative and awkward, but soon he was walking in a more natural gait. He moved around slowly, picking up various pipes and pieces of equipment, testing his strength, coordination, and balance. When he first tried to pick up something heavy, an axle assembly, he nearly fell over.

"Whoa!" he yelled, his voice muffled by the visor. "The suit itself is very strong. I can easily lift this axle"—he tried it again—"but I've got to watch the weight distribution. It's very easy to become overbalanced."

The professor quickly made some notes, then said, "Anything else?"

"I think it could use some more padding," Algert said, "particularly around the elbows and wrists."

Algert moved around for two or three minutes, and then the Steam Chamber began to run out of steam.

"That's to be expected," the professor said. "Once we perfect our stronger chamber, we'll be able to go for a much longer time."

"How much longer, Professor?" I asked.

"Oh . . . I should think . . . at least ten to fifteen minutes."

I blinked in confusion; that didn't seem like very long at all. I couldn't imagine any soldier wanting to wear the suit if it only worked for fifteen minutes. It just didn't seem practical to me. "That's not very long," I said without thinking.

"Long enough, my boy," the professor said. "Long enough to impress the emperor and get that fat commission. And that's all that counts. We'll be in the money for the rest of our lives."

Suddenly I heard a snapping sound followed by a clank, and the suit began to list to one side. I could see Algert trying to straighten up, but then we heard another *bink* and a *clank* followed by a stream of strong profanity from Algert. "Damn, damn, and bloody damn! I'm froze up. Can't move a foot."

"Hang on, hang on," the professor yelled, "we're coming."

We got Algert out of the suit and as I looked inside I saw that several nuts had slipped off the bolts attaching the hip braces and had sprung out, letting the cog wheels fall away from the clockwork drive.

"It's Dummy's fault," Corbin said quickly, pointing at me.

Everyone turned to look at him, then at me.

"He's too weak to tighten the nuts properly. I told you he was too small, Professor."

I shook my head in protest. "No, Professor. I checked and double-checked every nut and bolt."

"Obviously, you did not!" he said, glowering at me. Then he turned to Corbin and said, "He's your responsibility, Corbin. If this happens again, you're both out on your ears!"

Corbin looked cowed for a moment, and then he turned his hateful glare onto me. My heart dropped down into my stomach. I knew I would get a beating later.

That evening, after work, Corbin grabbed me by the back of my shirt as I was trying to get out of the workshop. "Not so fast, Dummy."

I looked around for help and saw Russell standing to the side.

Corbin must have seen the pleading in my eyes because he turned to Russell and said, "Got something to say, Bustle?"

Russell gave me a helpless look, then lowered his eyes and shook his head.

"Then get up to dinner, unless you want some of what I'm going to give Dummy."

I watched Russell trudge up the walkway toward the main house knowing he felt almost as bad as I did. Once he was out of sight, Corbin shook me hard and said, "Now, you little turd, the professor's none too happy 'cause of you!"

"I tightened all of my special bolts," I said in protest. "But those on the hip strut . . . everybody's supposed to tighten those."

Corbin's eyes grew wide and he cuffed me once hard. "Shut up! You keep your mouth shut. Don't nobody want to hear anything you got to say. You got this coming and you know it." He hit me again . . . then again. Then punched me in the stomach so hard it knocked the wind out of me. I rolled into a ball, making a strange honking sound, trying to catch my breath.

"The next time you cause the professor to even look at me hard, I'll beat you so you can't move. Got that?"

Then he walked away without another word.

I lay there, gasping for air, until Russell found me. "Hey, you okay? Come on, let's stand up so we can take a better look."

He helped me to my feet and brushed the dirt off. "There, not so bad, no broken bones, no missing teeth. Corbin must like you; he took it easy on you for some reason."

"Easy?" I croaked.

"Yeah, he nearly killed one lad about six months back, and broke that other guy's arm. I think they tried to fight back. It was good that you just took it." Russell looked me over more carefully. "All you got were some bruises."

"Why does the professor let him do it?" I asked.

"Corbin keeps us in line, makes us work, gets things done, I guess." He shrugged. "Remember, I told you that the professor wasn't much better than Corbin. He sounds all nice and cultured, but he has a mean streak, too. The only thing he really cares about is getting that commission." Russell shook his head. Then he patted me on the back and said, "Come on, supper's getting cold."

As we walked up to the main house, I began to wonder: had Corbin really gone easy on me? It sure didn't feel like it. Maybe it was because of my size. Maybe he was afraid he would kill me or hurt me so bad I couldn't work. Still, I didn't ever want him to beat me again, so I was determined to be even more careful to check every nut and bolt and connection to make sure everything was as tight as I could make it.

The next few days were filled with long hours of rushing about to get ready for the big appointment with the emperor. Everything had to be exactly right, all the plates of armor securely attached, all the cables and lever arms tightened properly, burner and boiler checked for leaks, and the steam compression chamber tested one last time for integrity.

Finally everything was ready; we had done all that we could do. Friday night I was upstairs in our attic room with Russell talking about what we might expect to happen the next day.

"I nearly soiled my trousers when the professor told us me and you were going, too," Russell said.

"I know," I said. "Do you think the emperor will really be there?"

"Oh, definitely. According to the professor, he's really got a thing for clockwork devices and steam engines and such. He wants to modernize the city, the army, the whole country."

"Yeah, I can see all that," I said, thinking, "but why a clockwork suit?"

"What do you mean?" Russell asked.

"You know, why build the suit in the first place? I mean, it looks brilliant and dangerous and wonderful and all that, but it will only run for a few minutes before shutting down. And even when it's working, it's clumsy and slow; Algert has a hard time just keeping his balance. I could probably push it over by myself. I can't see it ever being practical in an actual battle."

Russell got a strange look in his eyes. Then he got up and tip-toed to the door. He looked down the stairs, then came back in and made a point of closing the door quietly. He sat down across from me and held a finger to his lips. "They don't think I know, but late one night I was sneaking down to the kitchen to get some leftovers when I heard the professor and Algert in the study. It's all a scam. The professor knows the Clockwork Suit will never be practical, but he doesn't care. He just wants to get that big com-mission from the emperor."

"What!" I said much too loudly, and Russell made shushing motions.

"Him and Algert came up with this plan over a year ago. They're just after the money. The professor has spent his life sav-ings on this project and needs the money bad."

"But he's a professor . . . he lives in this big mansion . . ."

"He got kicked out of his university. And the house is not even his anymore; bank foreclosed last month. Everything's rid-ing on this commission. Once he gets the money, he'll pay off some stuff, maybe hang around for a few months, make some minor improvements to the suit just to keep the emperor in the game, and then they'll just disappear with all the money."

I was too stunned to say anything. The professor seemed like such a nice man most of the time, I couldn't imagine him doing anything so shady. I just sat there staring at the rough woolen blanket on Russell's bed. Then I thought of something. I looked at Russell and said, "But what about us?"

He shrugged. "We'll be out of a job, I guess."

"No, no! I mean, what do you think the emperor will do to us when he finds out we were in on the scam?"

Russell's eyes grew wide. "But, but we just—we didn't—he can't—we're just little kids!"

I shook my head. "Not going to matter. He's the emperor and he can do whatever he wants to us. When the professor hightails it out of here, we're going to be the only ones left to punish."

"I never thought about it like that." Russell sagged down into a dejected heap. We sat in silence for a while, and then finally

Russell said, "Oh . . . no." He grabbed me by the arms and shook me. "No, no, no. I can't go to prison. Donny, we have to do something."

"Yeah," I said, prying his hands off me. "But what?"

"We need a plan. We need to . . ." He started looking around like a rat trapped in a box.

"Maybe we can blame the whole thing on Corbin," I said, then laughed.

"Yeah! That's it," Russell said, joining in. "Let's blame the whole thing on that bastard. He deserves it."

"But the appointment is tomorrow," I said. "I was really looking forward to seeing the inside of the palace."

"Oh, right!" Russell said, hitting his forehead with his hand. "That doesn't leave us much time."

"Yeah. . . ." Suddenly I got an idea. "What if things don't go so well tomorrow? What if the suit doesn't work like it should? And the emperor doesn't approve the commission?"

"What do you mean?" Russell said, his face hopeful.

"I don't know yet," I said, the gears in my mind turning faster and faster, "but something's gotta happen—we have to *make* something happen to the suit. We have to show the emperor just how stupid this whole Clockwork Suit of Armor is. We've got to make him see the truth."

I jumped up and started toward the door.

"What are you going to do?" Russell asked.

"I don't know yet. I'll figure it out when I get down to the shop."

"I'll come with you," Russell said.

"No, you stay here, I can be quieter by myself." I started taking off my boots. "I used to sneak out at night all the time back home; never got caught once."

"Well, okay. I'll turn out the lamp, but I'll still be awake. Be careful."

I eased myself down the stairs, quiet as a mouse, my boots hung around my neck. I didn't want Russell with me because he was kind of clumsy and would have made too much noise. When

I slipped out the back door into the cool night air, the hinges didn't creak even once. I put on my boots, then headed on down toward the workshop, but as I got closer, I noticed a dim light moving around inside. *The professor must be up checking things over one last time,* I thought. *He probably can't sleep, either.*

But when I pressed my face against the window, I could see that it was Corbin moving around the suit of armor. *Corbin?* Now, what was he doing down here this late? He had a hacksaw blade in his hand and was climbing into the suit. After a moment, he started sawing away at something. I couldn't tell what he was working on from where I was looking, and the window was beginning to fog up from my breath in the night air, so I eased the door open a crack and slipped inside.

Corbin had his whole body buried up inside the suit and would never be able to see me, so I tiptoed my way along until I was crouching behind some big wooden crates only a few feet away.

I could hear the saw blade chewing away at something deep inside the suit. I watched Corbin's back for a moment from the shadows, trying to figure out what he was doing. I had never liked him much, but I had to give him credit for being so conscientious as to work so late at night.

I would have to wait until he finished, but I needed a better place to hide. I started to back away, but he chose that moment to climb out of the suit, so I slid down again behind the crates. He put the saw down and grabbed a small punch on the floor. He placed it against the bottom of the boiler on the back of the suit. Then he lifted a ball-peen hammer and hit the punch hard, as if he was trying to punch a hole in the boiler!

Suddenly I realized that he was doing what I had come down to do. He wasn't fixing anything; he was trying to wreck the suit. I couldn't believe it—Corbin was making it so that the Emperor's Suit of Armor would fail. All the work I had done over the past months, and now I wouldn't even get to see the suit working as it should. Then it hit me . . . it had been Corbin all along, going behind me and loosening all those nuts and bolts and compression fittings. He had set the whole thing up so that I would get the blame!

My temper flared and I could feel steam boiling up inside me. I stood up before I knew what I was doing and said, "Hey, stop that, you stupid bastard!"

Corbin dropped the tools and jumped to his feet. His eyes showed white and round in the dim light from the Ruhmkorff lamp lying in the suit. When he saw that it was me who had caught him, he said, "Dummy! I might have known."

Three quick steps brought him over to me and he grabbed the front of my shirt with both hands. "You stupid little . . ." He looked both angry and scared, as if he was trying to decide whether to take off running or start pounding on me. His eyes bulged as he looked around trying to see if anyone else was there. "Where's Russell? Anybody else hiding with you?"

I shook my head, too scared to speak.

"Always getting in the way," he said, dragging me out into the night. "Always being so careful to go back and check every single connection." He pulled me around behind the shop where we ate lunch. "Always telling the professor . . . everything!"

He smacked me in the head one, two, three times real fast. "Why couldn't you just . . ." He seemed to have trouble talking, his teeth clenched so tight I could see the muscles knotted in his cheeks. He shook his head, then smacked me again.

He was hitting me pretty hard, but I had been hit hard my whole life. "Now you're going to get what you deserve, Dummy." *Whap!* "I'm going to beat you so bad you won't be able to talk." *Smack!* "Then I'm going to tell the professor that I found you down here messing around with the suit." *Smack!* "And if you want to keep breathing"—*whap!*—"you'll keep your lying little mouth shut." *Whap!* "Get me?"

I had been beat up many times by boys and men bigger than Corbin, and I had learned how to take it, how to shield my head and ribs, how to give as each blow hit. I knew how to survive . . . and how to keep my mouth shut.

But each time he hit me my temper grew. There was just

something about the whole weird, unreal situation, about being blamed for every little thing that went wrong, Corbin saying I was too weak to tighten a bolt or compression fitting, calling me "Dummy" ten times a day, kicking, punching, smacking me and all the other boys every chance he got, and now he was going to blame me for what he did to the suit . . . blame me when it was him all along.

The steam valve inside me blew. I had taken all I was going to take from Corbin. I wasn't going to stand there and let him hit me anymore. He was bigger than me, but I knew where to hit big boys to stop them from hurting me. I raised my hands, took a step back, and said, "I won't say anything. Don't, don't hit me anymore, please." Then I kicked him as hard as I could in the shin.

And when he howled and grabbed his leg . . . I kicked him in the balls.

He made an "Oomph!" sound and fell to the ground, hands between his legs.

I didn't wait around to find out what else he had to say. I ran as fast as I could back up to the main house and all the way back upstairs to the attic room. I didn't even try to be quiet about it, either. By the time I shook Russell awake, lamps were being lit downstairs and I could hear voices echoing through the halls and up the stairs.

"What! What is it?" Russell said, wiping the sleep from his eyes.

"Corbin!" I said, breathing hard. "I kicked Corbin!"

"You what?"

"I saw him down in the workshop . . . he was . . . he was messing up the Clockwork Suit."

"He what?" Russell said, jumping out of bed. There was moonlight coming in through the dormer window, enough so we didn't light the oil lamp. "But you said that you were going to—"

"I know, but he was doing it first! I yelled at him and he caught me and started hitting me . . . and . . . and I kicked him . . . hard."

Russell looked at me more closely in the moonlight. He must have seen some blood and bumps from Corbin's beating because his eyes grew round. Then his open mouth turned into a grin. "You kicked Corbin?"

"Yeah," I said, smiling. "Right in the balls."

Russell let out a loud, barking laugh before grabbing his mouth and looking toward the door. "You have to get out of here. When Corbin gets up here, he'll kill you!"

"I know, I know." Suddenly I started crying. I couldn't help myself. I was scared and beaten and terrified about what might happen.

"Come on," Russell said, grabbing my hand, "maybe you can make it out onto the roof and down the gutter pipe before he gets here."

We rushed over to the window that led out to the roof and had just started to push up against the heavy frame when we heard Jarvis yell, "What the hell is going on in here?"

We both jumped and turned around, reflexively holding our hands behind our backs as if caught stealing.

Jarvis stood in the doorway holding an oil lamp in one hand, the other propped on his hip. "I said," he repeated, stepping into the room, "what the hell is going on?"

Russell looked at me, then back at Jarvis, then at me again. I didn't know what to do or say, so I just stood there.

"Either of you two," Jarvis said, walking toward us, "going to tell me what—" Suddenly he stopped and squinted at me, holding the light closer. "Donny, what happened to you?"

I knew I was in trouble, just how much trouble, I couldn't imagine, so I started talking fast, making sure to leave out the part about what Russell and I had talked about earlier.

"I went down to the workshop," I said in a rush, "just to make sure I had tightened all the nuts and bolts and screws and connectors 'cause Corbin says I'm too weak to get them tight enough and the professor got mad last time and I just wanted to do things right, and—and Corbin was there and he was working on the clockworks with a file and—and then he took a punch and knocked a hole in the boiler and I said, 'Hey, don't do that,' and then he was hitting me and so I—so I . . . I . . . kicked him."

Jarvis looked at me as if frogs had been jumping out of my mouth. He pointed at us and said, "You two stay right there. Don't move."

It didn't take long before the professor and all the boys were standing around in our room all talking at once. Finally the professor said, "Quiet! Everyone quiet down. Jarvis has gone down to the workshop to check on Corbin. We'll get all this sorted out when they return."

But they didn't return—at least, Corbin didn't. Jarvis hurried in by himself, his eyes wide. "Corbin's gone. Can't find hide nor hair of him, and there's one of those funny lamps on in the workshop."

The professor started to say something, then stopped. I could almost see the gears in his head turning as he thought things through. Finally he looked at me and said, "Donny, come along. I think we better have a look at the Clockwork Suit."

It wasn't just me and the professor that made it down to the workshop—everybody in the house came along to find out what had happened. I followed the professor into the special room where we kept the emperor's suit. Professor Widget grabbed the Ruhmkorff lamp Corbin had been using and cranked the handle until it shone bright. Then he leaned in close and went over the suit of armor inch by inch.

I pointed to the place where Corbin had been punching a hole in the Steam Chamber. I think everybody was holding their breaths as Professor Widgerty looked in and around the shining suit. I know I was.

Suddenly he stood up and bellowed, "Sabotage! That little bastard has sabotaged my creation. The whole thing would've blown up in the middle of our demonstration right in front of the emperor!"

I realized that Corbin had solved all of my problems. He had ruined the Clockwork Suit, and it would be months before the professor could get another appointment. Plus, he had gotten himself removed from the workshop and taken all the blame with him.

I should have been happy—things couldn't have turned out better. But I still wanted to know why.

"Why would he do it, Professor?" I asked.

The professor's face grew dark and I saw a look of hatred that scared me. "Schneider," he said. "That bastard must have gotten to Corbin . . . bought him with a bag of gold and silver, no doubt. He's been out to ruin me for years. He has had his spies watching my workshop from the very first day. He is an unscrupulous, untalented, shortsighted cretin. But thanks to you, Donny, we may have caught him in time. Russell, you know where Algert lives. Run and fetch him. You other boys, get some lamps lit and start up the boiler. No telling what we may need.

"Donny, you and I will get to work setting things right. We'll stay up all night if we have to, but we will get the Clockwork Suit running in time for the appointment with the emperor tomorrow."

It was a long night of everyone pitching in together to get the suit repaired in time for the appointment the next day. When Russell got back with Algert, we exchanged a few looks, but neither of us could figure out any way of stopping or slowing down the repairs. Both the professor and Algert were watching everyone closely and checking and double-checking everything we did.

I was deep inside the suit with a Ruhmkorff lamp just inches from my face, trying to tighten every bolt and nut and screw, when I saw where Corbin had cut a deep notch in the axle for the main cogset assembly. It wasn't enough to keep the clockworks from running, but I could tell that if it got under too much pressure, if Algert tried to lift something heavy, the axle would break.

Corbin was smart. He didn't rely on just one or two things to stop the Clockwork Suit; he made sure something would break or slip or fall apart sometime in the middle of the demonstration. The professor had found all of the other problems Corbin had caused, but this one, this was too far up inside and he would never see it.

I closed my eyes and thought for a moment, trying to decide whether or not to tell the professor. He would never be able to fix the axle before the appointment, too many cogs and sprockets connected to the assembly. But if he knew about it, he could just postpone the appointment, and we would have to do it all over again.

But what if I didn't tell him? What if I kept my mouth shut and left things as they were? The axle would break, all of the cogs and sprockets would slip out of place, and the whole thing would just stop. The professor would lose his commission; he would have to start all over with something else, something better . . . something really worth the emperor's money.

I looked more closely at the notch Corbin had made . . . perhaps . . . yes, as soon as Algert tried to pick up something heavy, the axle would break; I was sure of it. I nodded to myself and yelled, "Everything looks good in here, Professor."

As I climbed out of the suit, I said, "Corbin couldn't get to any of the nuts and bolts deep inside. They're all still tight."

"Excellent, Donny. Excellent," the professor, said rubbing his hands together. "Now, if Algert can get the Steam Chamber up to pressure, we may still make our appointment."

Algert worked almost until dawn sealing up the hole Corbin had put in the compression chamber. He stood back from his work and scratched his bald head. "Well, it's not as good as new, but it should hold long enough to impress the emperor."

"Excellent!" the professor said, clapping his hands together. "Capital!" He took a closer look at the patch and asked, "And you think it will hold long enough to do the demonstration?"

"I'll try not to slam around too much," Algert added. "Patches are never as secure as solid unbroken metal, but I'll go slow and easy just to be sure."

"We'll just have to be extra careful loading and unloading," the professor said. "I can make up some excuse for why we have to take things easy . . . or perhaps I could even tell the truth!"

He and Algert broke into a fit of laughter.

I looked at Russell and saw the worry on his face reflecting my own.

We got things patched up and in working order just in time to load the suit onto a strong wagon, then head off up to the palace.

It was a long worrisome ride for me and Russell. I kept hoping that the Clockwork Suit would just fall off the wagon. But no such luck.

We arrived just a few minutes behind schedule. As we were unloading the suit, I noticed that both the professor and Algert were trying hard to look confident and cool, but I could tell that they were nervous.

We were led into a big hall with a paved stone floor and told that the emperor would be with us shortly. We unstrapped the suit from its wheeled hand truck and stood it upright. Algert filled the boiler and lit the burner; it would take several minutes to build up steam.

Russell and I unlocked and swung open the chest and girdle plates so that Algert could get in. The whole insides with all the gears, cables, pressure plates, and levers were open to view.

Finally the emperor came in along with an entourage of attendants, advisers, and military men. We lowered our heads until the emperor was seated upon a raised dais. I don't think it was an actual throne, but it was good enough for me. He nodded and one of his attendants turned to us and said, "You may begin your demonstration."

I was standing at attention, kind of half bowing, waiting for the professor to tell me what to do. I looked around and saw that Russell looked as if he might faint, but the professor and Algert both had big smiles and looked as if they did this sort of thing every day.

The professor stepped forward and said, "Your Imperial Majesty, thank you for this generous opportunity, and welcome to the future. Today we will demonstrate only a fraction of the potential abilities of our wonderful Clockwork Suit of Armor. We must apologize to you in advance; late last night, a former employee damaged several, um, internal workings of the suit, particularly the Steam Chamber, and we have only just managed to put things right again. Have no fear, the suit will still function properly, only not for the full length of time we had planned, owing to the particular damage, as I said, to the Steam Chamber itself, which is essentially the pumping heart of the machine and which drives the suit."

Some of the military men and advisers began to grumble to each other, but the emperor's face maintained its look of mild interest.

"Again we apologize, Your Majesty. However, we will endeavor to show you what we can and hope that it is enough to impress you and your advisers on the absolute necessity of funding our research so that we can equip our soldiers with the very best equipment and protection to defend this great country of ours."

He looked at Algert, who was standing behind the suit as it *chug, chug, chugged* along, building steam. Algert looked at the compression dial and nodded back to the professor.

"Come along, lads," the professor said. "Help Algert into the suit."

We stood to each side so that Algert could put his hands on our shoulders as he climbed into the suit. Once he was in, we closed up the greaves, the cuisses, the thigh plates, the faulds, then the breastplate, and watched as the professor lowered the visor.

"Careful, now," the professor said just loud enough for Algert to hear, nothing too exciting.

We got everything snapped and locked down, then stepped away. The slow *chug, chug, chug* of the suit began to build until it was as if the suit had been sleeping and suddenly woken up. Steam began to rise and the clockwork mechanism began to spin as Algert and the suit took a step. The clang of his footstep rang throughout the hall even over the noise of the steam engine.

He took another step, then another until he was walking around the hall in a halting, unsteady gait. Finally he stopped in front of the emperor and bowed, then clanged over to the heavy hand truck we had used to load and unload the suit. With one hand he lifted it over his head and tossed it across the hall. The emperor and his advisers cheered and applauded.

Then the professor, smiling wide, nodded to Algert and said, "Your Majesty, as I said, this is only a small portion of what the

Clockwork Suit can do. I hope it was enough to satisfy both your curiosity and your requirements for a positive evaluation."

Russell and I ran over and began to release the snaps and locks so that Algert could climb out. The professor turned down the boiler and released some of the steam from the compression chamber. I'm sure he and Algert thought that the demonstration was over—I know I did—but just as Algert was climbing out, the emperor stood up and came down to the floor. His advisers followed.

"Tell me," he asked Algert, "how do you make it work? From the inside, I mean. Is it difficult?"

"No, Your Majesty," Algert said, bracing himself on my shoulder as he slid his left foot free of the suit.

The professor stepped up quickly. "You Majesty, if I may . . ." He pointed out the pressure plates and said, "You see those small plates there and there and there? They are designed to activate the cables and pistons automatically whenever you lift your leg or arm. And around back, we have a gyroscope, which helps to maintain balance."

The emperor nodded, tapping his lips with a ringed finger. "Could anyone, for example, one of my average soldiers, learn to operate this Clockwork Suit of Armor?"

"Unless he is either too large to get in or too small to reach the plates, yes, certainly."

The emperor nodded as he walked around the suit holding his chin and tapping his lips. "You and I are of the same size, are we not? Do you think I am smart enough to operate this suit?"

I saw the professor's eyes widen and his mouth open. The one thing none of us wanted was to have the emperor climb inside the suit. But the emperor had laid his trap well, and the professor had to bite his tongue before smiling and saying, "Oh, absolutely, Your Majesty."

"Good, then that is what I shall do."

We were not the only ones who thought this was a bad idea. All his attendants and advisers suddenly surrounded him, offering all sorts of reasons why the emperor could not possibility do such a thing.

"Silence!" The emperor gave everyone a dangerous look. "If I am to give this man such an enormous sum of money for his invention, then I will know all that I can know about it. I must be able to say, 'Yes, I have actually worn a Clockwork Suit and I know what it can do.' Now stand aside."

Worried looks passed through the crowd of advisers, and from Algert to the professor and back. Everyone seemed to freeze in place for a moment, until the emperor took off his fancy coat and said, "Well, help me into this contraption."

Russell and I automatically moved to stand on either side just as we had done with Algert, and before anyone could do or say anything, the emperor put his hand on my shoulder and stepped inside the Clockwork Suit.

Even as I was helping him get inside, I knew that it was the wrong thing to do. I started to tell the emperor that he shouldn't get in, that it wasn't safe, that something bad could happen, but Algert pushed me out of the way and began telling the emperor more about how the pressure plates and mechanisms operated.

I stepped back, my stomach twisting into knots, and watched as the professor hurried around to turn up the boiler and charge the compression chamber.

Finally Algert waved us over to close up the Clockwork Suit of Armor. As we fastened the chest plate, Russell looked at me and mouthed, "Do something!"

I wanted to, I really did, but it was too late. If I said anything now, the professor would know I had lied to him. He would beat me worse than Corbin had. I would just have to wait and hope the suit broke in a way that wouldn't hurt the emperor.

Algert looked both worried and elated, and the professor's face was practically glowing with excitement. I was sure he thought he had the commission in the bag.

I glanced at Russell. He looked as if he was about to cry, or run, or explode, and that made my stomach twist even more.

This was not what I had planned. The suit was supposed to fail, yes, but not with the emperor inside.

If the professor ever found out I knew about the axle, he would hurt me bad, but if I let the emperor get hurt, I might end up dead. I eased around back where the professor was watching the steam gauge. I took a deep breath, then reached out and tugged at the professor's sleeve.

"Not now, Donny," he said, his voice carrying a dangerous edge.

"But, Professor."

"I said, not now, you little cretin! Can't you see we've got the emperor in our suit!" His face looked as if it were lit with fire, bright and glowing, and hot. Beads of sweat rolled down his forehead, and he was in no mood to hear anything from me. "You and Russell get out of the way."

I walked over to stand next to Russell. "Did you tell him?" he asked in a loud whisper. I shook my head, and we both crossed our fingers.

The *chug, chug, chug* of the boiler began to build until finally the professor nodded to Algert, then moved around in front of the suit. He put on his biggest false smile and gestured for the emperor to take his first step.

The first step was shaky, but the next was more sure. Soon the emperor was walking almost as well as Algert. He made it over to where Algert had thrown the hand truck, then bent over and tried to lift it into the air. Algert had failed to warn him about how the added weight would disrupt his balance, and the emperor had to take two quick steps to keep from falling.

There was a loud *ping!* and then some grinding, clanking sounds. The added weight and the quick motions were apparently just enough strain to snap the axle in two. The Clockwork Suit began to shake and tremble . . . and then the emperor began to scream.

"Help! Help! Get me out of here. Something is wrong with this infernal contraption. The machine is eating me alive!"

Everyone moved at once. All the attendants, advisers,

generals, all of them came boiling down onto the floor around the suit. Everyone was yelling and cursing and the emperor was yelling and telling them to hurry. The suit was shaking and clanging and pinging, and Algert was doing his best to shut the thing down, turning valves, venting pressure, until we were all standing in an enormous cloud of steam.

When they finally pulled the emperor free of the suit, he was completely shirtless and bleeding from some nasty-looking cuts and scrapes on his back. His trousers had gotten caught on something and they had to rip and cut at the legs just to get him out.

I looked inside the suit and saw that when the axle broke, the gear cluster had shifted forward, and one of the big sprockets of the clockwork mechanism had somehow slipped down, gouging into the emperor's back, the points digging and twisting and winding around in the fine white cloth until the whole shirt was ripped right off his body.

The sprocket itself was covered in blood, and there were pieces of torn shirt and skin clogging up most of the clockworks.

The palace guards rushed in to surround the professor and Algert. There was a lot of shoving and yelling, the professor protested loudly that he was not to blame, that Schneider had sabotaged his creation, and that he still deserved the commission regardless of the emperor's injuries. "My research must continue! Science must move ever onward!"

He was still bellowing at the guards as they tugged him and Algert out of the hall. Russell and I stood beside the Clockwork Suit for a while in a daze, not knowing what we should do. Nobody seemed at all interested in us. I guess we were just too small and insignificant for them to worry about. We watched the surgeon tend to the emperor's wounds until a guard walked over and told us, "You lads run along home, now. We can handle things here."

We slowly made our way over to where another guard stood holding open the big double doors leading outside. I think we were both a bit shaken, surprised and amazed that we could just walk away. I wanted to break into a run, feeling I should get away before someone realized that we belonged with the professor, but I held myself back.

I could see it on Russell's face that he felt the same, that we had lucked out, that we should run as fast as we could and never look back.

But I did look back. The Clockwork Suit stood in the middle of the hall, a mechanical miracle of polished brass, copper, and steel, full of all kinds of advanced scientific wonders. But ultimately it was nothing more than a fancy gewgaw, a shiny contraption that moved around and made a lot of noise, designed for only one reason . . . to cheat the emperor out of his money.

The moment we stepped outside, Russell began to snicker and snort. I looked at him in shock. "Shut up!" I rasped though my teeth. "You want the guards after us?"

"I can't help it," Russell said through his fingers, trying to hold back his flood of laughter. "Did you see what that suit did to him? The emperor had no clothes on!"

The Steampiper, the Stovepiper, and the Pied Piper of New Hamelin, Texas

by Gregory Nicoll

**(BASED ON THE LEGEND
OF THE PIED PIPER OF HAMELIN)**

It was not so much the sound of the huge rats that awoke Stovepipe Montpelier as it was the *smell* of them, a foul, sickening, almost *burning* odor from the ragged fur of the three big rodents, their matted gray hair swarming with black fleas as they skittered past his bedpost. It stung Stovepipe's nostrils so fiercely that he jolted upright in his hotel bed. The lumpy, coarse canvas mattress yielded and pitched beneath him as the weak network of ropes beneath it strained to support his shifting weight. Leaning quickly to one side, he wrapped his fingers around the cool smooth steel of his Winchester's barrel and raised the rifle like a club.

Wham! Wham! Wham!

Through the threadbare sackcloth curtains of the hotel room's small window, moonlight dimly illuminated the carnage. Two dead rats, heads smashed flat against the rough boards of the hotel's bare pine flooring. A third rat wounded, bleeding, skittering for cover beneath the chifforobe across the room.

There was no time to fumble for a match and ignite the whale-oil lamp that tottered precariously on the rickety nightstand. Instead, Stovepipe flipped the Winchester muzzle-forward. He took a brief moment to daub some blood and chunks of rodent gore from its crescent brass butt plate, smearing them off with a corner of his bed's woolen shoddy, before bringing the rifle up tight against his shoulder. Furiously he cranked a tiny pewter dial inlaid on the dark walnut of the rifle's wooden stock. Blue sparks flashed from the dial's edges. There was a sharp metallic hiss, and then the weapon fired.

What emerged from the muzzle, however, was not a bullet.

In fact, the firing mechanism of Stovepipe's carbine had been hopelessly jammed for more than a week now. The soft shiny copper casing of a .44 rimfire cartridge, badly distorted, was still annoyingly visible atop the receiver where it had become stuck upon the closing of the lever. Instead, a beam of pure white light shot out from a narrow brass tube that paralleled the Winchester's barrel. In an instant it lit up the room with the heat and intensity of the midday sun.

Two small beady eyes gleamed like campfire coals from the darkness under the chifforobe.

Stovepipe wished desperately that the carbine would still fire. A single squeeze of the trigger, and that rodent would be splattered dead against the wall. But although its telescopic sight and its light-beam generator still worked perfectly, the customized Winchester would not shoot again until some serious gunsmithing was applied. Besides, a .44 load would likely penetrate the hotel's thin pine wall and cause unpleasantness for other guests.

Not that their sleep had been peaceful tonight.

Sounds of creaking doors and tramping feet came from the hall, heavy footfalls pounding along the corridor. They stopped outside his door.

Knock! Knock! Knock!

Without waiting for Stovepipe's response, the hotelier entered. The door exploded inward, iron hinges screaming. Reflexively, Stovepipe swung the muzzle of his Winchester in that direction, directing its burning bright light at the intruder who, startled and unexpectedly blinded, added a *real* scream to the cacophony. The solid oak door banged hard against the wall. The oil lamp tottered and tipped off the nightstand, bursting on the floor with a shower of tinkling glass and glittering crystal particles.

Darting from beneath the chifforobe, the injured rat escaped through a tangle of kicking feet.

Stovepipe swung the Winchester and pointed it up toward the ceiling, which softened the character of the light in the room. Blue sparks crackled from the dial on the rifle's stock, indicating that its charge was waning.

Glowering at him in outrage was the hotelier, Erik Kauffmann, whom Stovepipe had met several hours earlier when he first arrived in town. Fully dressed in his street clothes, Kauffmann carried a small brown Dachshund with his left arm, the little dog's lips curling as a low growl rumbled from its throat, mirroring its master's anger. Kauffmann took three steps inside the room, stopping only when a fourth would have planted his feet in the spilled whale oil. "Herr Montpelier," he said indignantly, "vee haff a problem here."

Before he could continue, Stovepipe kicked one of the rodent carcasses so that it rolled across the boards, gliding on a layer of slick oil until it slapped hard against Kauffmann's toes, its long pink tail whipping around the hotelier's ankle.

"Yes," Stovepipe declared. "We have a *rat* problem."

At that instant, the pewter dial on his Winchester spat out three final blue sparks. With a faint hiss, the rifle's light beam generator went dead, plunging the room back into darkness.

Breakfast was unexpectedly fragrant and delicious.

Stovepipe had arisen quite late, getting some much-needed rest after finally drifting to sleep near dawn, but not before adding three more rats to his kill count. Kaufman had eventually offered to move him to a different room, giving him his choice of three. Stovepipe was allowed to pick between one on the hotel's first floor and either of two on the hotel's third floor. He had insisted on seeing each room and testing each mattress very carefully before committing to a decision.

"Zee man must try *all three*," muttered the hotelier impatiently.

Stovepipe grinned. "That's how I am."

His new room, located on the highest floor, was smaller, noticeably colder, and had a musty smell about it, but at least it did not stink of whale oil and Stovepipe had at last slept undisturbed there. Only the sound of a late-morning firewood delivery, hundreds of split logs crashing from the back of a horse-drawn dray, had roused him.

As the sun moved toward noon, he belatedly enjoyed a hearty German-style morning meal in the hotel's modest little six-table dining facility. Seated nearby were several elderly bearded and white-haired Europeans, displaced here in the wilds of Texas but far from free of Europe's woes.

Or from its rats, thought Stovepipe.

A blond girl, barely twenty years old but big-boned and wide-hipped, her hair braided in long pigtails, approached him with a serving tray. Leaning forward, she lowered it to the tabletop, displaying neat rows of soft-boiled eggs, still in their shells, each standing upright in a brightly painted wooden cup. Stovepipe took one while trying hard not to stare at the girl's ample white cleavage, pleasantly visible as the neck of her gown hung slack while she hovered there. A direct ray of sunlight from the nearby window lit her bosom, the gown becoming almost translucent in the warm, bright aura. The effect was such that Stovepipe half expected to hear trumpets and choirs of angels.

"My name's Thomas Montpelier," he said, forcing himself to look up at her face instead. "But please call me Stovepipe. Everybody does, on account of me bein' so tall."

"I am Greta Freiburg," she said softly, a heavy Bavarian accent sweetening her English. "It pleases me to meet you, Herr . . . Stovepiper."

"Freiburg?" Stovepipe replied, grinning. "I take it, then, that you are not Herr Kauffmann's daughter?"

She smiled and shook her head. *"Mein* father is Fritz Freiburg, zee brewmaster. Haff you not zampled zee fine beers of New Hamelin, Herr Stovepiper?"

He shrugged. "As soon as I finish my breakfast, by all means bring me a schooner of your best."

Greta chuckled and batted her blue eyes, blond eyelashes fluttering. "Herr Kauffmann serves no beer, nor wine, nor spirits, here at his hotel. You vill haff to go to zee Alt Bamberg Bier Garten." Rising to her full height, she pointed through the window and up the street.

Wearing a ridiculous pink apron, Kauffmann waddled up to the table with a plate of meat and used a long, iron two-pronged fork to shovel fragrant strips onto Stovepipe's plate. Still hot from the pan, the beef strips sizzled. The aroma was pure heaven.

"Thanks," he said appreciatively.

Kauffmann bowed and, with an impatient gesture, urged Greta to the next table. Feigning sadness, she waved silently to Stovepipe as she carried off the egg tray.

Kauffmann turned back to Stovepipe. "Vill there be anything else, Herr Montpelier?"

"Not this morning," he answered, reaching into an inner pocket of his long slick coat. Without a further word, he produced a tiny pewter dome from within the coat and clicked a brass switch on its side. The dome began to emit a loud ticking sound, like exaggerated clockworks. Stovepipe placed it atop his boiled egg, where it spun completely around once and tumbled off onto the tablecloth, taking the top of the egg with it. Now upended, with its tiny blades pulsing uselessly, the little dome ticked all the louder for the indignity it suffered. Stovepipe switched off the device and, after adding a dash of black pepper to the open top of the egg, plunged his spoon inside.

Kauffmann picked up the little pewter device and turned it

over in his hand, admiring it with open astonishment. "Old Fooks would love ziss."

"Old folks?" asked Stovepipe, puzzled.

"Old *Fooks*," said Kauffmann. "Herr Fritz Fooks. He vuss a clock-winder back in the old country."

"Is he staying here? I'd be happy to—"

"*Nein*. He vurks out at the woodchoppers' camp now. Vee haff little use for clock-winders in New Hamelin, but vee haff much need for chopped wood."

Kauffmann placed the device carefully back on the tabletop and turned to offer his beef platter to another guest. At that moment, however, an enormous brown rat darted from the cover of a dangling tablecloth and skittered between Greta's feet, with Kauffmann's little brown dog in rapid pursuit. Greta screamed, tossing her tray skyward. Eggs flew in all directions, several of them connecting with Kauffmann's head. Stunned, he dropped his plate of meat, which shattered on the floor.

Stovepipe got to his feet. He pulled a large, thin, flat steel knife from the slender sheath on his belt. It required only a split second for him to adjust the center-mass weight on its double-edged blade before he threw the knife across the room. The knife spun like a wheel, turning exactly six rotations before the razor point of its tip connected with the rat's body at midspine, pinning the unfortunate pest to the floorboards and killing it instantly. The Dachshund approached it, tentatively sniffing its limp carcass.

Stovepipe walked over and retrieved his knife, taking note of the rat's partially crushed left shoulder blade and mangled left front leg. "This is the one that escaped from my room last night," he observed, turning to face Kauffmann. "I think that—"

He stopped in midsentence, staring in astonishment at the spectacle playing out across the room. The platter Kauffmann dropped had broken into dozens of irregular white fragments, but the fresh-cooked meat it carried had all landed between two dining tables. The rats were helping themselves to it.

Rodents of all sizes were darting from cover, seizing strips and chunks of it between their teeth, and then skittering away to enjoy the feast in private. In seconds, every bit was gone. Kauff-mann's dog charged into the midst of the shattered platter but arrived too late. The canine whined in frustration.

Stovepipe sighed. "I think you *really do* have a rat problem here."

The laughter of children seemed incongruous to him amid the gloomy gray streets of New Hamelin, but Stovepipe realized that they had adapted well, making a game of the rat infestation.

The sky had turned cloudy again and the air was cool, not unusual for so late in the year, but the dust beneath Stovepipe's feet was as powdery as any dry desert. He trudged up the street, boot leather plowing his path. He wore his shiny ankle-length fish coat and a wide-brimmed brown bowler hat with built-in sand goggles, although at the moment the goggles were retracted and concealed in the hat's brim. His Winchester carbine hung from a leather sling over his right shoulder, muzzle pointed toward the ground. Despite the customized weapon's mechanical problem, its familiar weight was a comfort in any unfamiliar territory, from the wide wilderness of Comanche hunting grounds to the dusty streets of little Texas towns.

Rats darted from beneath the boardwalks and porches of New Hamelin's many pinewood buildings. Whenever one appeared, several small boys—and occasionally girls—would leap after it, shrieking and cackling as they gave chase, armed with rocks and sticks, which they hurled furiously at the furry fugitives. Stovepipe saw one little fellow who had fashioned himself a small bow and several crude arrows from sagebrush wood. The child's well-practiced archery proved deadly to several fleeing rodents.

Stovepipe paused and watched them for a moment, regretting his inability to open fire and execute the fleeing vermin. Two potent clockwork grenades remained in his arsenal, and he wondered briefly what effect they might have if tossed into a large congregation of the pests.

A dog began to bark.

Then another.

From the hotel behind Stovepipe came the sound of a third, Kauffmann's little pet, yapping and turning itself excitedly in circles. More dogs joined in from farther up the street, some of them letting loose long, wailing howls.

The sound of a train whistle roared from somewhere in the distance, toward the east. It instantly brought the whole town to a stop. Riders and wagon drivers reined up short. Folks resting on sidewalks or chatting at doorsteps looked up, startled, pausing in midconversation. Shades rolled up in second- and third-floor windows, faces pressing against the glass. Doors flew open, curious heads poking out. The children stopped running and turned, facing toward the sound. Momentarily freed of all hostile pursuit, the legions of rats skittered for cover.

The choruses of barking, howling dogs grew louder and more frantic.

The faraway whistle sounded again, now accompanied faintly by the unmistakable chugging of a powerful steam locomotive. The ground began to shake.

Stovepipe knew what everyone was thinking and why the dogs were in such alarm. There were no rails within a hundred miles in any direction. The town of New Hamelin lay much too far west for the Great Northern Railroad and way too far north for the Texas Western.

So what on earth is making that noise?

The answer arrived a few minutes later. It rolled directly into town on wheels made of gigantic ribbed-iron drums, leaving two parallel trails of corduroy impressions punched into the sandy plain behind it. It was a massive thing, a land-ironclad, part locomotive and part battleship. Its sooty black boiler stood as tall as the Hotel Kauffmann's second story and was crowned by a row of smokestacks almost as high as the third. White clouds ballooned from some of these iron columns, while black smoke trailed from others. The tubes of an immense pipe organ, darkened with dust and webbed with verdigris, protruded like porcupine spines from the machine's rear.

Women screamed. Men ran for cover. Children fled up staircases. Dogs leaped and yapped as if possessed by demons. Horses whickered in terror, many of them rearing up on their hind legs and casting their riders into the dust. Near the hotel, a team of Percherons hitched to a half-empty lumber dray bolted in panic, slinging the wagon left and right, split logs spilling from the back end as it lurched forward.

The elbow rods connecting the ironclad's wheels churned more slowly as its speed slackened. Rolling over the spilled logs, the wheels cracked them like matchsticks and ground the resulting splinters into sawdust. Loudly losing momentum, the machine crunched to a halt in the center of New Hamelin, dripping rusty water and stinking of heated iron.

Huge metal letters, painted gold and bolted onto the sides of its cabin, spelled out the name of this remarkable conveyance: The STEAMPIPER.

The great ironclad bleated one final time, its whistle pitched lower now as the internal pressure of its steam decreased. Then it let out one last immense reptilian hiss, releasing a massive curdling cloud of white condensation, before its huge engine fell silent.

Several dogs continued to bark, but the canine cacophony quickly concluded. Wind whipped through the street, stirring the steam cloud. From within its white mists came the crunch of footfalls. Then the gust changed direction and lifted the white curtain, revealing a strange figure standing beside the machine.

He was short and portly, nearly as wide as he was tall. He wore red-brown Wellington boots and a knee-length beige coat whose heavily waxed surface glistened with condensing steam. Around the waistline of the coat was a heavy leather belt ringed with oversized cartridge loops, each of them carrying a corked glass tube in place of rifle ammunition. In each of these tubes were small crystals of green and blue, which sparkled as they caught the light.

The stranger's coat collar was folded up high, partly concealing his wide, puffy, beardless, and toadlike face. His eyes were hidden by heavy goggles, secured to his head by a black India rubber strap. Atop his head was a strange oversized flat cap, its upper surface sectioned off in triangular wedges, like great slices of pie, each decorated in a different brilliant color and beaded with glittering gemstones.

A circle of townsfolk advanced cautiously, surrounding the stranger and his machine. Standing closest to him was their apparent leader, Herr Kauffmann, still wearing his kitchen apron and holding his serving fork. He took a tentative step forward.

The stranger loosened the strap on his goggles and let them fall to his neck, revealing a pair of searing blue eyes. He extended his hand in greeting to Kauffmann. "The name's Crossley... Cruces Crossley," he said pleasantly, "and I have come for your children."

A nervous murmur rippled through the crowd.

"I have come *for the sake of* your children, that is," he chuckled. "I am here *for their benefit*. New Hamelin's vermin problem is the talk of the territory. You don't want to raise your progeny with *all these rats* capering about, do you?" He gestured grandly, making a complete circle. "Unhealthy! Foul! These rodents must *go!*"

The murmuring became louder.

Crossley raised a hand to silence them. Shaking his head with exaggerated theatricality, he added, "Allow me a moment to prepare my machine, and I shall gladly offer a demonstration of my services."

Turning, Crossley stepped back toward the Steampiper and seized hold of the handrails that extended down from its cabin. With surprising agility he propelled himself upward and swung himself atop the ironclad, landing with an acrobat's grace. The cabin was open at the rear, with the pipe organ mounted on a platform above the depleted cordwood stacks that served as the machine's fuel. Crossley scrambled up to the organ platform, turned a series of valves, and then flipped a small lever. With another hiss of steam, a metal panel retracted and slid into a hidden cavity, exposing a large semicircular keyboard surrounding a gold-framed, red-cushioned swivel chair.

Crossley bowed to the crowd and unbuckled the wide leather belt that cinched his coat. He unfastened the coat itself, swirling it in the air before draping it carefully over the back of the golden chair.

A murmur rippled through the crowd as the townsfolk beheld the garment Crossley wore beneath his coat. A perfect match for his pied hat, it was a grand tunic of many colors, assembled from triangular bolts of cloth dyed in varying hues, from the bright green of New Hampshire forest moss, to the sparkling blue of a Louisiana tidal pool, to the searing orange blaze of a Texas sunset.

Taking his seat before the keyboard, Crossley flexed his fingers and gently applied them to the ivories. At first there was just a hum, a great stirring from deep inside the instrument's mechanism, as he powered it up. Small trails of white steam began to fountain from exhaust vents on its sides. Then he struck a note, a single lingering organ note that wafted mysteriously in the air. Smiling with satisfaction, he began to play. For a moment he treated the crowd to a Mendelssohn overture, amply demonstrating both the organ's mighty sonics and his precise command of it, before easing seamlessly into a playful reading of an Irish novelty song, "The German Clock-winder." After two verses and two choruses, he stopped and returned to the single note with which he had begun.

The crowd applauded eagerly, many of the men whistling and cheering. Several women, staring from upper-story windows, shouted names of other tunes, pleading for Crossley to play them.

The strange little man raised his free hand and waved them to silence. Then he pressed it back to the keyboard and altered the held note, expanding and reshaping it in a curious manner so that it seemed to *bend* in the air. The crowd was so absorbed that it was some moments before anyone noticed the rats.

From every crack and crevice, every hole and hollow along the entire street, they came. Large ones and small ones, brown ones and black ones, old ones and young ones, rat mothers nursing rat pups. Every rodent in New Hamelin crept slowly from concealment and moved toward the Steampiper, transfixed by the odd sound Crossley coaxed from its pipe organ.

The townspeople stood, looking about in wonder, astonished by the strange tableau.

With his left hand, Crossley twisted a large knob on the instrument in a clockwise motion and then released the fingers of his right hand from the keyboard. The bent note continued to be played, as if his hands had never left the keyboard. The chubby little man made a great show of flexing all of his fingers high in the air as he walked a full circuit of the ironclad's upper deck, looking down proudly at the hordes of stunned rodents gathered on every side and the masses of equally dumbstruck townspeople. Then, with a flamboyant flourish of his arms, he stepped back to the organ and twisted the knob counterclockwise. The organ fell silent.

With their musical trance broken, the rats skittered quickly back under cover, completely disappearing.

Crossley stood up and lifted his voice high. "Ladies and gentlemen, *Dammen und Herren* of New Hamelin!" he shouted. "I can end this insidious infestation in a single day! The pipes of my mighty machine can clear these streets of all rats, ridding your town of their foulness once and forever!"

Stovepipe's voice cut through the ascending hubbub of the crowd, instantly bringing the townsfolk back to silence. *"Sure,"* he shouted, "but at what *cost*, Mr. Crossley?"

Crossley bowed in Stovepipe's direction. "A most prudent question, sir. For my services I shall require . . ." He paused, smiling. "I shall require wood—*much* wood and *much* water—to fuel my machine."

He paused again, emitting a nervous chuckle before he resumed. "And, beyond that, of course, I should like a generous fee . . . in an amount . . . an amount to be negotiated *after* I've had a good meal. Can your fair hamlet accommodate me in *that* small request?"

The murmuring turned to cheers as Herr Kauffmann

beckoned Crossley toward his hotel. A mob of townsfolk crowded around as the hotelier ushered the stranger into the first-floor dining room, some of them pressing their faces against the window glass. Everyone else slowly drifted off.

Stovepipe studied the immense land-ironclad for a moment. A crowd of small boys was gathering around the machine, daring each other to climb aboard. Something seemed suspicious to him about Crossley and his gigantic transport. Actually, *everything* seemed suspicious about them, but it was none of his affair. He was a stranger here himself.

Onward, he thought.

His goal this afternoon was to visit the beer hall at the far end of town, but he stopped briefly at the livery stable to check on his horse, a dapple gray he called Thursday. The mare's unusual name was always good for the same question, to which Stovepipe always gave the identical response.

Because that's how far she'll kick you.

New Hamelin's modest livery stable contained little more than two rows of undersized stalls, all of them stinking of wet hay and horse manure, and it seemed to be a favorite haunt of the town's rodent population. However, Stovepipe had no other options for housing Thursday. He found her about halfway back on the left. She seemed alert and in good spirits, blowing her lips as he approached and whickering eagerly, letting him know she was ready for the trail.

Stovepipe stroked her dense, soft mane as he leaned into her stall, giving the space a quick inspection. He was alarmed to discover bloodstains on his animal's hooves but quickly realized the blood was not her own. The flattened carcasses of a half dozen trampled rats attested to its origin.

Her kill count is higher than my own.

"Ziss one is a vine, vine horse," came a voice behind him.

Stovepipe turned and found himself staring into the eyes of Rittmeister Schell, the odd little fellow who ran the stable. Schell was middle-aged but had grown an especially long beard. He carried a pitchfork and wore a floppy straw hat, a white cotton blouse, and an enormous set of leather overalls that hung loosely about his small frame.

"She is, indeed," Stovepipe replied confidently.

"But I must ask you, Herr Montpelier, vat are zose strange scars on her zides? Each of her flanks has ziss small burnt zircle, where hair grows no more."

Stovepipe smiled. Turning both of his feet heels-inward, he deliberately formed a bow with each leg, pointing his boot heels' protruding metal spurs so that they nearly touched each other. "Watch closely now," he instructed Schell. Hoping there was still a sufficient charge left in both boots, he clenched his teeth tight and clicked the spurs against each other.

A shower of bright white sparks fountained from the intersection of the metal, smelling of sulfur and overheated steel. Schell leaped backward in fearful surprise, his straw hat flying off his head. Stovepipe leaped upward as the searing hot crackles of incandescence came uncomfortably close to his crotch. He had definitely overestimated the charge.

Schell was wide-eyed. "You haff spurs made of the lightning!"

Stovepipe composed himself, discreetly running a hand across the intersection of his trouser legs to verify nothing had been burned. No worries. His dignity was intact. "Lightning, yes," he said proudly.

The Rittmeister retrieved his straw hat. He regarded Stovepipe with an especial curiosity now, furrowing his brow and stroking his beard, as if contemplating a mystery.

"You look as if you may have another question for me, Herr Schell," Stovepipe observed.

The little man nodded. "Venn you vurst come into *mein* stable, you haff a large device vich you ask me to keep zafe for you. Vat is zee strange device vich your horse carries?"

"That's gear for walking underwater," Stovepipe volunteered. "Not much call for it out here, but it was plenty useful back East. Hope you're keeping it away from the rats. It wouldn't work well with holes chewed in it."

"Vawkink underwater?" asked the Rittmeister with disbelief. "I haff never heard of zuch a tink."

"I was with the Ohio Volunteers, back during the conflict," Stovepipe explained. "When word got to us about those Rebs in South Carolina who sunk a ship with a torpedo boat that traveled underneath the waves, it got some of us thinking. And once a man knows something's *possible* . . ."

"Vawkink under zee water," Schell repeated skeptically, shaking his head. He turned and headed off into the depths of the stable, his pitchfork propped on his shoulder.

Stovepipe gave Thursday a little good-bye pat and then headed to the street once more.

His hunger had been sated at breakfast and he was wide awake from the potent effects of Kauffmann's coffee, but now he felt a craving for a stronger libation. Besides, he had other questions about this little settlement and, based on previous travels, knew the best place to get answers was an ale house.

The Old Bamberg Beer Garden stood near the far end of New Hamelin's main street. The pub's outdoor garden was hardly that, just a sandlot outlined by a low flagstone wall that surrounded a shabby collection of round wooden tables, warped and bleached from the Texas sun. However, it afforded an excellent view of the distant snowcapped peaks of the Glass Mountains, with a winding bend of the Pecos River spread out in the foreground.

Several elderly couples and a few old men sat silently in the garden, sipping foamy beer from gray crockery mugs. Stovepipe trudged past them, nodding and tipping his bowler hat. One long-bearded fellow raised a mug with a brief, polite salute before hoisting it to his lips. Stovepipe smiled at the stranger and kept walking, quickly reaching the wooden steps that led to the interior of the saloon.

His left boot was on the second of the four steps, the fresh pine bending slightly beneath his weight with unexpected springiness, when a young serving girl came backward through the tavern's batwing doors. Both of her hands were gripped securely around a large tray laden with sloshing beer mugs. Clearing the doorway, she turned on her heel and ended up face-to-face with Stovepipe as he reached the top step.

The girl was Greta Freiburg, from the hotel dining hall.

Stovepipe grinned. "Hello again, Greta."

Strangely, she showed no signs of recognition. Looking away from him with mild annoyance and shaking her head, she eased past and carried the tray toward the customers.

Stovepipe watched. He started to call after her but thought better of it and turned back to face the saloon. At that moment he found himself almost nose-to-nose with another blond girl, considerably younger but similar in appearance, who stared straight into his eyes.

Startled, Stovepipe took a step back.

"*She's* not Greta," the girl announced flatly. She continued to stare at Stovepipe, taking the measure of him.

Stovepipe turned back toward the one he had believed was Greta.

Well, he thought, *she certainly looks like Greta. Same blond hair braided in pigtails, same face, same unforgettable eyes, same dress, same large and equally unforgettable bosom.*

Continuing to stare, he admired her as she bent over to place a beer mug on a customer's table. He felt a surge in his loins.

"Her name's *Gerdie*," the girl on the steps declared.

Stovepipe looked back at the younger one. He smiled as he removed his hat and bowed at her. "And what is *your* name, my dear?" he asked warmly.

The girl tried to maintain her dry and stony composure, but a smile crept up at the edges of her mouth. "I am Berta," she replied.

"Pleased to meet you," he answered. "I'm Stovepipe." There was a metallic whirring of clockwork as he returned the derby to his head. A set of sand goggles with dense black India rubber rims emerged from the brim, swinging downward. The goggles surrounded his eyes and gave them an immense, fishlike appearance.

Berta laughed sweetly.

Flushing with embarrassment, Stovepipe reached up and

squeezed the side of the derby. The goggles retracted, folding up invisibly into its brim. "Danged mechanicals," he muttered.

Grinning, the girl turned and beckoned for him to follow her inside. "Come," she insisted, "you must meet our father."

"Did you say *our* father?" he asked, suddenly baffled.

An explanation was soon forthcoming. Fritz Freiburg, father of three lovely blond daughters—the twins Greta and Gerdie, and their little sister, Berta—was the proud proprietor of the Old Bamberg. He was also its brewmaster, and he took great delight in producing the only locally brewed intoxicants available in the entire region. He ran the brewing as a two-person operation, assisted by his wife, Helga, an immense, muscular, pipe-smoking woman whom Stovepipe observed carrying barrels of ale on her shoulder that would have crushed most men flat.

Most important for Stovepipe's purposes, Freiburg was also a veteran who proudly displayed his wartime flag over his tavern's beer taps, Old Glory's thirty-three white stars arranged in concentric circles on the blue union in its upper left corner. It was the flag under which Stovepipe himself had marched during the final years of the conflict. Freiburg still wore his old unit's blue forage cap at all times, even indoors.

"Herr Montpelier," said the brewer cheerfully, "you must zample *mein* beer!"

Stovepipe unslung his Winchester and leaned it against the bar. He parked his butt on a padded bar stool and hitched a boot heel over each of its cross-rails. "So, tell me about your beer," he said.

"I brew three styles. Two of them are *Altbiers*, vich I produce in the cellar beneath zee tavern. Zee other is *mein Lagerbier*, vich must age and mature in zee cold, so I haff zee woodchoppers to guard zee barrels in a cave on the mountainside, at their camp."

"I'd like to try all three," said Stovepipe eagerly.

Freiburg frowned. "So sorry, *mein* friend, but vee haff only two available at ziss moment. I haff only one large brew kettle—zee metal I cannot get here—*und* New Hamelin is a very thirsty town. Perhaps on your next visit. . . ."

Stovepipe shrugged. "Well, let me have your best."

It was the most interesting—and most delicious—beer Stovepipe had ever tasted, a hearty ale with a strong smoky flavor. Freiburg explained that, for want of enough metal kettles, he had to brew in wooden barrels. Unable to boil the mix of ingredients over a fire because the wood would burn, he used an old Bavarian trick of heating large stones until they were glowing red and then dropping them into the barrel with iron tongs. The Pecos provided just the right stones, smooth and clean. This odd process produced excellent ale with pleasant flavors of caramel, minerals, and smoke.

Stovepipe was drinking his third mug of the fine brew when it occurred to him to ask how Freiburg kept his grains safe from the town's ravenous rats.

Freiburg smiled. "Berta," he called, "please to show Herr Montpelier our champion rat catcher."

"Yes, Papa." The young girl vanished down the cellar stairs. She returned a few moments later, carrying a large black cat that had white fur on its underside and paws. "This is Sofia," she said, holding the well-fed animal up for Stovepipe's inspection.

He stroked the cat, delighted by the unexpected softness of its coat.

Freiburg leaned down beside him to pet the animal. As the older man inclined his head forward, the Union army cap started to slip from his head. He reached up and adjusted it, pulling it down tightly against the backs of his ears, but not before Stovepipe had glimpsed evidence of a hideous wound. The brewer glanced back at him, realizing Stovepipe had noticed.

There was an awkward silence.

Stovepipe politely turned his attention back to his beer, but Freiburg felt a need to explain.

"I vuss scalped," he said bluntly.

"Scalped—but you survived. When did . . . I mean, who was—"

"It vuss zee Comanche raider, zee one called Crooked Scar."

"I know him," Stovepipe said grimly. "A week ago I was

tracking Crooked Scar when three of his raiders doubled back and surprised me. I took down two of them with my rifle before it jammed. Barely escaped the third."

Freiburg's eyes widened. "You hunt zee Crooked Scar?"

"That's what brought me to this territory."

Freiburg's eyes widened and he licked his lips. He raised one hand absentmindedly to the edge of the scar. "Your rifle," he declared, "it must be repaired!"

It was near dawn the next day when Stovepipe set out on his horse for the woodcutters' camp with a sealed letter from Freiburg tucked safely into the interior pocket of his ankle-length slicker. Kauffman had roused him at the appointed hour, knocking at his hotel room door to deliver a small ceramic pot of steaming-hot coffee, accompanied by a serving of beef and bread rolls.

Dressed and properly fed, Stovepipe had passed quietly through the kitchen and dining areas, puzzled that there was no sign of Greta or the other women. He slipped out into the cold, dark street, where the Steampiper's massive black bulk was framed against the setting moon.

Stovepipe found Thursday saddled and ready when he reached the livery stable. Schell had even rigged up the custom saddle extension and carefully lashed Stovepipe's precious diving gear to it, although he couldn't imagine why he'd need it. He slung the Winchester over his shoulder and carefully tucked a pair of clockwork grenades, the last of the dozen he had brought west on his travels, into the side pockets of his coat. Freiburg had insisted that Stovepipe travel armed. The brewer had even offered his own double-barreled shotgun, until a whispered aside from Berta convinced him otherwise, at which point Stovepipe assured Freiburg the extra firearm was unnecessary.

The horse was well rested, sprinting toward the distant mountain range as soon as Stovepipe applied his sparking spurs to her flanks. It was going to be a long ride, though, so he reined the animal in, slowing her to a pleasant trot. It felt good to be settled back into his smooth, well-worn black saddle, and to feel the mare's rocking motion beneath.

Stovepipe had not slept well. The town fathers' beer-fueled negotiations with Crossley, whom they were now calling "the Piper" or "the Pied Piper" because of Crossley's wildly colorful clothing, had extended from the previous afternoon into late evening. Their talks had moved from the hotel dining room over to Freiburg's beer garden and then back again, growing louder at each phase. The evening had ended with Crossley performing a brief concert in the center of town, playing J. S. Bach on the gigantic pipe organ atop the rear of his ironclad. Stovepipe recognized the Piper's tune as "Toccata and Fugue in D Minor" and found it no more conducive to proper sleep than the drunken haggling that preceded it. He presumed that New Hamelin's Council of Elders had eventually reached an agreeable price for the Pied Piper's service.

Either that or they had all passed out.

The sound of the pipe organ wrenched him from his morning reverie. He turned and looked back toward town, visible only as an irregular black silhouette on the starlit plain, its few early-morning lanterns hidden by swirling, drifting fog. The Piper was clearly preparing the instrument for its assigned duty, verifying that each reed was in proper tune.

Does the little man never sleep? Stovepipe wondered.

He was certain the beer had been flowing well past midnight, yet there Crossley was, up before the sun and at work on his strange machine.

Stovepipe turned toward the trail ahead and kept riding. He had been disappointed to learn that New Hamelin lacked a proper bathhouse. After another sweaty night wrapped tightly in a woolen shoddy, he felt grimy and wanted to scrub with hot water and strong soap. However, he was told that Herr Kauffmann's elaborate plans for an in-town bathing facility had been stalled for lack of enough metal pipe, as well as for any efficient means of heating the necessary quantities of water.

Local custom was to bathe away from town, at a distant bend of the Pecos.

Half an hour passed as Thursday bore him along the wide, desolate trail which led out of the town and toward the mountains. The sand was deeply rutted from the tracks of many heavy wagons, but he met no other travelers. For several miles this route roughly paralleled the river, from which great curls of morning mist drifted.

Eventually he reached a crossroads, marked by a simple sign pointing one way back toward New Hamelin and the other way toward Lost Draw, the only alternative being a side trail to the woodcutters' camp. This was indicated by an arrow-shaped board into which had been burned the image of an axe. Stovepipe reined Thursday to a stop and considered the options.

What I need most right now is a bath, he decided.

He touched one spur gently to the mare's flank and rode her up the trail a ways, reining her to a stop at a point where a small horseshoe-shaped bend created a shallow private cove. Here he dismounted and then disrobed, folding his garments in a neat pile and laying the Winchester atop them. He fetched a brush from his saddlebags and ventured tentatively into the water, wincing at its unexpectedly strong chill.

When his body finally acclimated to the cold, he submerged himself up to his chin and used the brush to scrub his body thoroughly. When this was complete, he tossed the brush ashore and let himself drift out toward center stream, enjoying the sense of near-weightlessness.

He was swimming slowly back when he thought he saw a flash of white from somewhere upriver, at the bend, and heard what was unmistakably laughter—*women's* laughter. Curious, Stovepipe swam back and turned upstream, dog-paddling slowly and quietly with his limbs concealed below the surface, so that only his head was exposed. Reaching the bend, he was amused to observe a most pleasant sight.

The ladies of New Hamelin had come here to bathe.

Under the watchful chaperoning of Helga Freiburg, approximately a dozen younger women—including Greta, Gerdie, and Berta—were splashing in the shallows. Many of them wore loose-fitting white bathing gowns, but Stovepipe noticed with pleasure that the three Freiburg girls apparently had no need for such modesty and had taken to the water, like himself, devoid of clothing. Their discarded dresses and petticoats littered the shoreline, some draped from the sides and the wheels of the ox-drawn wagon upon which the massive Frau Freiburg was perched. Squinting, the big woman scanned the horizon. A small corncob pipe protruded from her clenched lips, trailing fragrant smoke.

Stovepipe took careful note of the double-barreled shotgun lying across the big woman's lap, recognizing it as the weapon Herr Freiburg had intended to lend him yesterday. He had no doubt the pipe-smoking mother of three knew how to use it and that she would not hesitate to open fire on any predators, two-legged or four. He considered swimming back and putting on his submarine suit but knew that, were he to be discovered peeping from the deep water, its waxed canvas certainly would not withstand a volley of Frau Freiburg's buckshot.

A challenge Stovepipe set for himself was to devise some method of distinguishing the identical twins, Greta and Gerdie, apart from each other. After careful observation he discovered a charming secret. Although the twins' voluptuous bodies had identical shapes, Greta's skin was unblemished in any way. Gerdie, however, sported a small red-brown birthmark on her right breast.

Stovepipe doubted he would find much practical use for this knowledge, but knew his thoughts would turn back to its pleasant image many times in the future, as he hovered at the edge of sleep during lonely nights on the trail.

He reached the woodcutters' camp by midmorning, when the sun had baked the open plain enough to burn away the fog and briefly banish the seasonal chill.

The camp stood near the base of the mountains, at the edge of a huge stand of trees. It was a modest tent city, augmented by a few large lean-to structures built for maximum portability. Indeed, the last mile of the trail led through a graveyard of stumps where the town's wood supply had been previously harvested, and from which the nomadic lumberjacks had long since pulled up their tent stakes.

Everywhere he looked, men were hard at work, dragging fallen trees behind horses, cutting the trees into logs, and splitting the logs into practical sizes of firewood. Some carefully stacked the split logs into even cords underneath a large lean-to, while others harvested discarded branches for an immense crackling fire, over which the skinned carcasses of two deer rotated slowly and fragrantly.

Stovepipe's attention turned to the sound of a grindstone, and in the distance he spied an elderly man sharpening axes beneath the shadowing roof of another, much smaller lean-to. Sparks spat from the stone as it whirled, putting the necessary edge on each tool.

"Herr Fooks?" he asked.

The old man nodded and seemed to smile, although the details of his expression were nearly lost in the sprawling mass of dense white beard covering his face. Fooks wore an ancient floppy gray Tyrolean hat, a braided green cord serving as its hatband. This gave him an elfin appearance that his white shirt, green suspenders, and traditional leather pants served only to enhance. He rose to his feet and extended his hand to Stovepipe, greeting him in unintelligible German.

Stovepipe fumbled in his coat pocket and withdrew the letter of introduction that Freiburg had written for him. Bowing politely again, he presented it. Fooks broke the red wax seal and withdrew its contents. Fetching a pair of spectacles, he sat down to read.

As Stovepipe waited, he took notice of the many tools arranged carefully on the crude benches that lined Fooks's workshop. There were hammers, mallets, wedges, whetstones, and assorted other devices obviously staged for the maintenance of axes and saws, but what caught his eye was an array of much smaller and more refined tools. These were the tiny drills, miniature clips, odd-sized screwdrivers, tweezers, and finely compartmentalized trays filled with the springs that a man would need to repair a fine timepiece.

Or, perhaps, a rifle.

Eventually Fooks finished reading. "Bring me zee Vinchester," he said quietly, *"und* vee shall zee if I can mend it for you, Herr Montpelier."

Stovepipe unslung the rifle from his shoulder and handed it to the old man, who shouldered it as if to fire it and experimented briefly with its long brass telescopic sight, taking mock aim at various distant objects. Eventually he directed its muzzle toward the ceiling while he gently tugged at its lever. Finding the lever jammed, he emitted a low grunt of disapproval and set the weapon on his bench.

"Ziss vill take zum time to repair, Herr Montpelier."

"Good things take time," Stovepipe replied, nodding. "Oh, and please call me Stovepipe."

Fooks appeared to smile. "Herr Stovepiper, zo it is." He looked back at the rifle. *"Und* vat ist ziss?" he asked, pointing at the pewter dial in the stock.

Stovepipe gave him a quick demonstration of the light-beam generator, which had the bonus effect of not only lighting up the inside of Fooks's wooden shelter, but also igniting the old man's enthusiasm. Practically dancing with amusement, the white-bearded fellow slapped Stovepipe on the shoulder and babbled something incomprehensible, in German, which sounded like high praise.

The clucking of chickens sounded in the distance.

"You have hens here?" Stovepipe asked.

Fooks nodded. "For zee eggs, yes. I begin every day with a much-cooked egg."

Stovepipe smiled. *"Bitte,* please, get to work on my rifle. I must go and boil an egg for you now."

True to the innkeeper's prediction of the previous morning, Fooks was thrilled beyond measure with Stovepipe's little egg-cutting device and insisted on being served two additional soft-boiled eggs while he worked. Nearly an hour passed before Fooks emerged from the lean-to, cupping a small broken piece of metal in his right hand. He explained he would have to construct a replacement for it before the rifle could be reassembled. However, he added that he would be happy to lend Stovepipe a telescope and another rifle until he was able to complete the repair.

Hardly had the words passed from his lips when three younger woodcutters came striding up to the lean-to, each bearing a different weapon. One of them held a long-barreled Remington Rolling Block, a fine single-shot rifle ideal for long-range work. Another carried an old military-issue Spencer repeating carbine. The last man had a Civil War–era Henry repeater, definitely of early issue because its receiver was plain iron instead of the more familiar shiny brass.

Fooks gestured at the selection of firearms as the men held each of them forward for Stovepipe's consideration.

"Hard to decide," said Stovepipe after pondering the options for a moment.

"Herr Stovepiper," Fooks said pleasantly, "Fritz Freiburg writes to me zat you are zee type of man who must try all three."

Riding back toward New Hamelin, Stovepipe took great comfort in the solid feel of the old Henry repeater as it slapped against the side of his long coat. Fooks had rigged up a rope sling for it so he could carry it just as he had carried his Winchester, and he had been pleased to find it accepted the same .44 rimfire rounds. The rifle functioned flawlessly, as determined by the brief test he had conducted. Before Stovepipe rode out, Fooks even insisted on sharpening his throwing knife to a needlelike point. He was now fully prepared for battle with Crooked Scar's raiders.

It was not the rogue Comanches who crossed his trail that afternoon, but rather the Pied Piper. Stovepipe reined Thursday up short when he heard the sound of Crossley's land-ironclad chugging in the distance, its pipe organ eerily holding a single sustained note. The huge engine was moving at a moderate pace, billowing great clouds of steam as it deviated from the main road and cut across open prairie. A strange shadow followed along behind it, its bizarre shape shifting irregularly like a desert mirage.

Stovepipe pulled Fooks's telescope from his coat pocket, extended it to its full length, and carefully adjusted its focus. He could clearly see Crossley at the Steampiper's helm. The Piper was wrapped tightly in his rubbery coat, goggles secured over his eyes and pied cap pulled down tightly against his ears. What intrigued Stovepipe, though, was the shifting mirage trailing behind the machine. The optics of the telescope could not quite capture the image with sufficient clarity, but Stovepipe realized what it was.

The rats. . . .

Sure enough, the Piper had been true to his promise. He was leading a massive herd of them, so many that it appeared to be every rat from the town, maybe the entire territory. They spread out for a considerable distance behind the Steampiper, a roiling brown/black/gray mass of undulating fur and whipping wormlike tails. The metal treads on the huge machine's wheels pressed into the prairie's sandy surface, leaving deep corrugated impressions wherever it rolled. The pursuing rodents spilled into these indentations, pooling up until their numbers were so great that new arrivals simply skittered over the writhing bodies of the others and plunged into the next impression in the sand, where their own bodies formed the base of the next rat bridge.

Stovepipe lowered the telescope and wiped his brow. *But where is the Piper leading them?*

He kept his distance but changed course and followed, aligning his path with the rear of the ironclad, taking care not to be observed. It was a simple matter. The pipe organ blocked any rear view that Crossley might have had. Clouds of steam billowing behind the machine did the rest. Stovepipe donned his goggles and rode among the swirling mists.

The Steampiper chugged steadily along, eventually heading toward a small, craggy hill. Stovepipe noted that it was a considerable distance from town and the rats had finally begun to expire. The oldest and weakest were starting to collapse on the trail.

Stragglers. . . . The Piper's killing off the stragglers by simple attrition.

It occurred to him that an efficient means of destroying the rodents would simply be to bring the Steampiper to a full stop and reverse its direction, crushing the weakened creatures as it rolled back into its own tracks.

Is this the Piper's plan?

But when the ironclad slowed near the base of the hill, he saw a large entrance partially blocked by an immense coin-shaped stone and realized that the Piper had other intentions. Stovepipe reined his horse and took cover behind a small stand of trees, tying Thursday to one of the low branches. He carefully climbed up to a wide fork at the apex of its trunk and took a seat, bracing the telescope against a limb as he studied the distant scene.

The Steampiper rolled into the cave, still issuing that one peculiar sustained note from its pipe organ and leading the rats behind it. They continued to scamper in, although their weakened condition was evident even from a distance. Shortly after the last stragglers had made it inside, the pipe organ's bent note abruptly ceased, and the distinct chugging of the machine's massive engine was heard anew. The ironclad was building up steam again.

He's coming back. . . .

Stovepipe slipped down from the tree. Quickly tucking Fooks's telescope back into his coat pocket, he unhitched Thursday and led her into an arroyo a dozen yards away. He patted her dense gray fur to calm her before extracting the periscope from amid his diving gear. He extended the device to its full length, raised it up straight, and then peered up out of the arroyo to see what the Piper was doing.

The Steampiper reached the tunnel entrance and rolled to a stop. Her captain sounded three long separate sustained notes from the steam whistle and then swung himself down from its cabin. He walked out and stood in the open, hands on his hips, obviously waiting for something.

He did not wait long. Within minutes there was a rumble of hoofbeats, and a Comanche war party rode up, bringing their horses to a halt in a circle surrounding him. Clad in dirty buckskin and lumpy buffalo robes, they carried both bows and repeating rifles.

Stovepipe watched through the periscope, transfixed.

Is Crooked Scar with them?

He could not be certain. Some sort of negotiations seemed to be taking place. After a few minutes the affair was concluded, and the Comanches rode off toward the northwest, as if to circle around to the other side of the hill. Crossley returned to his machine and set it in motion.

Stovepipe pondered the potential meaning of the odd meeting he had witnessed. The Piper had made some sort of arrangement with the Comanches, but its brevity suggested a follow-up to something already in place. Stovepipe resolved to continue observing, but to wait a full hour before following Crossley back to town.

Gigantic clouds of prairie dust churned up by the Steampiper's huge wheels commingled with columns of steam from its boiler as the machine moved back and forth in front of the cave, until at last the mysterious operation was completed and the ironclad chugged off toward New Hamelin, the ground shuddering as it passed. The dust settled and the steam evaporated. Only then was it clear what the machine had accomplished.

He sealed off the cave.

Stovepipe was impressed. The immense coin-shaped boulder now blocked the entire portal, with piles of dirt and smaller rocks scraped up closely around the edges, sealing it so that any escape was impossible. The Piper had done his job well.

The rats will not be leaving here.

Stovepipe turned his head and looked at the image of the distant Steampiper, now just a speck on the distant horizon.

Well, all but one of them, that is. . . .

The aroma of sausages steaming in beer greeted him as he rode back into town. It was late on what had become a cool afternoon, with shadows growing long as the sun descended. From the beer garden at the hamlet's edge came the joyful sound of a horn band playing "Roll Out the Barrel." Stovepipe was amazed to find that the streets of New Hamelin decorated as if for Oktoberfest, with huge cloth drapes of blue-and-white-checkered Bavarian bunting hanging from every rooftop, gutter, railing, and second-story window. Similarly festooned tables had been set up on the boardwalks, wood groaning under the weight of iron cauldrons filled with steaming sauerkraut and neat rows of tall dimpled-glass mugs foaming with fresh ale.

Young women wearing festive dirndls moved through the crowds with platters of food and beer, making sure everyone was served and that no mug remained empty for long. Stovepipe spotted all three of the Freiburg girls hard at work on this happy duty, yet, despite the plunging necklines of their low-cut dirndls, he was still unable to tell Greta from Gerdie.

He smiled. *Perhaps, though, upon closer inspection . . .*

The Piper's ironclad stood at the center of town. The towering conveyance was nearly silent, its engine fire stoked low so that only the slightest huff sounded occasionally from its boiler. Rusty water puddled up in the muddy sand around the machine's immense wheels, fueled by a steady *drip, drip, drip* from the hot ironworks above. Its dark, hulking image might have appeared grim, if not for the long shimmering blue-and-white ribbons that dangled from its smokestacks and trailed from its external tubing and handrails.

Beside the Steampiper stood two empty lumber wagons from the woodcutters' camp and a third dray piled high with empty cooperage, the last vestiges of the barrels' contents drooling down their smooth wooden sides. The Piper's request for a great excess of wood and water in exchange for his services had clearly been met. Stovepipe wondered if Crossley's third demand had been similarly settled.

He let out a weary sigh. His had been a long and eventful day marked by many miles on the trail. He had nothing to celebrate. All he wanted was a buffalo hump steak, a pint of Kentucky whiskey, and, afterward, to bed down in a brothel.

However, he would settle for a bratwurst, a quart of beer, and to drift asleep dreaming of the Freiburg girls bathing upriver.

Someone was pounding on the door of his room.

He awoke in darkness at an undetermined hour, an autumnal chill nipping at him through the hotel bed's thin woolen shoddy. The night was curiously quiet, unlike when Stovepipe had slipped off to bed amid the boisterous sounds of the rollicking street party. He sat up, rubbing his eyes.

Knock! Knock! Knock!

"Herr Stovepiper!" cried a voice as he approached the sound. "Mama says you must help us!"

It was the twins. Greta and Gerdie stood in the doorway, dangling lanterns, each girl still in her festive dirndl, although they were now wrapped in shawls against the chill. They also wore expressions of great alarm.

"Zee Piper has taken away all zee children!" said one of them.

"He led them off behind his loco-motiff, just like zee rats!" cried the other.

"Berta was with them!" added the first.

Stovepipe gathered his weapons and gear by the light of their lanterns as the girls related the strange events that had unfolded while he was asleep.

Once all of the town's men and most of its women were hopelessly drunk, the Piper had demanded a final fee of three hundred United States gold double eagles, an amount that not even all the citizens of New Hamelin working together could possibly assemble. When Kauffmann explained this sad fact to him, the Piper had accepted the news quietly, making no protest. Then, in an unexpectedly charitable offer that caught everyone off guard, he announced that he would perform a special concert on his pipe organ for all of the town's children. The Freiburg girls could not describe the music he had played, saying only that it was neither familiar nor melodic, and that it involved a series of uncomfortably long sustained notes. The children, however, were instantly mesmerized and had gathered around the Steampiper with expressions of rapturous delight. Crossley then set the machine in motion and led them up and down the street two times, the little ones dancing happily as they followed along in its wake.

However, on his third pass Crossley abruptly steered the procession outside town and made a northeast course across the open prairie. More than two hours passed, and none of the children had returned. With almost all the townsfolk either drunk or asleep, the girls had come to seek Stovepipe's help.

Hurriedly he cranked the little generator that powered his spurs, charging them up for the trail. He had listened to the girls' odd story with a sense of growing dread, for it had come clear to him why the Piper was conversing with Comanche warriors.

He's going to sell the children to Crooked Scar. . . .

Not wanting to increase Greta's and Gerdie's already considerable panic, Stovepipe said nothing about his suspicions but instead instructed them to follow him.

Frau Freiburg waited for them in the street outside the hotel. Clad in a gray leather coat and wearing a green felt hunter's cap, she sat atop a powerful roan, clutching the reins in one hand and her long-barreled shotgun in the other. A bandolier loaded with cartridges crisscrossed her chest. There was no sign of her pipe tonight, her hands apparently too preoccupied with preparations for riding and shooting.

Fastened to the hitching rail was Thursday, ready to ride, complete with the special saddle extension and its diving gear.

Stovepipe briefly considered abandoning this heavy and perhaps superfluous equipment, but thought better of it when he recalled how useful the periscope had proven at Crossley's cave.

"Can you drive a wagon?" he asked the twins.

They both nodded.

He pointed to one of the woodcutters' lumber drays that stood nearby, its team still hitched to the traces. "Turn that wagon around and follow us as best you can. But first get some wool shoddies from the hotel, at least a dozen or two, and put them in the back."

One of the twins dashed inside to get the blankets. The other started for the wagon but stopped and turned back to ask a question. "Herr Stovepiper, why is zee wagon needed?"

Unfastening Thursday from the hitching post, he swung himself up into the saddle. A tap on his hat brim caused his goggles to descend over his eyes.

"To pick up the stragglers!" he shouted in answer.

Then he put the sparking spurs to his horse's flanks and set off after the Steampiper at a frantic gallop, with Frau Freiburg's roan thundering behind.

Even in the cold starlit darkness, the Piper's route was simple to follow. Crossley's machine forged its own trail, creating a corduroy passage wherever it traveled, as distinct as any road built by the Caesars. Stovepipe and Frau Freiburg rode to the left and right of it to avoid tripping their nimble steeds, but Greta and Gerdie drove the empty lumber dray, drawn by its oversized plow horse, right up the center. The wagon rattled fiercely, but its bench seat was amply cushioned by a huge pile of hotel bedding.

By watching the position of the stars, Stovepipe made a mental map, charting their position. The route seemed to be leading very near the cave where Crossley had entombed the rats. Grimly, Stovepipe recalled seeing the Piper direct the Comanche raiders in much the same direction.

It was not long before they found the first straggler, a small blond boy dressed in leather overalls, shivering and sobbing alone on prairie. The child was so tired and distraught, blubbering incoherently in a bilingual muddle, that questioning him was impossible. The twins wrapped the boy in a blanket and tucked him securely between them before slapping the reins and setting off again.

Soon there were more. Children clearly too small and too weak for a protracted march. Girls whose feet had become too blistered and sore to proceed, the pain snapping them from the Piper's musical trance. Boys who lost a shoe and stumbled behind. Numerous youths who injured their feet or legs on the uneven trail.

Leaving the retrieval of the abandoned children to Greta and Gerdie, Stovepipe and Frau Freiburg kept riding. Half an hour later, within easy reach of the hills close to Crossley's cave, they arrived at an open plain where unmistakable tracks revealed that the Steampiper had been turned in a wide circle and driven repeatedly around it. Within the great ring carved by its iron treads was a confusing mass of small footprints.

"The Piper was herding them here," Stovepipe shouted.

"*Varum?*" asked Frau Freiburg.

He shrugged. "I can't figure out why. Let's ride the circle and find where they left it."

This strategy proved difficult to follow. Although they each rode slowly around the circumference of the ring that the Steampiper's wheels had pressed into the prairie, they found no point of mass departure. Bafflingly, they found more small footprints leading *into* the ring, as if the mesmerized children had been joined by others who entered at random points from beyond the circle. Complicating matters was the odd detail that the Steampiper itself appeared to have come and gone from the circle several times, creating a variety of additional false exit (or where they *entrance?*) points.

"Zey all are loaded aboard zee loco-motiff, *yah?*" suggested Frau Freiburg.

Stovepipe shrugged. "I don't think so. Crossley could have done *that* as soon as he got them outside town."

The big German woman frowned. "Zee Piper makes them walk back to front?"

He smiled. "Backwards? *There's* an idea. Let's trace some of those tracks that look like they go *into* the circle . . . and see where they come *from!*"

They rode out in a wider circuit, straining in the darkness of the starry night to follow the separate trails of small, individual footprints across the rough surface of the prairie. Eventually, however, Stovepipe spotted hoofprints that paralleled one particularly large and obvious set of girl's prints, which he worried might belong to Berta Freiburg. He dismounted and took a closer look, running his hand in the sandy grooves of the horse's tracks.

This pony was unshod. . . .

He knew that could mean only one thing: *Comanches!*

Remaining on foot, he led Thursday by her reins as he carefully followed the footsteps and Indian pony's hoofprints until they merged and the girl's tracks disappeared. The hoofprints then changed character, becoming less deep and farther apart, as the animal had picked up speed. The horse's tracks were joined by other unshod pony tracks, which then merged with a set of impressions left by the Steampiper's wheels.

Stovepipe squinted and could barely make out the image of Frau Freiburg in the distance, off pursuing another lead. He unslung the Henry rifle, jacked the lever once, and fired it straight up into the air. The weapon's loud report instantly drew her attention and the thick, cottonlike cloud of smoke from its muzzle was as good a signal as any fluttering flag. She rode quickly toward him, reaching his side as he ascended back into his saddle.

"Crossley's been working with the Comanches, selling these children to Crooked Scar," he said. "I think he's taking them near a cave where he led the rats. *Follow me!*"

Stovepipe tapped the rifle's still-smoking muzzle against Thursday's side. The animal bolted forward, nearly throwing him from the saddle, and set off at full gallop. He glanced back and saw Frau Freiburg on her roan, keeping pace by using the barrel of her shotgun like a quirt.

Roughly half a mile from the rats' cave, the tracks of the Steampiper led through a narrow pass and down into what appeared to be a box canyon. Stovepipe diverted from the corduroy trail and rode to the east of the pass, until he found a spot where the steep outer wall of the canyon sloped less dramatically, at an easily scalable angle. Here he dismounted and, leaving Frau Freiburg with their horses, scrambled up the rough, rocky surface until he could peer down into the canyon. He heard the distant sound of strange music and saw the ambient glow of flickering lights. Retrieving Fooks's telescope from his coat pocket, he brought it up to his eye.

The children were there.

Crossley had corralled them in a large wood-railed holding pen where they all sat in silence, apparently still mesmerized by a peculiar warbling note from the pipe organ aboard the Piper's ironclad. The huge machine was parked at the edge of the corral, backed up near the gate, with its organ pipes as close as possible to the captives. A long row of Indian ponies was tethered just outside the corral. Several dozen Comanche braves were gathered around a huge bonfire that lit up the whole scene. In the distance, at a break in the canyon walls, was some nameless tributary of the Pecos. Its water flowed briskly past the camp, splashing against a ragged, sandy shoreline.

But what drew most of Stovepipe's interest was a second fantastic vessel, an immense silver-gray ascension balloon. It was similar to those he had seen used for military observation during the war, only much larger, and its immense hot-air bag was shaped like a giant lozenge instead of a bulb. Moored in place by a series of long ropes, it hovered silently several dozen yards over the camp, creating an eclipse of the moon that cast a massive oval shadow near the riverbank. Beneath it hung a large wooden carriage shaped like a miniature whaling ship, with long wooden fins protruding from either side. Mounted on each of these short wings was a three-bladed propeller. Small trails of steam wafted from the bulges in the wing behind each propeller, leaving no doubt as to how the device was powered.

Studying it through the telescope, Stovepipe made out the shapes of two small men, both clad in brightly pied garments, walking casually around the bizarre vessel's wooden deck.

After a moment he spotted the Pied Piper himself emerging from the cab of the ironclad. As the odd little fellow climbed down the handrails, a darker shape appeared, following him down the ladder. When the dim figure reached the ground and turned toward the firelight, Stovepipe was certain who this was.

Crooked Scar. . . .

Standing nearly seven feet tall and clad in ragged buffalo capes, his belt adorned with dozens of scalps, Crooked Scar had long been a terror of the region. Dead or alive, he carried a higher federal reward than any white outlaw. Apparently he and the Piper were still in the midst of negotiations.

Stovepipe dearly wanted to eavesdrop, but there was no time. Scrambling back down the outside of the canyon wall, he rejoined Frau Freiburg at their horses. "The Piper's got the children in there, but he has Comanches as guards," he told her. "Can you find the woodcutters' camp from here?"

She looked hesitantly in several different directions. Finally she pointed in what Stovepipe believed was the correct one.

He smiled. Swinging himself up onto Thursday's back, he said to the big woman, "Try to keep the North Star always ahead and to your right. Once you see the Glass Mountains, you'll know where the camp is."

"*Und* vut vill I say to zee woodchoppers?"

"Bring every man who can handle a weapon. Also, get them to bring a loaded log wagon and position it on the plateau above the canyon entrance. Whatever happens, we can't let the Piper drive his machine out of there!"

"*Und* vut vill you do here until I return *mit* zee woodchoppers?"

Stovepipe grinned. "I believe I'll go for a swim."

It was difficult to navigate the dark tributary that ran behind the Piper's camp, but Stovepipe slogged along beneath the surface of the rapid, chilly water. The speed of the current kept the river bottom clear of loose debris, so he stepped with sure footing, but he had to work hard to keep from being swept forward and pushed off his feet. He marched with awkwardness because of the long Henry rifle stuffed into the diving suit's left leg, between the canvas of his trousers and the heavily waxed cloth of the submarine costume.

Stovepipe bit down on the oval breathing valve, wrapping his lips tightly around its polished wooden surface, slowly drawing air and trying to calm his overworked heart and lungs. It tasted pleasantly of varnished pine as his teeth found the familiar grooves pressed there. Eventually he stopped and raised the periscope, studying the scene in the camp from the reverse of his canyon rim perspective, and from a much closer vantage.

The camp lay still, aside from the airship's occasional impatient tugs against its mooring lines. The flying machine's shadow created a natural pool of darkness at the water's edge. Beyond this was the Steampiper, still issuing its strange music, and on the other side of the ironclad stood the corral where the dazed children were imprisoned. It appeared that Crossley and the Comanches were all at the bonfire.

Stovepipe climbed out of the river, taking care to make as little sound as possible. Dripping and shivering, he lumbered stiff-legged across the sand until he reached the pool of shadow cast by the airship overhead. After struggling to shed his diving gear, he emerged in his boots, trousers, and shirtsleeves, with the Henry rifle slung over his shoulder and his throwing knife gripped in his right hand.

A small, slender man wearing a pied outfit approached, oblivious of him, carrying an empty bucket in each hand. Stovepipe watched silently from the shadows as the costumed fellow scooped both buckets full of river water and began retracing his steps. He did not make it.

Stovepipe made a quick adjustment to the dial on his knife and threw it with pinpoint precision, piercing the man's neck and dropping him in his tracks. The target fell, grasping at his severed jugular, and lay writhing on the ground between the drool from the spilled buckets. Stovepipe retrieved his knife, wiping the blood on a wide red triangle of the dead man's costume.

A whistle sounded from above.

Stovepipe looked up and saw a metal hook, about the size of an upside-down walking cane, descending from the sky on the end of a rope. Realizing that its purpose must be to raise the water buckets, he quickly packed both of them half-full of sand and, after a brief search of the accessories box on his diving suit, tucked one of his clockwork grenades into each one, winding the first bomb's fuse to its ninety-second setting and twisting the other to the two-minute mark. He covered the explosives with a final sprinkle of dirt.

The whistle came again from overhead.

What's the signal that these buckets are ready to lift?

Stovepipe stepped over to the dead man and made a quick search, discovering a metal whistle on a chain around the corpse's severed neck. Although the links were thick with spilled blood, the whistle was untouched. He raised it to his lips and mimicked the whistling from the sky. To his relief, the hook immediately began its ascent, carrying the two buckets aloft with their deadly cargo ticking inside.

He reached down and grabbed the pied cap from the dead man. He pulled it onto his head, hoping it would serve as a sufficient disguise, however briefly, from the eyes of whoever was aboard the airship. Acting quickly, he scampered over to the ironclad and climbed up one of its ladders, pulling himself hand over hand until he arrived at the cabin. Finding the machine unguarded, he scrambled over the scuffed metal ridge and landed with a dull clunk on its upper surface. A quick twist of the pipe organ's one protruding knob made the instrument falter and then fall silent, immediately breaking its spell on the corralled children.

Stovepipe could see the little ones snapping out of their trances, rubbing their eyes, getting to their feet, clearly baffled as to how they had arrived at this strange destination.

Swiftly he slid down the metal ladder on the opposite side of the ironclad, boot heels hitting hard against the sandy surface below. Staggering upright, he turned and ran toward the gate of the corral.

The first bomb exploded overhead.

The burst itself was not especially loud, but it echoed off the high canyon walls with a sound like a dozen cannons, and the flash of its detonation was like a bolt of lightning ripping through the night sky. The ponies panicked and reared, tugging against the thin rope line that secured them. The Comanche braves abandoned their bonfire and came running, all of them looking up in wonder at the wobbling airship.

Stovepipe threw himself against the tall wooden post at the edge of the corral gate. Unslinging the Henry rifle, he used its butt stock to push the huge latch up and free the gate to swing outward. It trembled, gravity opening it a few feet on its own before Stovepipe's kick sent it flying the rest of the way. He saw Berta Freiburg, towering above the other children, pushing her way through the mass of them as they came stumbling out.

"Herr Stovepiper!" she shouted excited. "Why are you wearing zat hat?"

Ignoring the question, he asked her sternly, "Can you ride a horse?"

She nodded. "Certainly!"

"Bareback?"

"Yes!"

He pulled his knife from his belt and extended it to her, handle forward. "Take this and cut loose a Comanche pony. Every child who can ride, get 'em aboard a horse. If they can't ride, they can hang on behind." He tugged the pied cap from his head and extended it to her. "Here. Now *you're* the Pied Piper. Lead 'em out!"

Berta snatched the hat from his hand, turned, and began waving at the children. *"Kinder! Kinder!"*

The second bomb burst overhead. This time, in addition to the lightning flash and the reverberating echoes, there was a ripping, wet human scream. Stovepipe suspected his explosive had shredded the metal bucket, blasting steel shards into some unfortunate crewman aboard the flying machine.

The Comanche warriors continued to run his way, but so far none of them had spotted him. Stovepipe dropped to his knees and, crouching behind the lowest rail of the corral gate, opened fire. Thick clouds of black powder smoke from his blazing rifle added to the chaos of the scene before him while behind him the children of New Hamelin ran for the row of ponies, following Berta Freiburg's lead.

With thick goggles protecting his eyes and a green kerchief guarding his face, Cruces Crossley stepped clear of the gun smoke clouds far to Stovepipe's right and ran for the Steampiper. Crooked Scar emerged a moment later, following fast behind the little man. Stovepipe started to turn and shoot at them, but at this point a fresh wave of Comanche braves, advancing on him with Winchesters and tomahawks, made a more pressing demand for his marksmanship. He laid down another volley with the Henry and then ducked as the braves' erratic return fire zinged around him, kicking up dirt and chipping at the wooden rails. A stray arrow whisked by overhead and another struck with a loud crack, its chiseled stone tip sticking into a post nearby.

To his left he glimpsed the children swarming over the Indian ponies. Berta had done an impressive job of rallying the little ones and was now hastily putting them atop the horses' backs, sometimes three or four per pony. So far the Comanches were too distracted to notice their animals being stolen.

The Steampiper's whistle roared.

Stovepipe saw Crossley at the helm of the ironclad, signaling to the airship above by means of semaphore flags. Stovepipe wondered fleetingly what the Piper's escape strategy was, and if anyone was still alive aboard the balloon to pilot it.

Behind Crossley stood Crooked Scar, rapidly inserting cartridges into the loading gate of a Winchester carbine. Stovepipe knew it was only a matter of seconds before the warrior would begin shooting at him from behind, trapping him in an inescapable cross fire. Then something astonishing happened.

Crooked Scar's head shattered.

In one moment the legendary warrior was working the lever on his rifle and bringing it up to his shoulder, and in the next his entire skull flew apart in every direction like an egg struck by a hammer. A second afterward came the distant sound of the rifle that had done the deed.

Stovepipe glanced up to the canyon rim and spotted the telltale puff of white gun smoke, revealing the shooter's position. As the cloud drifted, he thought he discerned the silhouette of Frau Freiburg perched at its source. There was another burst of white, then a third, and subsequently the entire canyon rim blossomed with cottony tufts. Bullets zinged into the camp, clanging as they bounced off the ironclad, cracking as they split railings, and thudding as they connected with Comanche flesh.

Although splattered with Crooked Scar's blood, Crossley was uninjured. He immediately set the Steampiper chugging, its iron wheels slowly beginning to turn. The huge machine crept forward, gaining speed as it turned toward the canyon entrance.

Way ahead of it was Berta, astride a pinto pony, leading the mounted children out through the escape route. The few remaining Comanches made no effort to fire upon them, but instead directed their shots at the canyon rim.

Stovepipe fired the Henry twice, taking out a brave with each shot. He drew a bead on a third, but the rifle clicked empty. Setting it aside, he scrambled from cover and ran toward the Steampiper, which was quickly reaching its top speed. Running alongside it, he managed to get hold of a handrail and swing himself aboard. He climbed quickly to the edge of the upper deck and took a tentative peek over the side.

The Piper was fumbling with his belt. From its big leather cartridge loops, he withdrew two of the glass tubes that held sparkling crystals, one blue and one green. He discarded the corks from both of these and, with his right hand, poured their contents into his cupped left hand. Stepping over to open the iron door of the engine's furnace, he cast the blue-green mixture into the fire and slammed the door closed again, levering it shut. There was a delay of approximately three seconds before a rumbling explosion sounded from inside, after which the great ironclad abruptly lunged forward at nearly double its original speed, dense black clouds spraying straight up from several of its smokestacks.

Stovepipe was shaken loose by the sudden change of speed and he fell to the ground, landing hard. He lay there gasping for a moment and then scrambled back up to his feet, watching with frustration as the Steampiper thundered toward its escape route, in pursuit of the fleeing children.

But Berta and her column of little ones had already ridden safely through, and just as the Steampiper inserted itself into the narrow pass, an avalanche of logs descended from above. They cascaded down the steep walls, some rolling like wheels, while others tumbled and bounced end over end. The logs piled up, blocking off the pass amid a colossal cloud of dust.

Under the influence of the magic crystal fire, the Steampiper was moving too fast to stop short of the obstacle. It collided with the makeshift barrier in a massive banging and twisting of metal, spraying of steam, and crunching of split lumber. Its pipe organ emitted one final, sorrowful note before it expired forever.

Stovepipe's elation at the machine's demise was short-lived, however, for almost immediately a giant shadow fell over the scene.

The airship was on the move.

Its mooring lines trailing along the ground, the immense craft drifted majestically toward the crash site. The impact of the ironclad's collision had knocked Crossley flat against the pipe organ, but he was now on his feet, signaling the flying machine with semaphore flags. The ship maneuvered itself in the air, propellers whirring, so that its foremost mooring line reached the upper deck of the wrecked ironclad. The Piper discarded his signal flags and seized this rope, ascending it with the agility of an inchworm.

Stovepipe looked back and observed that the airship's rear

mooring line dangled invitingly just a few yards away. He leaped at it, grabbed the rope, and clung to it as the airship turned and began to rise, hoisting him aloft. Crossley was now almost aboard the ascending craft.

The airship dipped and turned, then picked up speed as it rose above the canyon rim. Stovepipe was swung left and right. He tried desperately to climb the rope, but despite the firm purchase his hands found on its thickly knotted hemp strands, he could not manage to get it gripped between his boots. He dangled helplessly.

Whoever was piloting the airship must have observed his plight, for they began turning the craft erratically in an effort to fling him off. Finally they dangled him level with the canyon rim and proceeded toward it at top speed to smash him against the rocks.

But as the stony rim approached, Stovepipe let loose of the rope and tumbled free, mitigating the impact by dropping downward many yards as the momentum carried him forward. He struck a gravelly patch and came to a stop, winded and exhilarated, bruised but uninjured. Wasting no time, he climbed up and over the canyon rim, noticing as he did that to his left and right were woodcutters, armed with long-range rifles, finishing off the last of Crooked Scar's raiders. He scrambled down the outer wall of the canyon, making his way to where he could see, even through the starry dark of night, that several horses were tied off and waiting.

Thursday whinnied in greeting as he stumbled toward her. He was climbing into her saddle when a familiar voice cut through the dark.

"Herr Stovepiper!"

He was astonished. "Herr Fooks!"

The old man appeared from behind the other horses. He held up Stovepipe's beloved Winchester and thrust it toward him. "Zee repairs are completed!"

Grinning, Stovepipe caught it in midair. "Is it loaded?"

Fooks chuckled. "Vut use is a rifle vich is *not* loaded?"

Stovepipe levered a round into the chamber. He slapped the reins against Thursday's back and kicked his spurs dully against her flanks, the sparking charge in his boots long depleted. Thursday set off at a brisk trot that transformed quickly into a full gallop.

The airship. . . .

Stovepipe could barely see it now, a black oval against the starlight sky, but there was still a chance.

The horse thundered across the prairie, her rider bouncing hard in the polished leather saddle, struggling to rotate the small pewter crank embedded in his rifle's wooden stock. Eventually he turned the horse toward the steep upward incline of a hill, but instead of dismounting, he proudly rode Thursday to the peak of the rise. There he swung from the saddle and lifted the rifle to his shoulder. Bringing its telescope up to his eye, he triggered the light beam generator. The side of the distant aircraft lit up in its brilliant ray, providing a perfect target.

Stovepipe took aim and squeezed the trigger.

The hot, steaming water felt delightful against his bare skin, but at the moment his greatest pleasure was the company he kept. The laughter of the Freiburg twins was sweet music as they splashed him playfully and bounced in the deep, hot bathwater.

Stovepipe was still astounded by how quickly Kauffmann had converted the crashed ironclad's boiler into a source of steam for his long-planned bathhouse. Equally impressive was the speed with which Freiburg, following a tearful reunion with his scalp salvaged from Crooked Scar's belt, had so efficiently cannibalized the same twisted metal wreckage for the components of a massive new brew kettle.

"Zo, tell us, Herr Stovepiper," asked one of the girls, "zee Pied Piper vuss killed ven his flying machine was shot down?"

Stovepipe smiled. "No, he got out while it was still burning and ran for a cave in the hills, the cave where he'd entombed all of the rats. It was blocked with a huge stone, but he used magic powders from his belt to move that. I pursued him inside."

"Zat is where you killed him?" asked the other girl.

"I merely gave him a *push* . . . into a pit at the rear of the cave."

The twins looked at each other and then back at Stovepipe. "He's still in zee cave?"

"Well, I can't imagine there's really *anything* left of him by now." Stovepipe smiled and added quietly, "After all, *rats must eat.*"

One of the girls let out a shrill squeal and nearly leaped out of the water.

Stovepipe grinned. He was now certain she was Gerdie, for in these intimate circumstances he had no difficulty telling the two shapely young women apart. His only problem, in fact, was choosing between them.

The wooden door of the steamy bathing chamber creaked open, letting in a chilly gust. Stovepipe's breathing stopped and his heartbeat quickened.

Standing in the doorway was the Pied Piper.

Then a sweet laugh broke the spell.

Berta Freiburg stepped inside, still wearing the pied hat Stovepipe had given her, and wrapped in a bulky robe that oddly resembled the Piper's shiny coat.

Relieved, Stovepipe let loose his breath again. Then his brow furrowed. "Berta, uh, what are *you* doing here?"

Smiling widely, the youngest Freiburg reached up and unfastened her robe, casting it aside. Beneath it she wore a bathing gown, but this, too, she immediately discarded. She eased down herself into the steaming water to join them, whispering mischievously into Stovepipe's ear.

"Papa tells me," she said, "you're the kind of man who likes to try *all three.*"

The Mechanical Wings

by Pip Ballantine

(BASED ON "THE WILD SWANS" BY HANS CHRISTIAN ANDERSEN)

leanor stood in the shadow of her father and watched him slip the golden ring on the finger of the wickedest person in any of the floating cities. Her protestations, her scream of outrage lay still on her tongue like a painful stone. One that she would gladly have spat out into the world—but dared not.

Faine Escrew was tall, beautiful, and the richest women in all of the sky. She also had a heart as dark as a moonless, starless night, and not an ounce of pity for any living creature in her blood. As she turned and looked over her shoulder at Eleanor and her brothers standing on the steps of the palace below her, a smile lingered on her lips. It was one that some might have said was beautiful, but that the princess knew was more of a smirk than anything else.

King Ivan had long ago passed into Faine's iron grip—anything that Eleanor said now would be wasted on him. However, her brothers were not so circumspect. Iain, the youngest of the king's sons, and of the eleven the closest to his sister in age but furthest in temperament, could not keep his words to himself.

"Snake," he whispered under his breath, his blue eyes narrowed in hatred. Too late, Eleanor shot him a look to silence him. A slight shift in Faine's back told that she had heard Iain's comment.

All unaware, the aristocracy and common folk of the City of Swans watched their monarch marry his second wife. Perhaps they hoped he would not have quite so many children with this one, but more likely no thoughts at all occupied their minds. Madame Escrew had that effect on people. The dirigible city relied on her trade for its mere existence.

Every ship in this city, tethered one to another, filled the envelopes of their airships with gas mined from her mountain estate. Those ships that could not afford the precious æther from the Escrew Conglomerate would eventually be cut loose from the city as a whole and be allowed to drift downward into the boiling earth beneath the clouds.

It was a fair enough reason not to stand against her, but it didn't make it any easier for Princess Eleanor.

Farthest down the stairs stood Eric and Merion, the eldest of her brothers. They were whispering to each other, not bothering to even try to be covert. Eleanor had eleven brothers, and all of them were far too rash.

Finally the ceremony was over, and the priest proclaimed them husband and wife. As the crowd cheered—somewhat weakly, Eleanor thought—the couple retired into the bowels of the cathedral ship to begin the arcane rite of crowning Madame Escrew queen.

Eleanor released an angry sigh, spun around, and walked down the steps toward the knot of princes waiting for her.

Eleven brothers. The other cities, particularly Eagle and Owl, were jealous of the surplus of sons the King of Swan City possessed. Eleanor could tell them it was not everything that they imagined, especially for a lone princess. Much as she loved her brothers, sometimes it felt as if she were floating in a sky full of men. At times like this, in fact.

Instead of complaining, she led the way back to the palace with not a comment to her brothers except for a curt look. They fell into step around her, all varying shades of blond and brown hair. Just like that, her feelings toward her brothers changed. Instead of swallowing her, this phalanx of tall men were providing comfort. Now they were her own personal army.

She knew full well that was what Madame Escrew feared.

On reaching the palace, Eleanor ignored the throne room, drawing them all up to their study. It was here they learned of the history of the City of Swans, mathematics, geography, and navigation. Here and now, Eleanor would be the teacher, her brothers dutiful students.

Eric, the eldest at nearly thirty, sat himself on the window and peered down into the swirling clouds below. The palace ship was in the center of the city, but gaps between the ships meant that the reality of their existence could still be seen. "That woman—" he began, but his sister held up her hand.

Eleanor pinned up the long curls of dark hair into a far more utilitarian bun than the court fashion she'd worn to the wedding. Then she darted to her desk and withdrew the dragonflies she had spent the last week working on. This had been done out of the sight of Madame Escrew, naturally. While the brothers watched, she carefully wound up the five gleaming machines with the two tiny keys in their abdomens before releasing them. With a flicker of bright green, they leaped into the air and began to circle the room in a cloud.

They darted about from ceiling to floor. They had only been airborne for mere moments when one quickly grabbed something hidden on top of the bookshelf. The brothers all winced as a high-pitched whine echoed through the library, about as enjoyable as fingernails scratched down a blackboard.

The little gleaming predator pulled loose a long whiplike creature not much longer than itself. As the brothers watched wide-eyed, the dragonfly ripped it apart with its gleaming articulated legs. Eleanor smiled, but she waited until her creations had circled the rest of the library.

"We should be safe to speak freely now," she said, arranging her ridiculous dress as she sat on a stool.

"Eleanor," Alan whispered, his eyes following the continuing path of the machines as they buzzed around the room, "they are incredible. I didn't know you could build such marvelous things."

Their sister shrugged. "Neither did I, truth be known, brother. Something about that woman's presence in the palace just brings out the inventiveness in me. I remember seeing a plan of them in one of those books that old tinker showed us last summer."

"Finally that memory of yours is some use." Roger, who had been her childhood competitor, flicked a balled-up piece of paper on the desk at her.

"Madame Escrew might take you as her apprentice," Maximilian laughed.

Eleanor felt something like a hard sob form in her belly. Once they had been genuinely merrier. This very room had rung with laughter and learning.

"I blame myself," she whispered, even as she held out her hand for one of the dragonflies to return to her. "After Mother's death I should have taken better care of Father. I should have noticed he was so lonely. Madame Escrew would never have—"

"It's not your fault, Ellie." Alan grasped her hand. "We were all distraught when it happened. None of us ever thought—"

"No, we did not!" she snapped, yanking her arm free and turning away before they could see her tears. "That is what she counted on. She saw an opportunity and she took it. Now we must deal with the consequences." Out the window, their flag of a rampant swan fluttered in the always-constant breeze, seeming to challenge her.

"What can we do?" Alan went relentlessly on. "Father is utterly bewitched by her."

"We must find a way," she said with determination. "Not just for ourselves, but for the city itself. We must be like her, and find an opportunity."

The siblings looked on her, the silence as thick as the tension of the day. One by one, they retired to their rooms, choosing to miss out on the revels of the evening and avoid the new queen.

The next morning, Eleanor forwent any assistance by her

maid and dressed herself. The princess went down to breakfast on the very edge of being late. The less time she had to spend in her new stepmother's presence, the better. Apparently her brothers had either been down early or abandoned any thought of food whatsoever, because she was alone with her father and his queen.

The three of them sat at the long table while being served by masked servants. They served grilled flying fish, starling eggs, and expensive grilled bacon to the silent royals.

It was the new queen who broke the stillness, her voice like silk. "You are looking very pale, Eleanor. Are you well?"

"Not at all, thank you," the princess replied, concentrating on the food before her. She stabbed an egg with a certain misplaced anger.

"It is just that this is the season for insects, and I would hate to think you have been bitten by something . . . nasty." Madame Escrew's hard brown eyes locked with Eleanor's just-as-determined blue ones. The princess did not need to be told; the new queen had noticed that her listening device in the library had been removed.

"What could be nasty in our palace?" Eleanor asked mildly. "All is so wonderful here. If any such vermin were to infest our hallowed halls, Your Majesty, I would take action. Have no fear."

Eleanor's eyes flicked over to King Ivan, who remained oblivious of their verbal sparring. He was nothing like the man he had been before his real queen's death.

Madame Escrew tilted her head and smiled a smile like an iron barb. "Indeed, the palace is a wonderful place to grow up, but still . . ." She paused and placed her hand over the king's. "Even a princess should have a use. Don't you think, my love? It does not set a good example for the citizens to have your daughter seen idle around the palace." Faine leaned over and placed a kiss on the king's cheek. "Too long have your children frittered away their time without a mother's touch."

Eleanor's cheeks flamed red at the suggestion that she was idle and that Madame was anything like a mother. "Reading is not being idle. It is feeding the mind."

King Ivan jerked upright as if he'd been struck, and stared at his daughter as if seeing her for the first time; and Eleanor flinched. She had never seen her father look at her in that way.

"Yes," he rasped, "everything and everyone must have a purpose in the City of Swans."

Eleanor swallowed hard, feeling tears spring in the corner of her eyes.

She watched her stepmother rise, fighting the urge to pull free of her touch when she snatched up one of her hands, flipping it over as if it were a dead frog. "Look at that, as soft as cheese! By your age, my dear, my hands were scarred and toughened by tightening screws and forging parts for my father's machines."

The king nodded mechanically. "It would be good for Eleanor to see the other side of privilege."

"Yes, not all of your subjects can write with diamond pencils on golden slates," Faine said, her eyes still fixed on Eleanor as she returned to the king's side.

Her father grinned like an idiot, and pushed back from the table to stare at Faine. "What do you suggest, then, my darling? How can we make Eleanor aware how truly blessed she is?"

Madame scraped up the last of her bacon and starling eggs, dispatching it with neat efficiency. "My engineer, Stella, would make an excellent teacher for the princess. Some call her a witch, and it is true she has many secrets that should not die with her. She is, after all, old. Quite frail."

Eleanor's calm shattered as she leaped to her feet, knocking her chair over in the process. "Father!" she protested. "I refuse to be judged by this woman. Surely you can't mean to send me away? What have I ever done to deserve being used so ill?"

Thunder clouds gathered in her father's gaze, a darkness that she had never seen there before. Plenty of grief she'd seen in his eyes, but always lightened by his love for his children. He was a stranger to her in that moment.

"Done?" he growled. "Done, my daughter? You have done nothing! That is precisely the point. You will do as your mother suggests, and be grateful for the chance to improve yourself."

She knew a pointless fight when she saw one before her. "At least let me say good-bye to my brothers," she whispered, dropping her head.

"They are busy with their own work," the king muttered as he slurped down some tea.

Eleanor clenched her jaw shut hard. As she had grown older, her father had become a benevolent, if distant, figure. She had always been able to dream that he loved her in some kind of way. All through the brief courtship of Madame Escrew and the king, Eleanor had felt even that tenuous connection disappearing. In this particular moment, hard and brutal as it was, she realized that it was completely gone.

Now there only remained to think of salvaging the remains of her family and the rest of the city.

So she smiled in what she hoped was the manner of an obedient child and tilted her head. "Then I look forward to being of some use to you, Father. And will attend Miss Stella and learn what I can."

A bitter bile welled in her throat. Anyone remotely connected with Madame Escrew was not someone she wanted to meet.

Eleanor barely had a chance to wipe her mouth on the linen napkin before Madame was leading her to the door. A footman was waiting under the arch of the Great Hall, a small traveling case and an abashed expression across his face.

"Please do give sweet Stella my regards," Madame said, her voice full of false delight. The feeling of her hand pressed into the small of the princess's back was like a hovering knife. It made Eleanor think of her own desires the previous day and wish again for a blade of her own.

No, Eleanor decided, *I will have to wait a little while. Find out her secrets and a way behind all her defenses.*

Eleanor looked to her father one last time, but saw there was nothing to be had there. His eyes were elsewhere. He did not even bother to wave her off.

As she was escorted down the stairs, out the door of the palace, and toward the city dock, Eleanor's throat tightened. Maybe she hadn't expected to be allowed to see her brothers, but she had hoped one might come down the stairs by chance. With eleven of them, there was a decent statistical possibility. . . .

Nothing.

She shot a glance back at the gleaming spires of the palace, and a fear grew in her. Had Madame done something to them? Were they already dead?

No, the princess reminded herself, *Madame might be able to bend Father's will on me, but his sons—my brothers—are another matter.*

The ferry that waited for her was manned by a gray-faced old man, with one eye replaced by a battered onyx eye. She did not know him by sight but saw immediately by his expression that he would be no friend to her. Madame's minions had been infiltrating all levels of the kingdom for quite some time now.

Silently, Eleanor took up a place at the prow of the airship, setting her eyes to the horizon of gleaming silver clouds. The ferry pulled away from the City of Swans, and she swallowed hard on the realization that this was the first time she'd been away from the place of her birth. She'd previously dreamed of adventure beyond the safety of her father's kingdom; it was cruel irony that she was achieving her dreams at the hands of her enemy.

The ferry was old but not as slow as she wished it was. With the engines chugging and guided by the morose captain, they pulled quickly away from the city and found a fair current. It was as if Nature herself was against the princess. By the evening Eleanor no longer had the comfort of ignorance in her destination.

They were turning toward the distant crags where Madame held sway, and with every mile Eleanor could feel her stomach clench in an unhappy knot. The surface was a place no city dweller wanted to think of: contaminated, dangerous, a place your body was consigned to when you died, and a place no sensible citizen would ever travel to. However, it did provide some resources that were necessary to their lives.

The princess walked reluctantly to the prow of the ferry and watched the destination resolve itself before her. Ahead, the gray tips of the mountains were now becoming visible, rising out of the clouds like thick knuckles. As they drew even nearer, she could make out square buildings dotted over their surface, accompanied by chimney stacks billowing smoke out into the winds.

It was not a scene to inspire confidence. By the time the ferry pulled next to the dock and tied up, Eleanor's nostrils were filled with the choking sulfurous odor Madame's industry created. The bleak gray rock harbored no life, and the buildings had few windows to greet her. It was as far removed from the City of Swans as it was possible to get. It felt as though she had traveled for days to get here, and she was cut off from everything—including the love of her brothers.

It would be exactly what Madame Escrew had planned from the beginning. At that thought Eleanor straightened her back. She had to remember her royal heritage. She had to remember every detail of her trials so she could draw on them for strength in the battle yet to come. That memory of hers would be useful once more.

A tall, burly man, dressed in dusty gray clothing and covered by a leather apron, stood waiting for her. His eyes were as welcoming as the stone beneath their feet. The effect was only enhanced by the fact that he wore a filtering mask that completely covered the lower half of his face. He could have been grinning or leering beneath it, and she would never know. "Come," he muttered, jerking his head and turning away.

Eleanor contemplated what might happen should she refuse his curt command but decided this was a fight not quite worth fighting. Instead, she followed in his wake, past rumbling factories and ranks of dead-eyed men filing in and out of them. As she went she held her sleeve over her mouth and tried not to choke.

Finally they reached a building with a large door with a mechanical wheel attached to it that stood nearly as tall as Eleanor herself. Her nameless guide spun the wheel with some little effort and pulled the door open. The shriek it gave would have made the dead flinch. Without waiting to be asked, Eleanor stepped inside.

It was as she expected. Her guide slammed the door and spun the wheel behind her back. With a concentration of will, the princess did not flinch, but instead carefully examined her surroundings. Since the interior of the building was illuminated only by half a dozen dim lanterns attached to the walls, it was made that much harder.

However, she was able to make out ten long benches laid out at the far end of the cavernous space, a forge with all the tools necessary for casting metals. She and her brother Brian had shared an interest in metalwork, and, curious despite the situation, Eleanor stepped farther into the workroom. She ran her fingers lightly over the items she could now make out laid out on the benches.

Automatons in various shapes and forms were easy to identify. They covered half the workspace, while the other benches had cogs, gears, pistons, and pieces of boilers laid out in patterns she could not comprehend. She paused to examine them, her brow furrowed.

Automatons were becoming popular in the City of Swans, but they were still restricted to simple tasks: pouring tea, answering doorbells, and perhaps walking the dog. As her fingers traced over the inner workings, she began to perceive that whoever the maker of this was, they had managed to miniaturize so many of the parts that these figures when finished could take on far more varied activities.

"Interesting way of saying hello you have—rummaging around in my work!" The voice that came out of the shadows was so sharp and unexpected that Eleanor dropped with a clatter the flywheel she'd been examining. The figure that emerged from the rear of the workspace was as incredible as the works in progress on the benches.

Eleanor quite forgot her manners and stared. The woman was small and old, her gray hair tangled and matted as if she had little care for it. It was, however, only on one half of her head. The other portion was a construction of naked gears and cogs that approximated the remaining part of her skull. Her right eye was a bleary cataract-covered blue mortal eye, while the other was a gleaming gem that must have been the largest diamond Eleanor had ever seen. The strangeness was not, however, limited to her head, for whatever traumatic event had stolen this woman's face had also taken much of her body, too. The whole right side of her was a collection of gleaming brass. An articulated hand was wrapped around a wrench, and when the woman moved forward it was with a pronounced limp. Beneath the leather metalworker's apron, Eleanor knew there would be more wonders to behold. This, then, was the witch Madame had spoken of.

The princess swallowed hard and waved her arm to take in the work laid out. "I couldn't help myself, this is so fascinating. I do a little tinkering myself, but this . . ."

The woman's snort was an odd concoction of human and mechanical sounds, the wheezing of lungs along with the sound of air striking metal.

Eleanor cleared her throat and dared to venture, "Stella?"

Eyes, both flesh and jeweled, focused on her. "Indeed. I am guessing She sent you."

Eleanor had no way of knowing how deep were the clouds she was stepping out into, so the princess kept her tone moderate. "Yes, the new queen. She told me you were a friend of hers. . . ."

Stella lurched forward, throwing her weight unexpectedly toward the princess. Eleanor managed not to yell in shock, or to move—but it wouldn't have made any difference. A long chain, gleaming in the faint light, pulled the woman up short. It was attached to the good human leg she still had.

"Made it myself," she said with a bleak grin. "She challenged me to make a device even I could not break. And I—in my arrogance did." She rattled it once more. "Forged the steel with my own blood. Hard magic to break, that. I suppose I could saw my damn leg off, but . . ." She paused and shook her head. "I haven't quite reached that point. Haven't got much humanity left as it is."

The princess nodded, not quite knowing how to reply to that. In the end, she said nothing. It must have been the right thing to do, as Stella, once the greatest tinker to be found in any city, took Eleanor Princess of the Swans into her apprenticeship.

Unlike the older woman, she was not chained, but the door was locked securely, and only the faceless guard came to deliver food twice a day. They were a pair of prisoners.

However, soon enough Eleanor forgot all about that. In her father's palace she had toyed with mechanics and engineering, but under Stella's tutelage she was given total focus. Her new teacher would tolerate no idle moments, not even thinking of anything else. Nor was she shy about punishment. She would leave tools' hot or sharp edges bared so that the princess would burn or cut herself.

Soon enough, Eleanor learned to observe where everything lay in the workshop. She also learned the fine art of cogs, wheels, pistons, boilers, and the little magics used to bring them to the peak of their abilities. Stella, she soon discovered, was a mistress of weaving not just metals together, but also the magic of blood and flesh. It was this that made her prosthetics possible and would in time bring the automatons to life.

Eleanor would have thought the rough, sometimes verging on cruel treatment she received from Stella would have driven her mad, but the truth of it was she was learning, in addition to the witch's art, something of the witch herself.

Once, when Stella was fitting a flywheel into the housing of the most complete automaton, she caught a proud smile on her fellow captive's face. Eleanor, however, knew she was losing herself in the endless progress of days. She had lost count, and been so immersed in the interesting work that she'd not thought to keep a tally.

One morning—though she could not have identified which one—they sat on each side of the door eating their cold breakfast in silence, and the princess realized it was a different silence. Instead of being awkward and painful, the quiet was companionable. Somewhere in the uncounted days, they had reached an accord.

The question remained whether she could spin it out into something more than that.

The next night, cautiously, Eleanor began to speak. She drew her finger through the dust on the floor. "I confess I wonder what is happening in the outside world." She did not mention her brothers or the City of Swans, but she had to lower her head lest Stella see her thoughts in her expression.

Instead of speaking, the witch climbed to her feet and tugged her chain after her to the window. It was small, shuttered, and usually never opened, but Stella unhooked the latch and pushed the coverings aside. Moonlight flooded in, and Eleanor recognized with a start that it was night beyond the walls of their prison. She didn't want to see the outside world—especially the stained, bleak world of the rock—but Stella gestured her over.

Together then, they peered out into the night. The sulfurous clouds were still there, but a breeze was wafting them back and forward in front of the full moon. Eleanor felt a knot choke her throat, and would have turned away to the harsh reality of their work when Stella grabbed her arm and pulled her back. "Look!" she rasped.

The princess stepped back and turned her gaze to where the witch was pointing. She saw shadows against the moon. They were more solid than clouds and shaped like great birds. Eleanor shook her head, and with a frown tried harder to discern what they were. They could not be owls, for the City of Owls had been breached and sunk over a hundred years ago—and besides, these shapes were far too big.

They had long slender necks and huge wings. They were swans!

"What swans would fly at night?" she wondered out loud.

"Watch," Stella whispered, her rancid breath hot against Eleanor's cheek.

The group of swans turned in the moonlight, and the princess gasped. These were no creatures of feather and flesh. The light caught them and sparkled on brass and iron, etching each metallic feather in a gleam of white. The long articulated necks flexed beautifully with each downward beat. Eleanor was entranced at this display of the maker's art. The artistry of the work burned into her memory.

"They are amazing," she stammered, pressing her fingertips against the glass as though she could somehow reach through and touch them.

"Yes, they are," the witch replied, "but you are only seeing skin-deep. Do you not see how many there are?"

Eleanor didn't understand, but she did as she was bidden. Her gaze flickered over the slowly moving group. "Ten . . . eleven. . . ." She stopped immediately that the words were out of her mouth.

"Eleven birds. Eleven brothers," Stella breathed into the ear of the princess.

"No!" Eleanor flicked her head and stared at the witch. "She can't have—"

"As clever as we are in this day and age, there are some things that even the greatest tinker cannot do better than a living being." Stella looked out the window again, following the circling flight of the mechanical birds. "Sometimes a sacrifice is required."

"My brothers . . . ," Eleanor whispered, thinking of them all; some more beloved than others but all dear to her. They were her blood.

"Now they are her creatures," Stella returned. "They will be absorbed into the machine and eventually become part of it."

Eleanor's mind was spinning, but she watched her brothers for a moment until it came it to her. "Eventually?" She grabbed hold of Stella. "You mean they are not already?"

The witch shook her head, her brass jaw working, but sagged in the other woman's grasp. Finally she ground out, "No, not yet. It will take a month for the transformation to be complete, and the machine to take all of their humanity beyond the ability to get them out alive."

"Then there is a chance?"

Even Stella's jeweled eye could not meet Eleanor's, but she finally did manage to grunt out "Yes."

So there it was. Eleanor sat back and thought for a moment. She thought about how she'd always had to be the sensible one, and how her brothers had always come to her for advice, because princes were supposed to know everything. She thought about how—trapped as they were now in their mechanical swan bodies—they would most definitely want her advice, and yet for once she had to ask someone else for it.

Carefully, she cleared her throat and probed Stella further. "So, how would I go about getting my brothers back?"

The witch stepped away from the window and dragged her chain clanking behind her back to the workbench. She jerked a magnifying glass down on a boom arm, adjusted the gaslight brighter, and began to screw a tiny flywheel into the chest of the automaton—all the time as though nothing had happened.

Eleanor could hardly believe it; after all, it was Stella who had shown her the scene out the window in the first place. She walked over to the witch and stood behind her shoulder, silent and waiting. She was completely at a loss to know what words to use that would get Stella to help her. Perhaps the witch had only wanted to drag her fellow captive down into the mire of despair she had been in for so long.

However, it appeared that silence weighed on Stella, because after a moment, she sighed heavily and put down the screwdriver. "To break the magic and undo the machines, you would need to make skins for them."

"Skins?"

"Her magic and tinkering are strongest when creating creatures for the air, and you would need to counter that by building metallic vises to interfere with her workings. It is the only way to allow the men to come out of the machines."

"How do you know about my brothers?"

"I've always known who you are." Stella tilted her head. "She talked about you a great deal. Well, you, your brothers, and your father. I don't know why. . . ." The witch's voice trailed off as though she was thinking on something unpalatable.

Eleanor shuddered; however, she was not going to travel old paths with her fellow prisoner. She had to think of the future.

"So I can make the cloaks here, and we can save them?"

Stella flinched, presumably at the liberal use of the word *we*. "Even if I wanted to help you, I don't have the necessities here.

Spun silver must be used to make the cloaks—it is the only material that can bear the magical component."

"Silver?" Stella bit her lip. "The City of Eagles is the only place to get quantities of that."

Stella croaked out a laugh. "Even Madame dares not attack that city—at least not yet. However, there is more and worse to hear." She rubbed her finger on the rough edge of the nearby hacksaw.

The pregnant pause drove Eleanor crazy, but she managed not to snap.

"It is the silence, you see." Stella smirked, and for a second the princess worried that she could read her thoughts. "You have to bind a bit of your soul into each cloak, and every ounce of your being must be bent to the task. Every sinew and effort must be put into this undertaking. Should you speak you would destroy not only the materials but the magic, too." The witch shot her a gaze out of the corner of one eye.

"Silent the whole time?" Eleanor couldn't help an edge of dismay creeping into her voice. She could never remember having been silent for a day, let alone a month!

The other woman snorted. "You shouldn't have had so many brothers, should you!"

Eleanor frowned. "It wasn't as though I had a choice!"

Stella wanted to end the conversation there, but the princess would not be turned aside.

Eleanor spent the next few days trying to convince her fellow prisoner that they had to do this. The witch kept to her task of creating the automatons, but the princess could detect a change in her speed—as though other thoughts were tangling her concentration.

So Eleanor kept lightly on, discussing how much of a challenge making the mechanical cloaks would be, and how the person who would do it would have to be a master of the craft. She even sketched out from memory the workings she had observed on the surface of the mechanical swans.

Stella grumbled, "Don't even try to tempt me, girl!" Yet she could not hide the light of interest in her eyes.

Eventually, on the third day after she had pointed out the swans to the princess, Stella set down the gruel she had been eating and grabbed Eleanor's hand once more.

"If it is to be done, we must make our escape quickly. We will need every day that remains. If it can be done tonight, then it should be."

Eleanor blinked. "What about you? This chain is not going to stretch all the way to the City of Eagles!"

Stella stared down blankly at the finely constructed chain. "She imprisoned me here with my own work, but it is held together by her magic. She said I did not know the meaning of loyalty and friendship, but I would know the strength of my failings. It is unbreakable."

"Unbreakable? There is no such thing," Eleanor said with the firmness of one who had studied every book on metallurgy she could find from an early age. She dropped to the floor and picked up the chain. It was heavy, and she observed spots on Stella's good leg where it had rubbed for years. As she studied the chain, she realized that it was in fact made up of several strands of metal bound together tight, and that each was engraved with words. After fetching oculars and pliers from the workbench, she was able to read the words. *Proud. Arrogant. Friendless.*

The strands labeled *Proud* and *Arrogant* were strong and seamless. She pulled and tugged at them fruitlessly with the pair of pliers. Nothing. However, when she applied the pliers to *Friendless*, she felt it give a little.

With a grunt, she was able to bend one strand. So the weakness was in the strand that was inscribed *Friendless*. The princess stared through the magnifying glass at the hair's-width crack and then glanced up at Stella.

"It's hopeless, isn't it?" the witch muttered, and since they had spent so much time together, Eleanor was able to discern that the bleak disinterest her fellow captive had been wrapped in when she arrived was nothing more than an act now.

She managed to smother a smile, but dared to pat the witch's leg. "I am not leaving without you. We need each other."

Stella swallowed, but when the princess bent once more she saw that the strand now looked corroded. Now when she applied the pliers and tugged, the strand snapped.

"Holy steam!" Stella yelped.

One strand was all it took—even the remaining two could not hold themselves together without the third. While the witch watched, the princess pulled the chain rope apart and gently untwined it from her leg.

Stella stared at it a moment, her breathing unsteady. "I could have cut off my own leg," she muttered, "but she knew I would never do that."

"Now you don't have to," Eleanor whispered.

The witch's lips twisted, and her eye glittered dangerously. "She also thought me too far gone. Lost to humanity. She never was very good at judging kindness in people. It is a quality she knows little about."

The two women clasped hands tight.

"Then I think we should go and teach her how wrong she is," Eleanor said with a savage grin. "What do we need to proceed?"

"I'll show you."

Together, then, they raced around the workshop, taking the specialized tools that Stella pointed out and shoving them into a pair of large canvas bags. They took the sketches that the princess had made, and she saw with some pride that the witch had made some notations on them while she hadn't been looking. The last item that Stella insisted on was a jar of gleaming gems, tiny pinpricks of light that looked like trapped fireflies. "Starlight opals," Stella said with a grin. "We will need these for the cloaks."

Eleanor knew that a combination of tinkering and magic would be required, but starlight opals were the most rare stones to be found in the cloud mountains. That the witch had so many was heart-stopping.

Yet neither of them could afford to stop for anything. Stella picked up a mallet and tossed Eleanor a thick metal spike. It passed briefly through her mind that only a few weeks ago, she would not have had the strength and dexterity to catch it so easily. Yet she did.

Placing the spike on the bottom hinge, she glanced at the witch. She did not flinch when Stella struck it hard. The hinges broke away like children's candy, and the door fell out with a muffled bang.

The chill night air invaded the princess's chest and she gasped reflexively. Suddenly the task of freeing her brothers lay before her. Yet she paused for a moment, letting her eyes adjust to the weak moonlight. Thankfully, at night the factories ran on a reduced workforce and the clouds of poisonous smoke were lessened. Both woman pulled the front of their shirts up over the mouths.

"The ferry," Stella hissed. "It is the only airship we can manage with just the two of us."

Eleanor nodded. It looked quiet out there, and the ferry was not far. If they unhitched it and floated, they could start the engine once they were away from the mountain.

So the two of them scuttled in the shadows of the factories toward the ships. The whole place was so still that Eleanor could hear her heartbeat in her head, but their footfalls were softened by the thick layers of ash and they made it to the pier with no signs of pursuit. Quickly as they dared, they unhitched the ferry.

Eleanor began to breathe again—or at least it felt to her as if she did. She had just slipped onto the deck from the dock when a group of men stepped down from a larger airship on the other side. For an instant, the women and the men stared at one another in the moonlight. Then the men snatched up their rifles. Eleanor standing exposed on the deck made a perfect target, but when the rifles of Madame's soldiers came about, it was Stella who stepped before them.

Eleanor screamed, but the weapons fired anyway. The witch fell, but the soldiers had one more barrel to unleash, and they turned again on the princess.

That was when her own art—almost forgotten—saved her. A

cloud of gleaming green shapes darted down. They were sharp and metallic, and glowed in the dusky confusion of the clouds. Eleanor recognized the shapes—her little mechanical dragonflies that she'd made back in the palace.

Yet these little creations of the tinker's art did not come to their creator. The dragonflies, with their sharp, long legs, flew at the soldiers—straight for their eyes. It was the last thing they could have expected, and they actually shouted in surprise.

Eleanor saw in a moment that this was her only chance. She spun the wheel wildly, and let the wind grab hold of the airship. She heard gunshots fire after her, but it was dark and they flew wide. The cloud of dragonflies—now only four in number—came back to her, perching on her shoulders. The wind had its way with the airship, dragging it away and smothering it with clouds.

Eleanor slumped down on the deck and let her head fall into her hands. As she wept the eddies and currents of the air played with the ship. This tumult would give her some advantage. By the time they had prepared and stoked the engines of the larger airships, she would be on her way.

They would think that she would set course for the City of Swans and the comfort and refuge of her brothers. They would never guess that the princess was in fact aiming the airship for the City of Eagles—the traditional enemy of her home.

Finally, after shedding her tears, she crawled to her feet and made her way to the engine room to stoke the boiler to life. She had never piloted an airship, but her memory of traveling on her father's ships served her well.

Still, it took two days to find her way to her destination. They were chill, frightening days, in which she sat on deck rummaging through the two bags of tools that Stella had collected, and scanning the diagrams they had drawn. Her head felt stuffed and overfull. The idea that she was going to have to do this thing alone was enough to drive her brain to distraction.

It was almost a relief when the city itself came into view. The City of Eagles Eleanor had read much of, but naturally never seen for herself. Unlike the carnival of colors of the City of Swans, the Eagle airships wore cloth of silver on every single envelope. In the morning's light the collection that made up the city gleamed like the lights in her father's ballroom.

"No," Eleanor whispered to herself, using up her voice while she still could. "I mustn't think of Father. Only my brothers—they deserve my thoughts."

It also helped to think of Madame Escrew, and her face if Eleanor could just complete her task. That would be a sweet return.

The ferry was accompanied into the city by a squadron of ornithopters. Eleanor stood at the wheel, her mouth dry, and followed the shouted instructions of one pilot to follow him in. She couldn't help contemplating that if these were the City of Eagles' idea of a defensive perimeter, then they would have no chance against the mechanical swans Madame Escrew had constructed. It was not just her brothers she would be saving; the City of Eagles and all the others would be saved, too.

The squadron guided her toward a small dock, and the workers there helped her tie up her ship. She was lucky in that none of her clothing bore the emblem of her home and neither did the ferry.

The princess threw the two sacks over her shoulder with a grunt and then stepped out into foreign territory. The dockmaster came bustling over to her, wearing a brown coat bearing the eagle crest. "Two ducats a day," he snapped, not meeting her eyes, but instead scribbling down notes on the ferry.

"Actually," Eleanor interrupted, "I am looking to sell it and take up lodgings in the city."

The dockmaster's sharp blue eyes darted up to meet hers. "Lot of that these days. You should find Master Pettingren on the lower docks. He's been buying up airships of all sizes. People appear to think war is coming. We've had to lash in three dozen new ships this month at least."

Eleanor shuddered. The cities grew a little, but that many new arrivals seeking the perceived safety of the Eagle meant that the free travelers of the skies were also getting nervous.

She had to hurry. She sold the stolen ferry to the thin but

remarkably cheery Master Pettingren very easily, and earned a healthy sack of ducats; even in a time of approaching war, a ship was still an expensive object. Then she found herself a small workshop in the lower hull of an airship hulk.

It was full of desperate people, packed into tiny rooms in the lumbering ship. The place ran with gossip and contagion in equal amounts. Again, Eleanor forced herself to ignore all that. Instead she set herself to the calculations of what she would need. Then the princess went into the city and bought the strands of silver that Stella had said were required for the cloaks. She bought all she could find, but by her calculations she knew that it would only be enough for six cloaks. She would have to venture out later and find more.

Still, it was surprisingly cheap. That she had not expected.

Once she said thank you to the shop owner and gathered up her materials, she knew that had to be the last time she spoke. It was too important a task that she couldn't leave anything to chance. Stella had told her the magic and the crafting would require everything she had. She would have to give it that.

As she returned to her little cell, she weighed the remaining coins in her pocket. She hoped they would be enough to buy not only the remaining silver she would need but also the things a human body needed. Silver might be cheap in the City of Eagles, but food was not.

She would just have to do the best she could. In her cell she laid out all the tools from the two canvas bags. There were various sizes of little saws, some with diamond blades, and a set of gleaming screwdrivers that tingled on her fingertips. And then there were the starlight opals.

Eleanor sat back on her heels. She had been thinking about what might be required to interfere with the workings of the swan machines, and though she had many ideas it was the use of the opals that she was really guessing at. Their function was something Stella had not had time to explain. That was the sticking point, and the one thing Eleanor was least confident about.

However, doubts had to be left behind. First, Eleanor laid out and measured the silver tape and hoped her calculations were correct. She had only the glimpses of the swan machines she'd managed to catch from the prison window, and so she was forced to rely on her own sense of proportion.

The clockwork underneath the cloaks was the easiest part for her to do. She designed spikes that would drive into the workings of the mechanical swans, locking the skins on them tight—this was just in case Madame Escrew had set some defenses on her devices. The skins that would hold these mechanics were by far the harder to construct. The silver tape was flexible, but reluctant to give itself up to her. She knew that she had to weave the skin in just the right way. It had to be strong and yet conform to a shape.

The solution she settled on was one that drew inspiration from ancient armor—the kind that she had seen on display in paintings in her father's palace. It was called fish armor, though no one in any city had seen a fish for ten generations.

First she fixed the silver tape into a tiny loop of no greater circumference than she could make with her index finger and thumb. The next loop she threaded through the first and welded it shut. It was long, tiresome work that made her head, her eyes, and her fingers ache. It would have been nice to spare a curse word now and then, but she was careful never to do that. Always in her mind was the witch's reminder that she needed to put everything into it.

She ate little with her stinging fingers, but still ventured out to buy what silver she could find. A princess had no experience at thievery, and she dared not risk being caught—that would mean an end to her project. So instead she bought what little cheap food could be found. Though in times of war there was little enough of that.

So, as the days and weeks went past, Eleanor's figure began to dwindle, and her mind grew foggy with hunger. Now the cloak making was proceeding by sheer habit.

The role of the starlight opals was something that still eluded her, until one day when she was passing—or rather, staggering—through the market and saw an aristocratic lady with a cloak wrapped around her against the chill. Eleanor's head jerked up, and her gaze followed the woman. The garment was festooned with glimmering beads. Despite her weariness and hunger, Eleanor knew this would be the best way to add the opals to her own project.

She wobbled her way back to her dim rooms and set to work immediately.

However, a strange young woman who communicated with gestures alone had made an impression in a city on the verge of all-out war. Gossip was not something that Eleanor had calculated in her plans.

She was working at the inner cage of the fourth cloak when the flimsy door was kicked in. She hadn't eaten in three days, but somehow she managed to hold back a scream or any other sound.

"There she is—the witch!" The voice seemed to fill the tiny room, and Eleanor staggered a little as she rose to her feet. Her tools scattered on the floor, and she wondered how in the sky she was going to find them again.

Guardsmen struggled to enter such a small space, but all of them were pointing and shouting. None of them used the word *swan*, for which she was very grateful. Still, *witch* was not that much better. In a world constructed on floating airships bound together, the punishment was to see if the witch could fly. If she plummeted to her death, then she was obviously innocent; if she did not, then she would be weighed with stones until she did.

Eleanor stood tall and for a second almost spoke. Her mouth dropped open, but then she shut it with a snap. Her brothers' fate and that of all the cities that flew the skies depended on her strength of will. It would be weak of her to falter now.

"It is as they say," one burly guardsman rumbled. "She does not speak . . . even in her own defense."

The word *witch* was passed from man to angry man, and Eleanor knew there was no way out of this situation. They were blocking her way from the room, and where could she go without her works anyway?

The four dragonflies buzzed and snapped on her windowsill,

but the princess gestured them back. They would only create a worse situation. Brave little insects that they were, she didn't want them destroyed.

Then a voice from the back snapped, "Make way, make way!"

Suddenly the guardsmen were shifting, jostling, and some of them slipping out of the tiny room. They all hurriedly got out the way to make space for the man who demanded entry.

Eleanor was sure she was hallucinating. Though she did not know the tall young man with the military uniform who loomed in the doorway, she did recognize the silver badge on the scarlet sash over his shoulder. It was an eagle, with its wings spread. Only one person could wear such a thing. She had seen its like only on her father.

This was the king of the City of Eagles. Eleanor wobbled on her feet as her stomach growled and her brain struggled to catch up. This was the last person she wanted to seem weak in front of, but going so long on so little food had finally caught up with her.

Eleanor's vision blurred as her legs buckled. She tried desperately to prop herself up against the wall, but it was treacherous and she ended up sliding to the floor. Throughout it all she kept her jaw locked shut, refusing to let out even a pained sigh.

Through her graying vision she saw the king bend down toward her. He had startling eyes; they gleamed gold like a hawk's. He turned and commented over his shoulder, "She doesn't much look like a witch to me. And most certainly not a very good one."

"But, sire, you know the temple will . . ." From her place on the floor, she couldn't tell who spoke.

Darkness was washing over her, but the last thing Eleanor heard was the king saying, "We must keep an eye on her, that is for certain."

When Eleanor struggled back to consciousness, it was to find herself in a bed as soft as the one she had left back in the Swan City. For a moment, a blissful moment, she believed she had imagined the whole horrible Madame Escrew event, but then as she sat up she realized that she was not in the City of Swans, but the one of Eagles. It was the decorations that told her that immediately.

Great birds of prey were shown everywhere: in tapestries, paintings, and most disturbingly of all in sculpture, where a spread-winged eagle had a tormented swan in its claws.

That bought her back to reality with a start. So she slid out of bed and gently to her feet. Immediately the smell of food on a nearby table drew her over. Eleanor had devoured all of the soup and bread before she even worked out that it was onion broth and good millet bread.

Feeling her brain starting to work, like a furnace finally fed coal, she began to explore. The room was decorated in outrageously rich fashion—even more so than she was used to in her home. It was a two-room suite of some kind. Eleanor entered cautiously to find the second room was some kind of observatory. Her father had one very similar in his own palace. This was, however, even larger, filled with many long benches, and on these were all her tools, the cloaks in progress. Even the starlight opals were there and the four little mechanical dragonflies.

She rushed over and ran her hands over them to make sure she was not imagining it.

"I think you will find everything there." The king, standing in the window, overlooking the swirling clouds, had gone unnoticed by her.

A hundred questions bubbled in her mind, but she managed to hold them back.

"I imagine you are wondering," the king said, stepping toward her, those emerald eyes locked on her, "why I would give you this chance to complete your work, when you might be some kind of witch."

Eleanor looked away, totally unsure how to deal with a man without her tongue.

"Well," he said, picking up the jar of starlight opals, "you are a most unusual one, and I think perhaps you are silent by choice." The look he shot her was direct and probing.

The princess had never felt such a wash of warmness over her body for a man's sake. Certainly there had been suitors in her time, but with her the sole sister in a line of eleven brothers, not many had lingered long. Now she wished most fervently for the freedom to use her voice, to show him her wit and intelligence. Instead, all she could do was smile. Even writing was something she dared not attempt.

The king shook his head, as if emerging from a deep pool of water. "But where are my manners? I have not properly introduced myself! I am King Nikolai Swoop, of the City of Eagles." His fingers tweaked his cravat almost nervously.

A little confused herself, Eleanor picked up an end of the silver metallic tape and gestured for his permission to begin. The ticking of the clock in her head reminded her she had little time for embarrassment—or any other emotion, come to think of it.

Nikolai tilted his head. "They say I should see if you fly, but I am preparing a city for war from the King of the Swans and I cannot turn down this chance to see what you are building. None of my tinkers can fathom what this is all about. Maybe it can help my city survive."

He seated himself on a stool near the window, out of her way but near enough that he could observe what Eleanor was doing. And thus they proceeded.

He came and watched her every day while the dragonflies circled the observatory. Sometimes he sat silent and watched, departing without a word after no particular length of time. She imagined he had many things to deal with since they were—as he said—on the very edge of war. Part of her—the smallest portion that she allowed freedom in those brief moments she stopped to eat—was flattered at the king's attention.

For there were times he talked. At first they were words of a ruler: light matters of court, moments of his family history, and the minutiae of ruling that grated on him. However, as the days passed he delved deeper and, perhaps emboldened by her silence, told her things about himself. He revealed his fears, his hopes and dreams.

For herself, Eleanor yearned to tell him the same, but the work and the magic held her tongue.

The mechanical delivery system was ready—or as ready as it was ever going to be—but it was the cloaks that would wrap tight around the forms of the swan machines that were the most time-consuming.

As she sat on the floor, her fingers worn almost to nubs by the work, Eleanor's mind contemplated the thousand ways that this could have been made easier. If she had the voice, she could have asked Nikolai to get some of his subjects to help—but Stella had asserted that it must be done by the princess alone. Once when her fingers started bleeding, Nikolai tried to take the link work away from her and do it himself. Her frantic dismay had been enough apparently to keep from trying that again. He did, however, remind her to eat.

As she marked off the twenty-first day on the wall of her prison—something that made the king's brow furrow with confusion—Eleanor sighed.

Nikolai looked up from where he sat, in the sun, his gold hair gleaming. He looked so normal and wonderful that Eleanor risked another sigh. She slid down to the floor once more and picked up the cloak.

Despite her protestations, the cloaks were nearly done. In fact, she was working on the final one, confident that she was going to finish it well before the end of the month and the deadline that Stella had set. She only had to stay the course and finish the final loop work, as dull and painful as that was.

All would have been well had the bells not begun to ring. It was not in a happy way, but in a discordant chorus that spoke of imminent threat. Nikolai leaped to his feet even as Eleanor ran to the windows.

Together they looked out into a clear blue sky, and the princess felt her chest tighten and her throat close. The machines were so much more incredible and frightening when seen in the daylight.

Great wings of brass and bronze beat the air as the eleven swans descended on the City of Eagles. Eleanor and Nikolai watched as the city's ornithopters flitted out to meet them. Compared to the stout realism of the machines, the 'thopters looked like a child's set of paper planes. They lasted just about as long.

The elegant swan necks were bent toward the attackers. Above the desperate ringing of the bells could be heard a dreadful, constant stream of explosions. "Holy steam," the king swore, thumping the back of the chair.

The delicate wings of the ornithopters caught fire and crisped. Their descent was silent and dreadful.

"Wait here!" The king grabbed her shoulders and planted a kiss on Eleanor's silent mouth. It was sudden, unexpected, and made her blood rush to her head, but before she could react further, he darted out the door to see to his city.

The princess was left standing in the conservatory, the final cloak trailing from her fingers, and watching her brothers destroy a city she had come to see was no enemy. Eagle and Swan had been at odds for generations, but it had never broken out into real war.

Some of the smaller airships were punctured already, their envelopes sagging and collapsing in on them. People on the deck below ran backward and forward like disturbed insects, cutting the ties between the stricken ships and those still untouched, trying to save them. It seemed like a pointless attempt to Eleanor because soon enough the whole city would be in flames.

The princess knew, despite one of the cloaks not being completely done, that this was the only chance she would have. She cast about, grasped hold of a chair, and flung it through the nearest window of the observatory. It shattered, spraying glass out into the void, and the sound joined the screaming of the citizens and the rattle of the swan machines.

"There she is!" The guardsmen had entered the workroom, and at their head was a priest of the Sky God in his bright blue vestments. He looked as though he was about to have apoplexy right there and then.

"Witch!" he howled, his pointing managing to encompass both Eleanor and the devastation beyond the window. "She has bought these demons of the air down on us."

Eleanor knew she only had mere moments and that all of her

work of the last weeks hung on this few heartbeats. The four dragonflies, quiet for so many weeks, flew once more to her defense. Eleanor flung another chair at the advancing guards and spun away.

Then as they scrambled toward her, she turned to the window and screamed, "Brothers! Brothers!"

Something in her blood, something in the bond they shared, must have reached them, because the machines turned. For a long second they flapped in position, outlined against the bright blue sky, with the flame light of the airships below them reflected on their brass wings. Then they dived.

The priest and the guards screamed behind her, leaping back almost as quickly as they had surged forward. Eleanor stood there, one cloak held in each hand, and waited.

The swan machines, each about twice the size of a man, crashed through the glass of the observatory. Eleanor could see that her memory had not failed her. The details of the gears and workings of the swans were as she had seen them in the moonlight.

The swans all bent their heads to her, and she could see the weapons that Madame Escrew had fitted them with: devices to spurt flame, and repeating guns the like of which she had never seen. All of which could be turned on her in a moment.

If the remains of her brothers were truly gone, then this would be her last moment. Eleanor stood poised, knowing that she didn't have any chance should they turn on her. The articulated necks and gleaming jeweled eyes of the birds were all directed at the princess below.

"Come away. . . ." Nikolai's voice came soft from behind her back. He sounded as if he were calming a falcon, trying to put a hood on it.

Eleanor dared not glance back at him; one sight of his face twisted with concern and she would be quite undone. Yet she couldn't tell him what to do, not yet . . . not when she was so close to the end of her task. She just had to hope he would follow her lead.

With quick strides, she walked toward the first of the swans and flung the cloak over the metallic back. With eleven brothers she had to work fast, but then she heard the king himself step up and help her. He couldn't have known what he was doing, but her heart swelled at his trust in her.

Finally the swans all stood, covered in their cloaks.

"See, my liege," said the temple priest, finally collected himself, "the witch knows them."

"I think perhaps she does." Nikolai held up his hand, to stay the guards from making a move.

Eleanor took out of her pocket the largest starlight opal. The one worth a fortune in any kingdom. Every love meant sacrifice.

Dropping the gem to the floor, she pulled her mallet out from her other sleeve and bought the weight of it smashing down on the precious thing.

The white light within was freed, making everyone in the room flinch away. All except Eleanor, who watched it fill all the other gems in the cloak. They gleamed brightly, bringing power to the cloaks. She heard the creak of the gears, and the snap of the vises within as they locked tight on the structure of the swans. The machines threw their proud heads back, and great trumpeting screams broke the rest of the remaining glass in the observatory.

The machines shivered, the workings shaking themselves loose; something large and metallic ground against itself. And then the doors burst open and Eleanor's brothers—all eleven—staggered from within them.

They were gaunt, pale, and sweaty, but Eleanor didn't care. She rushed to them, called their names, embraced them.

After so long in silence her voice cracked and fractured on the words. Then she felt Nikolai's hand on her shoulder, and now she found she could look up into the king's eyes. She was free of subterfuge and the tenets of the cloak construction.

"These are my brothers." It felt so good to say it, though it came out husky. "I am sure you are wondering. Madame Escrew has my father in thrall, and she did this to them. The machines were swallowing them, and I had to work in silence to free them."

"That was not what I was wondering," Nikolai replied. "Your name is what I have wanted all this time?"

She smiled as she helped Brian to his feet. "Eleanor."

The princess and the king stared at each other while the brothers shook themselves and blinked.

The priest had turned white, while the guardsmen shifted on their feet, uncertain what to do. They could all tell that something had changed in the broken observatory.

"Now what do we do, Eleanor? What is the next move?" Alan pushed his hair out of his eyes, and she was aware that all of her brothers were once again looking to her for answers.

The king of the Eagles, too, was watching her, those green eyes expecting and welcoming. She turned and looked at the remains of the swan machines with an analytical eye.

"I say that we can learn a great deal from these machines. And then"—she smiled archly—"we turn her work on her, and take back the Swan City and my father."

The men around her nodded.

"And you shall lead us," Nikolai said, taking her hand. "A true Queen of the Swans."

Contributors

Paul Di Filippo began reading science fiction at the age of five, when he encountered his first Mighty Mouse comic. He published his first story in 1977, and has since become responsible for thirty books under his byline. He hopes to keep at this game for some time yet. His tastes in fantastika are omnivorous.

Nancy A. Collins has authored numerous novels, short stories, and comic books, including *Swamp Thing*. She is a recipient of the HWA's Stoker Award and the British Fantasy Society Award, and has been nominated for the Eisner, World Fantasy, and International Horror Guild Awards. Best known for her groundbreaking vampire character, Sonja Blue, which heralded the rise of the urban fantasy genre, her works include *Sunglasses After Dark*, *Knuckles and Tales,* and the *Vamps* series for Young Adults. Her most recent novel is *Magic and Loss*, the third installment in the critically acclaimed Golgotham urban fantasy series. She currently resides in Wilmington, North Carolina, with her fiancé, Tommy, their Boston terrier, Chopper, and an indeterminate number of cats.

Gregory Nicoll has created eerie, atmospheric horror tales for such anthologies as *Confederacy of the Dead, Cthulhu's Heirs, 100 Vicious Little Vampire Stories, It Came from the Drive-In, Gahan Wilson's The Ultimate Haunted House, Book of the Dead 2: Still Dead, Mondo Zombie,* and *Zombiesque*. Three of his works were selected for *The Year's Best Horror Stories* and another was chosen for the 2012 edition of *The Mammoth Book of Best New Horror*. Greg's long-overdue first foray into steampunk appears here in *Clockwork Fairy Tales*. He promises it will not be his last.

Steven Harper lives with his sons in southeast Michigan, where he teaches high school English, plays the folk harp, and spends a sadly enormous amount of time online. He recently discovered to his surprise that as of this writing, he's written more steampunk than any other genre. He's currently working on the Clockwork Empire series for Roc Books; the series includes *The Doomsday Vault*, *The Impossible Cube*, *The Dragon Men*, and *The Havoc Machine*. Visit his Web page and blog at http://theclockworkempire.com.

Jay Lake lives in Portland, Oregon, where he works on numerous writing and editing projects. His 2012/2013 books are *Kalimpura* from Tor Books, and *Love in the Time of Metal and Flesh* from Prime Books. His short fiction appears regularly in literary and genre markets worldwide. Jay is a past winner of the John W. Campbell Award for Best New Writer, and a multiple nominee for the Hugo and World Fantasy Awards. Jay can be reached through his blog at jlake.com.

Kat Richardson is the bestselling author of the Greywalker paranormal detective novels and models her stories on the work of such iconic detective writers as Dashiell Hammett and Raymond Chandler, with a dash of whimsy, horror, and an occasional ferret. A former theater brat and technical editor, Kat has worked in a variety of fields from music to magazine and course writing, as well as film, games, and gemology. She lives on a boat in the Seattle area with her husband and a goofy pit bull, as well as the ghosts of ferrets. Visit her Web site at http://katrichardson.com. for more information.

Philippa Ballantine is the author of the Books of the Order series with Ace: *Geist*, *Spectyr*, *Wrayth*, and *Harbinger*, the final book out soon. She is also the coauthor of the Ministry of Peculiar

Occurrences series with Tee Morris. *Phoenix Rising*, the first book of the series, won an Airship Award in steampunk writing. In addition, she has the Shifted World series with Pyr Books, with the first book, *Hunter and Fox*, out now. Philippa loves reading, gardening, and, whenever possible, traveling. With her husband, Tee, and her daughter, she is looked after by a mighty clowder of five cats.

G. K. Hayes has been writing award-winning fiction for more than thirty years, with recent short stories appearing in SF and Horror anthologies such as *Critical Mass*, *Zombiesque*, *Night Terrors II*, and *Dark Moon Books Presents: Zombies!* He is also the author of the six-book epic fantasy series, *Sleag's Quest*, a fun ride through a New World. You can visit him at gkhayes.com. He has been lucky to find his muse in his beautiful wife, Linda.

After residences in Los Angeles, San Francisco, England, and Spain, **K. W. Jeter** and his wife, Geri, currently make their home in Ecuador. He still grieves for the now-vanished Los Angeles in which he was born. His latest publications include the novel *The Kingdom of Shadows*, a collaboration with Gareth Jefferson Jones titled *Death's Apprentice*, and the first four books in a new thriller series—*Kim Oh 1: Real Dangerous Girl*, *Kim Oh 2: Real Dangerous Job*, *Kim Oh 3: Real Dangerous People*, *Kim Oh 4: Real Dangerous Place*, and *Kim Oh 5: Real Dangerous Fun*. More information on his books and stories can be found online at www.kwjeter.com.

About the Editors

Stephen L. Antczak is the author of the short story collection *Daydreams Undertaken* and the novel *God Drug*, as well as more than fifty horror, fantasy, and science fiction short stories, the play *Romeo's Ghost*, and the comic books *Nightwolf: the Price* and *Arkadian*. He coedited, with James C. Bassett, the horror anthology *Zombiesque*.

James C. Bassett's fiction has appeared worldwide in markets such as *Amazing Stories*, the Australian anthology *Shadow Box*, the German *Podgeschichten,* and the World Fantasy Award–winning anthology *Leviathan 3*. With Stephen L. Antczak he coedited the anthology *Zombiesque*. He is also an acclaimed stone and wood sculptor.